I'm an Irish author who is addicted to writing romances featuring damaged, moody, book boyfriends searching for their happily ever after.

Visit K.A. Finn online:

www.kafinn.com
(trailers, excerpts, artwork, playlists etc)

Facebook: kafinnauthor

Instagram: kafinnauthor

Additional links: linktr.ee/kafinn

Also by K.A. Finn

## Nomad Series (Space Opera)

Ares

Nemesis

Perses

Chaos

Mania

Cronus

Talos (TBA)

## Blackjacks Series (Paranormal Romance)

Breaking Phoenix

Reviving Davyn

Defying Shep (2023)

Defending Rhain (TBA)

## Broken Chords (Rockstar Romance)

Broken Rock (Tate)

Fractured Rock (Gregg)

Split Rock (all band members)

Crushed Rock (Luke)

Shattered Rock (Dillon)

## Twisted Legends (Folklore Retelling/Romance)

North Bound (Nick/Santa)

Shadow Bound (Damon/The Boogeyman - TBA)

Broken Chords #4

CRUSHED Rock

K.A. FINN

**Cover design by Deranged Doctor Design**

www.derangeddoctordesign.com

**Photographer: Shauna Kruse**

www.kruseimagesandphotography.com

**Model:**

Lance Jones

Published by Cooper Publishing

ISBN: 978-1-914177-52-1

Coming soon

*Broken Chords #5*

K.A. FINN

# Crushed Rock Playlist

Although I haven't mentioned any song lyrics in this book, that doesn't mean music didn't play a MASSIVE part in its creation.

This playlist was on every time I wrote, edited, or just read the book.

The bands, the songs, or the lyrics remind me of Luke and Maeve in some way. It's still a playlist I listen to regularly and it always reminds me of his story.

If you want to check out the playlist that I had blaring in the background while I was writing **Crushed Rock,** you can find it on my website (www.kafinn.com/crushedrock), by scanning the QR code below, or by searching the following songs.

Just make sure to play it LOUD!

*World So Cold*– 12 Stones
*The Permanent Rain* – The Dangerous Summer (Luke's Song)
*Not Alone* – Red
*Paino Song* – The Mile After
*Second Chance* – Shinedown
*The Phoenix* – Like A Storm
*Broken Heart* – Escape the Fate
*Until the End (Acoustic)* – Quietdrive
*Fears* – Twin Wild
*Call You Mine* – Daughtry
*Always December* – Citizen Soldier
*Would Anyone Care* – Citizen Soldier
*If I Surrender* – Citizen Soldier
*Hope* – Nathan Wagner
*I Met a Girl* – Nathan Wagner
*Wanted*– Citizen Soldier
*Tired Of You* – The Exies
*Still Alive* – Ashley Wallbridge, Evan Henzi
*Saving Light (Acoustic)* – HALIENE

*Falling Slowly* – Glen Hansard
*You Broke Me First* – Conor Maynard
*Grenade* – Boyce Avenue
*Easy's Never Been This Hard* – Citizen Soldier
*Never Really Loved Me* – Kygo, Dean Lewis
*Chances* – Backstreet Boys
*Wreckage* – Nate Smith
*What You Like* – Darren Hayes
*The Best Part of Letting Go* – The Dangerous Summer

Well, enough from me. I'll leave you in the Luke's more than capable hands – have fun!

# Intro

This series is based in the Republic of Ireland. The timescales, procedures, and context are reflective of local practices and policy.

# Content Information

This book contains strong subject matter that may not be suitable for all readers, including scenes that may depict, mention, or discuss:

- abusive relationship
- alcohol and drug use
- anxiety
- assault
- emotional abuse
- physical abuse
- rape
- sexual abuse
- sexual assault
- suicide
- violence

*To Luke*
*I'm sorry.*
*xxx*

## Luke

Pippa runs her hand over his leg, her fingers brushing against his dick. He swallows, but it's got nothing to do with excitement or pleasure. It's fear.

Pippa straddles him, pushing him back on the bed, her hands on his skin, touching, squeezing, rubbing. Then she uses her nails, scraping along his side, leaving a deep gouge in his flesh. He hisses in pain, but, instead of stopping, she smiles and does it harder.

'You like that, don't you?'

'Just go easy, please.'

She laughs as she climbs off him, undressing quickly before roughly pulling his boxers down his legs. When she takes the handcuffs from the bedside drawer, he wants to throw up.

'Pippa. I'm really tired. Can we do this tomorrow instead?'

'Oh come on. Luke. You like when I take charge.'

'Please Pippa. I need to get up early. I should get some sleep.'

But Pippa isn't in the mood for listening. She fastens the handcuffs in place, ignoring his pleas to not lock him up. She never listens though, and as soon as he hears the cuffs lock in place, he knows things are going to get a lot worse.

Pippa takes his dick in her hand, squeezing it hard. 'Oh Luke, what's going on here? Feels like I'm going to have to help you along.'

He pushes up the bed, trying to get his dick out of her iron grip, but she's enjoying herself too much. She massages his balls, squeezing them too hard. 'Pippa! Gently, please!'

'I like when you pretend you don't like this.'

He really doesn't like it. Everything she is doing to him hurts.

'We're doing this Luke. You dragged me to that boring band event. The least you can do is make it up to me.'

She straddles him, sliding him inside even thought he's not quite ready. He never is. She'll be waiting a while.

'Please, Pippa…' He doesn't know why he keeps begging her. It won't work. She won't stop until she's got what she wants from him.

The slap to his cheek stops any further protests. His wife leans over him as she rides him, grabbing a fistful of his hair and pulling hard. 'You're going to have to do better than that baby. You're supposed to be able to satisfy me, Luke. Why am I the one always doing the work?'

He tries to do what she wants, but it's not enough. Disappointed yet again, she climbs off and slaps his dick.

'What did I do to deserve a husband like you? You can't even have sex with me. What is wrong with you?'

'I'm just—'

When she grabs her hairbrush off the bedside table, he closes his mouth and curls into a ball to protect himself as much as he can, as she beats him.

Luke wakes up with a start, looking around him as the nightmare fades away. He pushes up the bed, gasping for breath, while he wipes sweat-soaked hair from his forehead.

He's alone.

No Pippa.

No handcuffs.

No hairbrush.

His stomach flips, so he leaps out of bed and into the en-suite, emptying his stomach. Thankfully, he'd only managed a small bowl of soup for dinner. His appetite is taking time to come back, but his thin frame is filling out again. Throwing up a few times a week isn't helping his progress, but at least it's not every night. A few months of being terrified to sleep, had taken its toll on him and his body.

Using the side of the bath, he pulls himself to his feet and shuffles into the kitchen. Moving on autopilot, he boils the kettle, then sits at the highly polished counter and drinks his coffee, as he watches the early morning Dublin traffic through the massive one-way windows, which line the entire wall of the apartment.

Since he was discharged from the centre before Christmas, he's felt like he's been wandering through his life with no control, no idea what he's doing, or even what he wants to do.

It took a lot of convincing for his family to let him out on his own, but they'd eventually agreed. That probably had a lot to do with the fact Dillon is in the same building. He's been living in the apartment under Dillon's for the last two months. It was an easy fix to a situation that had been giving too many people in his life sleepless nights.

Dillon actually owns the entire building. It's not common knowledge. Luke doesn't even think Gregg and Tate know. Dillon's sister Clara, looks after the property for him, but knowing the owner definitely has its perks. It's not as grand as Dillon's penthouse, but the three bedroom apartment has more than enough room for Luke.

It's an expensive address, with a spectacular view of the Liffey. It's not his home though. He doesn't have a home anymore. This is somewhere he's sleeping until...

He doesn't know what.

He'd managed to escape Pippa. It took too long and too many bruises, but he finally broke away from his wife, physically at least. Not that it solved his problems. Shame and embarrassment had stopped him from telling anyone about what she had been doing to him.

Dillon is his best friend, but Luke couldn't even tell him what had been going on for years. A part of him hadn't fully realised or accepted what his life had been like. A part of him still doesn't fully accept it.

The truth only came out after he had tried to take his own life. That was nearly six months ago. Six months of talking, of counselling, of trying to move on with his life.

And he still feels like he's in the exact same place.

He's still married to Pippa. Will be for another while, thanks to the rules in Ireland. And he's counting down every single day. He can't move on while she's still legally attached to him. He's in limbo and he hates it.

His two million Euro mansion is sitting empty, and that's the way it will stay. He has no intention of ever setting foot inside that house again. It had been his prison for years. It was meant to be his home, not the place he was hurt over and over again. Let the whole place burn to the ground! He couldn't care less.

At least the band is performing together again, and he can't be more grateful for that. Being on stage helped him feel more like himself. Well, the new him. The one that is still a little lost, but slowly getting there. Wherever there is.

And having Dillon upstairs helped. Even though his friend has another house by the coast in Wicklow, Dillon spent nearly every night in the flat. Luke knows it's so he can be close to his friend, but he's not going to argue. He needs the distraction, and if Dillon is happy to offer it, he'll take it.

Right on schedule, the doorbell rings and Luke lets Dillon in. He helps himself to a coffee and joins Luke at the counter. Dillon isn't the sort of friend who asks loads of questions, or makes meaningless small talk. He just sits and keeps Luke company. Which is perfect.

He does enough talking with his therapist. Not that it's really making a lot of difference. It doesn't matter how many times Luke hears that what happened with Pippa wasn't his fault, he knows it was. It had to be. He drove her to it.

'You all set for later?'

Luke blinks and looks over at Dillon. 'What's happening later?'

'Signing at the record shop.'

Luke nods. 'Yeah. Sorry, forgot.'

'You want to reschedule?'

'No. I just forgot. I'll check my emails again.'

'Okay, what's up?'

'What do you mean?'

Dillon pulls a bag of sour apple laces from his pocket and tears the end off one, chewing it, before he responds. '*I* don't read emails. *You* do. We switching places or something?' He winks, as he shoves the rest of the lace in his mouth.

He's got a point there. Dillon and Tate tended to miss or, more likely, ignore emails from their record company. Luke and Gregg didn't. Luke is the one the rest of the band tended to look to for information about where they're going, and what they're doing. 'I don't think I want to be you.'

'Fuck you!' Dillon pours himself another coffee, before topping up Luke's cup.

'Are you okay? You look tired.'

Dillon shrugs. 'All good.' He puts the kettle back on the counter behind them, but Luke catches him swallowing something while his back is turned.

Dillon's drug use is common knowledge. Has been for years. It's what he's taking that they still haven't quite figured out. Any questions or reference to it was met with a *fuck off* or *mind your own*

5

*fucking business.* Two of his friend's favourite replies.

The fact he uses in secret is the biggest worry. It's probably partly down to Tate's addiction problems and wanting to protect him, but Luke knows it's mainly because Dillon is one big secret. He's known him since school, but there's so much about his friend he doesn't know, or understand. And that's the way Dillon likes it. He can't let people get too close.

Luke checks his phone when it vibrates. 'Message from Sam reminding us about today. Shoot! We have to go in an hour.'

'Fuck!' Dillon downs the rest of his coffee, then rinses his cup. 'Better go glam myself up for my fans. We getting picked up or what?'

'They're sending a car for us.'

'Perfect. See you in an hour so.'

Dillon slaps him on the back as he walks past, shutting the apartment door behind him. Luke stares out the window again. He loves getting out and meeting their fans, but lately, the fear of being asked awkward questions has him dreading the events instead.

So far no one has even broached the whole Pippa subject, just telling him they're glad to see him back, and lots of other supportive things. But that doesn't mean it's going to continue forever. All he needs is one person asking the wrong thing, and he could very well fall apart in public.

With Dillon to his left, Tate and Gregg to his right, Luke stands in front of the massive poster of themselves and poses for photos.

'How many more fucking photos?' Tate mutters under his breath, the smile still plastered on his face.

'Ah you love it buddy,' Gregg says, smirking widely at the glare Tate doesn't manage to hold back.

'How about you try not to smile for a fucking change?'

Gregg's smile grows. 'Impossible. I'm just one of those naturally cheery people.'

'Irritating,' Tate says. 'You meant to say irritating.'

As Tate and Gregg do their usual back and forth, while the cameras keep flashing in their direction, Luke patiently smiles at everyone.

This is his happy place. Being with his best friends, being with their fans. It's the best feeling in the world. With all the stress and turmoil of the last few months, being here like this, makes it worthwhile.

It makes surviving worthwhile.

Sam puts an end to the photos, waiting while the band waves their goodbyes and disappear into the back of the shop. 'Good job everyone. I think you deserve some lunch now.'

'We've earned food? What a treat!' Sam throws a withering look at Gregg, then steps aside as Bria races over to him. He yelps as she throws herself at him, driving him back against the wall.

'So manly,' Dillon mutters, helping himself to a bottle of water from the table.

'You can shut up!' Bria says to Dillon, unwrapping her arms from around Gregg's neck. She gives Tate a hug, kissing him on the cheek. 'How's the dad to be getting on?'

'He's sick, after watching his sister groping his best mate. Can you two please keep all that touchy feely stuff to yourselves.'

She pokes him in the stomach. 'No way. I wouldn't be your sister if I didn't constantly annoy you.'

'And that is why I love her,' Gregg adds, wrapping his arms around her shoulders.

'And now I'm really going to be sick.'

'Funny! Oh and Mum wants you to call her.'

'What the fuck have I done now?'

'Wedding stuff. She needs to know if she can invite someone. I think it's a relative, but I wasn't really listening.'

Dillon snorts, then gestures towards Tate with his water bottle. 'That face there is one I want to remember. Stick the guy on stage, or

7

in front of a camera, and he's grand. Mention wedding stuff, and he looks like he's about to hurl.'

'You, shut it!' Tate says, pointing a finger at Dillon. 'And you!' he says turning back to Bria. 'The wedding is months away. I'm banning any talk of what distant relative will be eating food I paid for, until after the baby is born. The whole fucking house is full of baby and wedding magazines. I mean how many fucking magazines do you need? They're all full of the same shit. Buy one!'

Luke smiles to himself, as Gregg lifts his hands, standing in front of Tate. 'Okay people. I may be enjoying this as much as the rest of you, but clearly Grumpy here has reached his limit.'

Gregg yelps when Tate slaps him across the head. 'Hey! Watch the hair.'

'Fuck, would you both knock it off!' Dillon interrupts. 'I'm fucking starving. We getting food or what?'

'Sounds good, but I can't stay long,' Tate says. 'If Chloe goes into labour while I'm eating burger and chips, I'll be a dead man.'

Luke and Dillon take the lead, while the others follow them out into the rear car park, to the van. 'I'll just grab my shot. Give me a sec.'

Gregg hurries over to his car with Bria, while the others wait in the van.

Tate pulls out his phone, sending a message to Chloe.

'You okay?' Dillon asks Luke.

'Yeah. I love doing stuff like this. I like being busy.

'Glad to hear it. So, what do you fancy for lunch?'

Luke has lost track of the number of times he's been asked that question, but answering it doesn't get any easier. 'Whatever you guys want.'

Dillon gives him the look he reserves for when he's disappointed. Or at least, that's what Luke assumes it means. 'What do you want?'

He doesn't know. He never knows. 'Burger sounds good.'

Dillon takes a minute to look at him, running his tongue over his lip ring. 'Yeah. Fine. Burger it is.'

Gregg climbs in beside them and shuts the door. 'Insulin done. Let's eat.'

The van pulls out of the car park, taking a few minutes to drive past the screaming fans lining both sides of the street. As they drive by, Luke stares out the window. Why didn't he say a sandwich? Why can't he make a simple decision with his friends. Apart from his family, they're the people he's closest to. If he can't even speak his mind with them, what kind of a future is he going to have?

## Luke

He should be at home, watching TV, or messing around with his guitar. There's no way he should be parked at the side of the road, in the middle of nowhere, all alone, at half past nine at night.

But he doesn't want to be alone. After spending all day with the guys, the thought of going back to that apartment, and staring at the wall for the next few hours, isn't appealing. Especially when his mind is all over the place thanks, yet again, to Pippa getting to him.

She may be in prison, but she still has ways of getting her story out. No doubt one of her minions has access to her accounts and is posting on her behalf.

However she's getting her word out, it's working. Okay, so she's not contacting him directly. He's got a barring order, ensuring she can't go anywhere near him, but that doesn't stop her from putting lies online.

She'd been convicted of assaulting him. Why is she still protesting her innocence to anyone who'll listen?

Luke dumps his phone on the passenger seat and hits his head against the headrest. Because in her messed up mind, she is innocent. He drove her to it. Being a shitty husband had forced her to beat him.

Maybe that's true to a certain extent. He curses and shakes his head. 'It's not your fault. You did nothing wrong.'

Saying the words out loud doesn't help him believe them. He knows it wasn't his fault... mostly. Saying that Pippa has a problem, or talking about coercive control, doesn't help him accept that the woman he loves... loved, treated him the way she did.

Surely he must have done something? Maybe something insignificant to him, but important to her. Something that made her flip, like she had.

He absently rubs the side of his head. The scar in his hair line was left by her. She'd hit him with her hairbrush, hard enough to nearly knock him out. It's one of the many scars she left him with - ones you can see, but more you can't see.

He looks down at his ring finger. He only wore his wedding ring for a few weeks, but he can still feel it around his finger, weighing him down, a constant reminder of how gullible and stupid he is.

He closes his eyes. He's tired of everything. Tired of feeling like every minute of his life, is a fight he's not winning. And probably never will.

Luke starts the engine and pulls his Range Rover back onto the road. He should turn around and go to Dillon's flat, but his friend barely gets any time alone now, thanks to him hanging around. Tate and Chloe's baby is due any day now. There's no way they'd appreciate him dropping in on them.

Gregg and Bria are an option, but he reconsiders. They all deserve some time to be together, without him bringing them down.

Instead, he drives to Greystones, and parks around the back of the first pub he comes to. He grabs the cap off the back-seat and pulls on his leather jacket as he steps out of the car. Drinking probably isn't his best idea, but it's an idea, and he hasn't had many of those lately, so he's running with it.

He usually would have his security guard, Andy, with him, but had given him the evening off. Going to a bar without him is more than likely a terrible idea, but what the hell. Dillon has a habit of ditching his security when the mood takes him - which is usually all the time. Maybe it's his turn to be a little reckless.

Luke pushes open the door, then orders himself a beer at the bar, before choosing a corner booth at the far end of the room. It's away from everyone else and he should be left alone here. He'll have a few drinks, then call Andy, or a cab, to bring him home. Then he can figure out what to do tomorrow.

And the next day. And the next.

Performing again is amazing. He genuinely loves every second of it. But it's when he's not performing that brings him issues. He used to spend every free minute with Pippa.

Now it's just him. After being with her for so long, he hasn't got a clue what he likes to do. He'd given up everything he used to do before he met her.

His attention falls on the small wooden dragon attached to his keys. He carved it out of wood himself. For years, that was his way of unwinding, of relaxing. Seeing what he could bring out of a lump of wood, with just a few tools, and his own imagination, gave him such a buzz.

Carving wood, dancing, singing, playing the guitar. Four things he loves, or loved, until he was told otherwise. Carving made dust, so that had to go. As for dancing, well she didn't think it would work with the band.

Which is completely ridiculous. It's not like he was going to get on stage and dance. He did it in all the school performances, and he

12

didn't think he was too bad at it. But no. No time for that. He had to concentrate on her, and paying her credit card bill.

He grimaces and takes a long drink. Seems his bad mood is taking charge tonight.

But he's pissed off - at her and himself, for letting her do what she did. He lost so much because of her, nearly lost a lot more. Nearly died because of her.

She left him with nothing. Nothing in his life that's his.

He laughs wryly, then takes another long drink from his pint. He's heading towards his forties and has no hobbies, no idea how to spend his time. Hell, he doesn't even know what his favourite bands are. He knows nothing about himself. How pathetic is that?

That thought keeps him company as he orders a second drink. And a third.

## Maeve

Maeve steps into the pub and waves at a few of the regulars, as she makes her way through the crowd to the bar. After hanging her coat on the hook in the back room, she joins her brother, Mike, behind the bar and looks around the room. For a Wednesday night, it's surprisingly packed. 'Busy.'

'It's been like this all day. You're late by the way.'

She glances at her watch and grins. 'Barely ten minutes.'

'I should dock your pay.'

She wraps her arms around his neck and kisses his cheek. 'But my big brother would never do that. Would he?'

Mike pushes her off. 'Keep testing me and you never know. You can lock up tonight to make up for it. I've some paperwork to do.'

'Fine. So, anyone I should be keeping an eye on?'

Mike nods towards the far side of the room to the corner booth. She looks over, and frowns at the man sitting by himself. Thanks to the dim light in the bar she can't make out any details about the man, but from his posture, he's had a few drinks.

'How long has he been here?'

'About two hours. I've cut him off.' He takes her arm and guides her back towards the staff room, away from the rest of the customers. 'I can't swear to it, but I think it's Luke Daly.'

Maeve's mouth drops open, and she peers around the door frame to the darkened corner. 'Are you serious?'

Mike nods. 'I think so. He hasn't taken the cap off since he got here, so it's hard to see his face, but yeah. I reckon it's him. Keep it to yourself though. The last thing we need is a riot.'

Maeve couldn't agree more. Having a member of Broken Chords in the bar, all on his own, would absolutely attract attention. She glances at the other customers, but no one seems to be looking at him twice.

Probably because he looks downright miserable. That much she can tell. His shoulders are slumped, his head down, as he stares into his pint.

'We'll have to keep an eye on him. He arrived in that very nice brand new Range Rover in the car park. We don't need him smearing himself all over the tarmac, after leaving here off his head. Not sure what we do if he does try to leave though?'

'I'll have a look. See if it is really him.'

'Maeve,' Mike warns. 'Leave it alone!'

'Oh belt up, Mike! I need to check. If it's not him, there isn't a problem. If it is, we need to have a plan on how to get him out of here, without causing a scene.'

'Fine! But just confirm if it's him or not. I'm your brother. I know the history, okay?'

She rolls her eyes and fills a glass with water. 'It was a long, long, time ago.'

14

'Yeah, and you had a big, big, crush on him. Whopping crush. He's all you went on about, for about five years.'

Maeve snorts loudly. 'I think you'll find that's a slight exaggeration. And that was in school. He's like super famous now. I seriously doubt he even remembers me.'

'Whether he does or not, you do know he's married, right?'

'What do you take me for? Think I'm going to go over and jump on the guy? And for the record, he's separated. And his wife is in prison for hitting him. I think that would put an end to the relationship.'

'Exactly Maeve! He's still fucking married to a woman who hurt him. He's got stuff going on in his life. Serious stuff. Just watch yourself, Maeve.'

'Oh stop stressing about nothing.'

Mike looks less than convinced, as she squeezes past him and walks through the dwindling crowd. She stops in front of the man's table, and glances back to the bar.

Mike is facing her, his arms crossed. She waves, but he just frowns more. Maeve turns away from her brother, and looks down at the man in front of her. It's difficult to see any of his face under the cap.

'Hi.'

He completely ignores her, so she slips into the booth beside him, feeling Mike's disapproving gaze from across the room. 'Excuse me! Hello?'

He slowly lifts his head and blinks at her a few times. Maeve can't help but smile. It's Luke all right. It may have been nearly twenty years since she'd last seen him, in the flesh, but he hasn't changed a bit.

His chocolate eyes are a little unfocused, his brown hair hidden under the cap, but she'd recognise that face anywhere - whether he was famous or not.

She shuffles a little closer. 'Luke Daly. It's been a while.'

Her grand reunion falls flat. Luke frowns as he tries to focus on her, then gives up, and drops his head again. Well, that could have

15

gone better. Maeve slides the glass of water over to Luke, but he shoves it aside and finishes his pint instead. Once he's drained the last of the warm, no doubt flat, pint, he folds his arms on the table and drops his head again.

With no sign of any conversation heading her way, Maeve rejoins Mike at the bar and continues the rest of her shift, keeping one eye on Luke embedded in the corner booth. Every now and again he resurfaces, and takes a few peanuts from the bag she left on the table, then either slumps back on the table, or slouches against the back of the couch. He may look like the Luke she remembers, but he's not acting like him.

When the final customer heads for home, Mike and Maeve lean on the bar and face the drunken rock star.

'You think we should call someone?' he asks.

'Who exactly?'

'You're the one who knows him, not me.'

'Yeah, I know him. I mean I did know him, sort of. Okay, give me a few minutes with him. I'll see if I can talk to him.'

'Fine. I've got some paperwork to do. I'll head into the back and get started. You shout if he does anything he shouldn't.'

'I promise,' she repeats, then waits until Mike has gone before she slides into the booth beside Luke.

Maeve pushes the glass of water towards him again. 'You really should have some.'

'I don't want it.'

Okay, so maybe something has changed since school. His voice is deeper, and the smoky edge to it is far from unpleasant. 'Well, I disagree. We're closing now. Do you want me to call someone for you?'

He snorts and lifts the empty pint glass, slamming it back on the table when he realises there's nothing in it. 'Who exactly are you going to call, huh?'

'I don't know. Maybe you have a friend who can pick you up?'

16

He pulls a set of keys from his pocket and drops them on the table. 'My car is here.' He gestures absently towards the general direction of the door. 'It's there. Outside I mean. See. I'm fine.'

'No you're not. You've had too much to drink. There's no way I can let you drive home.'

He snorts again and slumps back in the seat. 'Home. That's a joke. I don't have a home.' He frowns and looks over at her. 'I know you.'

'We went to school together.'

Instead of commenting on that, Luke closes his eyes and shrugs. 'Fair enough.'

Maeve sits back and grimaces. She's seriously losing her touch. 'Okay, so should I call one of your friends?'

'No,' he mumbles without opening his eyes.

'Shit, that's not a great help is it,' she mutters to herself.

'It's all shit,' he responds even though she wasn't talking to him.

Maeve goes back to Mike and leans on the office door. 'Okay, so he's not budging. Can you give me a hand to bring him upstairs?'

'Not a chance in hell! I am not letting you babysit a drunk, married, rock star, that you used to fancy the pants off. Not happening.'

'So what's your big plan then? If you dump him in a taxi the driver would share his story. Imagine picking up an incredibly drunk Luke from your bar? I don't think that'd be great for business. He's a nice guy, Mike. Seriously. All I'm asking is for you to help bring him upstairs and dump him on the couch. Then he can leave under his own steam in the morning. No problems, and no publicity for him or for you.'

Mike gets up and glares over at Luke still slumped in the booth. 'Absolutely fucking perfect! Fine! But I'm staying over too. I'm not leaving you alone with a drunk.'

'Whatever. Will you help me move him, before he falls asleep here.'

'Fine! Just make sure you thank him from the bottom of my heart, for choosing my bar to get pissed in.'

## Luke

He groans as he wakes up. His stomach and head are having a serious dispute. One he has no control over. He gags and grabs the basin that's handed to him by someone, then spends who knows how long, getting up close and personal with whatever he drank last night.

Still too woozy to open his eyes, he collapses on the bed or couch or floor and buries his head under his arm. He doesn't do things like this. Not anymore. At least Tate and the guys weren't around to witness whatever he did.

Luke peers out from under his arm and frowns, as he looks around the unfamiliar room. Where the hell is he? He hears water running somewhere behind him, then footsteps, and the basin is lowered to the floor beside him again.

'How are you feeling?'

He rolls over faster than he probably should have, considering how he feels. There's a woman sitting on the armchair opposite him. She's familiar, but right now he's more interested in the basin than her. He holds up his hand to stop her talking, then lurches for the basin again. 'Sorry.'

She smiles at him, and he absolutely knows he's seen her before. 'It's fine. There's some water on the floor beside the couch.'

'Thanks.' Luke slowly sits up and wipes his hand over his face. 'Do I know you?'

She nods and tucks her purple tinted hair behind her ear. 'We had this conversation last night.'

'We did? Sorry. I don't remember.'

'Yeah, I'm not surprised. You had had a fair amount by the time I got to work. I'm a bartender.'

'Right.' He vaguely remembers going to the pub after the signing in town, but the rest of the night is a bit of a blur.

His phone rings in his pocket. 'That's been going for a while,' the woman says.

Luke pulls it out and frowns at the display, fully expecting it to be Pippa for some strange reason, but it's Tate. He swipes his thumb over the screen and attempts to sound less hungover than he is. 'Hey, Tate.'

'You okay?'

'Me? Yeah, sure. Why?'

'Cause we've been trying to reach you for hours. Dillon is doing his nut.'

'I'm sorry. I was asleep. Why were you looking for me?'

'You're two hours late for rehearsals.'

Luke glances down at this watch. 'Sorry. I lost track of time.'

'No problem. Are you sure you're okay. You sound a little rough.'

'I'm fine. Really.'

Tate is quiet for a minute which is never a good sign. 'How about you give this morning a miss? You good to meet after lunch?'

'Yeah. Sure. Sorry, Tate.'

'It's all good. See you in a bit.'

He ends the call and lies back on the couch rubbing his eyes. It takes him another few minutes to remember he's in a strange woman's house. When he looks up at her again, she's still in the chair opposite him.

'Right. So I have no idea who you are, or where I am.'

She smiles at him and Luke can't help but smile back. She's beautiful. Her black hair has purple highlights through it and is nestled into a loose bun, her pale skin is flawless and the sprinkling of freckles across her nose is adorable.

If he hadn't just been throwing up in her living room, he might have... He snorts loudly to himself. Would have what? Made a move? Asked her out? He doesn't do stuff like that. Wouldn't know where to start, even if he did.

'Are you okay?'

He attempts a smile, but has to reach for the basin as his stomach turns. Thankfully he gets it under control. 'Oh God! I am so sorry.'

'Seriously, stop apologising. It's grand, Luke.'

'So you know who I am?'

She hands him the glass of water from the floor. 'Yes, but not for the reasons you think. We went to school together. You were my physics partner for two years.'

Luke frowns over at her as the pieces fall into place. 'Maeve?'

She beams when he says her name. At least one part of his brain is still functioning. 'I'm impressed. You didn't seem to remember me last night.'

'I wouldn't take it personally. I don't remember last night, full stop. How did I end up here?'

'My brother Mike owns the bar you were... drooped over a table in. He helped me bring you up here. I live over the bar. Don't worry about your car either. It's still in the car park and the gates are locked.'

'Thank you. Really. I feel ... embarrassed.'

'Hey, we all go a little overboard from time to time. You do look rough though. Do you fancy grabbing a shower and I'll get you something to eat.'

'I'll just text my security guy. I'll need him to pick me up. I don't think driving would be a good idea.'

'Good thinking.'

He sends a text to Andy, asking him to pick him up and bring someone to collect his car. He needs to remove all evidence of his stupidity as soon as possible. On the ball as always, Andy replies within seconds saying he'll collect him in about an hour.

He stands up, desperate to try and redeem himself a little. Bad luck for him that his body is completely against that plan. He wobbles then crashes back on the couch. He holds his head as his brain takes another few seconds to catch up with the rest of him. 'That wasn't such a good idea.'

'C'mon. I'll give you a hand. You'll feel so much better after a shower.'

She helps him up and shows him to the small en suite attached to her bedroom. 'I've put fresh towels out. I'm afraid all the shampoo and stuff isn't exactly manly, but it's all I have.'

Luke leans on the sink and frowns at his reflection. He looks like he spent the night on the floor of the bar. Maybe he will feel better after a shower. 'Anything is better than stale beer, believe me. Thanks. I mean that.'

Maeve smiles at him again. 'I'll leave you to it.'

She shuts the door and he slowly peels off his t-shirt. He sniffs it and grimaces. Smells like stale beer too. It takes a monumental effort to get his jeans and boxers off. Maeve must have dealt with his boots while he was asleep. Either that or he lost them in the bar. Who knows? It's not like he can remember anything after the first few hours.

The hot water feels amazing and helps bring his brain back on line again. Unfortunately, it also brings the shame, humiliation, and total embarrassment with it. He can't go getting so drunk that a stranger ends up bringing him home with them. Who the hell does that? It's pathetic and something Ellen wouldn't be overly thrilled about.

He's lucky it was Maeve who found him, and not some random whoever, who would have sold the story to the highest bidder. Pippa would have loved that.

He angrily shakes his head. There he goes again. Thinking about Pippa, when he should be showering and getting the hell out of here, before Dillon comes looking for him.

He shuts off the shower and dries himself. Putting on the same boxers and jeans as last night feels horrible but he's got no choice.

'Luke?'

'Yeah.'

'I've left a clean t-shirt on the bed. It belongs to my brother so it should fit.'

'Thanks.' And he absolutely means it. He wasn't overly keen on putting his old one on again. As he gets dressed he looks around her room, spotting something by the mirror on the far wall. The notice board beside her mirror is covered with photos of friends and family.

He remembers her from school. How could he not? She was larger than life - even back then. He'd liked her. Quite a bit, but his shyness had been nearly crippling when he was in school. He only ever felt free on stage, which didn't help him relationship-wise when he was younger. Didn't help him now either.

He smiles and pulls the pin out of a photo of the physics club. As with most photos, he's in the back row with all the other tall kids. He's very different now to the boy in the photo. Looks different, mainly, but underneath so much has changed too.

If he'd known back then what was in store for him, he would have made a few different choices. But no one ever knows, and that's the problem.

He pins the photo back on the board and looks at his reflection. Black rings, unshaven, and looking a hell of a lot older than thirty-eight. He's surprised she let him through the door.

Not that he remembers how he got here to start with, and that's deeply embarrassing. He'd spent enough nights babysitting Dillon when he went overboard. It's not something he usually does himself.

Feeling a little more awake than he did a few minutes before, Luke walks back into the living room and Maeve gestures towards the table. 'Have a seat. I've done a bacon butty. Please say you're not a vegetarian?'

He shakes his head and winces. 'Ouch! Sorry, no. I'm not.'

'Phew! Oh, and I put a packet of paracetamol on the table for you. Might help with the headache. Do you fancy tea or coffee?'

'Coffee. Definitely coffee. Do you want a hand?'

'And risk you dropping everything? No thank you. You sit down. I'll be one minute.'

Luke takes two painkillers, washing them down with a mouthful of water. Maeve lowers a plate with a sandwich in front of him, and takes the seat opposite. 'Thanks. Again. You didn't have to do all this. I really do appreciate everything you've done.'

'Hey, I only passed physics because of your help,' Maeve says. 'It's the least I can do. Not that I'm using the subject in any shape or form.'

'You think I am?'

'Good point. Not sure international rock star and physics have a lot to do with each other.'

No,' he admits. 'Not really. Can I ask you something?'

She licks ketchup off her lips and nods. 'Go for it.'

'Why didn't you put me in a cab?'

Maeve shrugs and smiles at him. 'I didn't think you'd want everyone to know your business.'

23

'Thank you.'

'Just don't make a habit of it. My brother could do without the publicity too.' She sips her coffee as she looks at him. 'I can't believe who you are! I mean I know who you are, but the whole famous musician thing, is hard to get my head around. I copied my physics homework from you, and now you're a celebrity! That must be a claim to fame for me.'

Luke laughs at that. 'Not sure it's the best one. I reckon carrying me home from the bar, stupidly drunk, would work better.'

'I'm not going to tell anyone.'

He swallows the mouthful of sandwich before he answers. 'I wasn't implying you would.'

'I just don't want you to worry about that. Mike will keep it to himself too.'

'Thanks. Think the band has been in the press enough lately.'

'Okay, so tell me to mind my business if you want, but what happened last night? Why did you drink that much?'

Luke falls silent, focusing on his coffee, instead of her. How does he even go there? Does he even want to?

'It's okay,' Maeve says, when he doesn't answer. 'It really is none of my business.'

'I'm in a weird place. Having a few drinks seemed like a good idea at the time.'

'I get that. I'm sorry by the way. About you and your wife.'

And he absolutely doesn't want to go there. 'I had better go. I've got rehearsals.'

Maeve nods and smiles, but doesn't look happy. 'Of course. Your boots and jacket are in the hall.'

He gets up and brings his dishes into the kitchen, then sits on the chair in the hall to put on his boots. Maeve joins him when he's done, and holds out his keys. 'I'll show you down. It's a bit of a maze.'

'Thanks. And Maeve, I really do appreciate what you did for me last night. It... you saved me a lot of embarrassment.'

She rubs his arm, and Luke flinches before he can stop himself. Maeve pulls her hand away and crosses her arms. 'No need for thanks. I owe you. Come on, I'll show you out.'

He follows her downstairs and around the back of the building to his car. Andy is outside with Jason, Dillon's bodyguard. 'Wow! They're intense! Which one is yours?'

'The one on the left.'

'Well I wouldn't cross him. I'll unlock the gates.'

Luke hands his keys to Jason, who gets into his Range Rover and pulls out of the car park.

'It was good to see you again.'

She smiles, and he can't help but smile back. He doesn't know what it is about her, but he feels comfortable around her. Apart from the drunken stupor part, he's enjoyed meeting up with her again.

'Hey, not a problem. And you know where I am, if you fancy dropping in at any stage.'

'I'll keep that in mind. Thanks again.'

She winks at him. 'Any time. Bye Luke.'

'Bye Maeve.' With nothing else to say to delay the inevitable, he gets into Andy's car and they drive away. Luke glances back at Maeve, as they round the corner. It makes no sense at all, but he's already missing her.

*Luke*

He parks behind Dillon's Mustang, and hurries inside Tate's studio. He pauses at the door and closes his eyes, listening to the sound of the sea beyond the house.

Tate bought the incredible farmhouse for himself and Chloe last year, a few weeks before he proposed to her. It instantly became the new band hang out.

Having a purpose built studio in the garden was a big draw. Tate hadn't spared any expense, kitting out the three roomed studio to the highest spec. He'd even included a mini cinema so the guys could chill out in there, without getting under Chloe's feet.

Especially at the moment. At nine and a bit months pregnant, Chloe is overdue, and not in the best of form the last few days. Tate is seriously on edge too and Luke can't blame him. He could become a father any minute.

Over the last few months, Luke has seen a massive change in Tate. Fair enough he's still scared about being a father, but he'd come into his own. Luke couldn't be more proud of his friend.

He'd overcome his past and his addiction after a long and difficult battle. He'd managed to come out the other side with an incredibly loving and supportive fiancée, a baby on the way, and an amazing career.

Luke's smile fades a little. He'd kind of assumed he'd be the first to have all that. For a long time, he was the only one of the four who was in a relationship. Pippa had never wanted children though. She didn't want to ruin her figure. She was so against it, she'd even arranged for him to have a vasectomy. That should have been a red flag for him.

Too many of those flags were ignored, or not even seen in the first place.

He rubs his side, tracing the scar she left when she threw her jewellery box at him. A constant reminder of his naivety, of his stupidity.

'Hey. You okay?'

He jumps, then smiles at Chloe. 'Sorry. You scared me.'

She links arms with him, and rests her hand on her belly. 'Sorry about that. What are you doing out here?'

'Thinking.'

'Need to share anything?'

'No. I'm good. Thanks though. So, how are you doing?'

She blows out a long breath as she rolls her eyes. 'Big. Bored. Fed up. Uncomfortable. Did I mention big?'

'Yeah. You did. Do you want a hand back to the house?'

'I came out to stretch my legs, but now I'm out, I just want to lie back down. Would you mind being my crutch. This child is taking after its father. It feels like it's a giant.'

Luke laughs and takes a better grip on her arm, as they walk back across the garden to the main house.

'How's Tate getting on?'

She nods as she shuffles along. 'He's really good, Luke. Never misses a meeting or a phone call.' She goes quiet for a minute. 'The nightmares still get him from time to time, but he's coping a lot better than he was.'

'That's great.'

'So what about you,' she asks, looking over at him. 'How are you doing?'

He shrugs, as he helps her up the steps to the patio doors. 'I'm okay. Still finding my feet I guess.'

'How is it living under Dillon's place?' She grins, and he knows exactly what she's talking about.

'Surprisingly quiet. I don't think he's as... active as he used to be.'

'Perhaps his impending fortieth birthday is making him reevaluate things.'

Luke shrugs. 'I'm not going to try to figure him out. I gave that up years ago.' He helps her onto the couch and passes her a blanket. 'Do you need anything?'

She lies back and takes the remote from the arm of the chair. 'I need this baby out of me. Can you do anything about that?'

'Afraid not. Sorry.'

She grimaces and tucks the blanket around herself. 'Didn't think so. Get out!' she shouts at the bump, before sighing and turning on the TV. 'So bored with this.'

Luke kisses her on the head then gestures to the door. 'I'll leave you to it.'

'Thanks Luke. And make sure Grumpy has his phone on him all the time.'

'He's surgically attached to it. I promise. Take it easy.'

'I can't exactly do anything else. You better go. Have a fun rehearsal.'

Gregg opens the studio door, as Luke's walking back across the garden. 'How's the head?'

'Tate told you, huh?'

'Yeah, he might have mentioned something. You okay? You're not usually one to go on all night benders. You taking a leaf out of Dillon's book?'

Luke pours himself a cup of coffee and grabs a biscuit from the tin. He hears Tate and Dillon messing around on guitars in the inner room. 'No chance. I just got into my head a little and went to a bar.'

Gregg sits on the chair beside the coffee machine and rests his boots on the coffee table. 'What did she do? I'm presuming *she who shall not be named*, did something evil?'

'Just more nonsense online.'

'And you decide to deal with it by going to a bar? Alone? Why didn't you call me, Luke? I'm here for you, you know that. And since when do you get drunk? Is that a new thing now?'

'I've got a headache, so please don't lecture me.'

'I'm not going to lecture you. After everything you've had to deal with, I don't blame you for wanting a few drinks. It's the going alone part that I'm not happy about. How the hell did you get home?'

'I kind of didn't,' Luke admits, keeping an eye on the door into the inner room. The last thing he wants to do is have Dillon walk in on this conversation.

Gregg frowns, then grins widely and raises his eyebrows. 'Is that so? Do tell.'

'It wasn't like that. Well, I did stay in someone's house, but I didn't know until I woke up there.'

'I'm on my first coffee, Luke. You'll have to be less cryptic. You're confusing the hell out of me.'

'I went to Greystones and stopped at the first pub I found. Turns out it's owned by the brother of someone we went to school with.'

'Oh yeah. Who?'

'Maeve. She was in physics with me.'

29

Gregg nods slowly. 'Yeah, I remember her. Cute. Sort of nuts, but in a heartwarming and truly endearing way. Kind of like me.'

Luke laughs and sips his coffee. He needs all the caffeine he can get today. 'She's still nuts. Purple hair and tattoos. She works in the bar and lives over it. I must have passed out. And yes, I know, so don't say it. It was such a bad idea.' He shrugs and looks over at Gregg. 'Anyway, Maeve and her brother Mike, brought me up to her place, and I woke up on her couch, throwing up in a bucket.'

'Did you now? Quite the first impression!'

'I know, I know.' He rubs his forehead as the headache gives him a kick. 'God it was humiliating!'

Gregg waves Luke's concerns away. 'That's nothing, buddy. Believe me. I've lost count of the number of places Tate and Dillon have thrown up.'

'Oh, great. Well maybe if I keep this up I can beat their record?'

'How about you don't. So...'

'So what?'

'You woke up puking on her couch. And?'

'And nothing, so get your sordid mind out of the gutter. I had a shower, she made breakfast, then I left.'

Gregg nods slowly, while he ruffles his unruly hair. He's far from done with this conversation. Luke finishes the biscuit and takes another from the tin. His appetite is nearly back to normal, thankfully.

The weight he lost last year is back on, helping him look healthier than he has for a long time. Continuously living in fear of doing or saying the wrong thing, had made him physically sick. He still struggles with food from time to time, but it's getting better. Like everything else in his life, it'll take time.

'Do you like her?'

Luke splutters as the next mouthful of coffee heads in completely the wrong direction. 'What?'

'Do you like her?'

'No... well, yes. Maybe. I don't know. I was throwing up and trying not to die of embarrassment.'

'She works in a bar. I'm sure it's not a rare occurrence.'

'Thanks for that.'

'You didn't answer my question. Well, not really. Do you like her?'

Luke sits down beside him and shrugs. 'Yeah. I think so. I mean she's nice, but I don't know.'

'Not ready?'

He lies back and turns his head to look at his friend. 'I don't know if I'll ever be ready, Gregg. What if I can't...'

'Can't what?'

'Be with someone. Like that. Like any way at all. What if I freak out or...' he closes his eyes and sighs. 'I don't know.'

'Maybe you will freak out. I can't answer that. But if you find the right person, that doesn't matter, Luke. You deserve to be loved. You deserve to be treated right.'

'I'm scared, Gregg.'

Gregg nudges him in the arm. 'I know you are and that feeling won't go away easily. That doesn't mean it's not worth taking a chance on someone. And it sounds like she did right by you so far. Haven't seen any drunken photos of you on social.'

'Oh wow! Thanks!'

Gregg reaches for his coffee again. 'Any time.' Gregg slaps his leg, then waves excitedly at Luke. 'I've had an epic idea. How about we go to the pub for dinner?'

'I don't know.'

'It's just some pub food. If she's there you can thank her for last night. If she's not, we eat dinner and go home.'

'You won't leave me alone there?'

'Of course not.'

Luke glances over at the door again. 'What about Dillon?'

'What about him?' Gregg asks, frowning at the door.

'I'd prefer he didn't know about her. Not yet. I don't want to... with his feelings and all...'

Gregg catches on, nodding slowly. 'Got you. It's between you and me. If it turns out you want to see her again, you can tell him.'

'But what if he's angry?'

'What the hell makes you think he'd be angry with you?'

'I don't know. It's just weird knowing he has feelings for me. I don't want to hurt him.'

Gregg turns around to look him dead in the eye. Luke automatically drops his gaze. 'Hey, don't do that. Look at me.'

He forces himself to look at Gregg again.

'See,' Gregg says, smiling at him. 'Not so bad is it?'

'Sorry.'

'Nothing to apologise for, Luke. Ever. Now back to Dillon,' he continues, after patting Luke on the shoulder. It's a constant thing and Luke is taking time to get used to it.

The guys and his family are doing everything they can to make him feel valued, and he appreciates it. He just wishes they didn't have to wrap him in cotton wool.

'Now, granted, Dillon is in love with you, but he's said over and over again that it's his issue. Not yours. I promise you, he will not have a problem with you being interested in someone other than him. You're not gay or bi. He knows that. Seriously, stop stressing. He'll be fine.'

'You really think so?'

'Absolutely. But if you'd prefer we'll keep it to ourselves, until you know if there's anything there with the delightful Maeve. So, you on for the road-trip after work? Just the two of us. I swear I'll even try to use a napkin, but I'm not promising anything!'

32

Luke

He wipes his damp hands on his jeans, as he looks across at the pub. The lights are off in the apartment over the pub. Does that mean Maeve is at work? Maybe she's not home at all. That'll be the best option. He's not ready to go back in there again.

'It's just dinner.'

He nods at Gregg, not in the slightest bit convinced. The few minutes it takes for Gregg to give himself his insulin shot, only adds to Luke's terror. He can do this. He's walked out on stage in front of thousands of people. He can walk into a bar and talk to a girl.

'You all set?' Gregg asks as he packs away his insulin.

Luke nods and reaches for the door handle before he can change his mind. Andy and Ciaran meet them at the front of Gregg's

Defender. 'You really don't have to babysit,' Gregg says as he pulls on his jacket.

'Yeah. Right!' Ciaran says. 'You lot attract attention and more than your fair share of trouble, so don't even go there. We'll be subtle. You won't even know we're here.'

'If you're inside, I guarantee I'll know you're here. Seriously dampen my mood having you watching everything I'm doing.'

'Maybe if you all stop doing stupid things we won't have to continuously watch you.'

Gregg pouts at Ciaran. 'Hey! I'm one of the well behaved ones. It's Dillon and Tate who are the pains in the ass. We're the good ones, aren't we Luke?'

Luke is too busy trying not to throw up, to join in the chat.

Clearly realising he's about to make a run for it, Gregg nudges him in the side. 'C'mon. I'm starving.'

With Gregg leading the way, Luke follows him across the road and into the bar. It's half empty, so they easily slip in and find a booth at the back of the room. Andy and Ciaran stay at the side of the bar, keeping their clients in their sights.

'Is she here?' Gregg asks, as he hands Luke a menu.

'Don't think so.' But then Maeve comes out of the back room, a box of crisps in her arms.

Gregg grins widely and kicks Luke under the table. 'I take it by the look on your face that's the lovely Maeve? She's hot!'

'Would you stop it,' he hisses, terrified she'll hear.

Luke is still staring at her when she looks up and smiles at him. Maeve walks around the bar and over to them. 'Well, hello there. I wasn't expecting to see you again so soon.'

'Yeah. Hi.' He grunts when Gregg kicks him under the table again. 'I wanted to say thank you. For last night.'

She waves his comment away. 'Ah that was no big deal. Forget about it.' Her smile stays on her face when she spots Gregg opposite him. 'Gregg Egan! Would you look at your hair. I love it!'

He grins and nods to her hair. 'Look who's talking!'

She runs her fingers through her black and purple hair. 'Life is too short to be boring. Now, what do you fancy? Unless of course you came back to see little me?' She smiles at Luke and he swears she winks at him, but he dismisses it as a figment of his imagination.

'Food would be good,' Gregg says, drawing Maeve's attention away from Luke, allowing him to breathe again. 'What do you recommend?' Gregg asks, as Luke tries to focus on the menu instead of Maeve.

It's been a long, long time since someone interested him the way she does. The problem is, he's so out of touch with himself and how to act, he's completely lost and absolutely terrified.

'Burgers. Leave it with me. I'll sort you out. Drinks?'

'I'll take a coke,' Gregg replies, then she turns her attention to him. 'Em, coke too.'

She winks again, and this time he didn't imagine it. 'Okey dokey. I'll be back in a sec.'

When she leaves, Luke releases a long breath and collapses back in the seat. 'I can't do this.'

'Can't do what? Eat?'

'Talking.'

Gregg leans back in the booth and taps a beer mat on the table. 'Really? That's weird, because you do it with me all the time.'

'Yeah, but that's different. I haven't talked to a girl since before... her.'

Gregg's face changes. It does that every single time Pippa is mentioned or even hinted at. The hard lines appear around his eyes and mouth, a telltale sign he's pissed off. 'Don't overthink it. Just be you.'

Easier said than done. He doesn't know who he is anymore.

Maeve comes back over to their table with the drinks, and sits down beside Luke. 'Can you give us a minute, Gregg? I'd like to talk to Luke.'

Gregg smiles encouragingly at him, then grabs his drink and goes over to Ciaran and Andy at the bar.

'Sorry about that. I wanted to see how you're doing after all the puking.'

Luke can't help but laugh. 'Embarrassed.'

'I've never had a famous rock star throw up in my living room before. It was the most excitement I've had for ages.'

'I'm glad you enjoyed yourself. I didn't.'

She twirls a lock of purple hair between her fingers. 'That's a shame.'

'What is?'

'That you didn't enjoy yourself.'

'I was throwing up.'

'You know what, that's a good point. Okay, so forget about that part. It was great to catch up again.'

He nods. 'Yeah, it was.'

Maeve smiles at him and rubs his arm, removing her hand when he flinches. 'I'm sorry. Did I hurt you?'

He forces himself to smile, trying to put her at ease after his reaction. 'Of course not.'

Her smile comes back, but she doesn't make a move to touch him again. 'I prefer you sober though, so maybe lay off the drink today.'

Luke grimaces and points to the glass of coke. 'That's as hard as I'm going today. My head still isn't happy with me.'

'I'm not surprised. But no harm no foul. I've seen worse working here, I promise you.' She nods over to Andy, and Ciaran. 'Impressive heavies you have there. Do they go everywhere with you?'

'I'm meant to have Andy with me whenever I'm in public. I broke the rules yesterday with my solo drinking session.'

'Well I reckon there's no way anyone will mess with you, with him around.' She winks at him and smiles. 'Then again, you look like you could take care of yourself. You're hardly a small bloke, are you?'

He can't help but smile at that. He's not used to being complimented. 'Thanks.'

She slaps the table and pushes to her feet. 'Well, I better go get your food.' She winks and saunters away back to the bar. Luke stares after her, spending a little too much time focusing on her ass.

He clearly remembers her from school and she wasn't like this. Yeah she was out there, and didn't bend to peer pressure, or anything like that. Clearly that continued into adulthood. Purple hair, tattoos, and piercings. And she is completely captivating.

He hasn't looked at anyone since he left Pippa. Or she left him. He's still not quite sure how it ended. Neither one of them had actually said the words. The fact she's serving time for assaulting him, kind of put an end to the relationship.

'I like her.'

'What?' Luke asks as Gregg slips back into the booth.

'Maeve.'

'Yeah. Me too.'

Luke finds himself looking over at the bar as Maeve steps out from the kitchen carrying two plates. She places them on the table and waves for Gregg to move up.

'Oh you mean I can stay?'

'As long as you scooch up.'

Maeve sits beside Gregg and smiles across at Luke. 'I saw you in Dublin two years ago.'

'You did?'

Maeve reaches across and takes a chip from Luke's plate. 'Yep,' she says before popping the chip in her mouth. 'You were fucking brilliant!' She grins over at Gregg. 'Not too bad yourself.'

Gregg grins at her. 'Drumming God at your service,' he replies, before tucking in to his dinner... after moving the plate out of her reach.

She licks her fingers, all the while keeping her attention on Luke. He's not used to this. He's had plenty of attention from women. It went with the fame and all that, but he knows her. He's not used to people he knows looking at him like that.

'You deserved that award you won. You're a damn good guitar player.'

Luke coughs, as the chip goes down the wrong way. 'You know about that?'

'I'm kind of an internet snoop. I like to keep up with what everyone from school is doing. You two and your mates are by far the most exciting. You didn't go to the reunion a few years ago, did you?'

Gregg shakes his head as he chews on a mouthful of burger.

'We were on tour,' Luke says before Gregg can blurt out the real reason. None of them had wanted to go. Even if they weren't famous, they wouldn't have gone. The only people they wanted to mix with from school were each other.

She nods, then grins widely. 'Couldn't be bothered either.'

'Too right!' Gregg replies. 'Good riddance.'

Maeve nudges him on the arm, ignoring the glare he gives her. 'That's where we might actually agree Mr. Egan. God, I couldn't wait to get out of there.'

Luke catches a man waving at Maeve from behind the bar. 'I think your boss is trying to get your attention.'

She looks over her shoulder and gives him a gesture you wouldn't usually give your boss. 'It's okay,' she says, noticing the look on Luke's face. 'It's Mike, my brother. I'm guessing you don't remember him from last night?'

'I met him last night?'

Maeve grins and shakes her head. 'Not exactly. He moved your heavy, uncooperative ass up to my flat. He's *thrilled* you're back here again so soon.'

That's so not good. He didn't do embarrassing stuff like that. He left that to Dillon, and Tate every now and again. 'Back in a sec.' He goes over to Mike and leans on the bar. 'Hi.'

Mike's eyes narrow and he crosses his arms. He's the image of Maeve, except a lot less cheery. 'Great to see you in my bar again,' he says, his tone laced with sarcasm.

'Yeah, I wanted to apologise for last night. I had a bad day and took it too far. Maeve said you helped bring me upstairs.'

Mike nods. 'I appreciate you not throwing up on me.'

'Did I break anything?'

'No. To be fair, you weren't too bad. I get some obnoxious drunks in here. Apology accepted. I'm not about to turn down your money now, am I? Just do me a favour.'

'Sure.'

'Don't do that again. You could have ended up with some juicy pictures on the net.'

'I know. Believe me, I'm still getting over the hangover. I have no plans to get that bad again.'

Mike's frown finally breaks into a small smile. 'Don't worry about that. Maeve won't let you. Not while you're drinking here. You'd better go back to your mate. While you're there, can you kindly remind my sister I'm not paying her to sit and talk all night. There are tables that need to be cleared.'

## Maeve

Even though she would love to stay talking to Luke and Gregg all night, she can't deal with the constant dirty looks Mike is flinging in her direction. As she continues her shift, she finds her attention drawn to the corner booth continuously. Luke and Gregg are laughing and Luke looks genuinely happy. Very different to the depressed drunk from last night.

She knows a little about what he's going through, but has no doubts his management company have been economical with the truth. His wife is in prison for assaulting him, which is something she's still struggling to accept.

It's a pity she didn't remember that when she touched him earlier.

The poor guy visibly flinched, and she feels shitty about that. She hopes she hasn't scared him away by doing that.

Maeve leans on the far end of the bar and watches Luke and Gregg. The two men have been friends for as long as she's known them. The four band members had been lifelong friends. Time, and perhaps a lack of interest, had meant Maeve lost touch with most of her school friends over the years.

She wasn't one for the whole settling down with a nine-to-five job thing, like most people. As soon as school finished, she was off backpacking around the world, and didn't come back for three years.

Looking at Gregg and Luke, she can't help but be a little jealous. Luke has been through a lot and it's clear, even from the short time she's been back in their company, that Gregg cares about him.

She takes out her phone and enters Broken Chords in the search engine. As she scrolls through the multitude of images, she keeps glancing over at the booth where two of the four band members are eating burgers.

The four guys are good looking, but to her, Luke outshines the rest of them. It had nothing to do with the small detail of having a crush on him, since the first moment she saw him in school. The timid, slightly lanky teenager, had matured into a stunning man.

There are plenty of photos of Luke online. It seems the band aren't afraid to show off their bodies - not that she can blame them. The solid muscles, teamed with his pierced nipples and stunning tattoos, turns Luke's body into a work of art.

But it's his face that still gets to Maeve. His soft brown eyes, ruffled dark brown hair, and those lips that transform his face, when he smiles. As she watches him, he turns the stud under his lip, and her throat tightens.

Everything about that beautiful man gets to her.

She chews on the stud to the side of her mouth, under her bottom lip. Would he be interested in someone that looks like her? She's got her fair share of tattoos and piercings. Most of her stomach, side, and leg are tattooed.

She is as opposite to his wife as you can get. She's seen pictures of the perfect Pippa. Blonde hair, petite, designer clothes, and perfect make-up.

No ripped jeans, torn crop tops, ink and piercings, or purple tinted hair.

'What's the deep look for?'

Mike leans on the bar beside her, facing the booth with the rock stars.

'Just thinking.'

Her brother sighs loudly and clenches his hands together, the skulls on the back of each hand distorting as he tightens his fists. 'You still have a thing for him, don't you?'

She gives him a horrified look, then smiles when he raises his eyebrows at her. Mike knows her too well. 'Maybe.'

'Thought so. You're making a puddle of drool on the bar top.'

She glances down before she can stop herself. 'Oh ha ha. Don't worry, I'm not going to do anything. Like you said, he's in the middle of a shitty situation with his wife. Besides, I don't think I'm his type.'

'Ah now I wouldn't go that far. Fair enough, the timing probably isn't the best, but if you believe in all that fate shit that you seem to, maybe him walking into this bar last night was a sign. He could have gone into a few dozen different places. Why here?'

Mike has a point there.

'And as for the *not his type* part, yes you're not anything like his ex, but that's a good thing isn't it? And between you and me, I don't believe in that *type* nonsense. You don't build relationships with people because of how they look. It's how you are together.'

Maeve smiles at Mike and nudges his arm. 'Since when did you get so philosophical?'

'Old age. Now stop drooling over my customers. Finish your shift, then go and talk to him. He chose this place again tonight for a reason.'

# Luke

'She keeps looking over at you.'

Luke drops his head, focusing on his empty plate instead. He doesn't want to meet her eyes. Gregg wouldn't lie about it, but he honestly doesn't know how to react. He likes Maeve, but it's been years since he asked anyone out, and that hadn't ended well for him.

Maeve would probably know about what Pippa did. Not everything. He'd been able to keep a lot of it to himself, but the world knows she'd hit him. The world knows he was too weak to stop it from happening.

'Stop it!' Gregg grips his arm and squeezes it. It does the trick, pulling him out of his thoughts.

'Sorry.'

'Never apologise. You're allowed to think about it. Just don't let it stop you from living your life, Luke. You deserve to be happy.'

'Do you think Maeve knows about it?'

Gregg glances over at her, then shrugs. 'Maybe. Does it matter? You did nothing wrong. You have nothing to be embarrassed about. Sure I let myself be kidnapped by my stalker. Now *that* is something to be embarrassed about, believe me.'

He grins and Luke smiles back. 'You might have a point there. I don't know what to do though. I haven't done this for a while.'

'Well, from what I can see so far, you're off to a good start. It's clear she likes you.'

'Do you think she'd go for a walk or something with me when she's done? Or is that too much? Should I just—'

'Shush. You're going to talk yourself out of it. It's not too much. Far from it, buddy. I'd be amazed if she said no.' He finishes his coke and grabs his coat. 'I'm going to leave you to it.'

'What! No!' Whatever about talking to her with Gregg here, he can't do it alone.

'I'll wait outside with Ciaran. You can do this, but the last thing you both need is me hanging around. Andy will stay with you to watch your back.' He stands up and slips on his jacket. 'Have a bit of confidence in yourself Luke. You've got this. I'll be outside if you need a wing-man, but you'll be grand.'

Gregg winks, then walks away, waving at Maeve as he walks past the bar. It's now or never. He could wait here and hope Maeve comes over, but that could take hours if she's busy.

No, the only way he can come out of this in one piece, is to go over and ask her. She'll either say yes or no. Either way he'll know, and he won't be sitting here alone wondering for the next few hours.

Luke wipes his hands on his jeans, then picks up his jacket from the seat. Andy flashes him a thumbs up as he walks past. So many people have his back. He doesn't want to let them down. Or himself.

Luke picks a seat towards the far end of the bar, away from

everyone else. He doesn't think he's been recognised yet, and wants to keep it that way. He watches Maeve as she finishes serving. She's changed quite a bit since school, but he supposes they all have.

She was always a little crazy, not wanting to conform to what people thought she should. She's clearly carried that on since leaving school, and he really likes it. Quite a bit in fact. Her numerous tattoos and the piercing in the corner of her lip suit her down to the ground.

Pippa barely tolerated his tattoos and piercings. But he got them because he liked them. Over the years he'd begun to dislike them. Mainly because they were the source of so many arguments. Since he broke free, he's slowly learning to like things about himself again. Things like his tattoos.

She reaches up to a shelf behind the bar, and the short top she's wearing rides up, giving him a good look at the tattoo crawling up the side of her stomach. It looks like a rose with thorns, but it's hard to make out all the detail. It suits her though.

Maeve finishes what she's doing and walks over to him, smiling, which is a good start.

'Did your grumpy friend leave you alone?'

'Yeah. Well, I've still got Andy,' he says, nodding to his bodyguard.

'So you want another drink?'

'Can I get another coke?'

'Of course.' She takes out a clean glass and scoops some ice into it.

He launches in before he can talk himself out of it. 'What time do you finish?'

'About an hour. Why?'

'Do you... would you like to go for a walk maybe? With me, I mean.'

When she smiles over at him the nerves disappear. 'I'd love to. How about you stay where you are and keep me company until then.'

The next hour goes by quickly enough for Luke. In between serving the last few customers, Maeve made sure to speak to him as much as she could. He's not the best at talking to people. Even when he's being interviewed, he tended to let the others take the lead. But with her, he found conversation easy.

When the last customer finally leaves, Mike throws Maeve her jacket. 'I'll finish up here.'

She doesn't argue with him, slipping on her coat, then gesturing to the door. 'C'mon! This is a rare event. He never lets me go early. Better make the most of it.'

## Maeve

She keeps the massive grin to herself as they walk along the path beside the harbour. When Gregg had left without Luke, she'd hoped he would come over to talk to her. Being asked to go for a walk was better than she could have hoped for.

Luke isn't saying much yet, but she doesn't mind. He'd chatted easily enough while in the bar. Maybe one on one is a little different.

He seems less confident alone. His hands are stuffed in the pockets of his jeans and his head is down, the peak of the baseball cap hiding his features in its shadow. She noticed he tended to keep his head down, avoiding eye contact.

Perhaps it's as a result of whatever his wife did to him? He's different than she remembers. Quieter, but that's probably to be expected. Maeve takes a long deep breath of fresh sea air. 'I love that.'

'Love what?'

'The smell of the sea. Absolutely can't beat it. You know the first thing I do when I wake up?'

He shakes his head. Trying to get him to talk is proving difficult.

'I open my windows and take in a lungful. Best way to start that day. Well, that and a cup of coffee of course.'

He smiles a little, but that's as much of a reaction as she gets. She remembers him being painfully shy in school, but this is more than shyness. He's nervous. Maybe of her. Maybe of the situation.

'So, I've been dying to ask. What's it like?' She's going to keep trying to coax the conversation out of him.

'What's what like?'

'The whole famous thing. Being a celebrity. Is it amazing or annoying as hell - especially when you get people like me asking you questions like that?'

He smiles and Maeve nearly cheers for joy. 'It's really weird.'

'How?'

'I don't really know how to explain it. I don't think it's something any of us thought about, until it happened to us. I mean we hoped we'd do okay when we started the band, but we never thought about how things would change if we were ever famous. Fame and success are two different things.'

'I never thought about it like that.'

'One day I was just me, and the next I'm getting fans chasing me down the road.'

'Please tell me that's an exaggeration?'

He smiles over at her again. 'Nope. I was chased down the full length of Grafton Street by six screaming women.'

'Wow! That's a little intense.'

'It's surreal walking along the street and being recognised. I don't think I'll ever get used to it.'

'Do you like what you do?'

He nods enthusiastically. It's easy to see that the band is his passion. She loves the way his entire face lights up when he talks about it.

'I love it. I wasn't too sure about the band at first. I sort of got badgered into it by Dillon, but I'm glad I did join. I can't describe how it feels to be on stage singing and playing, while an entire room of strangers sing along with you. It's an amazing feeling. I think being on stage is...' he pauses and shakes his head.

'It's what?'

'Being on stage like that with my friends, is one of the few times I'm happy. I mean really genuinely happy. I'm not saying I'm not happy the rest of the time. But for the hour and a half or whatever, it's just us and the music.' He shrugs and looks out to sea. 'Sounds stupid.'

'Are you kidding me? It sounds amazing! Your family must think the whole thing is crazy. You have an older brother don't you?'

He nods. 'Alex.'

'Ah yes. My mate was completely besotted with him in school. He's all she ever talked about for nearly a year.'

Luke laughs again. 'Yeah. Alex was popular all right.'

'Is he still on the market, or do I need to break my friend's heart?'

'Sorry. He's married and has two kids.'

'I might keep that to myself. No point opening old wounds. So is he into music like you?'

'Finance. He works for a bank in Dublin.'

'How very civilised. Did you go straight into music when you left school?' She knows she's firing the questions at him but, not only is she interested, she likes hearing him talk.

'No, I did a business and marketing course. Worked in town for a bit until the band took off. What about you? Have you worked for your brother for long?'

Maeve shakes her head. 'Mike only bought the pub about two years ago. I have to admit, school and I didn't get on so well. I've never been one of those people who likes rules. I prefer to make my own way.'

'I think I got that,' he says with a smile.

'It's the purple hair that gave it away, huh?'

'Might have been.'

'And this coming from the guy who has a piercing in his chin.'

He shrugs, then smiles as he looks out at the sea again.

'Anyway, I did a dance course after school, then toured around for a few years with a dance company.'

'You kept that up? You danced in school, didn't you?'

Maeve is over the moon that he remembered that. 'Yeah. I've always loved dancing. Any dancing too. I honestly couldn't care. So I saw a bit of the world while I was doing it, which was amazing. But I guess I missed Ireland too much. When Mike told me he'd bought the pub I decided *what the hell*. I'll come home and irritate him for a while.'

'Do you like working for him?'

'Of course! What's not to like? I get to live over the pub for free, and I've got the sea outside my window. Besides, Mike is a big softy...well, most of the time.'

They reach the South Beach and walk down on to the sand. Maeve sits near the sea and after a brief pause, Luke joins her.

They sit in strangely comfortable silence for a while. Maeve has never really been happy to just enjoy someone's company like this before. She always felt like she had to fill the silence, but not with him.

'Luke, can I ask you something?'

'Sure.'

'Why did you come to the bar again tonight? Not that you shouldn't have. I'm so glad you did. But I'm curious. You must have dozens of pubs closer to where you live.'

He licks his lips and looks at the sand between his boots. 'Honestly, Gregg made me come. I don't mean that in a bad way. I told him I met you again last night and that you helped me. He insisted we come back here today.'

'Why?'

'So I could see you.'

His voice dropped quite a bit as he said it, but she heard every single word. 'Interesting.'

'I'm not sure what that means?'

'It means I'm glad Gregg brought you to see me tonight.'

'Really?'

'I know I was less than subtle when I was looking over at you every five minutes. You must have noticed that?'

'A bit.' He goes quiet for a few minutes, so Maeve leaves him to his thoughts. 'I'd...' he shakes his head and takes a deep breath. 'I'm sorry. I'm really out of practice. I'd like to see you again, Maeve, but I'm not... I mean I'm still married, Maeve. I can't get divorced yet. But I...'

The poor guy is seriously struggling, so Maeve decides to step in. 'How about as friends then, for now? We have loads of catching up to do. Decades of catching up. And I understand you're going through a shitty time, but I really would like to see you again.'

'You know about what she did? To me I mean.'

Maeve nods, just about stopping herself from taking his hand. 'Yeah. I know. I mean only what's been made public.'

'And that isn't turning you off?'

'Why would it turn me off?'

'I don't know. I just thought it might.'

'Nothing that happened was your fault, so why would I be turned off? I enjoy talking to you. You're genuine. Do you have any idea how many fakes and phonies there are out there? I'll give you a hint. There are a lot. I meet most of them in the bar. All smiles and sweet talk, but it's not real. You are. And I really like that.'

He smiles at her, his entire face lighting up. 'I like that about you too.'

Maeve nods and looks back at the sea, so he doesn't notice she's blushing. He's so fucking gorgeous, it's ridiculous.

'So, I'm starving! The takeaway should still be open. Fancy some chips?'

'Yeah. Sounds good.'

He gets up and holds out his hand, pulling her to her feet. 'Thanks.'

Luke looks her in the eye for the briefest moment, his hand still firmly holding hers. Maeve doesn't move. Even in the dim light she can see the sadness in his eyes and it kills her. Then he drops his gaze and releases her hand, stuffing his hands in his jeans again.

'Yo, Andy!' Maeve shouts, waving at the huge bodyguard watching them from the path. 'You want chips?'

'Too right I do!'

Luke and Maeve laugh, as they walk back up the beach to join him on the path. 'Is it not a bit unnerving having him around all the time?'

'He's really good at keeping an eye on me, without being in my face.'

They climb onto the path, walking under the archway leading into the town. It might be her imagination, but Luke seems to be walking a little closer to her. His arm has brushed against hers at least half a dozen times, since he helped her to her feet.

Usually she wouldn't notice something so trivial, but he makes everything so different. It's got nothing to do with that woman he was married to. It's Luke himself.

She tended to rush into everything she did. Patience wasn't one of her strong points. In fact it wasn't a point at all.

Luke is a calming presence. With him, she needs to slow down, and it's so refreshing.

'Andy! Get up here. I feel weird having you walking behind us.'

Andy pauses for a second, then joins them, walking to the other side of Maeve. She links arms with the two men, laughing when they both give her a strange look.

'Much better. So, I'm just going to state this for the record. I have a healthy appetite. I will be getting chips, a burger, and a battered sausage. And I won't be sharing any of it.'

'I wasn't planning on stealing your food,' Andy says.

'Right answer. I like you now.'

His eyebrows shoot up. 'You do?'

'That's a good thing. Myself and Luke have a lot of catching up to do. It's important we get on too.'

Andy looks at Luke who just smiles and shrugs.

'Fair enough.'

'Great,' she says, winking at Luke when he looks over at her. 'Would you get a load of me! I've got two strapping men protecting me. I feel like royalty.'

## Luke

He's going to be sick.

Luke closes his eyes and breathes out through his mouth, and in through his nose, over and over, until the feeling settles.

He can do this. It's not a big deal. He's got a long and stressful life ahead of him, if he freaks out at every potentially awkward situation.

When he opens his eyes and looks at Dillon's apartment door, the queasiness comes back. Hanging around out here like an idiot, isn't going to help. If he keeps delaying, he'll either chicken out, or throw up.

He rings the bell and holds his breath. Then the door opens and Dillon smiles at him. 'Hey. Come in.'

Luke smiles and steps inside the apartment, heading straight for the living room, so he can collapse on the couch, before he falls down.

Dillon joins him, giving him a strange look as he sits opposite. 'What's wrong?'

'I need to tell you something.'

'So talk.'

Luke wrings his hands together, stopping when Dillon notices. 'I've met someone. Well, kind of. I mean it's not serious or anything, but... I guess I like her. '

The silence hangs for a few minutes. At least he thinks it's a few minutes. It probably isn't because he's not breathing, so technically he'd be dead. He tenses as Dillon moves from the couch to sit beside him. 'Look at me.'

He can't and it's so stupid. Dillon is his best friend. But he's a friend who is in love with him. Or was at one time.

Ever since Dillon told Luke about his feelings, he's tried so hard to be respectful of them. Dillon can't help being in love with him, and it's certainly not a bad thing that he is. But Luke doesn't want to hurt him. Ever.

'Luke! Lift your fucking head and look at me!'

When he convinces himself to meet Dillon's eyes, he's surprised to see his friend smiling widely at him. 'Why are you smiling?'

'Why are you freaking out?'

'I thought...' If he finishes the sentence, he's going to sound unbelievably big-headed.

Dillon rests his hand on Luke's clasped hands and squeezes. 'You thought I'd be upset, or cross?'

'Maybe...'

Dillon licks his lips and looks at Luke's hands for a minute. 'Just because I have feelings for you, doesn't mean I want you to be alone and miserable for the rest of your life. I'm not a dick!'

He smirks and shrugs. 'Okay, so maybe I am some of the time, but not about this. Never about this. You have to believe that, Luke. I only want you to be safe and happy. That's all I ever want for you.'

'I'm sorry. I just... I don't know. I didn't want to hurt you.'

Dillon lies back on the couch, resting his arms along the back. 'I'm a hard nut, mate. I'm fine, really.'

Luke knows Dillon isn't as hard a nut as he makes out he is. He's been hurt so many times in his life, he's built a wall around himself, blocking everyone from the real him.

'So...'

'So what?' Luke asks.

Dillon gets up and grabs two bottles of juice from the fridge. His friend is trying his best to keep away from alcohol and drugs, but he's not fooling Luke. He's only keeping away from them when he's around the guys. Luke knows full well he still drinks more than he should.

As for the drugs, he has no idea how deep Dillon is into them. He knows Dillon went through a phase of using as soon as he woke up, and then again to help himself get to sleep. After Tate's relapse last year and Dillon's own stint in prison, he said he'd cut back.

But you were never sure if Dillon was telling you the truth, or what he wanted you to hear.

Usually the latter.

Dillon sits back on the couch opposite him and rests his feet on the coffee table. 'Who is she?'

'Maeve. She was my physics partner in school.'

Dillon frowns for a second, then smiles. 'Fuck! Not bad, Luke. She was hot.'

He smiles and nods. 'Yeah. Still is. She's also got purple hair, piercings, and tattoos.'

Dillon takes a long breath. 'Fuck, that's even hotter!' He lifts his bottle. 'I approve. Good work.'

'And you're really okay?'

'Jesus, Luke. Yes! I may think with my dick a little too often for my own good, but I'm actually using my brain on this one. I'm bi. You're straight. That's kind of a sticking point for any mad romance I may have had in my head. I accepted a long time ago that I have to get over you. So, stop stressing about me, and enjoy yourself. Are you seeing her again?'

Luke decides not to argue with Dillon. He's hurt. He can see it in his eyes, but there's not a lot he can do about it. 'Yeah. I think so. She knows I'm kind of all over the place, but she's happy to start as friends and see how it goes.'

'Sounds like you're on to a winner already. Where did you bump into her?'

'At a pub in Greystones. Her brother owns it and she works there.'

His eyes narrow slightly. 'Why were you at a pub?'

Luke was hoping not to go here with Dillon, but he's walked himself into it. 'I got into my head with that last rubbish Pippa's friends posted on the net. You know about her being innocent, and I'm just over reacting?'

'So you got pissed. Alone?'

He nods. 'I passed out, and Maeve and her brother brought me up to her flat. She lives above the pub. And I know it was a stupid thing to do. I just... I needed to forget for a while I guess.'

Dillon fixes him with one of his intense gazes. 'You don't forget by getting pissed by yourself. You hear me?'

'Yeah. I know. Believe me, it won't be happening again. My head was killing me.'

'Good!' He smirks to soften his reply, but Luke knows Dillon is right. It was a foolish thing to do. 'You feeling good about this?'

'Yeah. I am. I mean I'm nervous too, but a good nervous. She's so different to... she's different. And she listens to me. I like that.'

'That's the way it should be. Just take it slow. One day at a time and see what happens. Enjoy yourself.'

'But...'

'But what?'

'I'm freaking out about all the physical stuff. I mean we're nowhere near that yet, but I'm already stressing about it.'

'Has she touched you at all?'

'We were sitting on the beach and I helped her to her feet. I didn't even think about it - just held out my hand.'

'And...'

'It was fine. Nice even.'

'Great. That's good, right?'

'I guess, but that's a long way from actually holding her hand. Or kissing her.' His voice squeaks a little, as the panic sets in. He's not ready for this. He can't be intimate with someone. Not yet.

Dillon grips his face in his hands and forces him to look up. 'Breathe.'

'I can't...'

'Yes you can. Look at me and breathe.'

He focuses on Dillon, and copies him, breathing in through his nose and out through his mouth.

'You good now?'

He nods, so Dillon releases his face. 'Sorry.'

'You're getting way ahead of yourself, Luke. She knows that Pippa hit you. Even knowing that small detail, she's going to be careful around you. I fucking guarantee she's not going to jump on you, okay? From what I remember of her she's got her fucking head screwed on. Be honest with her. If she does something you're not comfortable with, tell her.'

'But what if that scares her away?'

'Then she's not the right one for you. Plain and simple. When you really like someone, you want to make them happy. If she truly gives a fuck about you, she'll understand. If she doesn't, then at least you'll know.'

Dillon sits on the coffee table in front of him. 'Not every woman in the world is like Pippa. Not every woman wants to hurt you. To

56

control you. Some will just want to spend time with you, because you're fucking awesome. And you're the easiest person to talk to. And genuinely decent. Maybe kind of gorgeous too,' he adds winking at him.

'You're biased.'

'Just saying it as I see it, mate. One day at a time, okay?'

'Yeah. Thanks Dillon.'

He slaps him on the leg and gets up, walking into the kitchen. 'Anytime. How about a coffee?'

'Yeah. That would be great.'

As Dillon disappears into the kitchen, Luke allows himself to relax, slumping back into the leather couch. That went so much better than he could have imagined. Dillon has supported him every step of the last few months. Why would he automatically assume Dillon would have an issue with him finding someone to be happy with?

It's early days. Very early days. And he still doesn't know what you'd call the relationship between himself and Maeve. All he does know, is that when he's with her he smiles, he laughs, and he's happy. He can count on one hand the number of times he's experienced that in such a short period of time.

It's probably silly, but now he's told Dillon, and his friend is happy for him, he can finally stop worrying about that, and enjoy getting to know Maeve.

# Dillon

It was bound to happen at some stage. He should have been prepared. Should have been building himself up to the pain of hearing it.

But he wasn't. Far fucking from it. As Luke sits on his couch, daydreaming about the new woman in his life, Dillon is trying to hold himself together in the kitchen, trying desperately not to beat his fists on the counter, and shout or scream.

He has no right to be an asshole about this. All he wants is for Luke to be happy. Fuck, it's all he thinks about. But the selfish asshole part of himself, was still hanging on to the slim chance it could be with him. That he would be the one Luke would choose to be with, to care about as more than just a friend.

It's a fucking ridiculous thought and he knows it. But that doesn't stop him wishing it wasn't the case. Doesn't stop him thinking about waking up next to the stunning man every morning. Of doing so much more than just sleeping with him, but that's mainly thanks to his fucked up imagination.

He still loves Luke. No, it's so much more than that. He's deeply in love with him. He's tried to ignore it. Tried to move on. Tried to force Luke out of his mind by fucking too many people. Nothing had worked.

Maybe Luke finding someone is a good thing. It'll force him to move on. Force him to stop fantasising about his straight best friend.

He looks down at his clenched fist on the counter. Seems he's got a bit of a way to go, before he's ready to let go.

It's time for Luke to move on though. Time for him to live his life without fear of being shouted at, beaten, or raped. Dillon is fucking surprised he's ready to move on at all, after what he went through.

His own heart was broken by a woman a decade ago, and he had sworn off women since that day. Probably overkill as usual, but it's kind of his thing to go to extremes.

But Luke seems to be ready, so it's his job as his best mate to support him. He'd been with Luke as much as possible, since he came round after his overdose. Sat by his bedside, visited him in the centre as soon as he was allowed to, sat in on a few of his therapy sessions.

Those were fucking torturous. Listening to Luke recounting

58

everything that bitch had done to him, had been the single most difficult thing Dillon has had to do - and that's even taking into account coming out to his parents all those years ago.

'You okay?'

Dillon squeezes his eyes shut, and drops his head to his chest. No, he's not fucking okay! 'Yeah.'

'Need a hand?'

Dillon unclenches his fist again, shaking his hand to ease the cramps. 'I'm good.'

He will be good. He has to be. Luke is one of the most important people in his life. He'll do anything for him - even if it means walking away, so he can be happy with someone else.

## Maeve

She shrugs out of her coat, and kisses Mike on the cheek as she squeezes past him. 'You've got a visitor.'

'Me? Who?'

'He's in the back room. Give me a shout if you need me.'

Mike's reaction to her visitor isn't filling her with happy vibes. Maeve opens the door to the office and her frown deepens.

Dillon Ryan is on the couch in the office, looking seriously imposing as he silently stares at her. She hasn't seen Dillon since school, but he still looks like the guy she saw around the school with Luke... well, with a few modifications.

His dark green eyes seem to interrogate her, as he chews on the black ring piercing the side of his bottom lip. The centre of his nose is pierced with a matching ring. She knows other parts of his body are pierced too, but that's between Dillon and the many people he has sex with.

He doesn't get off the couch, or make a move to greet her, so she sits on the chair behind the desk and spins around to face him.

'Well, this is a pleasure, asshole.'

That catches him out. 'What the fuck did I do?'

She loves that she completely caught him off guard by attacking him first. She knows he's here because of Luke, but that doesn't mean she's going to bow and scrape to the bad boy of the band. He may intimidate his fair share of people, but not her.

'The last day of school you threw me in the sea. Fully dressed with my school bag on my back. Ring a bell with you?'

Dillon grins. 'You know, I'd forgotten about that. Still holding a grudge, huh?'

'Oh, you have no idea how long I can hold a grudge. For you, Dillon, I think I can stretch it out for another few decades.'

'Ouch!'

'I can't believe you and Luke are still friends. He's nice. You're a dick. I don't get it.'

He opens his mouth to answer back, but reins himself in, smiling to himself as he looks down at his boots for a few seconds.

'What's going on with you and Luke?' he finally asks, hitting her with his full attention again.

'Are you seriously asking me what my intentions are? What year are we in?'

Dillon's cold eyes lock on to her, and she can't help but squirm a little. 'I want you to answer my question.'

'And what exactly does that have to do with you?' she asks, leaning forward, deciding to meet his glare head on.

'A lot.'

'Yeah well sorry, but I don't think it's any of your business.' She stands up and straightens her shirt. 'Now, I have to get to work, so please fuck off.'

Dillon meets her eyes and holds her gaze for longer than she feels comfortable with, but she'll be damned if she's going to be the one to back away. 'No. Sit down, Maeve.'

'Hang on one sec. I know you're some big shot celebrity, but that doesn't mean you get to be a rude, arrogant fuck. Luke is his own person. Whatever is, or isn't between us, has nothing to do with you.'

Dillon silently stares at her, then he laughs. Maeve stares at him in confusion, as he has a good chuckle to himself. 'I'm sorry. Can you please sit down for a sec.'

She slowly lowers into the chair and crosses her legs. 'You've got thirty seconds, before I call Mike to kick your rock star ass out the door.'

'I'm sorry, okay. I mean that.'

She narrows her gaze, hitting him with her own attempt at a deadly glare. He doesn't flinch, which irritates her. 'Fine. Apology accepted. Is that it?'

'Fuck me! You'd get on great with my sisters. They don't take any shit from me either.'

'Good. Glad to hear it.'

'Okay, I admit I came in all *bull in a china shop*.' He leans forward and clasps his hands together. 'Luke... well he's going through some stuff. Heavy stuff, and I guess I get a little over protective when it comes to him.'

'Over protective? No shit! So are you here to warn me off him? Is that it?'

'Would it do any good?'

'No.'

He smiles and she has a feeling it's genuine. 'Glad to hear it.'

'You what?' Now he's completely confusing her. This guy is the most irritating person she's met for a long time.

'Has he told you about what went on with his ex bitch?'

'Bits. I know she hurt him over a long time, and that she sounds like a right cow.'

61

Dillon nods. 'Yeah, that kind of sums it up. It's not my business to go into details. It's his story to tell, when he's ready. I just don't want him to get hurt again. And I mean any type of hurt. He's my best mate. I love him and I don't want...'

He looks away as his voice fades. Maeve's hostility towards Dillon diminishes. The pieces fall into place in that instant. This is more than the love you have for a friend. Dillon is *in* love with Luke.

He meets her eyes again and shrugs. 'I see by your face you've figured it out. And yes he knows, and no he's still straight. I only want what's best for him. I mean that. However fucked up our relationship is, I genuinely care about him.'

Maeve nods, his words taking the edge off her initial hostility to Dillon. However badly he may have begun this conversation, he has Luke's best interests at heart.

'Okay, I don't know what there is between us. I've only met him twice. It's not exactly a budding romance yet, but I like him, Dillon. Quite a bit actually.'

'You fancied him in school, right?'

She grimaces. 'Please don't tell me he knew?'

'Nah. Don't think so. He's never been good at reading signs like that.'

'Thank God for that! We're enjoying each other's company for now. It's early days.'

Dillon smiles at her. 'I've seen the change in him the last few days. He's happy, Maeve. Can't remember the last time I saw him happy. Thank you.'

Maeve moves from compassion to shock. 'Okay. I wasn't expecting that.'

'Yeah. My fault for interrogating you initially.' Dillon smiles and stands up. 'I'll get out of your hair. Wouldn't want your brother to come in here and deck me.'

'Ah Mike is a big softy.'

'Yeah right.' Dillon stops in front of her and peers down at her. 'It's good to see you again, Maeve. I mean that. I think you might be exactly what Luke needs.'

He winks, then leaves the room. Maeve slumps back in the chair and stares after him, only coming out of her thoughts when Mike sticks his head around the door. 'You okay?'

'Yeah,' she answers, nodding to herself. 'I think Dillon Ryan gave me his seal of approval.'

## Luke

He wakes from another nightmare when someone shakes him. 'Wake up!'

He opens his eyes, shuffling up the bed to get away from whoever it is. He rubs his eyes and frowns up at Dillon. 'What the hell are you doing?'

'I just got a call. Chloe had the baby!'

Luke shoves Dillon off him and sits up in bed. 'What? When?'

Dillon shrugs. 'Tate was a bit hyper. I think he said it was a few hours ago. I'm not sure. He wants us to come to the hospital. Get up!'

Luke showers quickly and throws on some clothes, before following Dillon down to the garage and into his friend's Mustang. Dillon pulls out into the Dublin traffic, heading towards the hospital.

'I can't believe Tate is a father.'

Dillon nods and grins. 'Yeah. It's fucking brilliant! Can't imagine him with a kid though.' He falls silent for a minute, but is chewing on his lip ring. Luke knows him well enough to know there's something on his mind.

'What's wrong?'

Dillon scrubs a hand over his face, and chews his lip ring again. 'Okay, so I have a confession to make.'

'What?'

'I went to see Maeve.'

Luke slowly turns to look at Dillon. 'You what? Oh my God! Why?'

'Because I'm an over protective asshole, that's why. I'm sorry okay, but I... when that bitch did what she did to you, I should have seen it. I just don't want...' He gives up and hits his palm against the steering wheel. 'Yeah, I'm an over protective asshole. Let's leave it at that.'

Luke isn't mad. How can he be? For such a long time, Dillon was one of the few people in his life he felt safe with. Yes, he's overbearing, overprotective, and would kill anyone who hurt him, but it came from his love for Luke. He could never criticise him for that.

'Okay.'

'You're not mad?'

'Why would I be?'

Dillon shrugs. 'You not worried I scared her away, or something like that?'

Luke smirks at Dillon. 'Scare Maeve away? You met her. Do you think that's possible?'

'She handed me my ass on a plate, feisty woman. God, I like her, Luke! She's a firecracker.'

Hearing that Dillon not only approves of Maeve, but that she handled him and lived to tell the tale, is such an unbelievable relief to him. 'I'm so glad you like her.'

'Like she so politely told me, it's none of my fucking business, but yeah. I do. She's genuine, Luke. Rare to find someone who says it as it is, without giving a fuck what anyone else thinks. So, you going to tell her everything?'

Luke had thought about it, but he's worried sick she'll run. 'I don't know. I want to... well, I think I need to, but I'm scared she won't want anything to do with me after.'

Dillon curses and swerves to the side, ignoring the scream of car horns as he cuts across two lanes of traffic before coming to a stop at the side of the road. He turns in his seat and hits Luke with an intense look.

'First, if anyone runs when you tell them what happened, good riddance. Let them go. You don't need assholes like that in your life. Second, I'd be fucking shocked if she ran. No one who gives a damn about you ran, did they?'

'No, but you're all family. She's an outsider.'

'Yeah, an outsider who knows some of the details. The press has been putting together some fucking works of fiction about you and the Bitch. That didn't turn her off so far. Luke, she genuinely likes you. You've got a shot at a decent relationship. But you can't be afraid to open up to her. YOU'VE. DONE. NOTHING. WRONG. Do I need to tattoo that on your fucking forehead,' he adds with a grin.

'I'd prefer you didn't,' he says with a smile. 'I don't think Ellen would like that.'

Dillon snorts. 'You think? She'd go fucking nuts! You've got to start believing you're the innocent party here. Please!'

Luke nods, wishing it was as easy as that. Dillon pulls back into the traffic, leaving Luke to think about Maeve again. He can't stop thinking about her and knowing that Maeve and Dillon have butted heads, and survived, is a massive weight off his mind. 'So what about you?'

'What about me what?' Dillon asks.

'You haven't said much about your private life recently.'

Dillon grimaces. 'Yeah well it's sort of bombed.'

'Why?'

'Just got other things on my mind. I still have two guys who get in touch every now and again, but that's it. I'm not really feeling it at the moment. I don't know. Maybe it's old age or something like that.'

'Are you okay? I've noticed you're drinking more than you used to.'

'You keeping tabs on me now?'

'You know I'm not. I'm worried you might be pushing it a bit. You're drunk a lot lately.'

'Wow! Thanks for that kick, mate. I'm sober now, if that's what you're getting at?'

'That's not what I was getting at, so stop being all defensive.' He's getting himself into a conversation he wasn't planning on having. Dillon is only going to get his back up, they'll fight, and Dillon will be in a foul mood for days.

'Yeah. I know. I'm in a weird place. I've got a handle on everything. I just don't fancy shagging everything that moves at the moment. I thought you'd all be happy about that.' He winks over at Luke, before focusing on the road again.

Luke doesn't try to get any more information from Dillon. He's giving off all his usual *I'm done talking* signals. His friend has an addictive personality. Always had. Sex, drugs, alcohol. Dillon was hooked on the three, and hearing that sex wasn't interesting him anymore, is like hearing that someone doesn't fancy breathing. It was part of him.

The last thing he wants to do is hurt Dillon, by flaunting a potential new relationship in his face. He'd never want to do that to Dillon.

'Are you okay about me and Maeve? Sorry. That sounded really bad.'

'Not at all. It's a legitimate question. To be honest, it means a lot you even thought about that. But I'm fine. Really.'

'I've known you most of your life. When you say you're fine it usually means the opposite.'

Dillon smirks at him. 'Got me there. Listen, I just want you to be happy, Luke. I mean that. I haven't seen you like this for years. You're genuinely happy. Anyone can see that. How could I ever have a problem with anyone who can do that for you? Granted, I wish I could have done that for you, but like I said in the hospital, it's my issue, not yours.'

'So you still feel that way?'

When Dillon smiles, it's one of his rare genuine ones, instead of the fake grin he gives the public.

'Yeah. I'm not going to fall out of love with you overnight, but there isn't a fucking chance in hell I'm going to let it get in the way of our friendship, or your relationship with Maeve. I can't promise I won't be watching her like a hawk though.'

Luke laughs and nods. 'I wouldn't expect otherwise. Thanks Dillon. You've been an incredible friend to me.'

Dillon reaches across and takes his hand. 'I meant it when I said I'd never let anyone hurt you again. That still stands. Always will.'

'I know.'

By the time they get to the hospital, Gregg and Bria are already there along with Tate's parents in a private family room. Tea and coffee is being handed out to the doting grandparents, while Bria and Gregg lounge on one of the sofas. Bria jumps to her feet when she realises they've arrived, quickly hugging both of them.

'About time! Did you walk or what?'

'We're here. Quit complaining,' Dillon says, smiling at her. 'So where's the new father?'

'He told me to bring you down when you arrived.' She leads them down the corridor to a room, with the recognisable hulking form of Liam standing guard outside. He nods at them as Bria knocks on the door, waiting a few seconds before she opens it and shows them in.

Luke barely recognises Tate when he sees him. Tate is one of those people he can't help but envy. He always came across as unflappable.

It didn't matter who was interviewing him, or what question he was asked, he remained cool headed. Or at least he did until drugs took over, but he's got a grip on that now.

The man in front of them is a far cry from cool headed. His dark hair is standing on end, his t-shirt more crumpled than usual, and he looks exhausted, black rings surrounding both eyes. But more than all that, he looks so genuinely happy. The grin is taking over his whole face, as he grabs them both, pulling them into a rib crushing bear hug.

'What the fuck took you two so long?'

'Speed. Limits. Ouch. Let. Go.'

'Sorry Dillon.'

'So? Where's the new arrival?' Luke asks.

Tate brings them around the side of the curtain to Chloe, lying in the bed with a small bundle in her arms. Tate sits beside her and smiles down at the baby in her arms. 'This is our son, Brandon.'

Luke hangs back, as Dillon compliments the couple on their new addition, his eyes transfixed on the tiny baby Tate is now holding in his arms. Brandon has Tate's shock of dark hair. He's like a mini version of him.

He always assumed he'd be the first to have a family. The guys always joked about him being a dad. He was always the one in a steady - if not messed up - relationship. It should have been him.

Now it's not even an option for him, thanks to Pippa arranging the vasectomy for him. Seeing the way Tate is looking at his son, seeing that instant love he has for him, it hits him that he'll never have that.

And he wants it. He's so far from being anything close to a steady and reliable father. But he desperately wants it.

Pippa crushed him in so many ways, but that's the part he can't get over.

Dillon pulls him into his arms as the tears pour out. He is such a pathetic mess, but he takes the comfort. It's either that or let Tate, Dillon, Chloe, and the baby witness him falling apart yet again. When

69

he finally gets a grip on himself, he wipes his face, trying not to look at the audience surrounding him.

'Sorry. I... I'm just sorry.'

'What the fuck are you sorry about?' Tate asks, sitting on the edge of the bed next to Chloe.

'I just... when I saw him... I mean he's gorgeous guys, really.'

'But you thought it would be you first,' Dillon says. 'I know mate. But to be perfectly blunt, would you have wanted a kid with *her*?'

He can't help but agree with that one. Being still married to her is bad enough. If they had a child tying them to each other for the next eighteen years or so, it would be a nightmare.

'It'll happen for you with the right person,' Chloe says taking his hand. 'And you'll be an amazing dad. Anyone with half a brain can see that.'

He doesn't bother correcting them. He's dampened the mood for Tate and Chloe enough as it is. 'Would you mind if I held him?'

'Of course we wouldn't fucking mind,' Tate says, grimacing when Chloe glares at him. 'Sorry. No cursing around the baby. Not that he has a fucking clue what I'm saying.'

'Yeah well I'd prefer his first word wasn't *fuck*. It would be great if he had a broader vocabulary that his father,' she says, poking him in the side.

Tate passes Brandon to Luke, settling him in his arms, before stepping away to give him space.

He's gutted he won't have this, but Dillon is right. Better not to have it, than with the wrong person.

He just wishes he'd met the right person a lot sooner.

## Maeve

She directs Luke down the track leading to the beach, hoping they have the place to themselves. He'd spent the morning with his therapist and then visiting with Tate, Chloe, and the new baby. From the sounds of things, Brandon has a powerful set of lungs on him - just like his father.

Luke's luxurious Range Rover makes easy work of the dirt track down to the beach. The car probably cost the equivalent of two years salary for her, but then again she didn't have the stellar career Luke does.

She hadn't seen Luke for a few days thanks to clashes in their schedules, but he'd spoken to her every day for a few hours. Maeve never had trouble talking the back end off anyone, but Luke was giving her a run for her money, easily talking as much as she was.

Once you got him started, he has no problem talking for hours.

Maeve had also used the time apart to do a bit of research on coercive control. She wanted to understand what he went through with Pippa, well, a little at least. No one would ever understand the true effect she had on him. But it gave her some insight into how, and why, he reacts the way he does, in certain situations. It also added fuel to the contempt she feels for his bitch of a wife.

'Is this it?' he asks, as they reach the end of the track.

'Yep.' She sits up in the seat and scans the beach. 'Yay! No one else here. I hate sharing beaches with other people.'

'So you want a private beach at some stage?'

'Doesn't everyone?' she responds, as she opens the door. Luke takes the blanket and basket of food from the boot of the car and follows her down the track to the stony beach. She picks a spot above the reach of the waves, where the stones turn to sand, and spreads out the blanket.

The sea is still, the sun sparkling off the ripples on the surface. 'Well that's settled,' she says, looking out at the water.

'What is?'

'I don't know about you, but it's too nice a day not to get in.' She pulls off her ankle boots and stuffs her socks into them.

'You're going in for a paddle?'

'Nope. I'm going swimming. You coming?'

Luke looks out at the sea, then back at Maeve again. 'Seriously?'

'Absolutely! You can't tell me that doesn't look inviting? There's barely a ripple. It would be a serious insult to the sea if we didn't get in.'

'Pretty sure the sea wouldn't mind.'

Maeve stands up and pulls off her t-shirt before she can talk herself out of it. She's swam in her underwear before, but that was in front of friends. Not Luke Daly. She shrugs out of her jeans and stands with her hands on her hips.

'Well? You joining me or not? Unless of course you're going commando under your jeans... Are you?' she adds, wiggling her eyebrows at him.

'No, I'm not. Going commando I mean.' He looks out at the sea again, and a few seconds later Maeve knows she won't be taking a dip alone. His kissable lips curl into a slight smile. 'What the hell!'

'Yay! That's the spirit.' He pulls off his boots and Maeve stares in stunned silence as his t-shirt comes off. 'Holy fucking shit, Luke!'

He frowns and looks at his chest. 'What's wrong?'

Maeve points a finger at him and nods. 'Nothing's wrong. I'm just wondering where in God's name that chest come from? You didn't have that in school, did you?'

He shrugs, his face reddening slightly, as he crosses his arms. Why does he have to be so goddamn irresistible? 'I guess I kind of picked it up over the years.'

'I'd hang on to if I were you.' And that's an understatement. That was a chest he worked damn hard for. Each muscle is defined and, if that wasn't enough to get her hot under the collar, the tattoos covering both arms, his chest, and his stomach will do the trick. She's seen his chest in photos, but in the flesh it's so much better.

Luke Daly, physics partner, may have caught and held her attention all through school. Luke Daly, seriously hot, tattooed, pierced rock star is a whole other being. Especially when he's standing in front of her wearing black boxers.

'We getting in there or what?'

She pulls her attention away from his body, and his pierced nipples that for some reason, she can't stop looking at. 'Absolutely! Yes! Great idea! Now you know we have to do the whole *run and dive under thing*? None of this one step at a time, and adjusting to the temperature, nonsense.'

He rubs his hands together and smirks. 'Count of three?'

Maeve stands beside him and tries to keep her eyes on the sea in front of her, instead of his body. 'One, three.' She breaks away from him and gets a few steps into the sea, before she hears him crashing after her.

## Luke

He surfaces a few metres further out and wipes his face. Maeve grins at him. 'Awww. Too slow! I think you lost that one.'

He stands up and grins at her. 'I don't think so. You cheated. What happened to two?'

She shrugs. 'Did I forget about two? Oops!' She dives under when he splashes her. 'Oooh - too slow!' she jests, splashing him in return. 'You see, I told you this was a good idea.'

'I can't remember the last time I was in the sea. It must be a decade at least.'

She gives him a horrified look, as she swims in circles around him. 'How can you say that? You live right near the sea.'

'I just never had time I guess. I was always doing other things.'

She changes direction, swimming the other way. 'Well maybe that's something you can change? I mean you look good in the sea,' she adds, before swimming a little further away from him, then lying back and floating.

Luke stares after her. He's not used to someone like her. There was little to no planning. She got the urge to do something, and she acted. After the stifling, suffocating relationship with Pippa, spending time with Maeve is incredible. He can't remember the last time he had fun. Just plain old, uncomplicated, fun.

She also makes him feel good about himself, and that's definitely something new. The throw away compliments give him such a boost. A year ago, he would have thought she was lying. He wasn't anything special and certainly not good looking. Pippa had made sure he knew exactly how little he was worth.

But now, after hours of therapy, he's beginning to believe people when they compliment him. Especially Maeve. She's not the sort of person who would say something she didn't mean.

Everything about her is genuine from what he can tell. If she says he looks good in the sea, whatever that means, to her he does. Maybe she likes seeing him with no top on. He certainly likes seeing her in the sea, only wearing her underwear.

She is really beautiful. He loves her tattoos, loves the way the thorny rose twists up her leg, along her hip, and stretches across her side and stomach.

'Luke Daly. Are you ogling at me?'

He blushes, thinking that he's going to be in trouble, but she laughs, then splashes him, before diving under the surface in a bid to get away.

Luke swims over to her, and pulls her against his chest as they catch their breath. Maeve slowly looks up at him and wipes her face. He knows he should move his hand from her back, but he likes holding her.

He never ever thought he'd like the feel of someone against his skin again, but he doesn't mind with her. She probably wants him to let go. But then she places her hands on his back just above the waistband of his boxers.

He desperately wants to kiss her. But he's scared to do something that will put an end to their friendship. She's the only thing getting him through his shit life right now.

It's been a long time since he just said *fuck it* and did something completely reckless. In that moment, in the sea with Maeve, he knows exactly what he wants to do. To hell with the consequences.

Luke lifts his hand out of the water and brushes her hair back off her face, threading his fingers through her thick locks.

Clearly a foreign part of his brain takes over. A part that's either been afraid, or forgotten about, over the last few years, because he pulls her close and kisses her.

As soon as he does it, he expects her to push him back, even though she hadn't said, or done anything to hint that she might. But when she wraps her arms around his shoulders, he can't help but be a little relieved.

He has no idea how long the kiss lasts for. All he does know is that it feels right. It feels safe. It's pathetic that, at his stage in life, he judges situations on whether he's safe or not, but that's what his life is now. Fear or safety.

And Maeve is the latter.

She pulls away, taking a step back from him. 'Oh God! I'm so sorry, Luke. I didn't mean to get all touchy feely like that.'

'It's okay.'

'I just reacted. Are you okay?' Maeve frowns as she looks at him. 'Why are you grinning like that?'

'I'm okay.'

She beams back at him. 'You are? Seriously okay?'

'Yeah. I think so.'

'That's brilliant! Yay! I would have been incredibly bummed if my impulsive hands scared you off. I promise I'll keep them under better control next time you kiss me. And by the way. Wow! That was one hell of a kiss!'

His stomach tightens at her words. 'Next time? You'd want to do that again at some stage?'

'I'm going to restrain myself and just answer with a hell yeah! I am entering this into the official records. You, Luke Daly, have full permission to kiss me whenever the urge takes you. Oh and you can absolutely keep smiling like that. You're sexy as hell when you smile.'

He goes full on teenage blush at that moment, but she doesn't draw attention to it, thankfully. Neither does she try to kiss him again. He wants to do it again, but he doesn't want to push his luck yet. Small steps.

Being with her is more important than rushing whatever this is, or more importantly, rushing himself.

He shouts when a load of water finds its way over his head. Maeve giggles, already making a break for it. Luke catches up with her, winding his arm around her waist again. Without thinking, he kisses her again. Not anything big or romantic, but enough for now.

Maeve points to the rocks a few metres ahead of them. 'Right so sexy rock star. Let's see how good a swimmer you are. Race you to the rocks.'

*10*

*Maeve*

She used to daydream about Luke a lot when she was in school. Typical teenage stuff. If he'd been famous back then, she had no doubts her bedroom walls would have been covered with posters of him. The crush had gone on for quite a few years. Probably most of her secondary school years, but as soon as they left school and he was out of sight, the infatuation had disappeared.

They'd spent close to an hour in the water, swimming and messing around, only getting out when they'd both begun shivering. Thankfully the sun is out, so they can just dry on the beach while they eat. It also doesn't hurt that the sexy man beside her is just in his nicely fitting underwear. God, that man should not be covered up!

Maeve has kissed her fair share of men over the years. She doesn't go around throwing herself at every guy who looks at her, but she wasn't exactly shy either. But for some reason, when Luke kissed her like he did, completely out of the blue, it was like the first time all over again. She wanted more. A lot more. The kiss was far too short, but the fact it happened at all was worth celebrating.

Sitting on the beach with him is so surreal. She's still attracted to him, more than she was twenty years ago. It would be impossible not to be, but they'd taken such different paths over the last two decades. They're not the same people, but also still are. When they talk, it's like they're back in physics class, him trying to help her understand a problem, and her messing around and making him laugh.

Except now it's a little harder to make him laugh, and even when he does, it rarely reaches his eyes, and she hates that. Hates that the happy boy she knew is so sad, so crushed.

The odd time, his genuine smile breaks out. Like right now. They're digging into the picnic she prepared. She has no idea what he likes, or doesn't like, so had gone completely overboard, buying dips, chips, nibbles, and anything else she could find in the shop.

Luke is smiling as he looks at the sea, and it's the best thing she's seen for a long time. He hasn't eaten much, barely picking at the food.

'Are you not hungry, or did I not pack anything you like?'

'No. It's great. I'm just... my appetite isn't great. Hasn't been for a while.'

She nods, not wanting to push him on the matter. As soon as she mentioned it, his smile faded. It must have something to do with what happened to him.

Maeve lies back on the blanket and stares up at the sky. 'You think Mike would believe me if I said I was sick and can't work tonight?'

It does the trick. Luke laughs and she seriously loves the sound of it. He really needs to laugh more. 'I don't think so.'

'Nope. I reckon you're right.' She turns over and looks at him. 'Okay, here's a question for you. What would you do if you could do anything you wanted? Go anywhere you wanted. Leaving aside the fact that you probably can of course, but play along. Humour me.'

Luke thinks about that one for a bit before he answers. 'Okay, so don't laugh, but I'd probably get myself a campervan.'

Maeve laughs and he frowns at her. 'I'm not laughing at that. I swear!'

'What are you laughing at then?'

'It's just that you've travelled all over the world. I presume you've seen some amazing places. Stayed in some of the best hotels. Yet you'd be quite happy with a campervan. I love that!'

He turns over and rests his head on his hand. 'Yeah, I've travelled all over, but we're surrounded by security and whoever else is attached to us. We stay in hotels or do self-catering, but it's not the same. It's not like we're relaxing. It's all for work. Which I love - I'm not complaining. But we barely get a second to ourselves.'

He plays with the stud under his lip as he picks at the food on his plate. 'When me and Alex were kids, we didn't have all the fancy holidays abroad like kids nowadays. We'd spend every summer camping. We'd park our caravan in the middle of a field near a beach and eat, swim, and read. It was simple, you know.' His smile fades a little. 'Simple sounds pretty boring right?'

Maeve shakes her head. 'No. Not for a second. Simple sounds amazing if you ask me. So why don't you do it?'

'Do what?'

'Buy a camper.'

He frowns and shakes his head. 'I can't.'

'Why not? I don't mean to get all carried away and tell you what to do, but it's like I always say to myself. Life is short. Putting stuff off could mean you don't get to do it at all. There's nothing wrong with being selfish every now and again, and doing something *you* want to do. Fuck what anyone else thinks.'

'I think I'm so used to not thinking for myself, it's difficult to know what I want.'

She gently takes his hand. 'But you do know what you want. A campervan.'

He smiles and tightens his grip on her hand. 'To be honest, I don't think I've thought further than today.' He laughs a little, but it's weak. 'Sorry, that sounds a bit silly.'

'Why would that sound silly? From what I hear, your life has been difficult the last few years. Day to day is absolutely fine. Whatever works for you. There's no right or wrong way to deal with what you went through. All I'm saying is that this is your time, Luke. Do whatever makes you happy and fuck everyone else!'

'You're right. It's just hard to change the way I do things. I am getting better at being selfish, if that makes sense? And I really would like a camper at some stage. Just get up one morning, pack a bag, and drive. No plan. No idea where I'm going.'

He smiles to himself. 'I don't think I've done anything spontaneous for years. Alone I mean. When I'm away with the guys, Dillon usually drags us into some random places and situations.'

'I don't doubt that for one second! I don't think I'd be surprised at anything he gets up to on the road.'

'I wouldn't be able to put half of it into words. He's a liability! Believe me.'

They lie in silence for a few minutes and she leaves him to it. She can't say why, but she gets the feeling Luke wants to say something, but either isn't ready, or doesn't know how to say it.

He keeps frowning and looking down, as he twists the stud under his lip, over and over again. It's his tell. A clear sign he's deep in his head.

Whatever he wants to say, she'll give him the time to get it off his chest. She's off until the evening shift, so has absolutely no issue sitting here with him for the next few hours.

He takes a deep breath and clears his throat. 'I need to tell you something.'

She smiles over at him. 'Sure. Go for it.'

'It's...' he sits up and rubs his hands on his legs, as he grimaces. 'It's not easy. I mean it's difficult to talk about. But you need to know. I mean you should know. I want you to know. You know... if we're... If you and me are...friends.' He smiles. 'Not doing a great job, am I?'

Maeve shuffles around to face him and takes his hand in hers. 'No rush. Just take a deep breath and talk. It doesn't matter if it makes sense or not. Half of what I say doesn't make sense.'

He nods and looks at the sea over her shoulder, as he takes another deep breath. 'Okay. I don't know if you're aware or not, but I sort of disappeared for a few months around the time Pippa and I broke up? My management company said I was stressed.'

Maeve nods, but doesn't want to speak in case she breaks his train of thought. She knew there was more to the *stress* story than the public were told. Luke was so laid back, she doubts it's even possible for him to be stressed.

'I was in a private hospital. The same place Tate was in for a few months.'

'You mean a rehab facility?'

He shakes his head. 'No. Well, yes, it is a rehab facility too. Tate was there because of his drug addiction. But they don't just treat addiction. It's somewhere people with various different problems go for help.'

Maeve licks her dry lips and nods. If he wasn't there for drugs, what the hell was wrong with him?

'Pippa...' He pauses and closes his eyes. Maeve runs her thumb over his hand. He's seriously struggling with whatever he's trying to say. 'She physically and sexually abused me for years.'

Maeve stops stroking his hand. 'Dear God.' She knew Pippa hurt him, but never like that. And not for years.

Luke pulls his hand back and hugs himself. 'Everything was great at first. Just like a normal relationship I guess. Then it changed. I don't really know when, it just sort of happened.

'She'd criticise me, just little at first, things like *I could dress better* or *do I really need to eat that slice of pizza? Why do I have to work so much?* Stupid stuff really, and I stupidly did what I could to keep her happy.

'Over the years it got worse, but I didn't see it. She'd shout at me a lot. Call me names. Blame me for everything that was going wrong. I could handle Pippa shouting at me. I mean I hated it, but I had sort of got used to it.

'But then she slapped me. After a while she'd hit me with her hairbrush, or whatever else she had to hand at the time. Every time she hit me, she said I pushed her to it. It was my fault. I let her down, disappointed her, embarrassed her. If I was a better boyfriend, a better husband she wouldn't get upset with me. Wouldn't have to hit me.'

Maeve swallows heavily, but keeps her comments to herself for now. Luke doesn't need to hear her curse his wife out, like she desperately wants to. He pauses and Maeve shuffles a little closer to him. She desperately wants to hug him, but doesn't want to crowd him.

'We went out with her friends one night. Rehearsals ran over so I was late, which didn't help her mood. It was a beyond boring night and I kind of got lost in my head a few times. I was going over some songs and she caught me singing to myself. Didn't go down well.

'She was furious with me when we got home. Said I'd ruined the night and embarrassed her as usual. I could make it up to her by... you know... being with her. I was tired though. I mean really tired, and had to be up early for work, so I said I didn't want to. But she wanted to.'

Luke falls silent and Maeve has to force herself to breathe. The direction this is heading is leaving a cold lump in her gut.

'What happened, Luke?'

He takes a few minutes to get himself together, before he speaks again, which doesn't put Maeve at ease at all.

'She had got these handcuffs as a gag present a few months before, from one of her friends. I tried to stop her. Kept telling her I was tired and didn't want to. But she wouldn't listen.'

Maeve feels like she's going to throw up. She wants to tell him to stop. That she gets what he's trying to say and he doesn't have to say the words. But maybe this is something he needs to do. It doesn't make it any easier to listen to though.

'I kept saying no. Even when she was handcuffing me to the bed, I kept saying no. But in the end I just lay there and let her... you know. I didn't see it as rape. I mean she was my girlfriend, the first time it happened.

'But after she let me go, I couldn't stop thinking about it. She didn't see what happened as a big deal. It was just a bit of role play between a couple. Most guys would love if that happened to them. What was I complaining about?'

'She said that?'

Luke nods, but keeps his eyes on the sea. 'From then on, Pippa liked having sex like that.' He unwraps the bandanna and leather cuff from around his wrists. 'I should have stopped struggling, but it really hurt. She was... rough with me. Sometimes she'd leave me locked in the room while she went out with her friends. I'd have water but no food.

'If she was in a particularly mean mood, I'd be left handcuffed to the bed while she went out. No food. No water. No way to...' he squeezes his eyes shut and shakes his head. 'I'd be trapped on the bed no matter what, unable to move for hours. I think she liked having that control over me.'

She's hearing everything Luke is saying to her, but she's struggling accepting that was his reality. Doesn't want to believe Pippa locked him in a room without food and water, and went about her day. He was a prisoner, living in fear of what his wife would do to him.

Maeve stares at the thick scars surrounding both wrists. She assumed the cuff and bandanna were part of his wardrobe, not worn to hide the wounds he was left with after his wife raped him. He wraps his wrists again, hiding the marks from her.

'It wasn't always bad, and I'm not just saying that. Things would be fine for a while, then I'd do, or say something, that would make her angry. It was usually when I had to go away, or do anything related to the band.

'She didn't like sharing me. Not that she was. I was in love with her. But she didn't trust me. Or didn't trust the guys, and thought they'd lead me astray, or something like that. Especially Dillon. She hated him so much.'

He falls silent again. Maeve slides her hand under his arm and grips his hand. Luke looks down at her hand in his, and glances over at her. 'She went crazy when I spent time with the guys, so I pulled away from them. I was caught between my wife and my best friends, and it was killing me.

'I saw them and it upset her. I spent more time with her and I was messing up stuff with the band. Every single day I was juggling both sides of my life, trying to keep everyone happy, and failing miserably.

'I didn't know what I was doing wrong, Maeve. I tried so hard to be a good boyfriend and husband. I really did, but it was never enough. I was never enough.'

He looks back at the sea and this time, rubs his thumb over her hand. 'I was nauseous all the time, and threw up when I ate. I wasn't sleeping. I lost weight. I was scared all the time. Scared of upsetting her. Scared of the guys or my family finding out I was messing up my relationship. I'd have to cancel photo shoots because of the bruises. I didn't want her to get into trouble.

'But when we came back from honeymoon, everything got so much worse. She told me I had to leave the band. Cut off all contact with Dillon. Not see him any more.'

Maeve discretely wipes the tears from her face. Her heart is breaking over and over for Luke. 'What did you do?'

'I agreed. I told her I'd leave the band. Told her I'd stop being friends with Dillon. I didn't know what else to do at the time. She let me go to see him, so I could tell him in person. But when I got to his place, I couldn't. I'm not sure it was ever an option. I think I just said whatever I had to say to keep her happy.

'She knew straight away. The second she saw me, she knew. She was so mad at me. Said she couldn't trust me. She took my car and bike keys from me. Wallet and phone too.

'Then she really lost it with me, hit and punched me. Got me on the side of the head with her hairbrush and sort of dazed me. When I fell, she kicked me, dislocating my knee, and stamped all over my legs with her stilettos.'

'Oh God...'

'So left me on the floor when she showered, got dressed, and did her hair and make-up. Then she told me she was going out and she'd think about if she could forgive me or not. She left and locked me in the room again.'

He faces her and he's crying. 'I didn't know what else to do, Maeve. I thought it was all my fault. I honestly thought I was a horrible person. That I was driving her to do those things, and if I wasn't around things would be better. For her. For Dillon. For everyone.'

Maeve grips his hand firmly in hers. She has a feeling she knows where this is going, but she could be wrong. She hopes she is.

'I dragged myself onto the bed and swallowed a load of Pippa's sleeping pills. Dillon found me a little while later and called the ambulance. Kept doing CPR until they arrived. If Dillon hadn't found me I wouldn't be here now.

'While I was unconscious, Dillon put two and two together. He saw the bruises, so it wouldn't have been too difficult for him to figure it out. Dillon told me what he thought was going on, and all I had to do was nod. It was such a relief to have it out there, and to be believed. But Pippa didn't want to let me go. She called the Garda and blamed Dillon for what happened to me.'

'And he was arrested. I remember reading something about that.'

Luke nods. 'He kind of jokes about that part now. But I think Dillon being arrested like that, sort of woke me up, if that makes sense? I either had to admit what Pippa did to me, or Dillon was going away for a long time. She was arrested, he was released and I went into the facility for a few months.'

Maeve doesn't have any words. What do you say when someone says all that to you? She thought Pippa verbally abusing and hitting him was bad enough. But to rape him and leave him so lost and alone, that he felt he had no escape but to kill himself, is beyond contempt.

Maeve wants to scream, to shout and curse his wife, but that won't help him. The fact he told her all of that - however painful it was for him, is something she needs to recognise.

'I'm so sorry, Luke. I don't know what else to say?'

He shrugs. 'Yeah, I get that a lot. I wanted you to know all that, because I'm kind of messed up. I'm starting from scratch, Maeve. I don't know who I am anymore. I've been the person she wanted me to be for so long, I've lost myself. I ate what she told me to eat. Wore what she told me to wear. Did what she told me to do. Apart from when I was on stage or doing band stuff, I was doing what she said.

'I'm thirty-eight years old and I don't know what my favourite breakfast cereal is. Or my favourite food, full-stop. I've just gone along with what she wanted, and what the guys suggested, for as long as I can remember.

'I don't know if I've had one independent thought for years. And I'm not having a go at the guys. I just mean that if we went out or ordered in, I picked what one of them had, instead of getting what I wanted. Not that I knew what I wanted.'

He turns around to face her fully. 'I like you, Maeve. For the first time in years, I've found someone I enjoy spending time with, outside my family and the band. But I'm still figuring myself out. I've got two appointments a week with a therapist and I'm talking about what happened. It's not a quick fix though.'

He smiles sadly and shrugs. 'I don't know if there is a fix at all, but I'm trying. I really am. I just don't know if I can be more than friends with you right now, as much as I want to. Physical contact sometimes freaks me out. I don't want to upset or offend you, by reacting badly.'

Maeve squeezes his hand, as she collects her thoughts. This isn't how she was expecting today to go. She wants a relationship with Luke. No question of that. She wants to hug him, to kiss him, to have sex with him. But more than that, she just wants him. She wants his company, loves spending time with him without anything sexual.

After hearing what she just had, she can hardly blame him for being unsure of a physical relationship.

But can she put all that aside to have him in her life? She smiles as she looks up at him. Of course she can.

'Okay, so first off. Thank you for telling me. I can't imagine how difficult it was for you, and it means a lot that you trust me enough to tell me. Second, I like you, Luke. Genuinely like you, and genuinely like spending time with you. Since you were so honest with me, it's only fair I return the favour.

'I want to be more than just your friend, but,' she adds quickly when his face drops a little. 'I'm more than happy not to label our relationship. Labels are boring and too restrictive. I would love to spend more time with you and, if all you can give me at the moment is your hand to hold, and the odd kiss, I'll take it. I'll take you however I can get you, Luke.'

'You mean that?' he says, the tears pouring down his face, each one breaking her heart over and over again. 'There's a chance I won't be able to give you what you want. At least not for a while. I don't expect you to stick around on the off chance I get myself sorted. That's not fair on you.'

'I understand. Let's take it a day at a time, and see what happens.'

When he drops his gaze, Maeve takes him in her arms, and holds him, thankful when he doesn't resist.

## Luke

He pulls into the car park opposite the pub and turns off the engine. Instead of getting out of the car, he sits and stares out at the boats in the harbour. He checks his phone again but there's no message from her cancelling their... what? Is it a date? A meeting? He's so out of practice he hasn't got a clue what to call it. Whatever it is, she still wants to go ahead with it. .

After he told her about Pippa, then broke down like a pathetic fool, he fully expected never to hear from her again. He wouldn't have blamed her. It was a hell of an info dump on the poor girl.

And it's not like telling her had been easy for him either. It doesn't matter how many times he says the words, it's like he's talking about someone else. He's not big-headed but he is fairly intelligent. He always thought out of the four band members, he was the sensible one. The one who had his head screwed on.

The one who allowed himself to be sucked in, to be used and abused. He fell in love and his brain switched off.

He jumps when Andy knocks on his window. 'Shit! You scared me,' he says when he opens the door.

'Sorry. I just wanted to check you were okay.'

He nods, trying to be convincing as he does too much of the time. Poor Andy signed on to protect Luke from other people, not check he's okay when he gets lost in his own head. 'Just thinking.'

'You need more time?'

'No. I'm fine, thanks.'

'Okay, so there are quite a few people here. You might want to deploy stealth mode,' he says with a grin.

Luke takes his sunglasses from the centre console and slips them on. 'Deployed. I'm still surprised the whole cap and glasses thing works.'

Andy flicks the peak of Luke's cap. 'It would work better if you didn't live in a cap all the fucking time. Maybe change your stealth mode disguise to a Stetson or something like that.'

'Yeah, like walking around Greystones wearing a Stetson wouldn't make me stand out at all.'

'Fair point. C'mon then. She's waiting for you.'

Luke climbs out of his car and follows Andy across the road to the door leading to Maeve's apartment.

'I'll be in the car. Any problems just give me a call.'

'Yeah. Will do. Thanks Andy.'

His bodyguard moves a little closer and smiles at him. 'She's a great girl, Luke. You don't need to know her for long to pick up on that. And she likes you.'

'You really think she does?'

'Yes! Listen, I know I'm paid to protect and look out for you, but this isn't coming from that guy who is paid. This is coming from the guy who considers himself fairly fucking lucky to have been assigned to you.

'You're a decent bloke Luke. And you're not nearly half as much trouble as your mates are. I enjoy talking to you. Enjoy spending time with you. And I'm not the only one who feels like that. I don't think I've come across anyone who doesn't like you. Now ring that doorbell, walk up that stairs, and spend the afternoon with Maeve.'

Luke faces the door, then straightens his shoulders and rings the bell. Maeve pulls the door open and he grins widely. She's wearing a vintage band t-shirt that's ripped, showing her stomach, with a pair of ripped and faded jeans. Her feet are bare, her fingers and toenails painted the same purple as her hair.

'Hey guys.' She surprises Andy by giving him a hug, barely reaching his shoulders, before taking Luke's hand. 'You want to check out my apartment Andy, or do you trust me with this sexy fellow?'

'I think I trust you. Have fun.' He winks and walks back over to the car park.

Maeve pulls Luke inside and shuts the door, nearly dragging him upstairs after her. 'Slow down! What's the rush?'

She pulls him into her kitchen and brushes her hair back off her shoulders. 'I wanted to show you this.'

Every free surface is piled high with everything from cereal to pizzas to packets of cheese to boxes of cakes. It looks like she's opened a supermarket in her small kitchen. 'You hungry?'

Maeve laughs and rests her hands on her hips as she looks at the food. 'There's a chance I may have gone a tad overboard, but I had to make sure I had enough of everything. This is important.'

'What is?'

She hands him a small brown paper bag. 'This is for you. Go on. Open it.'

Luke frowns as he unwraps a notebook. He reads the writing on the cover. '*Luke's Likes.* I'm confused?'

Maeve takes the notebook from him and opens the first page. At the top of the page she's written the word cereal. The next page is titled pizza. Then ice-cream.

'You mentioned that you don't know what cereal you like eating for breakfast, or what your favourite food is. It kind of stuck with me when you said that. So I had this ingenious plan. Well, I hope it's ingenious.' She hands the notebook back to him. 'I thought this could be a notebook of everything you like. As in you - not anyone else. The problem is you need to figure out what exactly you like, and for that I needed to get some provisions.'

Luke flicks through the notebook and tries not to get emotional. It's pathetic and irritating that he feels that way, but he doesn't know how else to react. He's floored and overwhelmed by the gesture.

Maeve steps up in front of him, then lifts his chin so she can look in his eyes. 'Worst idea I had, or is it okay?'

He nods and wipes his face. He's tired of always being on the edge of an emotional breakdown. 'It's okay. It's very okay. Thank you.'

Maeve's face breaks into a wide smile and she turns around to examine her purchases. 'Okay, so like I said, I may have gone more than a little overboard. There's a lot to get through. Where do you fancy starting? And please say you haven't pigged out on a massive meal before you came here?'

'No. Nothing since breakfast.'

'Thank God! This is meant to be fun, not make you sick. So, any ideas what you want to go for first?'

He opens the notebook and holds up to the first page. 'Guess I'm going for another breakfast.'

'Fantastic! Love a bit of cereal.' She gathers as many boxes as she can carry and brings them over to the table. 'Can you grab a few bowls. Second cupboard on the left beside the fridge. Spoons are in the drawer above.'

Luke finds everything they need and sits opposite her. Maeve pours two small bowls of Coco Pops. 'Now, I didn't go for all healthy options. It's about taste when it comes to cereal. And I figured you work out enough anyway, so you'll burn off the extra calories.' She passes one to Luke and pours in some milk. Maeve holds out her spoon and he knocks his off it. 'Cheers.'

'Cheers.'

Half an hour later, Luke is full of cereal and the table is covered in open boxes.

'I feel sick.'

She laughs and covers her mouth as she swallows her mouthful of cereal. 'But it's so good.'

Luke picks up the first packet they tried and reads the front of the packet. 'This is what Tate eats.'

'Tate eats Coco Pops?'

'He loves them.'

Maeve nods as she chews another spoon of cereal. 'He's got good taste.'

He looks at the cereal carnage on the table. The place is a mess. Maeve had knocked over a few of the boxes while she was reaching across the table. The surface and the floor are scattered in a rainbow of various cereals.

'Where's your dustpan and brush?'

She waves her hand dismissively at him. 'It's grand. No rush.'

'But there's cereal all over the floor.'

'It's not going anywhere. It'll still be there in a while.' Maeve frowns at him and leans across the table. 'Hey. Is it bothering you?'

It's not bothering him as such, he just isn't used to it. His house had always been spotless. As in sterile spotless. If he spilt anything Pippa would go nuts at him. 'Sorry. I just... never mind.'

'Talk to me.'

'I just... I don't know. I'm not used to mess.'

'Luke, life is messy from time to time. There's nothing wrong with getting a little food on the floor.' She reaches across and squeezes his hand. 'I will clear it up, but if I bend over right now, there's a strong chance I'll get sick.' She pulls a face and he laughs.

Maeve isn't bothered by the disorganisation. She's just happy being in the moment, and that's something he's not used to. His previous life had been so ordered and structured, he forgot what it was like to be free like Maeve is.

'What?' she asks around a mouthful of cereal. 'Why are you looking at me like that. Do I have food on my face?'

'I think you got it all in your mouth.'

She throws a Coco Pop at him and laughs. 'Smart arse. So, is that the winner?'

'Yeah. It's the winner.'

She waves her arms in the air. 'Woohoo! Pop it in the book.'

Luke adds the cereal to the first page, feeling oddly satisfied making the decision. It's a trivial thing. Most people would laugh at how much effort it took, but it is massive for him. Maeve pushes to her feet and goes over to the TV, scrolling through songs until she finds something she likes.

She moves back to the table, grabs another handful of cereal then dances her way over to the kitchen. He watches as she puts on the kettle, still dancing and singing to herself. Her short t-shirt rides up, giving him a perfect view of the large flower tattooed on her stomach.

'Coffee? Hello? Luke!'

'What?' He stops staring at her, and begins righting some of the overturned cereal boxes.

'Do you want some coffee?'

'Yeah. Thanks.'

She brings the two cups over to the table and uses her arm to clear some space, shoving boxes aside, knocking some on the floor. 'So,' she asks, settling back in the chair. 'Ready for the next page, or do you need a break?'

'I think a break would be good. I don't want to throw up.'

She sips her coffee. 'Good point.'

'Thank you for doing this.'

She waves his thanks away, covering her mouth as she belches. 'Excuse me! It's all the cereal.'

Luke bursts out laughing. Maeve is perfect.

That one thought stops him in his tracks.

She really is.

He thought Pippa was, but her perfection was different. It was fake. Forced. Maeve is honest and true. Her carefree way of approaching life is something he desperately wishes he could take on for himself.

But he can't. He doesn't even know where to start.

'A penny for them.'

'Sorry?' he asks, coming out of his thoughts when she speaks.

'You look like you're miles away.'

'I was just wondering how you do that?'

She pulls her feet up onto the chair, crossing her legs under her. 'Belching? It comes naturally,' she adds with a grin.

'You're hilarious!'

'Oh I know.'

'I meant the not caring bit. You are you, and you don't apologise. I don't know how to do that. I want to, I really do, but I don't know how. I'm used to...'

Maeve drags her chair closer to him and takes his hand. 'Used to what, Luke?'

'Not being good enough. Trying so hard to be someone who would meet expectations, but always falling short.'

Maeve takes a long breath, rubbing her hand over his as she thinks. 'Okay, so I kind of understand what you're saying. I wasn't exactly confident in my own skin for a long time.'

'Really? But I always remember you being so confident.'

'Confidence is a funny thing. It's easy to fake it when you need to. I don't think I fully believed in the whole *fuck it* way of thinking, until I was about seventeen. It was actually my brother who gave me the kick I needed.

'He was always this larger than life guy, who honestly couldn't have given a fuck what anyone else thought of him. If someone said he couldn't do it, he had to prove them wrong. I loved that attitude he had.

'One day I just looked at him across the dinner table. It was kind of like I was seeing him for the first time, which sounds random. I figured if he can do it why can't I? So I did.

'I'm only here once Luke, well, depending on your beliefs. But I really don't want to look back and beat myself up over not doing something, or doing something a certain way to keep others happy. All that matters is how I feel.'

She smiles widely at him. 'You Luke, have so much to be proud of. So so much. You told me on the beach that you don't know who you are anymore. This is the time to get to know yourself. Don't overthink. The only way you're going to figure out who the real Luke Daly is, is by experimenting. And I'll help you as much as I can.'

He places his other hand on top of hers. 'You already have, Maeve. So much. I mean I've never had so much fun eating breakfast before.'

'Oh eating should always be fun.'

Luke believes that now, but for so long it was just another thing he had no control over. Now, he's looking forward to exploring what else he likes, filling up the pages of his notebook. And it's all thanks to Maeve.

Luke leans forward, the urge to kiss her suddenly hitting and refusing to be ignored. Before Maeve, kissing hadn't been something he enjoyed. He didn't know he could. But with her, it's so different.

And it gives him hope that, maybe one day, he might enjoy doing more with her.

Maeve

She is so full she feels like she's about to burst. Maeve stretches out on the couch and groans. 'You know, there's a strong chance I'm going to be sick. You won't judge me, will you?'

'As long as you don't ask me to hold your hair.'

She grins over at Luke, stretched out on the other couch with a huge smile on his face. They'd successfully filled half a dozen pages of his notebook. It took about four hours, but for every minute of that time, Luke had been smiling and laughing. Genuinely having fun, from what she can make out. He'd even thrown a few pieces of cereal at her at one stage.

He's relaxed with her, and that means so much. This is the Luke she's seen in interviews or performing. He's happy. That seems to be the key with him. When he's on stage, singing and playing, he's truly happy. She just needs to get a bit of *that* Luke out.

'Can I ask you something?'

He opens his eyes and tuns his head to look at her.

'Are you ever going to sing for me?'

There goes the relaxed Luke. He pushes upright and frowns over at her. 'Sing? No. I can't sing.'

'Really? That's strange, cause I'm fairly sure I've heard you sing on more than one song.'

'Yeah, but with Tate. I can't sing unless Tate is there.'

'Ah, I've heard of that.'

'What?'

'Voices that only work when Tate Archer is nearby. It's actually quite common.'

He relaxes a little as he smiles at her. 'Do you have to be a smart arse?'

'Absolutely! Especially when the other party is being silly. I've heard you sing, Luke. You're so good.'

'I don't have a guitar. It'd feel weird singing without one.'

'I might just be able to help you out there.' She goes into her bedroom and comes back out with a guitar. 'I know it's just a cheap one compared to what you're probably used to playing, but it works. Mike plays it from time to time. You don't have to, really. If you really don't want to, it's fine.'

He reluctantly takes the guitar from her, and frowns at the instrument. Maeve wants him to do this - for himself as much as anything.

She's heard him sing on Broken's songs. Tate has an incredible voice, but she can easily pick out Luke's voice in the background when he sings. Whatever block he has about singing without the support of the rest of the band, he needs to get over it.

Luke plays with the stud under his lip, as he seriously struggles with the request. 'Okay, but can you sit behind me or something. I just feel a little weird singing like this.'

'Not a problem.' She gets up and leans against the counter behind the couch. Another few minutes go by, before he lifts the guitar off his knee and rests his fingers on the strings. She doesn't know why, but she feels that if Luke can do this, it will be a big step in the right direction for him. Playing and singing in situations like this, should be easy for him.

Then he sings, and Maeve is instantly transfixed. He starts off a little quieter than she's heard him before, but after a few lines, his confidence grows, and so does the volume. His voice isn't as deep as Tate's, but it's no less powerful.

Maeve slowly moves from the counter to the chair opposite him. Luke's eyes are closed as he sings, his fingers moving over the guitar strings from memory.

A shiver works through Maeve as she watches him. He is unbelievably sexy, and that's not a thought that is going to help either of them right now. He looks every bit the rock star he is. His plain black t-shirt and blue jeans don't distract from the stunning drawings on his arms. If anything, watching the muscles move under his skin as he plays, is only ramping up the sex appeal.

A sadness comes over her as she listens to him singing. She'll never understand why Pippa treated him the way she did. Luke is one of the kindest, sweetest men she's ever known. He deserves to be loved. He deserves someone who will listen to him singing and playing for hours. Deserves someone who will tell him how incredible he is. Someone who will love him for being himself.

Her eyes move to his wrists, to the scars hidden under the leather bands, and her thoughts darken further. That woman had slowly picked him to pieces. She'd hurt him so badly. Her insecurities had been thrown on to him. Had Pippa told him he's not a great singer? Had she not wanted to listen to him play?

He was never overly confident in school, but he had sang in front of people, as the lead in half a dozen productions. She doubts he would have joined the band if he had a problem playing in public. Maybe it was a strength in numbers thing? He was fine with the others around him.

He stops singing and slowly opens his eyes, smiling when he spots her in front of him. 'Hey! You're not behind me.'

'No. Appears not. And hey? That's all you can say after throwing that at me? Luke... wow! I seriously mean that. Your voice is... wow!' She holds out her arm. 'See. Goosebumps.'

They're partly down to his singing, and partly down to the fact she is unbelievably turned on, but there's no way she's going to mention that to him. 'I can see why Tate keeps you to backing vocals. You'd give him a run for his money.'

Luke laughs and her heart melts. It's the first truly genuine laugh she's heard from him. 'Yeah, well he has tried to get me to take lead on a few more songs but...' he shrugs and looks down at the guitar.

'But what? You should take him up on that.'

'I don't know. It's his thing. I'm happy backing him. Even just being on stage with the guys is enough for me.'

'You genuinely love it, don't you?'

'Every second. And I don't mean that in a big-headed way. Dillon is all about the fame stuff. He thrives on it. I just love playing and singing.' His smile fades a little, and he looks down at the guitar on his knee. 'I think for a long time it was the only place I felt... safe I guess. It was the only place she couldn't... Broken Chords is Tate, Gregg, Dillon, and me. No one else. It's ours.'

'You're lucky to have that.'

'I know. It was the one thing she didn't take from me.' He runs his hand over the guitar. 'She tried though. When she told me I had to leave the band and go solo, I couldn't deal with that. There was nothing good in my life without the band.'

Maeve doesn't want to think about his attempted suicide. She can't bring herself to imagine how bad it was for him. Can't imagine what would have happened, had Dillon not gone to find him that day. Doesn't want to imagine a world without Luke.

'But she didn't take it from you. And I don't think she would have been able to.'

'You don't? Why?'

'Because it's part of who you are. It's the same for the four of you. You were like that in school. You were all crazy about music. Okay, so you were top of all your classes. Quite sickening really,' she adds with a grin.

'But when you guys were unleashed in music class, you came into your own. Music is in your blood, Luke. I don't think there's one person who is in the least bit surprised Broken Chords has achieved world domination.'

He laughs at that. 'Except for the four of us.'

'Yes well, you're all surprisingly modest. Well, apart from Dillon!'

'True. He can't do modest. Thanks Maeve.'

'For what?'

'Understanding how I feel about the band.'

'Why wouldn't I understand? I'm the same with dancing. When I dance, nothing else exists. It's just me and whatever music I'm dancing to. It's how I relax, how I get rid of all the crap that builds up in my mind over the day. Sort of like a detox.'

His face lights up when he hears that. 'Yeah. That's how I feel. I'm happy when playing. Singing too, but I don't do that as much.'

And Maeve has a fair idea why. She's becoming familiar with his range of facial expressions. The frown is laced with fear. The poor guy is still scared of his wife. Time to take his mind off her.

She grabs the remote, scrolling through the music until she finds the right piece. It takes Luke a few seconds to recognise it.

'What are you doing?'

'I love this song.'

He smiles again, the lines around his eyes and mouth softening. 'You do?'

'Absolutely. And it's the only song you take the lead on, as far as I know?'

'Yeah. Tate wrote me a song and pestered me until I sang it. It was on the second album.'

She holds out her hand. 'C'mon.'

'What?'

'Stand up.'

He pushes out of the chair and stands facing her, looking like a deer in headlights.

'It's okay. I'm not going to bite.'

'I don't know. I saw what you did to the cereal.'

She laughs loudly and takes his hands. God she loves when he lets go and just has fun. 'Get into position. And don't look at me like that. I know you can dance. I watched you in enough stage shows at school.'

'I haven't danced in years.'

'Are you telling me that if someone took your guitar from you for years, you'd forget how to play?'

'Of course not.'

She wiggles his arms, trying to loosen his tense muscles. 'Exactly. Now don't make me unleash teacher mode. Position please.'

He goes through one hell of an internal battle, before he lifts his arms, sliding them under hers. She keeps the massive smile to herself. Victory! She wasn't bigging him up to give him a confidence boost. Luke can really dance.

He'd shown off his moves in show after show, mastering each of the complicated fast contemporary routines with ease. He was lead in the musicals every year for a reason.

She guides him through the steps, which, as expected, he picks up impressively fast. 'If all my students were as good as you, I'd be out of a job.'

'Stop talking, I'm concentrating.'

'Sincerest apologies.'

He grins at her, and she could swear some of the rigid tension in his body ebbs away. She could be mistaken, but she'd put money on the fact the rock star is enjoying dancing. He was like this in school too, always joining in the school shows and productions.

It kills her to see him withdrawn and unsure of himself. The crippling fear of doing the wrong thing is always there. He gets past it sometimes, but she has no idea how to help him shed it once and for all. Maybe it's a part of him now, something he'll have to live with.

His hands move down her back ever so slightly, then he draws her closer to him and does the last thing she was expecting. He sings along with himself on the stereo, adding a harmony that has the goosebumps out again.

God, this man can sing and dance at the same time! Talk about serious sex appeal. And his smell isn't helping. She can't explain it, but he smells like a coastal breeze coming off the sea. It's comforting and exciting at the same time. As he holds her, she takes a deep breath, surrounding herself with everything that is Luke. His voice. His scent. His body.

Realistically, the song only lasts three or four minutes, but in his arms like that, Maeve swears it's a lot longer, but also far too short.

'Would you... can I sing something else for you?' he asks when the song ends.

Maeve nods enthusiastically. 'That's not a question you ever have to ask me. The answer is always going to be yes.'

## 13

### Luke

He taps his fingers on the steering wheel as he waits at the red light. Dillon is slouched in the passenger seat, his sunglasses on and a large travel cup of coffee in his hand. 'Late night?'

'Just taking a while to get going today.' He glares over at Luke. 'Why the fuck are you so happy? It's too early to be that happy!'

'Can I not be happy for a change?'

Dillon swallows a mouthful of coffee before he answers. 'Of course you can! I'm guessing you saw her again yesterday?'

'Who?'

Dillon glances over at him, and rolls his eyes behind his glasses. 'Don't go all innocent on me. Maeve!'

'Yeah. I spent a few hours at her place. She got me a notebook.'

'You what?'

'I told her that I'm trying to figure myself out. I mentioned I don't know what my favourite cereal is, or my favourite food. So, she got me this.' He pulls the small notebook from his back pocket, passing it to Dillon who takes the next few minutes flicking through the pages.

'Fuck! She did this for you?'

'Yeah. She got loads of food and we did a tasting session. I felt as sick as a dog after, but I figured out some stuff about myself I didn't know. Then, I sang her a few songs.'

Dillon pushes up in the seat and stares over at him for a few seconds. 'You sang? Alone?'

'Yep. Just me and a guitar. Her brother plays a bit, so she had one in her apartment. I really enjoyed it, Dillon.'

'Fuck me! About fucking time!'

'What?'

'You singing without Tate. We've been telling you for years you can sing on your own. I'm fairly sure Tate's been badgering you to take the lead on a few songs too.'

'I know. I guess I just got used to...'

'Got used to her telling you you couldn't do it. Well guess what? You fucking can! I'm proud of you, Luke. That's fucking brilliant!'

'And I danced.'

If Luke wasn't driving and had a camera to hand, he'd give anything to record the look on Dillon's face at hearing that. 'It's too fucking early for all these revelations! You danced? As in, like you used to in school?'

'Yeah, but I haven't done that for years.'

'Fuck me! I can't keep up with all of this. Think I need another coffee. So I take it you danced with Maeve?'

'She's a dance teacher now. You should see her dance, Dillon. She's incredible!'

'I can believe that. She was a pretty amazing dancer in school. You were too. Did you make an ass of yourself, or did you still know what to do?'

'Funny! And yes, I remembered what to do. No making an ass of myself. At least I hope not. She seemed to think I was holding my own.'

'I'll bet you were,' Dillon says, before taking another drink from his coffee. 'You okay with her holding you like that? When you were dancing I mean?'

Luke nods. 'I actually think it might have helped a little. I was so busy concentrating on not tripping over my feet, I sort of forgot that she was touching me. And when I realised, I liked how it felt, a lot.'

'Sounds like a good thing you met up with her again, if that's what it took to get you used to someone touching you again? There's no fucking way any of us would have danced with you.' He winks, and Luke laughs at the thought of Dillon or Tate dancing. Gregg possibly, but definitely not the other two.

'Yeah, I think you're right there. You're not really the dancing type.'

'That's putting it mildly.' He takes a couple of tablets from a packet, then washes them down with his coffee.

'You okay?'

'Painkillers. Raging headache. I'll be grand when we get to Tate's. So you going to volunteer to take lead vocals now? Tate wouldn't have a problem.'

He'd be lying if he said a part of him isn't tempted, but it's a big step moving from singing with Tate, to singing out in the front alone. It's one thing in Maeve's living room. It's another on a stage in front of people. 'I'm not sure I'm ready for that yet.'

'You should try it, just with the three of us with you. See how you feel and go from there? And, it's not like you'll be alone. Tate will sing with you. You've got me and Gregg with you too. It's always the four of us performing together. We've always got your back.'

Luke sits on the couch next to Dillon, feeling like he's on top of the world. Their rehearsal had gone well. The new songs Tate wrote are amazing, but then again, they always are. When it comes to writing songs, the guy is a genius.

But when Dillon had told him to get off his ass and sing, he'd done it. And it felt amazing! It wasn't a stage, but it's a start.

He'd taken lead vocals, managed to get through the song, without forgetting the words or the chords, then earned himself a round of slaps on the back and hugs from the guys when he was done.

Tate drops on to the couch opposite him, and rests his boots on the coffee table. He yawns and scrubs a hand over his face.

'Long night?'

He nods and reaches for his coffee. 'I reckon Brandon slept for maybe an hour at the most. I'm too old for all this late night stuff. How the fuck did we go on all night benders?'

'We had alcohol,' Dillon says. 'Always helps.'

Gregg nudges Tate. 'Shift your arse. You're taking up the whole couch.'

'It's my fucking couch!'

'You want me to sit on you? Cause I will.'

Tate curses, then shuffles up, so Gregg can sit beside him.

'You guys see the email from Ellen?' he asks, as he digs his bag of gummy bears from his pocket.

Luke had seen it, but he knows Tate and Dillon won't have. They're not overly reliable when it comes to things like emails, or any other band stuff that doesn't involve the actual songs or performances.

'We in trouble again?'

Gregg grins at Dillon. 'Have you done something we should know about?'

'Why the fuck are you assuming I'm the one who's in trouble?'

Gregg raises his eyebrows, and Dillon shrugs. 'Fair point. So, what's wrong with our delightful manager?'

'We're off to the UK next week for a couple of TV appearances.'

Luke zones out, as the others discuss the email and the details. He's not as enthusiastic about the weekend as they are. He's done a few appearances since he was discharged from the centre, but he's still nervous about what he's going to be facing.

They'd been sticking to mainly performances, but this will be an interview. Thankfully, Tate is the one who usually takes the lead on those, but the rest of them will be there, so there's a chance he'll be asked something.

Ellen will prep him as she always does, and the interviewer won't be allowed to mention Pippa, but that doesn't stop the fear that someone will break the rules, then he'll be in front of an audience having a meltdown of some sort.

He jumps when Dillon kicks his foot under the table. 'You okay?'

'Yeah. Sorry.'

'We've got you, you know that, right? Anything happens you're not happy with, we'll step in. We've got your back, Luke.'

'I know. Thanks.'

Tate yawns again. 'Fuck. Sorry. Think I need another coffee. You going to ask Maeve to go with you to the UK?'

Luke looks from Tate, to Dillon, then Gregg. 'What? But I can't.'

'Why not?' Tate asks.

'Because we're not... I mean we're just friends.'

'And? How many friends do you know who would turn down an all expenses paid trip to the UK?' Gregg says as he searches in the bag of gummy bears. 'Answer - none.'

They look around as Chloe opens the studio door and comes in with Brandon. 'You having a break?'

'Yeah. You want me to take him for a bit?'

'He's asleep, but every time I try to put him down, he wakes up. If

I don't get a shower and something to eat, there's a strong chance I'll either cry or scream.'

Tate takes his son from Chloe and kisses her on the forehead. 'I'd prefer you didn't do either. We're pretty much done here, so take your time. Why don't you have a nap too?'

'Would you mind?'

'Of course not!'

'Thanks. Love you.'

'Love you too, babe.'

Tate lowers back onto the couch, moving slowly so he doesn't wake Brandon.

'Aww. Would you look at you, being all cute and all.'

Tate slowly turns to glower at Gregg. 'Just because I'm holding him doesn't mean I won't deck you.'

'Threatening violence in front of a minor. I'm shocked.'

'Yeah well keep that up, and I'll be looking for a new best man.'

'You wouldn't dare! I'm your oldest and dearest friend. And I'm dating your sister. That makes me extra special.'

'Keep thinking that.'

'So,' Dillon says, turning back to Luke. 'Back to the weekend. If you want her to come, ask her. There's no pressure, mate. Might be nice for you two to spend some time away from here. Show her a bit of the real you.'

Luke looks at his friends. They've only ever had his back. Through everything that's gone on over the last year, they've never led him astray. Not once. But he's really not sure about this. It's a massive step.

'What if she says no?'

Tate points to his coffee on the table. 'Pass me that, will you?' Luke carefully passes Tate his coffee, making sure not to bring the mug anywhere near Brandon. 'Cheers. And if she says no, it's not a big deal. At least you asked.' He adjusts his position on the couch, grimacing when his son stirs.

He enjoys seeing Tate with his son. Tate had been so worried he wouldn't be a good father because of his past, and his addiction issues, but he's risen to the challenge. He's such a natural, his intensely protective side coming into its own, to make sure Chloe and Brandon didn't want for anything.

It didn't matter what Tate did in his past, he was loved for who he is now.

Just like Maeve with him. Okay, so it's not love, but she likes him for being himself. And that's a good place to start. 'I mean is it not too soon? You really think I should invite her?'

'Yes!' they all say at the same time, quickly looking at the baby in case they woke him.

'We have to stop doing that,' Tate says. 'If we wake him up, Chloe will have my neck. And yes, you should ask her. Dillon and Gregg said she's decent. Have you told her everything?'

'Yes. I told her what it was like with Pippa. Told her about what I did to... you know... get away. I told her that I'm still figuring a lot of things out.'

'And?' Dillon asks. 'What was her reaction?'

'She said she'd take me however she can get me.'

'Jesus, Luke,' Gregg says around a gummy bear he shoved in his mouth. 'You're going to get me all teary. That's a lovely thing to say.'

'I know. I just don't want her to get her hopes up for more. I don't know if I can give her more.'

Dillon grabs another biscuit from the tin on the table. 'Exactly.'

'What?'

'You don't know. Right now anything physical turns you off. Understandable. But you don't know if that's always going to be the case. Don't write this off until you've given it, and yourself, a decent chance. What's to say Maeve won't be the one to help you rediscover all the really fucking amazing physical stuff? Cause it is really amazing, Luke. And that's not just my opinion.'

'I wouldn't know at the moment,' Tate grumbles. 'I'm sharing my fiancée with another man, and he's winning.' He smiles down at his son, before snapping out of it and looking back at Luke. 'But Dillon is right. What you had with the *Bitch*... that's not how it should be. Just take it day by day. Don't rule anything out.'

'What they said,' Gregg agrees. 'It sounds like you've found someone who gets you.'

Luke turns his mug in his hand. Maybe this isn't as crazy an idea as he initially thought? 'I have kissed her.'

The guys all look at him, each one grinning widely. Dillon slaps him on the knee and laughs. 'Fair play, mate! Who initiated?'

'I did.'

'Wehey!' Gregg shouts, grimacing over at Brandon who doesn't even flinch. 'Sorry buddy.'

Tate glares at him, before looking back at Luke. 'You realise how much of a fucking massive step that was for you?'

Luke nods. He does know. 'I got the urge to kiss her. We were swimming and I just kissed her.'

'Well that's settled,' Gregg says. 'You have to invite her along now. Bria will be there too, so she won't be the only woman. I take it Chloe is staying put?'

Tate nods. 'Mum will give her a hand with this guy if she needs it.'

'Should I get two rooms?'

'What do you want?' Dillon asks.

Since he left the hospital, that question is being asked a lot. And he knows why. They're trying to give him control of his decisions. Doesn't help him to know if he's making the right or wrong ones though.

'Maybe two, just in case.'

'Two it is.'

## Maeve

She checks the screen on her phone, and looks back at the cottage facing her. This can't be right. There's no way *that* Dillon lives in this house. There's no flare. Nothing Dillon about it.

She rides her motorbike slowly down the gravel driveway, then smiles when she sees the deep red classic Mustang parked outside. It is the right place.

Maeve takes off her helmet and swings her leg over the saddle. As plans go, she's not so sure this is her best one. But she wants to help Luke and, without help, she's just second guessing everything she's doing.

Before she loses her nerve, she rings the doorbell.

An attractive woman in her early to mid fifties opens the door, and smiles politely at her. 'Can I help you?'

Maeve pauses for a few seconds, thrown off by the woman answering the door, instead of Dillon. 'Sorry. Yes. I'm looking for Dillon Ryan.'

Her eyes narrow and the smile turns a little less friendly. 'And you are?'

'I'm a friend of Luke's. I went to school with Dillon and Luke, and I bumped in to them again a few weeks ago. I need to speak to Dillon if he's around.'

The woman's smile widens and she steps aside. 'Maeve?'

'Em, yeah.'

'Don't look so worried. Dillon's told me about you.' She holds out her hand and Maeve shakes it. 'It's so nice to meet you. I'm Dillon's sister, Clara. Come in.'

Keeping her surprise to herself, Maeve follows Clara into the living room and instantly falls in love with Dillon's home. The cottage is spacious and immaculate inside with vast beams and a flagstone floor. It's beautiful.

'Would you like a drink?'

'Water would be great, thanks. This is stunning. Do you live here with him?'

'You're kidding, right? You couldn't pay me enough to live with my brother! No, I'm married and live in town. I just pop over occasionally to irritate him and make sure he's eating food that didn't come entirely from a packet.'

Clara gets her drink, and gestures to the couch beside the enormous fireplace.

'He just went for a swim. He seems to enjoy throwing himself in the freezing Irish Sea every day for pleasure. Personally, I'd prefer a coffee and a good book. I'm surprised he hasn't caught pneumonia yet.'

Maeve laughs. 'Sorry. You're just very different to him. He's a little intense, and you're normal. I'm so sorry - that sounded a lot harsher than I intended.'

'No, I get that a lot. Dillon has a way about him, and people automatically assume I must be so over-the-top to be related to him. Surprisingly, he's actually very mellow... most of the time,' she adds with a grin. 'So, how are things with Luke?'

Maeve looks down at her hands and shrugs. 'I honestly don't know. I like him. Really like him, but I don't want to do something wrong, or scare him or... I don't know. I'm lost, and that's why I need Dillon's help.'

'I hope he can help. I love Luke to death, I really do, but he's in limbo and will need someone to help him out of it. Dillon was with him on quite a few of his sessions. I'm sure he can give you some advice.'

'I really hope so.'

Clara reaches over and squeezes her knee. 'You already sound like a winner.'

'Thank you, Clara.'

They both look around as Dillon comes in the back door and stares at them. 'Hi.'

'Good swim?' his sister asks, as he keeps his attention on Maeve.

'Yeah. Cold. What are you doing here?'

'I need to talk to you, if that's okay.'

'Right.' He keeps the frown in place for an awkward few seconds then drops his wet towel on the floor. 'I'll just grab a shower. I'll be out in a minute.'

Clara throws the towel at him as he walks away. 'Put this where it belongs.'

'Stop fussing over me.'

'I'm not fussing. Just looking out for you. I've filled your freezer with enough meals to last the week, and there's a roast dinner in the fridge for later. Just needs to be reheated. I brought over some groceries too.'

Dillon opens the fridge and takes out a carton, glaring at the packaging. 'What the fuck is this?'

'Almond milk.'

'What's wrong with regular milk?'

'Nothing. I just thought you might want to try that.'

'I'll drink it, if you point out where the nipple is on an almond?'

She grabs the carton from his hand and glares at him. 'You're infuriating!'

'I know.' He smiles at his sister and pulls her into a tight hug. 'Thanks for the food, but you can take that shit with you.'

'Asshole! And you're welcome. And wet. Get off me!' She laughs and shoves him away from her. 'Have a shower before you catch a cold. I'll call you later. Nice to meet you Maeve.' She picks up her bag and walks over to the door, the carton of almond milk under her arm. 'Don't forget to eat, Dillon.'

'Fuck off Clara!' he adds with a smile as she closes the door. He turns back to Maeve. 'I'll be five minutes.'

When he joins her less than five minutes later, he's in a pair of joggers and a t-shirt, his hair still wet and ruffled. Very different to the public version of him she's used to seeing, with the stylish clothes, jewellery, and perfect hair. This is more like the Dillon she knew in school.

'You want something to drink?'

'Clara sorted me out, thanks.'

He grabs a packet from the cupboard and turns the kettle on. As he waits for the water to boil, he pulls a green liquorice lace from the bag and chews on it. He offers her a lace, but she shakes her head.

'I'm not a fan.'

'Not many are. So, I take it you're not here to reminisce about school? Is Luke okay?'

She nods, as she tries to get comfortable, but something about Dillon always puts her on edge. He makes a coffee, then sits opposite

116

her. He lounges back on the couch, with his feet on the table in front of him.

She knows without a doubt that he will be protective of Luke, and after hearing the truth of what Pippa had been doing, she completely understands. 'This is a little weird for me.'

'What? Talking to me?' He grins, but his green eyes are interrogating her as usual.

'No, not that part. You're Luke's closest friend and it's a bit strange talking to you about this.'

He pulls another lace from the packet and tears a chunk from the end. 'Talking about what? You're not saying much. Sounds like a lot of stalling. I'll let you in to a little secret. Not much fazes me. Just say what you want to say, and stop making it harder on yourself.'

'Are you always so direct?'

'From what I remember, you can be too.'

'I guess you're right.' She clears her throat and he raises his eyebrows as she clearly stalls, yet again. 'Okay. So, I like Luke.'

'No shit! I figured that bit out already.'

'I mean really, really, like him.'

'And you're not sure what to do about it? Physically I mean?'

She nods, grateful that he got what she was trying to say...badly. 'Being with him is so different to anyone else I've been with. He's spending time with me and he calls and texts me, but I don't know how to move us on. I don't want to mess it up, or hurt him, by doing or saying the wrong thing.'

'He told us he kissed you.'

She nods. 'Yeah. It completely took me by surprise when he did that. I just sort of froze when he did though, and I don't want to do that either. I'm second guessing everything I do.'

Dillon finishes the lace he was chewing and wipes his hands on his legs. 'Got yourself all tangled up thinking about this, haven't you?'

'Over thinking probably.'

He nods, then rests his arms on his legs, as he clasps his hands together. 'Just to clear one thing up. He likes you too. Nothing to second guess there. And it's not just as a friend. There's not much chance he'll show you though.'

'Right.'

'It's not you. It's what she did to him. His confidence is destroyed, and he seriously thinks he's worth fuck all.'

'But how do I fix that?'

Dillon shrugs. 'Might not be able to. The fact he kissed you at all, is a fucking miracle. And a damn good sign. For a while there, he flinched every time we even brushed off his fucking arm.'

He sits back again and crosses his legs at the ankle. 'I went to a few of his sessions when he was in the centre. It was made perfectly fucking clear, that we all have to go at Luke's pace, whenever possible.

'That doesn't mean we can't give him a nudge if he needs it. I'm not a fucking expert in any of this, but I reckon being with him, the way you want to be with him, is going to take time. Probably a lot of talking too. You'll have to be the one to tell him how you feel.'

'So I'll have to take the lead?'

'Yeah.'

'But isn't that what she did with him?'

Dillon's eyes harden, and he clenches his fists. 'No! It's absolutely not. She abused and manipulated him. Taking the lead with someone you genuinely care about, isn't the same thing. You want to help him. She wanted to tear him apart.'

He gets up and sits on the coffee table right in front of her. His knees brush off hers as he shuffles closer. 'I'll never be able to forgive myself for not seeing what she was doing to him sooner. Years sooner. I let him down, and I'll have to live with that for the rest of my life.'

'Dillon—'

'Don't interrupt me.'

She closes her mouth and forces herself to look at him.

'She had such a firm hold on him, had him trained to believe he deserved everything he got. I nearly lost him because of what she did. Fuck, I don't think he's come back to us yet. He's lost, Maeve. Trying to figure out who he really is, after being trapped and controlled for so long, and he's struggling.

'I'll be there for him. All the guys will - no question. But we're struggling too, and I don't mean that in a dick way. I mean he's stalled. We got him so far but...' he shrugs. 'I don't know. Realistically, I don't think we're what he needs.'

'What do you mean?' she asks, realising a little too late that she interrupted him again, but he doesn't pull her up on it.

'I saw the notebook you made for him. He was blown away. Me too, which doesn't happen often. You did a good thing for him, and it's brought him on so much. It was hands down exactly the right thing to do. You figured that part out for yourself, and it was fucking inspirational.

'I guess what I'm saying is, just keep doing what you're doing. We didn't get him as far as you did in the last few weeks. You get him. You see the *real* Luke. I have no fucking doubt you care about him, and only want to help him.

'It's not going to be easy, Maeve, but all you can do is go by your gut. If you like him, you're going to have to tell him. If you want to kiss him, tell him. You want more, tell him. Talk to him about what you want. Show him what you want. Try to get him to make the decision himself, but don't be afraid to give him a gentle push. His go to position will be to go along with what you want.'

'Then how am I going to know if it's really what *he* wants?'

Dillon shrugs. 'I get the impression you'll know.' He drops his eyes and chews his lip ring. 'As for sex - and this next bit is strictly between you and me. You can't ever hold him down, restrain him, no power games of any kind. He's not going to be able for that. I'd be surprised if he even lets you straddle him. Best to avoid that too, unless he says otherwise. Initially at least, he's going to have to be on top. In control.'

She nods. 'I know. He told me what she did to him.'

'Sex was fucking terrifying for him. She chained him down and hurt him, to get herself off. You need to show him he can enjoy being with someone. That being touched by the right person is the best fucking feeling in the world. That isn't going to be easy. It's going to be frustrating as hell for you, and probably embarrassing for him. The two of you are going to be doing a hell of a lot of second guessing, until you figure it all out.'

Maeve sits back and rubs her hands over her face. She knew Dillon wouldn't have all the answers, but nothing he said is helping her to feel like she's the right person to help Luke.

She wants to be - desperately wants to be with him. But if she takes a wrong step with him, it could do more harm than good. And she can't live with that thought.

'Hey!'

She looks up at Dillon again. For the first time he's not looking at her like he's interrogating her. His eyes don't seem as cold as they usually are.

'You know what I remember the most about you from school?'

'What?' she asks, not sure where he's going with this.

'You had balls.'

'Okay. Thanks, I think.'

He laughs and it throws her off track a little.

'You never ever gave a fuck what anyone thought about you. You just did your own thing and stuck your finger up at the rest of the world. Do you have any idea how much confidence that takes?'

She shrugs and smiles. 'I kind of like being me.'

He smiles again. 'Exactly!' Dillon looks away, and chews his lip ring again for a minute or two. After being shouted at for interrupting earlier she lets him have his silence. 'Okay.' He looks back at her. 'I've never ever said this to anyone, and if I hear it repeated, I'll know where it came from.'

'Maybe it's best you don't tell me.'

'I trust you, so I'm going to tell you. I think you need to hear it. So... I came out in the final year of school. Luke figured out I was bisexual a few months before I probably even admitted it to myself.

'Telling my parents and sisters wasn't something I considered. I had kind of accepted I would live a lie and pretend I was *normal*. My mum's phrase - not mine. Anyway, Luke was a big part of my decision to stop hiding who I was.' Dillon looks up at her. 'But you were too.'

She stares over at him for a long few minutes, waiting to see if he laughs off what he said, or takes it back. But he keeps his eyes locked on her, and she realises he's telling the truth. 'Me? How?'

'Like I said, you were you. I remember you being bullied because you had the wrong hair colour. Fucking blond phase was boring as hell. And you didn't wear your skirt up around your arse. And you didn't fuck around in class. You actually listened and did your work. Well, apart from physics, but I guess you were distracted by Luke. Anyway, I figured that if you could be yourself and say to hell with everyone else, I could too. So I came out.'

'Wow! I'm not sure what to say?'

'I'm not looking for you to say anything. What I am trying to say is, all you need to do, is be yourself with him. Keep doing what you're doing. Keep listening to him. Keep encouraging him to talk. I have no fucking doubts you are the best thing that's happened to him for years.'

He pauses again and frowns. 'I've been in love with Luke for a few years. It's one sided, so don't worry. I'm over protective of him because of that. Probably too much, but that's my issue. I want him to be happy, Maeve. He is with you.' He scrubs his hand over his jaw, and smiles briefly. 'Not going to lie, I'd prefer that was my job, but Luke is all that matters.'

He straightens and gestures to the kitchen.

'Fuck, I need a drink!' He smiles quickly, then walks back into the kitchen, taking a bottle of whiskey from the cupboard. 'Drink?'

'What? No. Sorry. I'm good.' She silently watches as he pours himself a large whiskey. Everything he said to her is taking time to process. Hearing all that from Dillon has really impacted on her.

Coming out must have been incredibly difficult for him, and hearing that she had helped give him a little confidence to be himself, is humbling and such an amazing thing to hear.

'Can I ask you something?'

'What?'

'Did Pippa know how you feel about Luke?'

He glances at her over his shoulder. 'I think she figured it out, just before she got me arrested. It's not exactly something I wanted to make public. That's still the case.' His glare has the desired effect.

'I'm not going to say anything.'

He leans back against the counter and crosses his arms. 'You want me to keep away from him?'

Maeve laughs, but his frown stays in place. 'What? Fuck no! Jesus Dillon, you're his best friend. And I would never ever tell him who he can, or can't have, in his life. I can promise you, if he pulled that trick on me, I'd put an end to it fairly sharpish.'

'So it doesn't bother you that I'm in love with him?'

'Should I be bothered?'

Dillon's frown deepens, then he smiles. 'No. Besides, Luke is straight. That puts up a bit of a barrier.'

'Yeah, I guess it would. Luke needs his friends and family around him. That's you. I would never come between the two of you.'

'Fancy staying for lunch?' he asks, his sudden change in topic surprising her.

'No. I'd better go. I've taken up enough of your time.'

'Luke is coming over. You should stay.'

'No. Really. It would be weird.'

'How? You're having lunch with Luke and his friend. Where's the weird? He won't have a problem. I'll give him a buzz and give him the heads up. Trust me. It's all good.'

'I don't know...'

'Fuck's sake, Maeve! It's just food. Stay. I promise I'm nice... most of the time. It'll make his day.'

'I'm not sure—'

'You're staying. If it makes you feel better, you can help reheat the roast dinner Clara made.' He pulls out his phone and points to the kitchen. 'Go! I'm fucking starving, and if I scoff any more liquorice I'll be bouncing off the walls.'

## Luke

He follows Maeve out into the back garden, and sits on the bench next to her. Lunch had been incredible. It felt normal. Safe. It's been a long time since he enjoyed himself so much. Dillon and Maeve really get on well together, which is a plus.

Dillon doesn't warm to many people, tending to go for guarded, abrupt, and a little rude around new faces. He's different with Maeve though. Maybe it's because she's not intimidated by him. There was a good ten minutes over lunch, when the pair were tearing strips off each other.

Dillon had never been like that with Pippa. He would barely stay in the same room as her. Luke lost count of the number of times he wished he could spend time with both Dillon and Pippa together. But that was never going to happen. Maybe Dillon knew all along what she was like.

Maeve sips her coffee and looks out at the sea. 'God, this place is stunning. I see now why Dillon picked it.'

'Yeah. He says he picked it because he can unwind here. Just be himself without anyone around watching him. He loves it. And you being here is a big deal.'

'What do you mean?'

'He never lets anyone bar us and his sisters, in the house. He's super private about it.'

'Wow! That is a big deal. I'm honoured he's added me to the list.' Maeve sips her drink. 'I hope you don't mind me staying for lunch? I didn't plan it. Dillon is very difficult to say no to.'

Luke laughs. 'Yeah. He's stubborn. And of course I don't mind. It was great to see you.'

'Really?'

'Of course.' He pauses and looks out at the sea, as he figures out what to say next. The fact Maeve had come over to see Dillon threw him a little. He wasn't expecting it, but he'd thought about it over lunch, and thinks he knows why. There's nothing going on between them. He knows that much. So, they must have been talking about him.

'I'm sorry I spoke to Dillon behind your back. Are you cross with me?'

That saves him having to bring up the topic himself. He wasn't sure how to broach the whole subject with her. 'I have no problem with you speaking to him. Why would I?'

Maeve turns to face him and twirls a lock of her hair around her fingers, as she pauses for a moment. 'Okay. So, cards on the table. I may like you quite a bit. As in a lot, actually. But I don't want to... you've been through too much.' She winces. 'I don't know how to explain myself without sounding terrible.'

'She doesn't want to hurt you, by moving too fast, or too slow. Pushing you into something you're not ready for.' Dillon places a tub of ice cream on the bench between them and hands Maeve two spoons. 'She gives a shit about you.'

Dillon disappears inside again, leaving Maeve blushing as she stares after him. 'Well, that's not embarrassing at all,' she mutters, sipping her drink again.

'Thank you.'

She lowers her mug and frowns at him. 'For what?'

'Being so great about all this. I was dreading telling you what happened to me. I thought it would turn you off and you'd run.' He laughs and shrugs. 'A bit of me is probably still waiting for that to happen.'

Maeve reaches across and rests her hands on his. 'Did you know I had a crush on you in school?'

'You did? I didn't know.'

'Seriously? You didn't figure it out? I excelled at every subject except physics. Did it never occur to you why I had trouble with it?'

'I thought it was because you were copying from me.'

She nudges him in the side and laughs. 'Yeah right! I knew you were top of the class, so figured if I was struggling, I might be paired with you. And I was. Cunning plan success.'

'So you liked me before all this fame stuff?'

'Oh sure. Although, I have to say I much prefer you dressed like this, to the awful grey school uniform. That uniform was tragic!'

He laughs, then clasps his hands together to stop himself from fidgeting. He never suspected Maeve had a crush on him. He kind of thought she might like him a little now, but he'd put that down to his status.

People seemed to be attracted to band member Luke, more than regular Luke. He'd kind of forgotten how it feels to have someone like him for being himself. Not that he's truly been himself for years.

'I spoke to Dillon, because the last thing I want to do is hurt you, or make you wary in any way. I've never had to think about how I am with someone - physically I mean. I just act, or react, to the situation. But I can't do that with you, so needed a little help.'

'Was he any use?'

'Yes and no. It appears there's no manual.'

She grins and he smiles at her. 'Yeah. I've been looking for one of them myself. It would come in handy.'

'So I guess what we're left with, is figuring it out together. If you want to, of course?'

'I'd really like that. And I'll help you as much as I can, but I don't always know what will freak me out beforehand.'

She shuffles a little closer and laces her fingers with his. 'We'll go slow. I promise.'

The silence continues and he can't convince himself to fill it. Instead he stares out at the sea and keeps his mouth shut. Does this mean they're seeing each other? Or are they friends? Does it need a label? Probably not at this stage.

His head is still messed up. It'll take more than a few months of therapy to fix the years of damage, but she doesn't seem to mind. He's been honest with her. She knows everything that happened - well the shortened version, but it's enough.

He looks at their hands and smiles. This might just be the second chance at the happily ever after he's been longing for, wishing for.

She gently squeezes his hand. 'What are you thinking?'

He smiles at her words and squeezes her hand in return. 'Can I ask you something?'

'Of course! You don't have to ask, if you can ask. Just ask. I'm not sure that makes sense? There were a lot of asks in that sentence.'

He grips her hand a little tighter, loving how it feels. 'We're heading to the UK in a few days to do some chat shows. I was wondering if maybe you fancied tagging along?'

Maeve's mouth drops open. 'Are you freaking serious?'

'Yeah. It'll be two nights and I'll cover the cost, but it could be fun. I don't know? It was just a thought. You don't have to.'

'I'll repeat - are you freaking serious! That's a yes by the way, just in case you had any doubts.'

'Really? You want to come?'

She turns around to face him. 'I've been dying to see you perform. Will you be performing? Please say you will?'

'Yeah. I think we'll be performing twice.'

She wiggles in the seat. 'That's so freaking exciting!'

Her reaction is better than he could have wished for. Pippa always complained when he had to perform. Maeve's reaction is what he always thought it should be like.

He's seen Chloe and Bria at their performances. They completely got behind what Tate and Gregg were doing. Supported them. Were proud to see them like that. Even knowing that Maeve is so excited about a chat show performance is such a great feeling. 'Is that enough time to sort out work?'

'I work for my brother. Believe me, it's fine. Oh this is so exciting! What do I need to do? What should I bring? Where are we going from? How are we getting there?'

Luke laughs and holds up his hands. 'Whoa there! I'll get you all the info. I think Bria is coming too. Is that okay?'

'Does she bite?'

'Not that I'm aware of.'

'Does Tate bite? I've heard he's a bit grumpy.'

'You can handle Dillon. Tate will be easy after that.'

## 15

### Maeve

'I'll be ready to go in a minute,' Maeve shouts from her bedroom when she gets out of the shower.

'Take your time,' Luke replies from the living room. Getting the message from him earlier had been a very welcome and pleasant surprise. Every time she says goodbye to him, a part of her expects it to be the last time she sees him.

He asked her to go with him to the UK in a few days, but that doesn't stop her from worrying that he'll back away from her. His life is so complicated, she wouldn't blame him if he decided to suddenly go to ground.

Instead, this beautiful man keeps coming back. And she's more than happy to open the door to him. Maeve opens her wardrobe door and shuffles the hangers from side to side. 'Luke? I don't suppose there's a pair of jeans hanging around out there with you, is there?'

'Apart from the pair on me?'

God, she loves when he jokes like that. 'Yes, smart-arse.'

'Yeah. There's a pair on the couch.'

'Chuck them in will you?'

She tightens the towel around her, as she walks to the far side of the bed to get clean underwear, stubbing her toe on the desk.

'Fuck it!' Maeve hops on one foot, momentarily forgetting about the towel, and the sexy rock star she's just invited into her room. The first drops to the ground, as the latter opens the door and stares, as she hops on one leg, bare ass naked.

'Hey.'

Luke stares at her, his dark eyes travelling over her body before he blushes, and turns his back to her.

'Sorry. I didn't mean—'

She holds the towel up in front of her, but the damage is done. He got one impressive eyeful.

'It's fine, Luke. Don't sweat about it. I stubbed my fucking toe and the towel decided to screw with me. I'm covered up again.'

He holds out the jeans behind him, but keeps facing the door.

'Luke? I'm not going to wave my boobs in your face. I promise.'

'I'll let you get dressed.'

Suspecting something is wrong, Maeve hurries over to him, wincing as her toe complains. 'Hey,' she says as she stops in front of him. 'What's up?'

He shakes his head, but refuses to look at her face. 'I'm really sorry. I should have knocked first.'

'I told you to come in. And it's just a naked body. Not a big deal. We've all got one,' she says, trying to make light of a situation that's clearly troubling him.

Then she looks down and bites her lip to stop herself from smiling. He's either hiding a hard on behind his hand, or he's afraid she's about to kick him in the nuts. 'Luke?'

'Yeah?' he answers, still focusing on something in the living room.

'Can you please look at me?'

She probably could have got dressed twice in the time it takes him to convince himself to look at her. He's embarrassed. The poor guy got turned on when he saw her naked, and doesn't know what to do about it.

'Are you turned on?'

Colour touches his cheeks and he glances towards the door. There's even odds he's about to bolt.

'It's okay if you are. In fact, I'd be pretty darn flattered if you are.'

He frowns and meets her eyes again. 'You would?'

'Are you kidding me? If seeing my naked ass waving in your face while I hopped around my bedroom got you excited, I'd call that a good thing. Wouldn't you?'

'I don't know. I don't... ' he shakes his head and attempts a smile but fails miserably.

'You don't what?'

'I don't do this.'

The look he gives her is full of shame, but it's got nothing to do with seeing her naked. His body's reaction is what's bothering him. 'Get turned on you mean?'

He pauses, then nods once.

Maeve takes a second to process that, but she can't. How can someone like Luke not get turned on? He's surrounded by people who want nothing more than to be with him. Surely even one of those adoring fans would have caught his eye and got him hard. Not that he would have cheated, she knows that for a fact. But even getting turned on? Something? Anything?

At a loss for words, she sits on her bed and pats the duvet. 'Okay, sit.'

He shuffles back and sits, resting his hands on his knees, when he doesn't need to cover his crotch any longer.

'Right, so when you say you don't get turned on, do you mean you can't, or...'

'I can, but not since... you know. And even then, it wasn't all the time. I haven't...'

She takes his hand when he begins picking at the rip in his jeans. He needs to talk about stuff like this. He shouldn't feel shame about anything that happened to him.

'Haven't...' she prompts, hoping he'll keep talking to her.

'I haven't been with anyone except her.'

Maeve wasn't expecting that. She unfairly assumed with his job and celebrity status he'd had more than one sexual partner.

'I... when we were together... it was when she wanted. I think I just got used to ignoring myself, if that makes sense?'

'No, that makes sense.' God, his wife is a real bitch. 'So you haven't felt that way for what? Months? Years?'

'Years probably. I didn't like it. Not until...' He winces and shakes his head.

'Until what, Luke?'

For the first time since he began talking, he looks down at her. 'I don't want you to hate me?'

'Hate you? Luke, I'm not going to hate you. Well, unless you're going to tell me you've killed someone, or something like that. Have you?'

He grins briefly, easing some of the heavy tension in the room. 'No. Nothing like that. I went to see Dillon after he was released from prison. I was in a weird place. In my head I mean. Pippa wanted me to leave the band, and said I wasn't allowed to see Dillon again. I went to say goodbye to him. I don't know what happened, or how it happened, but I...'

He closes his eyes and curses under his breath.

'You kissed?'

His eyes shoot open, and he stares at her with a strange look on his face. 'What?'

'It's just a guess. Am I right?'

He nods once. 'Do you hate me?'

'Not a chance in hell! You kissed your mate. It's not a big deal at all. I kissed a few of my mates over the years.'

'You did?'

'Yeah. It doesn't have to mean anything. Experimenting isn't a bad thing, Luke. Did you do anything else with him, or just a kiss?'

'Sort of...'

'Was it good?'

He frowns at her, then the small smile comes back. 'I don't have a lot of experience kissing guys, but it was good. It's Dillon.'

She nods. 'I can believe that. The guy has a reputation for knowing how to use what he has. So I'm guessing this not terrible kiss, might have hit other parts of your body?'

He nods, but it's not followed by his usual pause. Good. He's getting that what happened isn't the end of the world, or some terrible crime. 'I freaked out and ran when it happened,' he says, nodding toward his groin. 'I just wasn't used to that.'

'Used to what part exactly?'

He runs his tongue over the back of his piercing and clasps his hands together.

'You know you can tell me anything Luke. I'll never ever judge you.'

'Towards the end of Pippa and I... my body.' He pauses and shrugs. 'It didn't respond... you know?'

She wasn't expecting that, but it makes sense. Sex with that woman sounds terrifying. No wonder he couldn't get it up. 'That's completely understandable. So I'm taking it that wasn't a problem with Dillon?'

He shakes his head.

'Okay, I'm not surprised you were turned on. From the sounds of it, you were experiencing an intimate moment with someone you love, as a friend or more. The contact, the connection with him, knowing that he was as in to it, as you were, in that moment, you'd have to be dead not to have been. Was is a peck or tongues?'

'Maeve...'

'What? It's nothing to be embarrassed about. And I'd be lying if I said the image of you and Dillon making out like that, isn't hot. I need details!'

He gives her a strange look and she shrugs.

'What? You're hot. He's not too bad. You and him... well, it's an image my head is enjoying imagining. So, was it a peck or tongues?'

'You really like that?'

'Eh, yes! Luke, I'm fairly free and easy when it comes to sex. I believe it's something you should enjoy and experiment with, as much as you can. You can say anything to me. I swear I won't think badly of you. So answer the question.'

'Tongues. We were touching each other too. Well, he was touching me... below the waist.'

'Interesting. And nice.' She drops her towel onto the bed and crosses her legs. She's not usually so brazen, but Luke has made her feel unbelievably comfortable from day one. His eyes travel down her body but he's not leering at her. He's admiring her.

'Between you and me, I'm turned on right now.' She leans closer to him. 'You have that effect on me Luke.'

'What? Really?'

'Oh yes. I'm naked in front of you. That in itself is turning me on. Believe me.'

He raises his eyes from her body to her face. 'It is?'

She laughs. 'Yes. How about you?'

He pauses, then nods slowly.

'There's nothing wrong with that, Luke. Just like there's nothing wrong with what happened between you and Dillon.'

'But I knew he had feelings for me. It was cruel.'

133

'You were in a strange place. I seriously doubt he's holding it against you. I'm right, aren't I?'

'Yeah. He understands. He always does.'

'So are you attracted to him, or was it just the totally hot scene that got you all worked up?'

He blushes, but doesn't drop his eyes from hers. 'I love him, but not that way. He's a good looking guy and I'm flattered. I'm attracted to women though. Only women.'

'Well I for one, am delighted to hear that. Definitely works in my favour being a woman and all. So it was the totally hot scenario that got you all excited?'

He shrugs, which Maeve takes as a yes.

'Right, well that's perfectly normal. It sounds hot.'

He smiles at her, still a little unsure, but relaxing into the conversation.

She brushes her fingers over her groin, and his eyes instantly lock on to what she's doing. 'The thought of you turned on like that, is kind of getting me turned on.'

'Right,' he says quietly, watching her fingers as she rubs herself.

'Are you turned on right now?'

He pauses, then nods.

'Again, phew! So, do you want to do anything about it? Do you want to touch yourself?'

# 16

## Luke

He peers over at Maeve, unsure how to answer that one. Of course he wants to touch himself. Her body is stunning. Absolutely beautiful in every way. And of course he wants to do something about the fact he's so turned on.

But he's scared.

How freaking pathetic is that? He's scared of touching his own dick.

'When you masturbate, what gets you off?'

Luke swallows, his throat suddenly tightening. He knows it's probably a perfectly normal topic of conversation between adults, but it's not one he's ever had. Well, apart from joking with the guys, but never in a serious way with a woman.

Yet again, the lump refuses to leave his throat, as with every single other time she has brought up something sexual like this. He's thirty-eight years old. Surely he should know these things?

But he doesn't, and that makes him feel like he's an inexperienced teenager again.

'What's wrong, Luke?'

She hasn't laughed at him yet, so what the hell. 'I don't really do that.'

Her eyes narrow as she stares at him. 'Okay. So, do you not want to play with yourself, or have you just never done it?'

'It's not that I don't want to. I've just got used to not doing it. I wasn't allowed to.' He'd been trained not to do it. Pippa had walked in on him once and went crazy. Apparently his dick was for her and her alone. If he wanted to get off, he had to ask her.

Even admitting that to himself, makes him sick.

Maeve's face takes on that strange hue she gets when she's pissed off. Dillon turns a similar colour when he talks about Pippa. Luke has no doubts they'd beat some sense into Pippa, if they ever got their hands on his wife.

'Sorry. I don't want to keep mentioning all that stuff.'

'Hey. Stop. I want you to. Luke, you can talk to me about anything. And I mean anything. No judging... well, no judging you.'

'Yeah, you just made that face.'

'What face?'

'The *I want to deck Pippa* face. Dillon makes that face a lot. I'm well used to it.'

Maeve grins widely. 'Oh *that* face! I have no control over that I'm afraid. But back to the main point. Okay, so when you say you weren't allowed...'

'She only wanted me... satisfied by her. Basically, no jerking off. Ever.'

'Interesting.' Maeve purses her lips, her eyes darkening as she glares at the ground. She takes a minute to shake herself out of her thoughts, smiling at him again. 'Now, forgive me for being blunt, but what about when you're on tour? You could go weeks without seeing *she who will not be named*. How did you go that long without... having to relieve some pressure, so to speak?'

'It was never a problem for me. I just didn't. I ignored it.'

Maeve taps her chin as she looks at him. 'Do you think it's wrong... you know, playing with yourself?'

He shakes his head. 'Of course not. It was just the way things were with me.'

She grins and looks down at his body. 'Fancy giving it a go again?'

'What. Here?'

'Well unless you'd like to go down to the bar? To be honest though, I don't think Mike would appreciate that.'

'Not really no. I meant the bar part.'

Maeve lies out on her bed, her gorgeous body on display for him to admire. He can't explain why, but he suddenly gets the urge to kiss his way up the rose tattoo trailing up her leg, along her side, and across her stomach. He licks his lips as he pulls his attention from her body to her face.

'I like the way you were just looking at me.'

'Sorry.'

Maeve laughs. 'Luke, I said I liked it. That's a good thing.' She pats the bed beside her. 'Why don't you join me?'

He wants to. Desperately wants to, but he's scared. Of what he doesn't know, but the feeling is always with him.

'I have an idea.' She climbs off the bed and stands in front of him. 'Close your eyes.'

'Why?'

'I promise I'm not going to bite you. Just trust me.'

He closes his eyes and frowns when he hears music playing. Maeve takes his hands and puts them on her bare skin. 'You want to dance?'

'Keep your eyes closed and move with me.'

He hasn't got a clue what's going on, but he's not complaining. He likes touching her skin. Her hands move down his back and grip the bottom of his t-shirt. Luke immediately tenses, but recovers quickly. It's Maeve. He wants her to do this, whatever this is.

She pulls off his t-shirt, her hands resting on his skin sending a shiver through him. Okay, this isn't bad. Far from it.

'Stop thinking. I can see the cogs in your head turning.'

'Sorry.'

'Don't be. But sometimes it's all about just feeling.'

He nods and forces himself to stop thinking. Which isn't exactly easy, considering his mind is always going at full speed. Then her hand rests on his belt buckle and full speed hits a higher level.

'Dance with me, Luke.'

He concentrates on not tripping, as she slowly unfastens his belt, then the button on his jeans.

She traces her fingers up his chest, leaving his jeans on, but unfastened, for now. The next few minutes are spent just dancing, his eyes closed, her bare skin touching his chest as she moves closer to him.

When she pushes his jeans down his legs, his nerves have evaporated completely. He steps out of his jeans, then decides to take the next step himself, kicking off his boxers and sending them across the room.

He hasn't been naked with anyone else except Pippa. Ever. He's been told his body isn't too bad, but that was coming from photographers and fans. It's what they do.

Only one other woman has ever seen him naked and she didn't seem overly impressed by his body. What if Maeve doesn't like his body?

'Look at me.'

He keeps his eyes closed for what seems like ages before he gets the courage to look over at her. She's openly staring at his groin. Luke tries to cover himself, but she keeps hold of his hands. 'What's wrong?'

'What's the look for?'

Maeve grins and lifts his arm, spinning under it before taking him in hold again. 'That look is my impressed one. And I mean seriously impressed. You have seen it, right? I mean like really seen it?'

'Well... yeah.'

'So you know it's...'

'It's what?' he asks, panic building as he looks down at his dick.

'Well, I'm not saying I'm an expert or anything. Far from it, but I have seen one or two in my day. That one you have there, Luke, is rather impressive.'

He holds her away from his body so he can look at it properly, not seeing what's so impressive about it.

'Actually, I must say your body as a whole is rather appealing.'

'Rather appealing?'

'Fucking amazing! But I was trying to be all posh.'

He laughs and pulls her closer again. 'We're dancing naked. What's to be posh about?'

'Valid point,' she says, brushing her hips against him in a way that feels too good. 'You okay?'

He nods. He feels more than okay. No shame. No embarrassment. Nothing but seriously turned on, but he's trying not to think about that part. It's not going to help calm him down.

'Do you trust me?'

He turns his head to look at her. 'Yes,' he replies without hesitation.

Maeve lies down, then pats the bed beside her. He stretches out on the other side, as she reaches into her bedside drawer, then takes his hand, squirting some lube onto his palm. 'This will make it feel so much better.' She rests her hand on top of his and guides it down his body. She places it on his dick and wraps his hand around it. Unable to look at her, or what she's doing, Luke looks at the ceiling as she guides him.

He can't remember the last time he touched himself like this. For too long, sex had come with a lot of pain - either because he was so scared his body didn't respond to Pippa, or she hurt him trying to get him to respond. Either way it was far from enjoyable.

'Take a deep breath and relax.' She rests her forehead against the side of his face. 'Close your eyes and just do what feels right. It's your body. No one knows it better than you.'

He takes a breath, then closes his eyes. Maeve lifts her hand off his, leaving him to explore his own body.

Once he relaxes, his body begins to respond to what he's doing. And instead of pain, it's so good. The lube definitely makes a difference, helping his hand glide over his dick.

When he hears a low groan from Maeve, he opens his eyes and stops what he's doing. She's playing with herself, her hand massaging her pussy as her eyes watch everything he's doing.

'What?' she asks when she realises he's stopped. 'You don't expect to have all the fun, do you?'

Luke continues, his attention focused on Maeve and what she's doing. His dick hardens in his hand. He thought it was hard before, but watching Maeve is turning things to new levels for him. His body is responding in ways it hasn't for years. Luke gasps as he rubs precum along his dick.

'You like that?'

'Yeah.'

'Oh God, Luke! I love watching you do that. Keep going. Please!'

He doesn't think he could stop, even if he wanted to. It feels too good and hearing Maeve talk to him like that, is only adding to the sensation. He knew sex was supposed to be good. But this is so far beyond a mere *good*.

His breathing quickens as his balls tighten.

'That's it Luke. You like that, don't you?'

He nods, unable to speak. He's so close to coming. He's desperate to come. To experience how it should have been all along.

'Look at what you're doing to yourself, Luke.'

He looks down, the sight of his hand around his dick not filling him with shame.

'I'm so close Luke.'

'Me too.'

Maeve arches off the bed as she orgasms, her moans hitting him straight in the groin. Luke comes with a shout, his orgasm rolling through him again and again. His cum hits his stomach, coating his skin. When he opens his eyes, Maeve is peering down at him, a huge satisfied grin on her face.

'Welcome back! How was that?'

Luke peers down at his body and smiles. His dick is still twitching and there's cum on his stomach and the sheets to the side of him. 'Wow!'

She laughs, then kisses him on the cheek, before flopping back in the bed. 'You made a bit of a mess there.'

He drops his hand onto his chest and sighs contentedly. 'Yeah. I know. Sorry about your sheets.'

She waves her hand dismissively. 'Whatever. It was so worth it to see you do that. There's a strong chance it may have contributed to my rather enjoyable orgasm.' Maeve peers over at him and winks, before closing her eyes again. 'So can I take it that wow meant you liked that?'

'Yeah. You can. Thank you.'

Maeve rolls over to face him, one hand under her head as she smiles at him. 'No need for thanks. You did that yourself. I might have just given you a gentle nudge. So, any guilt, or shame, or anything like that?'

He considers that for less than a second. 'Nothing. I loved it!'

'Glad to hear it. Pleasuring yourself is perfectly normal. That stunning dick of yours is just that. *Yours*. Play with it as often as you like. Maybe not out in public. You could get a name for yourself that way.'

'I'll keep that in mind.'

Maeve suddenly jumps off the bed and disappears into the bathroom, reappearing a minute later with a washcloth. She kneels beside him and cleans his body.

He's never had anyone do that to him before, but he's not going to stop her. It feels really nice, her touch gentle as she wipes the cloth over his skin.

It hits him in that moment. She cares about him. Genuinely cares. Even though that's not a bad thing, he can't help but get emotional about it. He's not used to it. It shouldn't be a new thing, shouldn't be something unfamiliar.

What she just did for him, was far more than just helping him jerk off, for the first time in years. She gave him back control over himself, over his body. He can't remember the last time he had that.

'Hey. What's wrong? Did I hurt you?'

He doesn't realise he's crying, until she points it out. He wipes his face, horrified that he's crying in front of her. 'No. Sorry. It's nothing bad. I just... ignore me. I'm a mess.'

'Can I give you a hug?'

He nods, so she wraps her arms around him and hugs him. 'I don't know why I'm crying. I feel like such an idiot.'

'You are not an idiot. What just happened... it was a big deal for you. Of course it's going to be emotional.'

'I swear I don't cry all the time. I know it seems like I do, but I swear I don't.' He wipes his face again and attempts a smile. 'I'm good now.'

'You sure?'

'Yeah. Sorry. Not sure what came over me. It's just been so long since... you know.' He still feels like a blubbering fool, but she's not looking at him like he's a sad case.

It was such a release - and not just a sexual one. Being able to so something as simple as jerking off, without having to ask for permission, is such a relief. One he didn't know would be as freeing as it was.

Maeve is right. It's his body. His dick. What just happened is another step to learning about the new him. Or the real him. The one who's been cowering in the corner, hiding all these years in fear.

But no more.

'Thank you.'

The stunning woman beside him kisses the tip of his nose, before lying down beside him and stroking his arm. 'Any time, sexy.'

## 17

*Luke*

He takes Maeve's hand as they sit on the beach, looking at the waves lapping on the sand. He loves meeting her for breakfast on the beach. Apart from a few dog walkers, they have the place to themselves. Maeve groans as she stuffs the bacon, sausage, and hash brown baguette into her mouth. She must have one hell of a metabolism. She can put away more food than he can.

'What?' she asks around a mouthful of breakfast baguette.

He reaches across and wipes ketchup from the side of her mouth, sucking it off his fingers. 'Just admiring you.'

She grins and he laughs loudly. Maeve swallows and wipes her face with a napkin. 'I am quite a sight, aren't I?'

'One I can't get enough of.' He grimaces as the words come out without any thought. 'Sorry. That was a bit cheesy.'

'It was fucking beautiful.' She kisses him on the cheek. 'You're an old softy aren't you?'

'Apparently. So, why did you ask if I'm free today? You have something in mind?'

She wiggles her eyebrows at him. 'What a question to ask with you sitting beside me. But no, I'm not going to jump on you... well, not until I've digested this lot.'

'I appreciate that.'

'I thought you would. Seriously though, I'm working today and thought you might like to tag along?'

'To the pub?'

Maeve takes another bite, swallowing before she speaks again. 'I meant my other job.'

'Dancing!'

She laughs at his slightly high-pitched squeak. 'Yeah, Luke. Don't worry. I just thought you might want to watch. Not join in. Well, not unless the urge to move that sexy ass overtakes you, and you can't resist.'

'Oh I think I'll be able to resist. Me and dancing.... Yeah, we don't mix.'

'Actually, yeah you do, so don't even try to go there with me. Are you afraid of damaging your hard-ass rock image?'

'I don't have a hard-ass rock image.'

'Of course you don't.' She leans closer and whispers in his ear. 'By the way you totally do.' Maeve scrunches up the wrapper for her breakfast and drops it into the paper bag. 'So, if I promise not to do your image any long lasting damage, will you come with me?'

He wants to see her dancing. The thought has him grinning from ear to ear.

'I am absolutely going to take that grin as a yes.' She stands up, wiping her hands on her jeans. Maeve dances in a circle around him, her body moving hypnotically. 'Oh, you have so got it bad.'

'Got what?'

She holds out her hand, pulling him to his feet and wrapping her arms around his waist. 'You fancy me.'

'You're only just figuring that out?'

Maeve smiles as she reaches up to pull his baseball cap off his head, slipping it over her hair. 'I might have picked up on it before. Having you look at me the way you just did, brings it home though. I hope you know I'm a little attracted to you too?'

He straightens his cap on her head. For some reason she looks so damn sexy wearing it. 'Yeah. I know.' And he does.

It's got nothing to do with her telling him either. Well, not just down to that. When she looks at him, he can see it. No one else has ever looked at him the way Maeve does. 'That suits you.'

She turns the cap backwards and winks at him. 'Good, because I'm keeping it.'

'No you're not.'

'Want to bet?' She smiles and takes off up the beach. 'You want it, you'll have to catch me!'

It takes ten minutes of chasing her around the beach, to finally reclaim his cap. Maeve holds his hand, as they walk all the way back down the beach towards his car. 'How the hell did you run so fast after just eating?' He's knackered, and has a stitch.

'All the dancing. I can go for longer. You can apply that to various different scenarios,' she says with a mischievous smile.

'So where are these classes you teach?'

'In Greystones. It's mainly twelve year old's and up. We're putting on a production in a few weeks, so need to up our game a little. Loads of practising to do.'

'Are you sure I won't distract them by being there?'

'Are you kidding? I doubt anyone will recognise you.' She pulls a face and looks up at him. 'Yeah, they totally will! But I'm sure it won't be too distracting. So will you come with me?'

'Of course I will. You might want to change your top first? You've got ketchup on you.'

'That's not a good look. Come on then. Back to mine, quick skin to skin cuddle, cause you know you can't resist, then off to entertain some rowdy kids. Perfect way to spend the day.'

'Are you sure this is such a good idea?'

Luke peers in through the glass panel in the door at the room full of children, screaming and shouting. Give him a stadium filled with thousands of fans any day of the week. He's never seen so many mini dancers in the one room before. It's like being back in school again.

'Ah they're not a bad bunch... mostly. I'm a very strict teacher. They know better than to get on my wrong side?'

'Yeah, I can believe that.'

She takes his hand and squeezes it. 'You'll be fine. I'll mind you.'

'You'd better.'

Maeve opens the door and leads him into the room. As soon as the door opens, the class falls silent and turns towards them. He holds his breath, waiting to see if he's recognised. He's not expecting may of the children to know who he is. Their fan base tends to be a little older.

But he's wrong.

The scream is deafening as they realise who has just walked in with their dance teacher. Maeve stands in front of him and waves her arms, trying to get their attention. It takes her a good few minutes, but eventually the sound level returns to a less painful level as they calm down.

'Everyone sit on the floor! Now!'

They do as they're told and drop to the wooden floor, but all eyes are still on him.

'Everyone silence! Now, I'm guessing by the screams that you know who will be joining our class today. This is my friend Luke, and he wants to see what you lot can do. Are you ready to give him a run through of the show?'

The scream is ear-splitting, but their smiles hit him more than their shout does. They're genuinely happy to see him.

Maeve turns and smiles at him. 'I think that's a yes. So Luke. Are you excited to see what they've been doing?'

'I can't wait.'

He laughs as they cheer again, only stopping when Maeve claps her hands and ushers them to the end of the room.

'Right, so Luke if you want to grab a seat. I'll get this lot on stage and they can show you what they've been doing.'

The next hour is spent watching the group of children dance around the stage, following Maeve's instructions. For every minute of the performance, Luke has been completely transfixed. The kids are phenomenal, each one dancing incredibly well.

But it's Maeve who captures his attention the most. Not only is she a natural teacher, watching her on stage with the kids, completely in her element, is so heartwarming.

This is her passion. Right here and now, she's at home more than he's seen her so far.

When they've finished the run through, Luke stands and gives them a round of applause as they take a bow. 'Well done! That was amazing!'

'Did you hear that?' Maeve says, climbing down from the stage. 'A rock star has given you his seal of approval. And he knows what he's talking about. Luke used to dance in shows when he was at school, didn't you.'

'One or two.'

She snorts loudly. 'He's being modest. Everyone get yourselves a drink and have a quick break.'

She walks over to him as the kids talk excitedly amongst

themselves. 'So,' she says, keeping her voice low. 'What did you think?'

'It was brilliant, honestly. You're an amazing teacher.'

She playfully pushes him on the arm. 'As if there was any doubt of that. Of course I am.' She smiles as she looks over at the kids. 'Do you have any idea how much you've made their day? Their week even! Never mind sending them home with a sugar rush. They've got a Luke Daly rush. Thank you.'

'For what?'

'For agreeing to come here on your day off.'

'I'm with you. It's not exactly hard work.'

She gives him a strange look, but doesn't respond.

'What did I say?'

'Just the right thing as always. You have a great knack of doing that. You're an incredible person Luke.'

He blushes and turns away before he attempts to kiss her. Meeting a celebrity is one thing. Seeing him kiss their teacher is another thing entirely. 'So what now?'

'Now you get to watch us do it all over again. Lucky you.'

# 18

## Maeve

She paces the small yard at the back of the pub and glances at her watch. Again. Not even a minute has passed. She shakes her arm trying to get the time to go a little faster. Maybe the battery is flat. Or maybe she's over-excited and needs to calm the fuck down, before she embarrasses herself.

She's going away with Luke. Okay, so the rest of the band will be there too, but that's just adding to the excitement level. Having this time with Luke and his friends is something she's really looking forward too.

Even in the few weeks since she met up with him again, she can see the change in him. He's still reserved and quieter than he used to be, but those times when he lets himself relax are happening more and more. He's breaking out little by little.

She checks her watch again. He should be here soon. Then it's off to Newcastle, and a private helicopter to the UK in time for the band's first TV appearance tonight.

She is so looking forward to, is seeing Luke on stage with the band. She's watched him so many times on TV over the years, but had only been able to bag herself tickets to one of their shows. They tended to sell out seconds after being released. She absolutely can't wait to watch the confident performer get on stage in front of the world, and do what he loves more than anything.

That's the real Luke. This shy, reserved man she's been spending time with is a temporary version. Someone he became, to deal with what life had thrown at him. Deep down, she knows the larger than life man with a guitar in his hands, is the true Luke. And she can't wait to see more of him.

She fails to suppress the grin, when a brand new black Range Rover pulls into the car park. Luke climbs out, looking as irresistible as he always does. Wearing a pair of jeans and a shirt, with his cap on backwards as usual, he looks comfortable and happy.

'Morning.'

'Morning sexy.' His grin grows and he blushes as he looks at the ground for a second. God he's so fucking adorable. 'Well isn't this fancy!'

He shrugs. 'Easier than leaving my car at the airfield. You ready to go?'

'Absolutely. I've been up since four.'

'What? Why?'

The driver gets out and takes her bag, loading it into the back. 'I was excited. I'm surprised I slept that long. I honestly thought I'd be up for the night. And just to warn you, I may have had three cups of coffee already. I'm kind of buzzing.'

He opens the door and she hops in, fastening her seat belt as Luke walks around the other side and gets in beside her.

The driver pulls out of the car park and drives through Greystones towards Newcastle. She reaches out and takes his hand, smiling when he squeezes it in his.

'Did you sleep okay, or were you up all night like me? Do you get nervous when you have to do things like this? Jesus, I'm babbling! Blame the coffee.'

He laughs, then reaches out to brush some hair from her shoulder. With previous boyfriends she doubts she would have paid the gesture any attention. Coming from Luke, it sends shivers through her. She's like some loved up teenager. It's ridiculous.

'I was up for a bit. I'm kind of excited too. I love performing.'

'I am so freaking excited about seeing you on stage. I know it's not like in a concert setting, but still, I'm buzzing about it.'

'Are you sure that's not just the coffee?'

She laughs, nudging him on the arm. 'No. It's genuine excitement. But the coffee will keep the babble coming.'

His full face smile is perfect. She desperately wishes he did that more often. 'I love that.'

'Love what?' she asks.

'How enthusiastic you are about seeing us live. About seeing me perform live.'

'Of course I am. It's a big deal.'

He slips on his sunglasses, peering out the window as he squeezes her hand tighter. He doesn't respond, so she leaves him to his thoughts. The urge to pull him out of his head is difficult to ignore. But he needs his silence too.

She rubs the back of his hand with her thumb as they drive through the quiet streets. Luke keeps to himself until they get to the airfield and she squeals aloud, startling both him and the driver.

'You okay?'

She grins at Luke, pointing out the window at the sleek black helicopter. 'It's a freaking helicopter!'

'I did tell you that part, didn't I?'

'Well, yes! But look at it. It's massive. Is this just for us?'

He nods, as the driver pulls up at the side of the field and turns off the engine. 'Dillon is already over there, and Tate will follow in a few hours with Gregg and Bria. I don't think Tate is keen on leaving Chloe and Brandon.'

'Aww. Why is he called grumpy all the time? He's a softy.'

Luke snorts at that. 'Oh he's grumpy, but yeah, I think being a dad is maybe lessening the grump.' He frowns at that. 'Can you lessen a grump? Does that even make sense?'

'Absolutely.' She squeals again, when the driver opens the door for her. 'I am going to expect this from now on. I want someone to open my car door for me all the time.'

'You have a motorbike,' Luke says as he climbs out of the car. 'No doors.'

She walks to the back, but another man is already half way to the helicopter with her bag. 'Minor detail,' she says to Luke, as he joins her and takes her hand in his. 'Do you do stuff like this often?'

'Take a beautiful, kind, amazing, woman away with me?'

She pulls him to a stop and turns him to face her. 'Are you actually trying to make me cry or what?'

He shrugs, colour touching his cheeks. 'It's the truth. This feeling right now, the excitement, the... pride I guess... you know, pride in myself. I'm not used to that. So no, I don't do stuff like this often, but I really hope I get to do it again.'

She wipes a tear away. Fuck, she doesn't cry at soppy stuff like this. Damn man has broken her, and she freaking loves it.

'C'mon sexy. I think it's time to show me your crazy rock star world.'

# Luke

He's never been big-headed or conceited. It would be easy to get carried away and lose perspective. When you're surrounded by people who throw compliments at you constantly, surrounded by fans who follow them around the globe, inundated with letters and gifts from strangers who love them, it would be ridiculously easy to let that go to your head.

The four of them had made an agreement when they were first signed. They'd keep each other grounded. Make sure no one got carried away. And so far, they've managed to do that.

Fair enough, Dillon splashed the cash around from time to time, but he's also sensible, even though he keeps that side hidden, in case it ruins his image.

From the minute the car pulled up outside Maeve's home and he saw her face, he'd felt a surge of pride he's only ever felt when he's on stage. He was proud of who he is, proud of what he does.

He doesn't have to play it down, or try not to talk about it in case he upsets her. Maeve wants to know about the band. She wants to know all of it. Actually asks him about it.

It's the way it should be. The way it is between Tate and Chloe. The way it is between Gregg and Bria. It should have been like that with Pippa, but... well, it wasn't. Far from it.

That's why Maeve's reaction to this entire weekend is like a dream come true for him. This is what he's wanted since they played their first gig. He wanted to be with someone who supported him. Someone who wanted to watch him on stage, doing what he loves more than anything in the world.

Pippa wanted his fame and his money, that's it. She wasn't in the slightest bit interested in what he did to get all that. Unless the venue had a private box for special guests, she didn't want to go. Standing backstage with the crew was beneath her.

He turns to look out the window of the helicopter as they near the hotel. Why is all this stuff only registering with him now? Why hadn't he seen it at the time? The red flags were obvious from the start. Damn it, they'd been waving in his face for years.

But he'd been blind to the warning signs. Trained to ignore them over the years with her. He was her property, her meal ticket, not her husband.

Luke looks over at Maeve, pinned against the glass, taking in everything around her, like it's the most amazing thing she's ever experienced. She turns to smile at him. Every single time she smiles, he smiles himself. She has that effect on him. A few weeks with Maeve in his life, and he's probably smiled more than he did for his entire relationship with Pippa.

He leans over, resting his hand against the side of her face and looks her in the eye for a few seconds, before kissing her.

Opposite him, Andy clears his throat and looks to the side, but Luke doesn't care.

'What was that for?'

'I wanted to do it. Do you mind?'

'I told you I have no problem with you kissing me whenever you want. In fact, the surprise ones are the best. It's good to catch a girl off guard every now and again. Keeps things exciting.'

'I'll keep that in mind. I want to thank you for coming with me this weekend. I'm really looking forward to spending some time with you like this. Give you a bit of an insight into this side of my life.'

'Me too. Although I will say I'm not used to slumming it like this. You're really going to have to up your game Mr. Daly.' She winks and sticks out her tongue.

'I'll keep that in mind. Try to do better.'

'I should hope so.'

# Maeve

She is doing everything possible to at least come across as cool and collected. But she's doing such a lousy job. The posh car collecting her from her flat. The helicopter ride to the UK. The gorgeous celebrity sitting next to her.

It's all like something out of one of those cheesy romance films she sometimes watches, but will never admit to. If he throws one more thing at her she seriously believes she'll pop.

As they come down to land at the heliport, she has to clamp her mouth shut to stop herself from squealing. Another black SUV is waiting for them, ready to whisk them away to their hotel.

He must be used to it at this stage, although she has no idea how you could ever get used to this kind of extravagance. Wearing ripped jeans and a t-shirt, Luke is completely relaxed, like he'd done this sort of thing thousands of times before. Which he probably has.

'Are you okay?'

She nods, unable to hide the grin any longer. 'Yep. Why?'

'You're kind of rocking back and forth a little.'

'Okay, so there's a massive possibility I'm so freaking excited about all of this. How are you so calm?'

He squeezes her hand and smiles. 'It's kind of normal for me I guess.'

'Normal? How is any of this normal? We're in a freaking helicopter and there's a car waiting for us! A rather nice car at that. None of this is normal.'

His response is cut off as her door is opened and she's helped down from the helicopter by Andy. As someone deals with their bags, Luke takes her hand and leads her over to the car. Once everything is loaded, the driver pulls away from the helicopter and weaves his way from the heliport to the main road.

When they're on the road, he turns to face her again. 'I know this all seems like a bit much, but this only happens when I'm doing something band related. The rest of the time I drive myself, and don't have people waiting on me like this. I'm kind of throwing you in the deep end. Giving you the full experience.'

'You think! But that's fine. Really. It's just really weird for me. I know the non-celebrity Luke, not this one. I'm afraid there will be a lot of squealing. I promise I won't do it in public though. Actually, how should I be in public? With you I mean. Are we together, or would you prefer I keep my distance?'

He shakes his head. 'No way! You're here with me. My marriage is over, Maeve. I know I haven't made anything public about that, but the fact she's serving time for hitting me, puts an end to that. But maybe no loud squealing if you can manage that.'

'I'll do my best.' She pauses before asking the question that's been on her mind for a while. 'Luke? Can I ask why you haven't said anything about what Pippa did? I'm not having a go, really. I'm just curious.'

He shrugs and picks at one of the rips in his jeans. 'I'm embarrassed, I guess. I don't want the rest of the world to know how stupid I was.'

'Luke—'

'I don't want to talk about her right now. I just want to be here with you. Please.'

'Of course.' She squeezes his hand and smiles, even though she isn't entirely thrilled about his answer.

It's absolutely not her place to tell him how to handle the public side of his relationship with Pippa. He has Vox to help him with that. But a part of her can't help thinking that if he just told the world what she did, it would help him move on from it. He shouldn't be hiding the truth like he has something to be ashamed of. Pippa is the one who should be doing that.

But what does she know? She's never been treated the way he was, nor does she have a whole record company managing her life. All she can do it keep quiet and support him.

'So,' she says after a slightly awkward pause in the conversation. 'Is there an itinerary for the weekend?'

Luke nods and digs out his mobile. 'Sorry, I meant to send it to you. It's just two TV interviews and performances. There will be a lot of sitting around I'm afraid.'

'Oh don't worry about me.'

'If I'm not with you, Sam from the record company will make sure you're okay. She looks after us while we're away.'

'The poor woman!'

He laughs and nods enthusiastically. 'You can say that again. She's got her work cut out for her.'

'Is there anything I won't be allowed to go to?'

He shakes his head. 'Access all areas for you. Well, not on the actual stage for the interview or the songs, but everything else, yes.'

'Damn it,' she mutters, jokingly. 'I was hoping to make my singing debut with you guys.'

'I love how excited you are about all this.'

Maeve turns to face him as much as the seat belt will allow. 'Of course I am. I'm so excited about all of this!'

'I've always...' he pauses and licks his lips, as he gathers his thoughts. 'Chloe is like this with Tate. Bria too with Gregg. I always wondered what it would be like to have that.'

'Pippa didn't enjoy watching you?'

He shakes his head. 'Not really. I don't think she liked other people around me. I don't mean that in a big headed way. She was just...'

'Possessive?'

'Yeah.'

158

'Well I can promise you this irritating, slightly over the top excitement is totally genuine. And I can't wait to see you in action on the stage.'

'Thanks, Maeve. That means a lot.'

When they get to the hotel, the red carpet treatment continues. The valet opens the door, and they are guided into the hotel by a man in a crisp three piece suit. Without having to stop and do something trivial like checking in, they are brought straight to the elevator and up to their rooms.

He pauses at the door to her room which thankfully, is next door to his. 'I'm just going to grab a shower and then we could maybe order room service if you want? We've got a few hours to ourselves before we have to head over to the studio.'

'Sounds good. Unless...'

'Unless what?' he asks.

She waves her hand at Andy, shooing him away. He rolls his eyes, but smirks as he takes a few steps away from them. 'I was going to have a shower too. Want to save on the water?'

Luke swallows thickly and looks down at her. 'You mean like have a shower together?'

She shrugs. 'It's just a thought. It's entirely up to you. If you don't want to, I'm not going to get upset.'

He runs his tongue over the back of the stud in his chin for a few seconds, then smiles. 'It would save on water.'

'Exactly!'

'Andy? Can you give me a shout when they want me?'

'Will do. Have fun,' he says as he walks away, whistling to himself.

## 19

*Luke*

He hasn't showered with anyone. Ever.

It's a random thought, but it's the first thing that popped into his head as soon as she asked him to join her. What the hell do you do when you share a shower with someone? A beautiful woman wants to shower with him, and that's all he can think about. He hasn't got a clue what she's really asking him.

Is it just a shower, or will she want more? He can't give her more. He's not ready for that. Maybe it is just a shower though.

He's going to freak himself out if he keeps letting his mind run away with him. It's Maeve. She's never ever done anything he didn't want her to do. It's a damn shower! That's it. So what if he's never done it with someone before? It's another thing to mark off his to-do-list.

And he really, really, wants to do it.

Maeve walks around her suite, her eyes wide as she takes it all in. She seems to like it. He'd asked for the best room for her, not caring about the cost. If she was taking time out of her schedule to come here with him, he's going to make sure she's spoiled rotten for every single minute.

'Oh! My! God! This is bigger than my fucking apartment!' She opens the double doors into the bedroom and squeals again. 'And there's another room. What the hell! This is like one of those rooms you see in movies. Yay!'

Luke hesitantly follows her into the bedroom, not sure if he should stay in the living area and leave her to it while she explores.

Maeve launches herself on to the bed, giggling to herself. 'You could fit the whole band on the bed! Not that I'm suggesting we do that,' she adds quickly. 'But it's massive.'

'So I'm guessing from your reaction that you like the room.'

She sits up and shuffles to the end of the bed. 'Well, it's not quite what I'm used to, but it'll do I suppose.'

'Slumming it again, huh?'

'Absolutely!' She stands and he watches in awe as she undresses, slowing uncovering her body in front of him. 'Come on Mr. Rock Star. I want to see that bod of yours.'

She turns on the shower, leaving him to get undressed before joining her in the bathroom. She steps into the shower and crooks her finger at him, beckoning him in.

'Get that sexy ass of yours in here.'

He steps under the water, mesmerised as he watches the water running down her smooth skin, darkening her tattoo. 'I love that.'

'Love what?' she asks.

He traces his fingers along the ink, following the line of the twisted rose stem up her side. 'Your tattoo. It's beautiful.'

'Coming from someone with as many tats as you do, I'll take that as a compliment.'

'You should, cause it is.'

Maeve places her hand on his chest, gently caressing his pecs as she traces his own ink. 'You're quite the work of art yourself. You're stunning, Luke.' She kisses his skin, slowly making her way across his chest.

It feels so good he actually gasps, startling her.

'Is that too much? Do you want me to stop?'

He shakes his head. 'No. I like it.'

'Good.' Maeve continues kissing his chest, water cascading over her hair, the black and purple locks clinging to her skin. He reaches out, brushing them aside so he can watch her. He likes watching her touching him.

Really likes it. This is all so new to him, he needs to learn what to do himself. He wants to be able to touch her, do things to her like she does to him.

He's a thirty-eight year old virgin. Pippa didn't count. The longer he's with Maeve, the more time he spends with her like this, the more he comes to accept that truth. Even from the beginning of his relationship with Pippa, sex hadn't felt right. It was never gentle or even enjoyable. It was never as it should have been.

But this is.

He enjoys this. Really enjoys being naked with her, enjoys her touching him.

Maeve smiles up at him, her hand resting on the centre of his chest. He wants to touch her too, but his head stops him again. He's just so terrified of making an idiot of himself in front of her.

But as always, it's like Maeve is in his head, sensing what he's thinking. She gently takes his hand, placing it on her chest, between her breasts. 'You're holding your breath. Just breathe, Luke.'

He nods and forces himself to take in a bit of oxygen. 'Sorry.'

'No apologising.' She moves her hand on his chest, brushing over the piercing in his nipple. Luke gasps, his dick jumping in response to her touch. 'You like that.'

'Yeah. A lot.'

'Well I have to say the fact your nipples are pierced is so unbelievably hot. As in the hottest level of hot.'

'Really? I got them done for a dare.'

'Seriously?'

'We kind of dare each other to do things like that when we're bored.'

'As in getting piercings?'

'Or tattoos. Depends on our mood.'

'I really feel for Sam now. The poor girl must be run ragged by you lot.'

He nods, his attention on her thumb as it grazes over the bar again. Feeling a little more confident, he copies what she's doing, moving his hand to her breast. Maeve groans as he caresses her nipple, squeezing it gently between his thumb and forefinger.

'Oh fuck Luke! That's so good.'

Confidence growing, he leans over and kisses her breast, slowly moving down to her nipple. She sucks in a breath when he pulls it into his mouth.

Then he stops thinking. All he wants to do is touch her. To taste her. To feel her.

His hands and mouth explore her, tasting, licking, kissing her soft skin, following the line of the tattoo down her firm body. Maeve lifts her arms above her head, giving him free access to her. Her eyes are on him, watching everything he's doing. But instead of embarrassment, having her looking at him encourages him to keep going.

His hands slowly travel around her back to skim over her ass. She groans again, her body moving hypnotically under his touch. God he loves when she dances. In the shower, the water trailing down her body, his hands and mouth on her, the movements are so much more breathtaking.

Her hips sway under his hands, his palms sliding over her slick skin as he kisses along her side and back up her body. She slides her finger under his chin, directing him up towards her face again. 'I want your mouth on mine, sexy.'

He kisses her, brushing her hair over her shoulder, tracing his hand down her back. Now he's in the shower with her, he can't stop touching her. He's turned on, but he's not sure he's ready to act on it. Not yet.

But how does he tell her that without upsetting her or making her think he's not interested in her?

Maeve cups the side of his face as she smiles at him. 'Well I don't know about you, but I'm shrivelling up like a raisin.'

He turns off the water and passes her a fluffy robe from the back of the bathroom door. Maeve bundles into it as he dries himself, still unable to take his eyes off her.

'What are you thinking when you go quiet like that,' she asks, rubbing her hair with a towel.

He leans back against the edge of the sink, watching as she finger combs her hair. 'I thought you'd want... that you'd want to take things further. I didn't know how I was going to...' He can't even say the sentence to her.

She stands in front of him, her hands rubbing up his arms. 'You're not ready, Luke. I know that. I told you on the beach that I'd take you however I can get you. I'm enjoying what we're doing. Enjoying just getting to know you.'

'Thank you.' Hearing her voicing his concerns and being accepting of them, is a weight off his shoulders. Saying what she did on the beach was all well and good, but a few weeks down the line, she might have changed her mind.

'Hey. You don't ever have to thank me for that Luke. We're a partnership. A team. We will take things step by step at your speed, together.'

He nods, not sure he'd be able to speak without breaking down.

'Now, I'm fairly sure you mentioned room service to me when we arrived?'

'Yeah. I did, didn't I.' She's changing to subject, clearing seeing that he was about to have a wobble. 'Let's get you some food.' He takes her hand and leads her back into the bedroom so they can check out what room service has to offer.

## Maeve

She keeps a firm grip of Luke's hand, as they are led through the studio to the dressing rooms. Tate, Gregg, and Dillon are in front of them with Sam, their PA, checking things off her clipboard, as she hurries to keep up with Tate's long strides.

Maeve is trying damn hard to give off a cool and collected vibe. But she's failing in every single way. This is far beyond the most excitement she's had... well, ever. In a few hours, she'll be watching the gorgeous man beside her, step on stage, and sing with the rest of the band.

And she can't wait! She's watched the band on TV enough times to know they have a definite look they go for, when making public appearance together.

Everyday Luke is sexy as hell, but she's so excited about seeing the performer side of him too. Witness that confidence he keeps hidden, until he's doing what he loves best.

He guides her through a door along the corridor, with his name stuck on the outside. Once the door shuts, blocking out all the commotion from outside, he smiles and pulls her arm, drawing her closer. 'You've been smiling like that since I picked you up this morning? Your face must be killing you by now.'

'Can you blame me? This is easily the most excitement I've ever had! And I so can't wait to see you on stage. I'm so freaking excited about that! I mean ridiculously excited. You probably can't tell though?'

The smile he gives her is unlike anything she's seen. He's smiled before, but this time, his entire face lights up. 'I've done this too many times to count. I've been to so many venues all over the world. But this time it feels different. Having you here, seeing how excited you are about it. I really like it.'

She rises to her toes and kisses the tip of his nose. 'So what now?'

'Now, I need to get changed, then someone will come in and do my hair.'

'But I thought you always wear a cap on stage?'

He smiles again, and she could swear his cheeks redden a little. 'I love how you know stuff like that. They like to give me the works. It's what they do. It's all part of the lead up to getting in front of the cameras. Make sure we all look our best - including my hair, which will be hidden anyway. Actually, I don't know why they waste their time with that?'

'Do you want me to leave you while you get ready?'

'You can if you want, but I think you've seen it all at this stage? I don't mind if you stay.'

She sits on the comfy couch and crosses her legs. 'So, do I get a striptease, Mr. Daly?' Maeve laughs hysterically at the horror on his face. 'Relax! That was a joke. You can strip in private. Or in front of me if you want, but you don't have to go for the whole stripping thing.'

'Good,' he says taking off his cap and throwing it at her. 'Because you'll be waiting. That's more Dillon's kind of thing.'

'Yeah, why doesn't that surprise me! He's not exactly what you'd call a wallflower, is he?'

Luke grins as he pulls off his t-shirt. 'No. Not exactly.' He grabs a packet of crisps from the basket on the counter and hands them to her. She checks the bag. It's her favourite flavour.

He unzips a clothes bag hanging on a hook on the wall and takes out a pair of jeans and a shirt.

'So,' Maeve says as she munches on the smoky bacon Tayto crisps. 'Is there a plan for after the show?'

He slips out of his jeans, standing in front of her in a pair of black boxers, and nothing else. 'I think there's a drinks thing after? Sam mentioned something about it.' He glances up at her, when she doesn't reply. 'Are you okay?'

'Oh yeah. Just a smidge distracted for some reason. You said something about a drinks thing?'

Luke walks over to her, leaning down to kiss her. 'You want to meet some celebrities?'

'Sounds like fun.'

He kisses her again. 'You taste good. I like that flavour of crisp.'

'It's the best. Is that on your list?'

'Yeah. Last week. I'm filling up the pages.' He straightens, then goes back to his clothes, leaving her with her crisps, as he finishes getting dressed.

Maeve gets to her feet when Luke turns to face her. There he is and he's out of this world! Celebrity rock star Luke Daly has just appeared in front of her, and he is fucking gorgeous. 'Oh wow!'

The black ripped, fitted jeans and black boots, are teamed with a fitted black shirt and waistcoat. He rolls up the sleeves of the shirt, showing his tattoos. Whoever dresses the band for public appearances, certainly knows how to show them at their best.

When he grins, the level of gorgeous ramps up. 'Wow? Really?'

'Oh yeah.' She walks over to him, and takes a long time just to look him up and down. 'Okay, I'm so sorry. I'm gawping at you like you're a piece of meat. Wow, Luke. I mean *everyday you* is hot. *This you* is hot on another level.'

'Glad you approve,' he says with a wide smile.

She holds out her hand and he frowns at it. 'What?'

'Dance with me?'

She expects him to pause, or to think about it, but he surprises her by taking her in his arms, drawing her closer to him. 'I'm about to go on stage. I could do without a black eye because I tripped over my own feet.'

'I won't let you trip. I promise.' Maeve slowly rocks her body, moving her hips from side to side. His cologne is all she can smell, the feel of his hard body against hers, as addictive as his scent. Then Luke takes her completely by surprise by spinning her, before holding her close again.

'What exactly was that?'

He shrugs. 'I think you're unlocking my inner dancer again.'

'Is that so? Well, I have to admit that makes me all warm and fuzzy inside.

Then he completely floors her by singing, his low sexy voice matching the timing of the dance perfectly. If she wasn't turned on before, she is now.

As he sings, he adjusts his hold on her body, moving closer to her, until they're pressed firmly against each other. He picks her up, his hold perfect as he spins, before putting her back on her feet. He leads her, like the inner dancing pro he is, moving through the routine they'd done years ago in school.

With a little more space in the room she'd really give it her all, but in the confines of his dressing room, she keeps the movements somewhat restrained.

His body was meant for dancing, for leading a partner. His lifts are effortless, his toned body well able to support her weight for longer than any other dance partner she's had.

He slowly lowers her from another lift, and she wraps her legs around his waist, before he can place her back on the ground. He's still singing softly but, unlike the last time, he's doing it while looking her in the eye. And it's hands down the most sexy thing she's ever experienced.

He finishes and smiles at her. 'Not sure where that came from?'

'Oh I know.' She rests her hand on his chest. 'That came from in there. That was your inner dancer being unleashed, and it was fucking awesome. You really haven't lost your rhythm have you?'

'I'm kind of surprising myself. I don't get much chance to dance like that on stage. It doesn't really go with what we do.'

'Oh. I wouldn't know about that. Your music, and my choreography, sounds like a match made in seriously hot heaven.'

'Yeah, I guarantee if I run that by Tate, he'll piss himself laughing.' He places her back on the ground when there a knock on the door. 'Yeah!'

Sam opens the door and peers inside. 'It's time, Luke. You ready for hair and make-up?'

'Yeah. Thanks.'

'You too Maeve, if you want to be pampered?'

'Really? Me?'

'Of course.'

Maeve takes less than a few seconds to make her decision. 'It would be completely rude to refuse such a fab offer. I'm in.'

## 20

### Luke

He's lost count of the number of times he's sat in a room in a studio or back stage, waiting to go out and perform, or do an interview. Since the band took off about six years ago, situations like that became commonplace.

But, having Maeve sitting on his knees, her arm around his shoulder, is a new situation he could more than get used to. She laughs loudly, slapping Gregg on the shoulder, as they laugh at something Gregg said.

This is how things should have been all these years. It's something he longed for more than he knew, until this moment.

They're due on in about twenty minutes and he can't wait. Maeve and Bria will be in the front row of the audience, watching them. Apparently, watching from a monitor backstage wasn't what Maeve came all this way here for. She wanted to see him do his thing in the flesh.

Whatever his thing is.

Her fingers play with his hair, running over the nape of his neck, soothing the nerves he always has before going in front of the camera.

'Are you okay? You look miles away.'

He nods. 'Yeah. I'm just glad you're here to watch me.'

Maeve kisses him, before smiling widely. 'How do you think I feel! I'm so excited about this.'

'Ah the first performance excitement,' Gregg says from beside him. 'I remember when you used to get all excited like that.'

Bria swats Gregg's hand away when he tries to tickle her. 'Get off me! And I do still get excited. It's just I've been watching you lot for a long time, so I don't need to appear as excited.'

'Yeah but now you're watching your studly boyfriend do his thing. That's got to add to the excitement level.'

Tate curses under his breath from the other couch, and closes his eyes. 'Give me strength.'

Bria gets up and kisses Tate on the cheek before opening the door. 'I'm off to the bathroom before you lot go out there.'

'I'll go with you,' Maeve says, pushing off Luke's knee.

Gregg nudges Luke in the arm. 'Ah the good old piss posse. What is it with women, huh? Why can't you go to the toilet alone?'

'Because it's more fun to talk about you lot with someone else.' Maeve says, winking at Luke, before she closes the door behind them.

'So buddy,' Gregg says, when they've gone. 'How are things going so far? You good?'

'Yeah. It's going really well. I've kept the two rooms just in case, but... I don't know. I'll see how things go later.'

'Good plan,' Dillon says from beside Tate. 'Play it by ear. Got to say though, it's about fucking time you have someone with you at one of these things, who actually looks like they want to be here. Makes a fucking change!'

'I know. Her excitement is rubbing off on me. I can't wait to get up there and sing now with Maeve watching.'

'Does she know?' Tate asks, glancing up from his phone. He's been glued to the device since he arrived. Chloe has been sending him photos of Brandon, but he's clearly missing his son.

'No. I mean she knows we're performing, but not that I'm singing one of the songs.'

'She's going to freak!' Gregg says, beaming widely. 'Bria too.'

'You didn't tell her?'

He shakes his head, his hair flopping over his face. 'Nope. Sworn to secrecy and all that. Not a word to anyone. I'm not going to ruin your moment.'

'What are you smiling about?' Maeve asks, as she comes back in the room with Bria.

'Just looking forward to getting on stage,' he says, wrapping his arms around her again.

'You and me both! Now, should I throw my bra at you when you get on stage, or leave that until later?'

Luke blushes, not quite believing she just said that in front of the guys, but they just laugh. Probably more at the look on his face, than what she said.

'Maybe leave that until later,' Dillon says. 'His folks always watch him when he's on TV. Then again, it would be fucking hilarious!'

'Don't you go giving her ideas,' Luke says, glaring at Dillon who, as usual, doesn't take any notice.

Any further comment of flying underwear and his parents is thankfully cut short as Sam joins them. 'You guys ready? It's time.'

# Maeve

'Oh my God! Will you quit squirming!'

Maeve smiles apologetically at Bria. 'Sorry. I can't help it. I'm really trying to remain all composed and nonchalant, but I'm failing miserably.'

Bria laughs as she brushes her strawberry blonde hair back from her shoulder. 'Between you and me, I feel the exact same. I've been watching the band since they first began performing. Watching my brother on stage singing is such an amazing feeling. But now I'm with Gregg it's so different.'

She leans closer so the people in the row behind them can't hear her.

'I can honestly say watching Gregg performing is without a doubt the sexiest thing I've ever seen. I mean seriously hot.'

'Really? I've seen Luke on YouTube and he's sang for me a few times, but I've never seen him like this.'

Bria links arms with her. 'You're in for a treat, Maeve. Believe me.'

The first few guests the host brings on barely hold her attention, but being in the front row, she does her best to appear engrossed.

Then the host announces his next guest. Or guests. The excitement builds again when he introduces Broken Chords, her own applause being drowned out by the rest of the audience. The lights go up on the stage to the side, and there he is.

Maeve's mouth hangs open when she realises he's not where she was expecting him to be. Instead of Tate at the front, taking the lead, Luke is there.

'Oh fuck!'

Bria nudges her in the arm. 'You didn't tell me he was singing lead vocals.'

'I didn't know!'

Her stunning boyfriend looks directly at her and smiles. Luke Daly is on stage and smiling at her. Talk about a surreal situation. Gregg gets the song going, followed by Tate, Luke, and Dillon on their guitars.

He's going to sing. She wasn't expecting this for a moment, and she's so freaking proud of him.

Luke looks at her again and the magic happens. His stunning voice bursts out of him, and she smiles widely. He's confident, playing and singing as if he was born to do it. The audience gets right behind him as he sings. It's almost like they're all at a private concert.

But it's better than that for her, because he's singing to her. His brown eyes haven't moved from her since the lights went up. It's a private concert all right. Private between herself and Luke.

The song ends far too soon and again, the audience swallows up her applause. Luke is taken aback by the response. She can tell that much from here. He's blushing slightly, his waves of thanks a little tentative and shy.

He winks at her, before swapping places with Tate. There's a brief wait while the mics are changed, then the front man takes charge again. And boy does he take charge. Tate can sing!

His voice is breathtaking, but even though she's hooked on his performance, she can't take her attention from the stunning man to his left. This is the Luke she's been yearning to see, and he's not disappointing her.

When they wrap up the next song, the audience goes crazy again and the band waves, as they move over to the seating area for the interview. As front man of the group, Tate takes the lead in the interview as usual, with only a few questions being directed at the other three members.

Maeve knows that's what Luke wants though. He mentioned he was nervous about the interview part, but in all fairness to the

174

presenter, he keeps the questions far from Pippa, concentrating on the new album, future tour, and Tate's upcoming wedding.

As the interview wraps up, he audience rise to their feet, applauding the band as they leave the stage. About five minutes later, Sam comes out to get them, bringing them backstage to sit with the guys again.

As soon as the door opens, Maeve rushes over to Luke and jumps on him, wrapping her legs around his waist. She kisses him, then pulls back so she can look at him. 'You're a dark horse Mr. Daly, you know that?'

'I wanted to surprise you.'

'Surprise! I nearly wet myself. You were fucking amazing! Really, really amazing!'

Tate slaps him on the back, nearly knocking Maeve from his arms. 'I totally agree. You blew us all away, Luke. Well done.'

'Seconded!' Gregg says as he separates himself from Bria for a second.

Dillon slaps him on the other shoulder. 'Fucking proud of you!'

'Thank you, now can you please stop whacking me.'

They walk away, taking up positions on the couch as they talk about their performance amongst themselves. Luke lowers her to the ground, but keeps his arms around her. 'Having you in the front row, watching me, was such a boost. Thank you.'

'No, thank you! I wasn't expecting you to sing lead like that. I'm so, so, proud of you. You were... I have no words other than amazing, fantastic, and seriously fucking hot.'

He blushes again and she groans. 'See? You keep doing that and I want to get all over you.'

'How do you do that?'

'Do what?' she asks, confused.

'Make me feel about twenty foot tall. I'm not used to that.'

She takes his hand, pulling him over to the couch. 'Well you better get used to it, cause you're an amazing man, Luke. And I fully intend to accompany you as often as I can.'

He sits down, sitting her on his knee and holding her against his chest. 'I'd really like that, Maeve.'

She snuggles against his chest and closes her eyes. She could get used to this so easily. Get used to being by his side as he does what he loves.

Luke stops outside her hotel room door and leans against the wall. 'Thanks for tonight. It meant a lot having you here. Nice to have a friendly face in the audience.'

'Are you kidding? Every face in the audience was a friendly one. They love you, Luke.'

He smiles a little, but she's not fooled. He doesn't believe it for a minute. 'So, you fancy meeting for breakfast?'

'It's a buffet isn't it?'

'Yeah. You'll have to fight Tate for the food though. He's a big fan of buffets.'

'Who isn't? And I can take Tate.' She purses her lips, then shrugs. 'Yeah, I probably couldn't take him, but I'd give it a damn good try.'

'I don't doubt that. I better let you get some sleep.' He leans over and kisses her on the cheek, but doesn't straighten again. Maeve swallows thickly as his warm breath tickles her ear. Luke slowly pulls back and his lips part, but he doesn't kiss her.

*Please, please, please, ask if you can come in!* She says the words over and over in her head, hoping a part of him will hear her.

But Luke doesn't ask to come in. Instead he pulls back and smiles.

'Do you want to come in? You could have a drink. Or even stay. Just sleep - nothing else.'

He hesitates for a moment, then slowly shakes his head. 'I better not. Goodnight, Maeve.'

'Goodnight, Luke.'

And then he's gone.

Maeve closes her hotel room door and leans back against it. What is she supposed to do? She's crazy about him. Super crazy.

But how does she take things further, or even hint at it, without potentially scaring him, or making him feel threatened? It's such a fine line between encouraging him and forcing him, and she's terrified of crossing it.

She pushes away from the door and stands in the centre of her suite. Then there's a knock on the door. Maeve slowly opens it, smiling when she sees Luke. 'Hey. Morning already?'

'You know what you asked me in the corridor... about staying with you?'

*Oh shit!* 'Yes.'

'Is the offer still on the table?'

'Of course it is.'

He smiles down at her. 'Do you snore?'

'How dare you! Of course I don't snore. Do you?'

'I don't think so. Are you sure about this?'

'It's just sleeping, Luke. I think we can manage it.'

He smiles widely at her. 'Yeah. I think we can. I'll just go grab my stuff. I'll be back in a few minutes.'

'Perfect. That'll give me time to... get us some drinks.'

'Your clothes are all over the bed, right?'

She sticks out her tongue. 'Smart arse.'

He grins and turns away, so Maeve hurries into the bedroom and looks at the mess of clothes all over the bed. He knows her better than most people do, and that's scary.

Luke is staying overnight with her!

She jumps up and down, silently clapping her hands together. This is massive. Epic massive. Instead of randomly stuffing her suitcase with clothes, she carefully folds everything, and has just cleared the mess, when she hears a knock on the door again.

She steps aside and the stunning rock star steps into her room. He's still in his stage outfit of head to toe black, which makes him look so far beyond sexy. There is a difference in him, since she saw him in the dressing room earlier.

Dressing like he is, seems to give him confidence. The performer Luke Daly plays to countless people without a second thought. That's the man standing in her suite at the moment.

'Drink?'

He sits on the edge of the couch, and nods as he looks around.

'What are the guys doing?'

'Dillon went out somewhere. Jason is with him, so hopefully he won't get up to anything. Gregg and Bria went back to their room, and so did Tate. He was itching for a video call with Chloe. He's seriously missing Brandon. It's the first time he's been away from him since he was born.'

She passes him a coke and sits beside him on the couch. 'You know I never imagined Tate as a father. It's crazy, but so darn cute.'

'I know. I reckon out of everyone he was the last one I'd have had money on. Probably thought I'd be first.' He pauses briefly then shrugs, bringing himself out of his thoughts before they take hold. 'Being a dad suits him. He's happier than he's been for years.'

'And so he should be. Do you want to take these into the bedroom? We could see if there's anything on TV?'

'Sounds good.'

She sits a little off centre on the massive bed and waits to see what he'll do. After kicking off his boots, Luke sits on the bed, moving over so he's right beside her. Maeve flicks through the channels, stopping at a reality show.

'Oh God no! Seriously?'

'What's wrong with this?'

Luke gestures to the TV with his glass. 'How long have you got? It's all fake!'

'Yeah well I know that, but it's still good. Hey, have you ever been asked to do something like this with the band?'

'Yeah. About two years ago. We all flat out refused. No way we were letting random strangers into our lives like that.' She grins over at him and he turns his head to frown at her. 'What?'

'I thought you said it was all fake, so what does it matter?'

'You know it's okay if you don't listen to everything I say all the time. I won't get offended.'

She laughs and nudges him in the arm, gently pushing him to the side. 'I'm always listening.'

'Yeah. I got that.' She grabs a packet of crisps from the bedside table and opens the bag, offering it to him. 'Where did you get these from?'

'I always travel with crisps. Never know when you might get a case of the munchies. I get seriously grouchy when I'm hungry.'

'Where do you put it all though?'

The way he looks at her is as more than just a friend. It might be time to give him a little nudge. 'I'm not comfy. Fancy getting into the bed?'

He hesitates and, for a moment, she fears she might have gone too fast. But then he nods. 'Yeah, but on one condition.'

'What?' she asks.

'Have you got any more crisps? I'm starving.'

# 21

## Maeve

After cleaning her teeth, Maeve checks her reflection in the mirror over the sink. She's about to spend the night with Luke. Okay, so it's just sleeping, but it's a massive step for him. For them.

She walks out in to the bedroom, smiling when she sees the gorgeous rock star lying on his side in the bed, looking at her. How exactly is she meant to keep her hands off him and just sleep? It's going to be an interesting night.

She slides in beside him and turns off the light. 'Should I set an alarm?'

'We don't have to be at the next location until tomorrow evening. No rush to get up.'

'Well, apart from the buffet of course.'

'Or, we could get room service?'

She smiles to herself in the dark room. Is he planning on spending a lazy morning in bed with her? No problem in the slightest. 'We could. But then I don't get to fight Tate for the bacon.'

'True,' he answers. 'But I'd really like to see that.'

She rolls over to face him, his faint outline visible in the dim room. 'Actually, I think I like the room service idea. I may have to order a ridiculously obscene amount of food though.'

She holds her breath as his fingers touch her arm, slowly moving along it until he finds her hand, lacing his fingers with hers. 'Whatever you want. I'm not getting in between you and food. I'm not that stupid.'

She squeezes his hand, loving how it fits so perfectly with hers. 'Glad to hear it.'

He falls quiet for a moment, and she doesn't interrupt. She has no idea what he's thinking when he goes quiet, but the way his grip tightens on her hand, hints that he's not in a bad place. His breathing seems to be a little faster too.

Maeve wants to roll onto him and kiss him, but remembering Dillon's words about trapping him, instead moves onto her back, gently pulling his arm over with her. Luke hesitates for a moment, then follows her, his hand still gripping hers.

He hovers over her, his nose inches from hers. He smells like the sea and she really likes it. Maeve isn't new to this by any means, but for some reason, Luke is making her incredibly nervous. Maybe because this is such a big deal for him. Maybe because she genuinely has feelings for him.

She lies still, afraid to scare him away. She wants to wrap her arms around him, or run her fingers through his hair. But she's terrified to do anything that'll make him change his mind.

'Can I kiss you?'

She smiles and nods, delighted that he's comfortable with the closeness. 'I told you before. You never have to ask.'

He hesitates, then brushes his lips against hers. The contact sends a shiver through her. Then his lips touch hers again, for longer this time, and she kisses him back.

It's so difficult to restrain herself, but this is about Luke and he's in control. He's holding his body above hers, his lips the only part making contact with her. But he's enjoying it. The kiss is different, more urgent, more heated than before.

Maeve can't help the groan that escapes, when his tongue slides into her mouth for the briefest of moments.

He pulls away and looks down at her. 'Are you okay?'

She nods quickly. 'Absolutely. No complaints in the slightest. That was nice. I mean really, really, nice.' *Dear God above! What the sweet fuck was that?* Did she really just tell Luke Daly that his kiss was nice? Nice? Who the hell says nice after being kissed like that? It was freaking amazing!

He opens his eyes and looks her straight in the eye. He hasn't done that before, tending to keep his gaze downward, instead of directly on her. The intensity of his gaze hits her, even in the gloom.

'I can do better,' he says.

'Sorry?'

'You said the kiss was nice. I can do better. Can I try again?'

'Yes. No problem. Absolutely.'

When he kisses her again, it's with more confidence. She takes a chance and moves her hand, slowly, tracing her fingers through his hair. Luke's tongue glides against hers again, hesitatingly at first.

He pauses for the briefest of moments, and Maeve fears he might be about to pull away. But he doesn't. Instead his pierced tongue invades her mouth.

Maeve doesn't try to stop the groan this time. She's only human, and Luke is driving her fucking crazy. She desperately wants to grab him, and run her hands over every inch of his spectacular body. Trace the lines of the tattoo on his stomach, down below the waistband of his boxers.

Holding back is adding to her frustration, but it's so worth it.

He's coming out of his shell, exploring what he likes. Being a part of that is something she's so grateful for. His hand grips hers, his fingers locking with hers. Then he lowers onto his elbow, his chest pressing down on her. His solid body feels so freaking amazing against hers.

'Can we maybe do this...' He clamps his mouth shut, then moves away from her.

'Do what, Luke? Tell me what you want to do.' He sits back on his legs and scrubs his hand over his face. Maeve turns on the bedside light and sits up. 'Luke?'

'I was just wondering if we could maybe do this...without clothes?'

Maeve grins widely. 'Oh hell yes! C'mon then sexy. Strip.'

He reaches over and turns off the light again. Let him do this by feel first, if that's what he wants. She's bloody shocked and thrilled he wants to do this at all. Who cares if the light is on or not?

Luke slips off his boxers while she removes her underwear in record speed, lying down where she was, before he's even finished undressing.

Luke lies over her again, but takes a few minutes before he actually makes skin contact with her. And when he does Maeve freaking loves it.

His thick, hard, warm dick rests against her thigh, and it takes an impressive amount of willpower not to move so that it's on her groin. God she wants it there so badly.

His body feels too good against hers, solid, hard, and fucking perfect. His breath tickles the side of her face as he moves closer, kissing along her neck down to her collar bone. His dick twitches against her leg as he moves lower, lifting his body away from hers so he can reach her breasts.

Maeve gasps, when he gently swipes his tongue across her nipple.

'Should I stop?'

'Don't you dare! Please, keep going, Luke.'

And he does.

The slow, careful, gentle way he's being with her is so fucking hot, driving her crazy like she could never have imagined. His lips and tongue caress her skin, sending shivers through her entire body. Her heart is racing, her breath coming in quick pants. He's barely touching her, but it's so unbelievably intense.

He stops at her waist, heading back up towards her head again. She wishes he'd continue lower, but touching her like this was way off in the distance as far as she was concerned, so she's not going to complain.

Maeve buries her hands in his hair, pulling him closer, so she can kiss him. This time he rests his dick over her groin, pressing it against her, slowly moving his hips to grind against her.

She keeps still, resisting the urge to spread her legs and let him in. Holding back is nearly as much of a turn on, as the act itself. She'll go at his pace, earn his trust.

But maybe this is the time to give him a little nudge.

She reaches between them, brushing her fingers along his dick. 'How about you kneel up on the bed.'

He gives her his trademark frown. 'Why?'

'I want to do something I think you'll like. Trust me. I'll stop if you don't like it.'

He pauses before straightening, and sitting back on his legs. Maeve turns around, getting on all fours facing him. She glances up at Luke, towering above her and smiles. 'It's okay. Just relax.'

He nods, but doesn't look relaxed in the slightest. At least his dick is still with her, standing proud, waiting for attention.

Keeping her eyes on Luke's, she slowly runs her tongue over the tip of his dick, licking the precum from him. 'You taste amazing, Luke.'

But he doesn't respond. If it wouldn't ruin the moment, she'd laugh at the look on his face. He wasn't expecting her to do that.

'Are you okay?'

He nods quickly, then swallows before answering. 'Yeah. Yeah, I'm okay.'

She does it again and this time he groans. It sounds so fucking hot, so she slips the head into her mouth. Luke gasps, his dick pulsing in her mouth.

'Do you want me to keep going?'

He nods and it's all the answer she needs. Maeve grips the base of his dick in one hand and takes him deep into her mouth. Luke's spectacular body goes rigid in front of her, his hands clenched on his knees as she sucks him.

But Maeve doesn't stop what she's doing. He told her he's okay, and she trusts he wouldn't lie to her. She just needs him to trust she won't hurt him.

That thought threatens to ruin the moment, but she pushes it to the back of her mind. This is about showing Luke sex shouldn't hurt. That it should be an incredible experience that blows his mind. And that's exactly what she's going to do.

She places her free hand over one of his, squeezing it as she slowly runs her tongue along him, teasing him, before taking him into her mouth again. She takes her time, just letting him get used to what she's doing.

Then it happens. His fist unclenches under her hand, his fingers digging into his leg, as he releases the breath he was holding.

Encouraged by his reaction, she stops going slowly. Time to show him what he's been missing. She grips him tighter in her hand, and runs her tongue along his shaft as she sucks him.

It doesn't take long for him to tense again, but it's the right kind of tensing. His breathing quickens, his stomach tightening and relaxing as he nears orgasm.

She glances up at him, instantly turned on by the look on his face. His eyes are fixed on what she's doing, his lips parted, his head tilted slightly to the side.

His free hand drops to the bed, gripping the sheets. 'Maeve... I'm going to come.'

She has no intention of having him come anywhere, except in her mouth. Maeve releases pressure from the base of his dick, then pushes him over the edge. Luke comes in her mouth, his deep moan of pleasure sounding so fucking hot.

She groans as she swallows everything he gives her, loving the taste of him, the feel of his cock in her mouth, the sight of him towering over her as he comes.

In no rush to finish, she slowly releases him, then licks her lips and smiles at him. 'Yum!'

Luke wipes a hand over his face and shudders. 'Wow!'

'A yum and a wow. That's pretty good.'

He falls back on the bed, draping an arm over his face. 'Wow! I mean really wow!'

She drops down beside him and rolls over to face him. Maeve slowly lifts his arm and peers underneath. 'How you doing in there?'

'Wow,' he mutters again, his eyes closed and a lazy smile on his face.

'So now we're on four wows and a yum.'

'Yeah, I'm not so sure about the yum?'

'Oh it was yum, believe me.'

He lifts his arm and looks at her. 'You mean that?'

'Absolutely! Should I take it from all the wows that you enjoyed that?'

He nods, the grin on his face stunning. 'Yeah. I really did. Thank you. I've never... I didn't know it could be that...'

'Wow?'

He laughs and rolls over, wrapping his arms around her. 'Yeah. It was really, really wow.'

## Luke

He can't remember feeling so relaxed in such a long time. He wasn't going to come back to her room. He'd talked himself in and out of it so many times, as he walked down the corridor. But no matter how many times he convinced himself it was probably a bad idea, he kept coming back to the small detail of wanting to spend the night with her.

It'd been a long time since he actually wanted to share a bed with someone.

Maeve rests her head against his arm, but instead of the contact filling him with dread, he gets butterflies in his stomach. Good ones.

He's been told so many times, that what Pippa did to him wasn't his fault. He did nothing wrong. But hearing, and accepting, are two different things.

Deep down he desperately wants what Tate and Gregg have. He wants someone to look at him the way Chloe and Bria look at Tate and Gregg. His friends aren't scared of their partners. They don't flinch whenever they touch them. They don't dread being alone with them. If anything, they can't get enough of the girls.

It's not his fault he picked someone who wanted to control him. To hurt him.

Maeve wouldn't do that to him. Even after this short time with her he's certain of that. She's being so patient with him. Most women would have run, as soon as he told them about what happened.

He didn't feel safe with anyone apart from his family and the band. Not until he met her.

Maybe it's time to show her.

He wants to hold her, to wrap his arms around her, like he's seen Tate and Gregg do with the girls so many times. But that would mean him making a move, and he hasn't done that for a hell of a long time.

But he wants to.

And it's not like they haven't done stuff together. She'd given him a blowjob an hour ago, and it was beyond amazing. It was the way he thought it should be. An intense, incredibly pleasurable feeling. No pain. No having to pretend he liked it. He didn't need to. He loved every second of it.

So why can't he make a move on her? Why is he so terrified of doing something wrong?

He closes his eyes, takes a deep breath, then slides his arm around her back and pulls her closer. Maeve instantly snuggles in against his chest and rests her arm across his stomach, then quickly moves it off him again. 'Sorry.'

'It's okay,' he says. 'I like that.'

She puts her arm back where it was, hugging him to her. Luke tucks her head under his chin and smiles widely, as he watches the worst reality show he's ever seen, loving every single minute of it.

## Maeve

Through her dreamless sleep, Maeve hears a whimper. Just one at first. But then again, louder this time. She pulls herself awake, lying in the dark and just listening.

Then she hears it again. She turns on the bedside light and rolls over to face Luke. He's curled in a ball, his head buried under his arms, which are wrapped tightly around him. He whimpers again, his whole body tensing, as he moans in pain.

'Luke?'

'I'm sorry, Pippa. I won't do it again.'

Maeve wipes the tears from her face and leans over him, making sure to keep far enough away, so she doesn't touch him. 'Luke! Hey, it's Maeve. Wake up!'

But it doesn't work. He's so deep in his dream he's not even acknowledging her. With no other ideas coming to her, she grabs her phone from beside the bed and searches for Dillon's number, calling him.

'What the fuck! It's two in the morning.'

'I'm sorry, but Luke just had a nightmare. He's all spaced out and I can't get through to him, Dillon.'

'Your room or his?'

'Mine.'

'Give me two minutes.' Maeve throws on her underwear and Luke's t-shirt, then hurries into the main room and opens the door, peering out into the corridor. Less than a minute later, Dillon appears barefoot, wearing a pair of joggers and a t-shirt. He flashes her a tight smile, as he steps into the room, walking past her to disappear into the bedroom, as she locks the door again.

Dillon sits on the bed in front of Luke, keeping away from him so as not to spook him. 'When he's really bad like this, you might just have to get physical with him. Pull him out.' He turns his attention back to Luke. 'Luke, it's Dillon. You're safe, mate.'

Maeve wraps her arms around her, as she watches Luke. He's frozen to the spot, curled into a protective ball, *hiding* from his wife. And she hates it so much, it makes her feel nauseous.

Dillon moves a little closer and touches Luke's arm, ignoring his friend when he flinches. Dillon pulls Luke into his arms, holding him close to his chest, even though he struggles against him. 'You're safe, Luke. It's Dillon. I've got you.'

The tears pour down Maeve's face as Dillon slowly rocks Luke in his arms, running his hand over Luke's hair, as he quietly talks to him.

She watches what Dillon does, taking note, so she can help Luke herself the next time. She knew he suffered from nightmares, but never imagined they could be this severe. His fear is so visible, and it's tearing her apart.

The rage builds deep inside her. She'll never show him how angry she is. It's not his fault she's angry. It's Pippa's. Dillon glances over at her. He knows exactly how she feels. She can see the same look in his eyes. Give either of them three minutes alone with Pippa, and she'd regret ever laying a finger on him.

When Luke finally wakes and lifts his head, Dillon releases him from his arms. Luke looks at Dillon, then over at Maeve.

'Hey, mate. You good?'

Luke nods. 'Yeah. I'm sorry.'

Dillon shakes his head. 'No worries. Fancy talking about it?'

Luke rests his head on his knees, still drawn up to his chest. Dillon nods towards the bed, silently telling Maeve to sit down. Trusting he knows what he's doing, she sits beside Dillon. He takes her hand and rests it on Luke's and he takes the other.

'It was...' Luke stops talking and looks down at the hands, holding onto his own. 'It was that last time. It's always about that last time, when she broke my leg.' He pauses and frowns, then shakes his head and attempts a smile. 'Sorry. I didn't mean to wake you both. Hang on. Why are you here?'

'I called him.'

'And I wasn't asleep,' Dillon says, which is clearly a lie, but Maeve isn't going to argue.

Luke looks over at her, the embarrassment in his eyes killing her. 'I should go back to my own room. Let you get some sleep.'

'No you will not,' she replies, squeezing his hand. 'We're going to get back into bed and go to sleep here.'

'I probably won't sleep again. I don't want to keep you up.'

'I can survive on very little sleep, believe me. I want you to stay, so stop arguing and lie down.'

Luke nods, finally straightening his legs, slipping them back under the duvet.

'You too, Dillon,' she says when Dillon turns towards the door. 'Get in the bed.'

'You what?'

'You're here, so you might as well stay. I'll go make sure the door is locked.' She's not in the slightest bit surprised when Dillon joins her in the living room.

'You want me to stay? Why?'

'Because he needs you,' she answers, keeping her voice low. 'He was terrified Dillon, and I couldn't do anything for him.'

Dillon pulls her further away from the bedroom. 'I'm the last fucking person he needs. You get back in there and stay with him. He'll just sleep now, so you'll be fine.'

'That's exactly what I'm going to do. But I'd like you to stay with us. Please, Dillon. He's comfortable with you around.'

He crosses his arms and peers down at her, one eyebrow raised.

'I have no ulterior motive, Dillon. Please. Just sleep in the same bed. That's it.'

He nods. 'Fine. But don't you go getting any ideas,' he says, smirking at her.

'Oh I think I can resist.'

They both walk back into the bedroom and climb into bed, one to either side of Luke. Maeve takes his hand, hugging his arm to her chest, as Dillon settles in behind him.

'What's going on?' Luke asks, glancing over his shoulder to Dillon.

'He's staying with us.' She kisses Luke's forehead, then brushes her hand over his hair. 'Close your eyes and get some sleep, Luke.'

'We've got you,' Dillon says from the other side, before turning onto his back and draping his arm over his face.

Maeve smiles as Luke closes his eyes and pulls her hand tighter against his chest. She continues brushing her hand over his hair, until his breathing steadies as he falls asleep.

Maeve shuffles up the bed and peers over Luke to Dillon, still lying on his back.

'I know I'm irresistible, but you're going to have to resist. Go to sleep.'

He grins, opening one eye to wink at her, before turning his back to her.

'Asshole,' she replies, lying down and snuggling up to Luke.

She opens her eyes and smiles when she sees the image in front of her. Well isn't that one hell of a sight to wake up to? Luke is asleep beside her, on his side, one arm under his head and the other draped over her waist.

And they're not the only arms she can see. Dillon's arm is thrown across Luke's stomach, hugging him. Asking Dillon to stay had absolutely been the right thing to do. Luke has known him forever. If he feels utterly safe with anyone, it's Dillon.

With Maeve and Dillon keeping an eye on him, Luke had slept the rest of the night without any more nightmares disturbing him.

She pushes onto her elbow and looks at Dillon, pressed up against Luke's back. The tough guy is a lot less intimidating in his sleep - especially cuddling Luke like he is.

She absolutely doesn't agree with Pippa's reaction to Luke and Dillon's relationship, but a small part of her can't help but understand why Pippa felt the way she did.

Pippa was clearly insecure in their relationship, or else she wouldn't have needed to control Luke the way she did. Dillon's closeness to Luke would have been viewed as a threat to her marriage. Something that would have played on that very insecurity.

But Maeve could never object to Dillon. Their relationship is beautiful in its own special way. Dillon's love for Luke is so pure, she knows he'd never get in the way of Luke and his happiness.

He had done nothing except encourage her. Went out of his way to help her understand Luke, and how best to help him. He's part of their relationship, and she's more than okay about that.

Dillon mumbles in his sleep and tightens his grip around Luke's waist.

God, they are fucking adorable! A thought that would no doubt irritate Dillon.

She lies down and rests her head on her hand, as she watches the men. She could look at Luke's body all day and not get bored. Her eyes focus on a scar on his side, peeking out from under one of his tattoos. She's not going to ask him about it, but she has no doubts Pippa gave this beautiful man that scar.

She wishes there was something she could do, to help him break free for good. Being stuck married to that cow won't be helping him to move on. Until he's allowed to divorce in a few years, she's dating a married man.

Although some people would frown on what Maeve's doing, whatever relationship there had been between Luke and Pippa, had been beaten and put down so many times, it no longer existed. Pippa had made sure of that.

The only thing connecting Pippa and Luke is a piece of paper that says they're married. That and a lot of money. His money. Maeve wouldn't want to hazard a guess at how much Luke is worth.

Dozens of albums, constant number one songs, sell out tours. He's got to be worth a fortune, but she has no interest in that side of him. Unfortunately, it's that very side, that will make the break from Pippa all the more difficult. He could very well be left with nothing if she gets her way.

If they still allowed public stockades, she would happily shove Pippa in one. Hopefully she'll rot in prison for a long time. Bitch!

Luke sighs and opens his eyes. He smiles widely when he sees her and her heart melts a little. 'Morning Maeve.'

'Morning Luke.' She lies on her stomach and rests her head on her hands. 'What are you looking so happy about?'

'Waking up next to you. I like it.'

God, this man is doing things to her no one else had. She'd had people say things to her before, but she never fully believed any of them. There was something about Luke that makes those words completely believable. He genuinely means what he's saying and that makes the world of difference.

'Keep saying things like that to me, and I might have to sleep with you again.'

He smiles, then peers down at the large arm hugging him, and the smile fades a little as he looks back at her.

'It's okay, Luke. I called him when I couldn't bring you out of your nightmare.'

He frowns and grips the pillow under his hands. 'Yeah. I forgot. I'm sorry about that last night.'

She takes one of his hands and squeezes it. 'Never apologise. I'm just sorry I couldn't help you. But I watched what Dillon did. Hopefully I'll be able to help you next time.'

The look of shock on his face nearly has her laughing out loud. 'You want to sleep with me again? Even after that happened?'

'Of course! Ideally, I'd like it to be just the two of us as much as possible, but your mate isn't too much of a bed hog. And he doesn't snore, which is a definite bonus.'

Dillon's hand lifts from Luke's stomach, the middle finger up and directed at her. 'You do,' Dillon mumbles sleepily from behind Luke.

She slaps Dillon's hand. 'Fuck off! I do not.'

'You kind of do,' Luke says, laughing when she glares at him. 'It's cute snoring though.'

'Speaking of cute,' Maeve shoots back. 'Have you two seen each other, all cuddled up like that. Absolutely adorable.'

Dillon pushes onto his elbow and glares over Luke at her. 'You what?'

'Two big, tattooed, pierced, guys like you, getting all snugly. I love it!'

Dillon shakes his head before lying back on the bed and rolling over. 'I'll respond to that after I've had coffee. It's too early.'

Ignoring Dillon, Luke pulls her into his arms, brushing his nose against hers. 'I really am sorry about last night.'

'There's nothing to be sorry about. Do you have nightmares often?'

He shrugs. 'Every now and again. At first it was nearly every night, but not as much anymore. They seem to hit worse when I'm tired.'

'So if it happens again, and I just talk to you like Dillon did, that will help?'

'Yeah. If it's really bad it might take me a few minutes to wake up, but talking to me helps. Thank you for wanting to know all this stuff. For wanting to help me.'

'Why wouldn't I? When are you going to accept that I like you.'

'I'm trying. And I like you too.'

Dillon groans and climbs out of bed. 'Excuse me, I need to throw up.' He locks himself in the bathroom and Maeve laughs. 'Oops.'

'Ignore him. And thank you for being okay about...' he points over to the bathroom. 'He's not trying to do anything, I swear.'

She kisses his nose. 'Hey, I know that. He cares about you and there's nothing wrong with that. The way I see it, you need people around you who truly love you for the amazing person you are. I will never ever keep you two apart. And like I said, you're cute together.'

Luke kisses her, his hand resting on her cheek, as his tongue teases her lips apart.

Dillon knocks on the bathroom door, cracking it open a bit. 'You decent?'

'Yes. It's safe,' Luke answers, pulling Maeve into his arms. Dillon comes out of the bathroom and smiles at them. 'Now who's being adorable?'

'Aww, you are an old softy aren't you?'

He sneers at Maeve, but adds a quick wink, as he walks around the end of the bed. 'Well, I'm going to leave you two alone and head back to my room for a shower.'

'Do you want to join us for breakfast?'

'Thanks for the invite, but I'll pass. Watching you two gushing at each other over breakfast will put me off my grub. I'll see you both later.'

Maeve quickly jumps out off bed, catching up with him before he leaves the suite. 'Hey, Dillon! Wait.'

He turns around, his eyes darting back to the bedroom and Luke. 'What?'

'Thank you. For staying I mean.'

'No problem.' He chews his lip ring for a second, then steps closer to her, towering over her. 'You are the best fucking thing that's ever happened to Luke. Any idiot can see that. I'm here for both of you. Day or night.' He smiles, then turns and leaves the room.

Maeve stares after him, floored by what just happened. In any other situation she wouldn't have cared in the slightest if he approved or not.

But this is so different.

Gregg, Tate, and Dillon are his extended family. She wants to get on with all of them. Dillon was always going to be the biggest hurdle though, and she understands why.

'You want breakfast?'

She smiles over at Luke, sitting up in her bed looking sleepy and gorgeous. 'I think that sounds like a great idea.'

## 23

*Luke*

He pulls into Tate's driveway and looks at the impressive farmhouse. Tate's house isn't as imposing as his and Pippa's monstrosity, or as sterile. But, this is the sort of house he wanted. Or Dillon's place. Anything but the embarrassing heap he still owns. No doubt that'll be another fight to have with Pippa when they finally get divorced.

The house cost him close to two million Euro when he bought it. With prices the way they are, it's bound to be worth more now. But he doesn't want it. It was his prison every day he lived there. He never wants to see the house again.

Chloe answers the door, Brandon in her arms, fast asleep. 'Luke! Hey. So nice to see you. Come in.'

'I don't want to disturb you. Is Tate home?'

'He went for a ride on Jove. He was at his therapist this morning. It's his way of clearing his head after.'

'Oh. Sorry. I'll give him a call later.'

'Hey! Wait. Don't be silly. Please come in.'

'No, I probably should leave him to it. The last thing he'll want is more talking after that. Believe me, I know.'

Chloe pushes the door open wide and steps aside. 'Get in here and stop being silly. He's been gone for nearly two hours. If someone doesn't drag him back in soon, he'll be getting saddle sores.'

He follows Chloe into the impressive kitchen/dining room and out into the back garden. She walks with him over to the gate in the hedge, and looks each way down the beach, nodding to the left.

'There he is. Right down at the far end. Once you get onto the beach he'll see you.'

'Are you sure he won't mind?'

'Not for a second.' She rocks Brandon in her arms, then looks up at him. 'Are you okay? You look like there's something on your mind.'

'No, I'm fine. I just want to talk with Tate. I think he might be able to help me with a few things going on in my head.'

She smiles and reaches up to kiss him on the cheek. 'I think you might be able to help each other.'

Chloe turns and walks back to the house with Brandon, leaving him on the grass verge at the edge of the beach. He steps onto the sand, and walks down the beach towards Tate and his horse in the distance.

It takes about five minutes before Tate notices him, then shortens the distance between them at an impressive speed.

He pulls his huge black horse to a stop a few metres from Luke, and waits until Jove actually decides to stand still, before he acknowledges him. 'Just stand, Jove. Sorry, he's all wound up.'

'I don't think I've ever seen him calm.'

Tate laughs at that. 'Yeah. You might have a point.' He climbs down from the saddle and rubs the side of Jove's neck.

'Chloe said you were down here. I hope you don't mind?'

'Why the fuck would I mind? Was Brandon asleep, or screaming his fucking head off?'

'Asleep. He looks more like you every time I see him.'

Tate smiles and nods. 'A mini me. Just what the world needs, huh? Do you want to sit, or go for a walk?'

'A walk would be good, if that's okay?'

'No problem.' He pulls up the stirrups, then shortens Jove's reins, before gesturing back down the beach the way he came. Jove follows patiently behind them like an obedient dog.

'How did today go?' Luke asks. 'You can tell me to mind my own business if you want.'

Tate turns the ring on his thumb, a sure sign he's stressed. 'It was okay I guess. But I don't need to tell you how crappy some of the sessions can be. Talking about what's in our heads is fine and all in theory, but I fucking hate it.'

He nods. 'Yeah. I know. Are the sessions helping though?'

'Seem to be. Nightmares are hitting maybe once a week now, instead of every fucking night. I'm sticking with it this time.

'I'm getting married in a few weeks, and I've got Brandon to think about now. Chloe deserves a husband she can trust, and I'm going to make fucking sure Brandon will have a father he can be proud of.

'I can't undo what my asshole father did to me, or erase my heroin addiction from my past, but I can make sure I'm the father he needs me to be. Kind of added incentive, I guess. How about you? Getting anywhere with your sessions?'

'Yeah. It's just hard, you know. My therapist... well, she suggested that maybe I should... that it might be an idea to talk. To you I mean. You know, about it.'

Yeah well that was a disaster. He thought after months in the facility and in therapy afterwards, he'd have got the hang of it by now.

Tate turns the ring on his thumb and nods at him. 'Chloe mentioned the same thing to me a few weeks ago, but I didn't want to piss you off by suggesting it. Thought it would be better to let you come to me, when you were ready, if at all. Fuck knows, I wasn't keen on talking about what happened to me, for a long time. I know how irritating it is to be pushed when you're not ready.'

'So you don't mind?'

'Jesus, Luke! Of course I don't mind. We're friends. I'll be here for you however you want me to be. Day or fucking night. You hear me?'

'I don't want to upset you by asking you to talk about what happened to you, just so you can make me feel a bit better.'

Tate rubs a hand over his face. 'I hate talking about what my father did to me. Hate it more than I can ever put into words. But it's part of the deal. We both know that. We have to talk, or the shit in here won't let us go,' he says, tapping a finger against the side of his head.

'We both know how bad it can get. We've both done things to make it go away, no matter the cost to ourselves. And we were both given another chance to get it right. If it helps you even a small bit to talk to me, you use me.'

'But what your dad did... it was so much worse than what happened to me—'

'Hey you stop right there,' Tate interrupts. 'Abuse is abuse. What the fuck does it matter who was responsible?'

'You were only a kid though. You couldn't stop what was happening.'

Tate stops walking, turning to face him. 'Did you know Pippa was abusing you?'

'No. Okay, so maybe towards the end, I knew it wasn't right. But while it was going on, I just thought it was something I was doing wrong.'

'I thought the exact same thing, Luke. When my father came home drunk and beat me, it was because I was too noisy. Or irritating. Or

201

just there in the first place. It was my fault. And when I was really an irritation, things turned... sexual. That's how abuse is. What does it matter if you're six, or in your thirties? We still think it's our fault it's happening. That's part of the abuse. Part of the control she had over you. You didn't know how bad it really was.'

He knows Tate is right. He's heard it enough times over the last few months. But hearing it from Tate does help. He knows Tate. Trusts him. 'I guess you're right. It's just difficult sometimes to see where it all went wrong, you know. I mean I was happy with her once. It wasn't always like that.'

'Of course it wasn't. We could all see that you genuinely loved each other once. You wouldn't have lasted so long together, unless there was something real there to begin with.

'But the fact it went so wrong, isn't your fault. Just like it wasn't my fault with my dad.' Tate pauses and smiles at him. 'You know, seeing you coming out of all this, is really helping me.'

That surprises Luke. 'How?'

'I didn't give a fuck about my dad. He was related to me by blood, but that's as far as the relationship went for me. Pippa and you were in love. I've tried to put myself in your shoes a few times since we found out what was going on. Tried to imagine Chloe doing something like that to me, and how I'd feel if she did.

'But Fuck, Luke. I can't get my head around it. I do know it would completely devastate me. I know I'm not the emotional type, but I am so fucking proud of you. I'm proud of you for surviving the abuse while you were living with it, and I'm proud of you for fighting the after effects.'

'Thanks, Tate. Did you see when it went wrong for Pippa and I? I'm just curious. I've never asked anyone that.'

Tate shrugs as he looks out at the sea. 'I saw you disappearing into yourself a bit, but I had no idea why. But I'm probably the worst person you can ask. I wasn't a fan of Pippa's. We didn't see eye-to-eye.'

That's an understatement. Pippa tolerated Gregg, but tended to avoid Tate and Dillon whenever possible. 'Can I ask you something?'

'Sure.'

'What really happened between you and Pippa?'

Tate freezes for a second, before he answers 'You know what happened.'

'I know what you told me happened when she slapped you, but I had blinkers on when it came to Pippa. They're gone now. The slap was the final straw for you, but something else happened that night. It takes a hell of a lot to get you worked up. Slapping you was unacceptable, and I've always been upset with her for doing that, but I need you to stop protecting me and tell me the truth.'

Tate blows out a long breath and, when Luke sees him playing with the ring on his thumb, knows he was right. Something else had happened and Tate had been keeping it from him.

'Please, Tate. She's gone, but I need to know. I feel like it's this thing between you and me, and I don't want that.'

'We're grand, Luke. Always have been.'

'Please tell me.'

Tate scrubs a hand over his jaw, then nods. 'Fine. It was the same night as the slap. I went upstairs to the toilet, and I guess she followed me. She barged into the bathroom before I had a chance to lock the door.'

Luke swallows, a part of him regretting forcing Tate to tell him this.

'I politely explained that I needed to piss, and would she get the fuck out. She...'

'She what, Tate?'

'She tried to kiss me. Tried, Luke. I pushed her away before she got close. I mean that. Even back in my arse-hole days, I would never do that. You know that, right?'

'Of course I do,' Luke replies truthfully. He trusts the guys in the band more than he trusts most people in his life. Tate would never do that to him.

'Well she wasn't giving up that easily. It was probably drink, but she was all over me. She grabbed my dick. Through my jeans, not that it makes a difference. Then she started going on about how great a singer I am, then she started laying in to you, while feeling me up.

'I'd reached the end of my patience at that stage, so I shoved her off me. Bit harder than I meant to, but fuck it. I was done being polite. I ripped in to her — verbally, even though I wanted to do more. I didn't hold back, and she didn't take it well. Stormed out, I had a piss, then came back downstairs again.

'Then she started having a go at you, for needing to go away again. So I told her she was a money-grabbing leech, and I'm guessing the slap was her way of getting back at me, for what didn't happen upstairs. I was going to tell you, but I let the *Bitch* talk me out of it. She came to me the following day all apologetic. Said she'd had too much to drink and that she loves you. So, I let it go.'

Luke thought slapping Tate had been bad. But, coming on to him like that... 'I'm so sorry.'

'Hey! What the fuck are you apologising for?'

'I don't know.'

'You're done apologising for her, you hear me? Never apologise for her again. Not ever. It doesn't make us weak by admitting we're victims, Luke. My dad. Pippa. They're the bad guys. They're the ones who should be apologising. But, not fucking likely considering one is dead, and the other is rotting where she belongs.

'But we're here, Luke. Fucked up as we are, we're still here and considering everything, we're not doing too badly.

'You know what? You're right.'

Tate smiles and starts walking again. 'It happens from time to time.'

## Luke

He always considered himself a romantic kind of guy. Long walks, dinners out, just sitting alone with the person you love for hours, and listening to each other. Being with someone, spending time with them because you enjoyed it. That was what he loved.

Or did.

The last few years things didn't go to plan. He went from wanting to be with the person he loves, to being terrified of being alone with them.

Sitting on his motorbike, following after Maeve on her own bike as she speeds down the road, Luke can't stop the grin that's plastered on his face. This is what being in a serious, decent, healthy relationship means to him. She had arrived at his door with a bag full of food, and they had hopped on their bikes. Just like that. No planning. No schedule or itinerary. Just them and their bikes.

The fact she has a bike is such a turn on for him. He is being bombarded by various images, all involving her sitting on the bike, and him touching her.

She indicates, pulling him out of his thoughts. He follows her down a forest track, twisting through the trees until they reach the car park at the end. She pulls into a bike space and he parks beside her.

He'd been to Avondale years ago when he was kid, but not since then. Doing regular things like this is exactly what he wants. Pippa only wanted to go shopping, or out for fancy meals. Taking a drive, or going for a walk weren't ever things she wanted to do.

His attention is drawn to Maeve as she swings her leg over the saddle of her bike. She pulls off her helmet, ruffling her hair, and his dick twitches in response, something that catches him by surprise.

It hasn't done that for ages - or at least not out in public like this. He adjusts himself in the saddle, hoping Maeve doesn't notice what he's trying to hide.

Maeve walks over to him, looking really sexy in her tight jeans and short leather jacket. 'Hey Gorgeous. Fancy seeing you here.'

'Yeah. Strange that. I haven't been here for years. Myself and Alex got lost. We spent hours wandering around trying to find our parents. I don't think I've been here since.'

She links arms with him. 'Well don't you go worrying. I'll keep you close. Wouldn't want you wandering off on me. I know it's not exactly quiet here, but there are loads of trails. We can avoid the crowds. Nothing worse than heading out for a bit of nature appreciation, and being surrounded by people. No thank you very much.'

He slips on his sunglasses and cap, then locks his helmet onto his bike. Maeve finishes securing her helmet, then holds out her hand. 'Ready?'

He smiles as he takes it, loving the way her hand feels in his. There are plenty of people around, but they either don't recognise him, or are enjoying the scenery too much to notice him. And that's just fine. He's here with Maeve and doesn't want anyone to interrupt that.

'I'm glad we could do this.'

'Yeah,' he says. 'Me too. I like seeing you on a bike.'

She smirks over at him. 'Do you now? I have to say seeing you on your bike was rather nice too. We should do this more often. Just pack a lunch, jump on our bikes, and head off for the day. I love doing stuff like that. I'm not one for making rigid plans.'

That couldn't sound more perfect. After years of being stifled by plans he had no part in making, the freedom she described is exactly what he wants. 'You don't have to try and convince me. We should make it a monthly thing at least. Just head off and see where we end up.'

She hugs his arm and smiles up at him. 'That's the sort of plan I can commit to.' She holds out her hand and he shakes it. 'Monthly road trip.'

'Monthly road trip.'

They walk in silence for a few minutes, enjoying each other's company and the scenery. Then Maeve suddenly pulls him off the path onto the grass. She stops in a clearing a few metres away from the walkways, sheltered by a line of trees. 'Yep. This is the place.'

'What place?' he asks, looking around.

'The perfect place for food! I'm starving.' She shrugs off her backpack and opens it, taking out a blanket which she spreads out on the grass.

Luke joins her, placing his bag on the ground and sits down beside her. 'I'm not about to keep you from your food. I wouldn't want you to get grumpy on me.'

'Me, grumpy?' she says, feigning shock, before laughing. 'Yeah. I would totally get grumpy. What can I say? I love my food. All food. Any food. It's hands down my favourite meal.'

He can't explain what comes over him, but he can't resist the urge to kiss her.

'I like when you do that,' she says, taking his hand in hers. 'You continually surprise me. Keeps me wondering what you're going to do next.'

'I think that's called me being indecisive?'

She laughs and hugs him. 'No. I'm calling it being romantic. Indecisive? Please! Don't knock yourself like that. You, Mr Daly, are a romantic. I can tell these things. You know how I know?'

'How?'

'Because you're a rare breed of man. Well at least in the group of men I've associated with. That might have just been my taste though?'

She shrugs. 'Whatever! You're one of the good ones. Taking your time, not rushing things, it's a good thing. Everyone is so eager to jump into heavy relationships, or into bed with each other.'

'What's wrong with getting to know each other? There's more to a relationship than all the physical stuff, which, for the record, I like. I'm not knocking that. But I'm also enjoying doing things like this with you too. This is just as important.'

'I like all this too, I really do. I'm just worried you'll get bored.'

She shuffles closer, taking both his hands in hers. 'One word. Impossible. Completely, totally, and utterly impossible.'

'That's more than one word.'

She sticks out her tongue. 'Smart ass. I won't get bored with what we're doing. Please don't ever think that. Now pass me your bag so I can eat.'

He passes her his backpack, and she unpacks the picnic they brought with them.

'Can I ask you something?'

'Anything, sexy.'

He can't help but smile when she calls him that. It's such a small thing, but it means the world to him and his beaten down confidence.

'My brother is having a barbecue at the weekend. It's something he does regularly over the summer. Would you maybe want to come with me? My parents will be there too.'

'Oooh - meeting the parents. That's a big step.'

He shakes his head, wishing he could take the damn question back. He knew it was too soon for something that big. 'You don't have to. It was just a thought.'

'Hey! I wasn't saying no. Not at all. I was just joking with you.'

'I'm sorry. I'm still trying to figure all this out. You know, the timing of everything.'

She wraps her arms around his neck and pulls him close for a kiss. 'You're doing great. Don't mind me. And by the way, I'd love to go. Who doesn't like a barbecue?'

'And you're okay about meeting my family?'

She lays out the tubs of salads and sandwiches. 'Absolutely! And parents love me. I'm instantly lovable.'

'I know that.' Okay, that wasn't meant to come out of his head. Maeve glances up at him and smiles, but thankfully, doesn't comment on what he said.

'So who will be there?' she asks, passing him a sandwich.

'Alex and his wife Jackie, their two sons, and my parents. That's it. And they're all really nice.'

'Sounds fantastic! Count me in.'

He tucks into his lunch, surprised that he actually has an appetite for the first time in ages. He usually just eats because he has to, not because he wants to.

Maeve stretches out on the blanket, as she reaches for her second sandwich. He really can't wait to introduce her to his family. Her bubbly personality is so infectious, it would be impossible not to warm to her. There is no doubt in his mind that they'll love her. She's right. She is instantly lovable.

He loves her.

It's too soon to say anything to her, but he knows what he's feeling is real. He's falling in love with Maeve. It happened a lot faster than he expected.

When he was in the facility a few months ago, he would never have considered being with someone ever again. But so much has changed since he met her. It's like she's slowly pulling him out of the darkness.

That's the only way he can describe it. He's still hiding parts of himself, but with her help, with her support, that veil is slowly lifting, allowing him to discover things about himself he'd forgotten or dismissed.

'What are you smiling at?' she asks, wiping her mouth with the back of her hand.

'I'm just thinking how glad I am that I got drunk in Mike's pub that night.'

She kisses him on the cheek. 'And I'm glad I brought you back to my flat so you could get sick in my pudding bowl.'

He laughs and takes another sandwich from the lunchbox.

'You're right. I am romantic.'

She taps her sandwich against his. 'Too right you are.'

## 25

Luke

'So, who is she?'

Luke knew Alex would fire the questions at him, as soon as they were alone. From the minute he arrived at his brother's house with Maeve, Alex kept hitting him with questioning looks.

'She's a friend.'

Alex snorts, and passes him a knife. 'Cut up some tomatoes and cucumber while you're there. And what sort of a friend?'

Luke sits on the bar stool and concentrates on the vegetables, hoping Alex will drop the subject.

'Who's your friend?' Their mother comes into the kitchen, instantly veering towards Luke. 'She's lovely! When you said you were bringing someone, I assumed it would be Dillon. Jackie has bought enough food to feed him and his voracious appetite.'

'Sorry. I should have said who it was.'

His mum hugs him, barely giving him enough time to drop the knife he's using. 'It's brilliant honey! Really. And she's so nice.'

'Can I get back to the salad?'

She releases him, but the interrogation is far from over. His sister-in-law, Jackie, hurries into the kitchen. 'Spill the beans, Luke! What's going on?' she asks, as she piles some chips and dip onto a tray.

'Would you all keep it down! I don't want her to hear.'

Jackie waves away his protests, as she picks up a Dorito and smothers it in dip. 'She's busy hearing about your childhood. Your father is filling her in on some cute stories.'

'Oh please don't say that! What's he telling her?'

She eats the crisp, and shrugs. 'Something about a camping trip and you sleepwalking in the nip.'

'Please say you're joking?'

She grins and waves a Dorito at him. 'Don't hold back on us. Who is this mystery Maeve then?'

'We went to secondary school together, and bumped into each other again a few weeks ago. I like her, okay, so please don't scare her away with naked sleepwalking stories. I'm already giving her enough reasons to walk away as it is. I don't need you guys helping.'

'Why would she walk away?' Alex asks, crossing his arms the way he does, when he's going into big brother protection mode.

'I'm not without baggage, Alex.'

'Has she hinted that she has a problem with anything you told her?'

'No!' he says, shaking his head emphatically. 'Not at all. She's helping me figure out a lot of things about myself. Things I've forgotten, or didn't know in the first place. And she knows everything. I told her from the start, but she still wants to spend time with me. She's been really great actually.'

He pulls the notebook from his back pocket. He never leaves the house without it, taking every opportunity to fill another page, whenever possible.

'She bought me this a few weeks ago. It's somewhere I can write a list of things I like. You know like food wise. I've been struggling with food for a while, and she's helping me figure out what I like, and don't like. It's been great fun filling out the pages with her. The first day she must have bought every type of cereal you can get, so I could try them all.'

They all silently look at him for a ridiculous length of time, before his mum sniffs and wipes her face.

'Mum, don't cry. It's good, really. I'm happy.'

'I know. I think I just realised how much I missed that. It's been too long since I've seen you truly happy. I think she's a star, just for that alone.'

After much gushing and hugging, Luke finally manages to extricate himself from his emotional family, and head back outside to his dad and Maeve.

His dad generally gets on with everyone, but seeing him lounging back in a deckchair, beer in hand, chatting away to Maeve like they've known each other forever, is hands down the best thing he's ever seen.

His family and Pippa never got on. Thinking back, it's difficult to think of anyone she did get on with. Doesn't look like he needs to worry about that with Maeve.

'Hey there! I hear you were putting your salad chopping skills to work.'

He pulls up a chair next to her. 'Yeah. It's all done.'

'Speaking of done,' his father says, pushing out of his chair. 'Time for me to check on the barbecue. No point having salad with no meat.'

'I like him,' Maeve says, as his dad checks on the rest of the food. 'He's got a wicked sense of humour. I'm trying to put on a good impression and all, but he made me laugh so much, cider came out my nose! I'm not taking responsibility for it. Totally his fault.'

'Well if it's any consolation, you're doing better than I did, first impression wise. I got drunk in your brother's bar. I think you're winning. And they all really like you. Trust me.'

She winks at him. 'Of course they like me! I'm fucking adorable,' she says before taking a drink of cider.

Luke laughs, reaching out to hold her hand. She's not wrong there.

## Maeve

Luke parks at the far end of the car park, away from the crowds gathered around the coffee shops and ice cream stalls at the far end. He grabs his sunglasses from the centre console, before getting out of the car and walking around the passenger side to Maeve, opening the door for her.

'Why thank you! You know I could get used to being spoiled like that.'

'Spoiled?'

'You opening the door for me all the time. You're a proper gentleman, you know that?'

'My mum would be happy to hear that. She's a stickler for manners. Dad too. Kept drumming it in to Alex and I growing up.' He gestures over to the ice cream stand at the far end of the car park. 'Do you want anything to eat or drink?'

'Are you serious?' she asks, rubbing her stomach. 'After what I just ate, I'm going on a diet for the next month. Your father and sister-in-law can cook!'

He laughs, then leads her down on to the beach, heading away from the car park. 'Yeah, Jackie tends to go a little crazy when she's cooking. The two boys can eat a hell of a lot, so she's always prepared. I wanted to say thanks for coming today. I really appreciate it.'

'Don't be silly! Your nephews are amazing. You have a really lovely family. It was great to meet them.'

'You think so? I meant the lovely family part.'

'Of course! Why do you sound so surprised?'

'I don't mean to. It's just nice to hear you say that.' Luke looks as if he's about to say something else, but stops himself.

It didn't take long to figure out why he does that. It's always Pippa related. 'She wasn't a fan of your family?'

Luke shakes his head. 'Not really.' They walk along the shore, just above the breaking waves. 'I don't know if she didn't like them, or didn't like how I was with them.' He shrugs and glances over at her. 'Who knows what was going on in her head?'

'Well she was missing out.'

Luke smiles widely at her. 'Yeah, she was.'

'You know it was great to see you interacting with your nephews today. It was a side of you I hadn't seen before. You're a natural, you know that?'

'They're great kids. It's easy to spend time with them.'

'Yeah and spoil them. You don't hold back, do you? I wish my uncle brought me a present every time he visited.'

He shrugs and looks out at the sea. 'I can do it, so why not? It's nice to be able to do things like that for them.'

'So I take it you want your own family one day?'

He goes quiet and adjusts his baseball cap, but doesn't say anything. Something is wrong. She pulls him to a stop and faces him. 'Hey. What's wrong?'

Luke plays with the stud under his lip for a ridiculous amount of time. When he finally speaks, she can barely hear what he's saying. 'I can't have kids.'

'Oh Luke! I'm sorry. I had no idea.'

He smiles briefly and shrugs again. 'I haven't told anyone. It doesn't really come up in conversation, and the decision was only made last year.'

It takes Maeve a second to realise what he said. 'The decision? You mean you've had the snip?'

He nods.

'But why, if you want to have children?'

'Pippa didn't, so...' he shrugs again. 'She booked it for a few weeks before the wedding.'

Maeve turns away from him, so he doesn't see the horror and anger on her face. How dare the bitch make such a life changing decision for him like that? Use a fucking condom like other people do! But Pippa was all about controlling him, and this was one hell of a way to show him who was the boss in their relationship.

When she calms down enough to face him again, he's looking at the ground in front of him. 'Did you want to have a vasectomy?'

'No point regretting it. It's done.'

She takes his hand, bringing him down to the shore, away from any members of the public. 'Sit down for a second.' He lowers onto the stones next to her, and takes her hand when she offers it to him. 'Did you want to have the vasectomy? Honest yes or no answer.'

'No. I didn't.'

Maeve nods, focusing on the sea, so he doesn't see her silently cursing out his wife. 'Okay,' she says, back in control of her emotions. 'It's not necessarily a no going back kind of thing. If you want, you could see if you could get it reversed. There's a chance you could be a father... if that's what you want?'

He lifts his head and she sees unshed tears in his eyes. 'I never thought about that. I should have, but once it was done, I just accepted that was it.'

'So you want to have a family one day?'

He nods and the sadness in his eyes kills her. 'More than anything. When she... when I had the procedure, a bit of me died that day. A part of my future disappeared, a part I had been thinking about for a while. I think I'd be a good dad.'

Maeve cups the side of his face, running her thumb along his cheek. 'A good dad? That's a fucking understatement, Luke. You'd be incredible!'

'Yeah. I would, wouldn't I?'

'Too right you would! So maybe you should think about having a chat with your doctor? See what your options are.'

He nods, the smile that comes out lighting up his face. 'Yeah. I'll do that. If there's even a small chance I can have kids one day, I have to try.'

She hugs his arm, snuggling up against his side. 'Couldn't agree more. The decision shouldn't have been made for you like it was. I'm so sorry, Luke.'

'I'm sorry I let her make the decision for me. Anyway, I don't want to talk about her anymore. I had a great day with an amazing person. I just want to focus on that.'

Maeve grins against his arm. She loves when he says things like that. It's so genuine when it comes from him, it's difficult not to get swept away. 'Is that right? What amazing person would that be then?'

He kisses the top of her head. 'Might be you?'

'Might be? You better try that again mister.'

He tilts her head back and looks at her. It's the first time he's done something so assertive with her, and she could get used to it. Luke kisses her, his fingers tracing down the side of her cheek.

'Is that better?'

Maeve nods, clearing her throat. 'That? Yep. That was good. Better. Consider myself convinced.'

He drapes his arm across her shoulders. 'I hope so. You mean a lot to me Maeve. I know I haven't been good at telling you. But you do. I love spending time with you. You make me believe I can get over everything that happened. I want to get over it so... I don't know.'

'Hey don't stop now. You can't leave me hanging like that. Say what

217

you want to say.'

He takes a deep breath before he answers. 'Okay. So I've had thoughts about being with you long term.' Luke grimaces and rubs his forehead. 'Why am I so bad at this?'

'You're not bad. Just out of practice.'

'Very out of practice. What I'm trying to say, in a really bad way, is that when I'm with you, I can see the future for me. For us. I haven't been able to look further than tomorrow for a long time.'

'Wow!' And that's a ridiculous understatement, if ever there was one. Talk about completely blindsiding her. 'To elaborate on the wow, I would like to add that I feel the same about you, Luke. You're an incredible man and every time I'm with you I have so much fun.'

'I'm fun? I haven't been called fun for a long time.'

'Of course you're fun! I think I'm seeing the real you coming out, and I can't get enough of that. You're kind, and gentle, so easy to talk to, to be with. And it totally helps you're hands down the sexiest man I've met... well ever.'

When he blushes, it just reinforces her last point.

'Thank you, Maeve. I thought going into the bar that night and getting drunk alone was a really bad idea. Who knew it would be my best.'

Lost for words, Maeve lies against him, enjoying the weight of his arm across her shoulders as they sit in comfortable silence watching the sea.

## 26

Luke

The sound of his knee shattering is nearly as bad as the pain that follows. His stomach flips on itself, sending the little he'd eaten that day onto the spotless, plush beige carpet in their master suite. Whether down to the pain or the sickening sensation of his destroyed knee, he doesn't know.

Everything else that happens after that is a blur of shocking pain. He curls into a ball as she shouts at him. Tells him how he's forced her to do this. How he's a terrible husband, an embarrassment.

Then she showers and leaves him alone, locked in the room, bleeding and broken on the floor.

Despair, loneliness, pain. It's all consuming as he cries on the floor, wondering if it would be better for everyone if he wasn't alive any more.

Someone holds him, taking him in their arms as he cries. No one was in the room with him, but he's so lost, he hangs on to whoever it is, collapsing against them as they talk to him, telling him to wake up.

Luke opens his eyes, the bedroom in his old house disappearing to be replaced by Maeve's room. He wipes the tears from his face and pushes back from her. 'I'm sorry.'

She kneels up in the bed and smiles at him as he dies of embarrassment. 'Why are you apologising? You had a nightmare.'

'I didn't mean to wake you.'

'Luke. Stop. Please.'

He nods, then shuffles around to sit on the edge of the bed, rubbing his knee. The long scar will be a constant reminder of what Pippa did to him. A constant reminder of how she kicked his leg until his knee snapped.

Maeve appears in front of him, a glass of water in her hand. She places it on the locker beside him then rests her hands over his. 'Would you like to talk?'

He shakes his head. 'I'd prefer to forget. It was just the same dream. When she gave me this,' he says, nodding to the scar. 'Did it take long to wake me up?'

'A little while. I just did what Dillon told me to do. I got you some water. Is there anything else you want?'

'Can you... would you just hold me. Please.'

Maeve climbs back onto the bed behind him, then takes him in her arms when he lies down beside her. His knee hurts, but he knows it's just in his head.

Maeve runs her fingers through his hair as she holds him. Apart from Alex and Dillon, he's never felt safe with anyone else before.

Now the initial embarrassment of having a nightmare has faded away, he allows himself to be comforted by her, eventually falling asleep in her arms, listening to the steady beat of her heart.

# Maeve

As she brushes her teeth, she looks over her shoulder at Luke in the shower behind her. His fabulous body naked, wet, and covered in suds. Can you ask for a better morning image?

After the nightmare last night, he'd quickly fallen back asleep in her arms, and hadn't woken again until nearly ten.

The next hour was spent touching, holding, caressing each other. She never thought being naked with someone, taking time to appreciate their body, could be so fulfilling. It was all about sex before she met Luke. Not bad sex, but nothing as deep as what she feels she has with him.

He's growing more comfortable with her. His touches becoming less timid, more confident. Building trust is taking time, but it's time she's more than happy to give. If it means she can help heal him, she'll wait however long it takes.

Having his hands on her, even just touching her skin is such a turn on, in a way she never could have expected. The build up is intense and, hopefully, they'll be able to take things further at some stage. But there's no rush at all.

Maeve watches as he gets out of the shower, dries himself, then pulls on his boxers, transfixed by his body as the muscles shift under his skin.

Not for the first time she has to remind herself there's a real life super famous musician naked in her bedroom. Luke Daly from Broken Chords is in her room, getting dressed!

That's the part she still struggles with. To her, he's Luke. A guy she met in school and liked for years. But to the rest of the world, he's a celebrity. Someone they watch on TV, listen to on the radio, put posters of him on their walls. She needs to keep reminding herself of that at times. Especially when he's like this with her.

'I have to work tonight, but I'm free today,' she says as she ties her hair back in a ponytail. 'Are you working?'

Luke pulls on his t-shirt, hiding his impressive chest from her. 'No. I'm off today. Do you want to grab an early lunch? I'm guessing you're hungry?'

She playfully nudges him on the arm, as she passes on her way to her wardrobe. 'Are you saying I'm always eating?'

'Nope. I'm saying you're always hungry.'

'Okay. That's fair enough and very true.' She grabs the first top she finds and puts it on, glancing at her reflection quickly in the mirror. 'That'll do. So where do you fancy for brunch?'

'How about I take you to Dún Laoghaire? There's loads of choice there.'

'That sounds perfect.'

She slips on her shoes, then grabs her bag and follows him down to his car. As usual, Luke opens the door for her, closing it after she's climbed inside. His mum raised a good one there.

Maeve takes his keys from the centre console and holds up a small wooden dragon keyring. She runs her fingers over the wood, tracing the intricate details carved into the surface.

'I've been admiring this for a while now. Where did you get it? It's incredible. Do you think it's real wood, or one of those mass produced things?'

He smiles as he glances sideways at her. 'It's real wood. You really like it?'

'It's beautiful. It matches the tattoo on your arm. What came first - the keyring or the tattoo?'

'The tattoo. Do you...' he stops himself, and looks back out the windscreen.

'Do I what?'

'I have another one... if you want one for yourself? You don't have to though.'

'Why wouldn't I? That would be great. Thank you.'

He grins at her. That just made his day. He looks behind him, then moves into the next lane, turning off the main road. 'Where we going?'

'To get you the keyring.'

'Now? But what about bunch?'

He smiles across at her. 'It's five minutes from here. Then you can eat, I promise. You know, you're as bad as Gregg. Or Tate. Actually Dillon too. They're all like gannets when it comes to food.'

'I'm not surprised. You're all big guys.'

Luke looks over at her as they come to stop at a traffic light. 'I'm going to take that as a compliment. I think.'

'Oh it's one hundred percent a compliment.'

Luke's phone vibrates in the holder on the dash. 'Speak of the devil! Dillon. He wants to know if my parents survived meeting you.'

Maeve glares at the phone, acting hurt at the message. 'How dare he! Wait till I see him next. We'll see who survives.'

'You know, I'm impressed how you don't take any shit from him. I know he's a bit...'

'Intimidating.'

'I was going to say he's difficult to get to know. You think he's intimidating?'

Maeve shrugs. 'Not anymore, but initially yeah. He was a little. Once you get him to smile, he's genuinely decent. I like him. I think we're okay with each other, but it's hard to tell with him.'

Luke laughs and pulls away from the light. 'Yeah. Dillon doesn't bullshit. But once you get used to that, you actually realise it's a good thing. He never builds you up or compliments you, or even spends time with you, unless he wants to. After everything that's happened lately, having someone that transparent in my life is... well, I need it.'

She reaches across and squeezes his hand. 'I know. I'm just

223

terrified of meeting him when I'm having a bad hair day. That could be painful.'

'Oh God yes! He will absolutely tell you, believe me. But seriously, I am glad you two get along. He's really important to me. He's done a lot for me. You both have.' Before she can answer, he turns into a self-storage facility and turns off the engine. 'Time to get you a keyring.'

Maeve looks out the window and frowns. A self-storage unit wasn't quite where she thought he'd have a stash of keyrings, but she gets out of the car and follows him inside. Luke stops at one of the padlocked shutters and slips a key from his keyring into the lock. He pulls up the shutter and turns on the light.

Maeve stares into the unit and her mouth drops open. Inside the large room are the most incredible wooden sculptures she's ever seen. There must be at least two dozen, ranging in size from a few feet tall, to well over seven feet.

She goes inside and stands in front of the largest sculpture of a dragon sitting on a tree stump. The creature's wings are stretched over its head, as if it had just landed. She traces her fingers over the scales on its head, and along its jaw. The level of detail is staggering.

Her eyes travel over every inch of the creature, stopping when she notices something on the base under the dragon's foot. The initials *LD* are carved into the wood.

She points to the initials as she looks over at Luke. 'Oh my God! LD, as in Luke Daly? You did this?'

He nods once, but his expression isn't that of someone who's proud of their work. If anything, he looks a little nervous.

'Luke. I'm speechless. Well, not entirely. I'm going to keep speaking, but this... wow! I mean seriously wow! I had no idea. How the hell did you make this? Make all of these?'

'I did woodwork in school. I liked it, so kept it up after school, as a hobby.' He joins her in the unit and looks down at a carving of a snake. Its body not only twists around the chunk of wood it's carved out of,

224

but Luke had also managed to make it look like it was coming out of the wood. 'Carving these was my way to unwind after work, or after touring.'

'But how did you do all this?'

'Chainsaw for the bigger pieces. Then hand tools for the detail. You really like them?'

'Are you freaking kidding me? How could I not?'

She walks around the back of the dragon and stops in front of what looks like another dragon, but this one is hatching from an egg. Only a portion of the sculpture is completed. 'Like dragons I see.'

He smiles and shrugs. 'You figured that out, huh?'

'I'm clever like that. Why didn't you finish this one?'

Luke leans against the wall and stuffs his hands into the pockets of his joggers. 'Didn't get around to it. There were other things to do.'

Maeve is learning his expressions and knows the one on his face right now. 'Pippa, right? She not like you spending time working on these?'

He shrugs and looks at the unfinished sculpture. 'They didn't match the furniture in the house. And she didn't like the smell. Or the dust. Sawdust got everywhere, even when I was careful. That's why I moved them here, but I was here too much, so...' He shrugs again and looks up at her. 'Keyring. Nearly forgot.'

He goes over to a metal set of drawers and opens the top one. He takes out a keyring and hands it to her. 'I made a few of these when I was practising for the bigger sculptures. It's not the same as mine, but... is it okay?'

Maeve smiles at the small dragon. 'I love it! Thank you.' She takes out her keys and slips it on next to her house key.

Maeve stays quiet as Luke walks around the room. The more she hears about Pippa, the more confused she is. She doesn't get her. Not that it's a bad thing. Does she really want to understand someone like that?

All it takes is one minute in this room, and anyone with half a brain, would see how incredibly talented Luke is. Beyond talented. How could anyone stop someone who clearly has so much passion for something? It's criminal. Along with a lot of other things Pippa has done to him.

'So, which ones are you bringing back to the flat?'

'Sorry?'

'Your flat. Your furniture. And come on, you can't leave these stunning pieces here. It's not right.'

Luke frowns as he looks around the room. 'You think I should bring some back?'

'I don't see why not. I can't imagine the amount of time and work that went into each of them. They shouldn't be locked away where no one can see them. Show them off.'

He looks around the storage room and his smile grows. 'Yeah. I think I will.'

*Luke*

'You don't have to help me. I can drop you home if you'd prefer.'

Maeve looks up from the keying he gave her. 'Oh no. It's grand. I've got nothing planned. It's a shite day and it's kind of my fault you've got a car full of wooden statues. The least I can do is give you a hand.'

He wants her to come back to his flat, but it'll be the first time anyone bar the guys and his family have been there. He doesn't even know what state it was in when he left that morning.

Luke parks beside Dillon's Mustang and takes out the key for the service elevator. There's more room in it, and that means less trips. Maeve helps him load the lift, then squeezes in beside him, as they travel up to the level below the penthouse.

The lift opens on his floor and he locks the elevator door so it won't close before grabbing one of the larger statues. Maeve follows him around the corner to his door, a dragon carving under each arm.

'This is very fancy. How many neighbours do you have?'

'None. My apartment takes up the whole floor.'

Maeve whistles. 'Wowzers! Very nice indeed. So I presume Dillon lives here too? I noticed his flashy ride in the car park.'

Luke pushes his door open with his hip, struggling to fit the statue in through the door frame. 'Yeah. He's in the penthouse.'

'But of course!'

He laughs at the haughty look on her face. 'He doesn't like to make do. And he owns the whole building.'

'He what!'

'That's how I got this level. He didn't want any random strangers living under him, so kept it empty.'

'So Dillon is your landlord?'

'Yep. Lucky me, huh?'

He manages to get the statue down his entrance hall and in to the living room. Maeve follows behind, turning in a circle, when she joins him in the living room.

'Again, wowzers. My whole flat could fit in this room alone. And Dillon's place is bigger?'

'Quite a bit, yeah. His is on two levels. He's got a roof terrace thing.' He places the statue on the floor and gestures to the couch. 'You can lie them there while we get the rest.'

It takes twenty minutes to move everything from his car up to his apartment. Once he's closed the door behind them, he faces the stuffed living room, completely lost.

He's never decorated anywhere before. Pippa had hired people to decorate their house. He just had to pay the bill. No input at all.

Dillon had said he can go mad in the apartment, decorate it

however he wants. But he doesn't know how he wants it. It's not his home.

But maybe it could be, for the moment at least.

He looks around the white and grey walls, deciding he does actually like the way Dillon decorated it. He's never really thought about how it looked before.

'You know, I like this.'

He smiles over at Maeve, lying on the polished wooden floor with her arms behind her head.

'Why are you on the floor?'

'Why not? You get a good view of the place from down here.' She taps the floor, so he shrugs and lies down beside her.

'You're right. The place looks very different from down here.'

'So,' she says, shuffling closer so their bare arms are touching. 'Where are you going to put your stunning sculptures?'

'I don't know. Where do you think?'

She turns her head and smiles at him. 'No you don't! This is your home. Half of the fun is deciding yourself where you want them. There's no right or wrong answer, Luke. If you want to put them all sitting on the bathroom floor, that's cool. Might make using the facilities interesting, but hey! It's your home.'

He sits up and looks around the living room. The huge floor to ceiling windows take up one wall of the living room, and the kitchen next door. The entire floor space in front of the window is clear.

'The bigger ones could go to the side of the window I guess. And there's an empty corner in my bedroom. Maybe another one there?'

She pushes to her elbows and nods. 'You know what? That sounds like the beginnings of a plan.' She playfully slaps him on the leg and holds out her hand. 'Help me up.'

'I was thinking you could help me up?' he says, grinning over at her.

She slowly turns and stares at him. 'Seriously? Have you seen the size of you compared to me. I'm aware physics wasn't my strong subject, but even I know that's not going to work. Get your arse off the floor. We've got work to do.'

He gets up and pulls Maeve to her feet, not so accidentally drawing her against his chest when she stands. 'Thank you.'

She tilts her head back to look up at him. 'You're the one who helped me up.'

'No, I meant for all this. I have fun with you. We're moving carvings around the place and I'm still having fun. I didn't think... it's all new to me and I'm really enjoying myself.' She bites the corner of her lip, sucking the piercing into her mouth. Why does he love when she does that?

'You want to kiss me, don't you?'

'I'm thinking about it.'

'Is that so? Very inter—'

Luke kisses her, cutting off whatever she was going to say. He moves her arms from her side, placing them around his waist. Maeve accepts his invitation, holding him close as they kiss.

## 27

*Maeve*

She finishes making them a coffee, then leans back against the counter top to admire his temporary home. His incredible sculptures add that missing personality to the apartment. Every single one is a piece of Luke. A part of what makes him so special, went into every one of them.

It had taken a little encouragement, but he eventually found his confidence. She knows without a doubt he would have preferred if she took charge, and arranged the pieces where she thought they should go. But he got there himself.

'Can I borrow you for a sec?'

'Sure.' She shoves the packet of biscuits under her arm, then picks up the two cups. She finds him along the corridor in the massive master bedroom. 'What's up?'

He stuffs his hands into the pockets of his joggers. 'I need your help with something else.'

'Sounds intriguing. How can I be of assistance?'

Luke opens the two wardrobes and stands back beside her again. 'I probably should have done this before I moved in here, but I didn't think about it until recently. I bought everything in there. Problem is I don't know if I want most of it. A lot wasn't chosen by me.'

Maeve nods, understanding what he's saying. He wants to purge Pippa from his wardrobe. Fine by her. And by the looks of the stuffed wardrobes, there's a lot of sorting to do. He must easily have at least ten times the amount of clothes as she does.

'This sounds like the perfect way to spend a rainy day. I'm game. So, how do you want to do this?'

'I don't know. What do you think?'

She runs her hand over the clothes, most of which must be designer, judging by the feel.

'Well, I've seen this done on TV a lot. Gotta love daytime TV. Apparently, what you're supposed to do is make the decision quick. Like less than a few seconds. First reaction is the right one.'

'Okay. I can do that.'

'I can hold up each item and you say nay or yay. Maybe we could put everything you want to keep on the bed and the stuff for charity or selling or whatever, on the floor? That sound okay?'

He nods.

'Fair enough. Why don't you have a seat on your bed and I'll do the holding up part.'

Luke sits down and rests his arms on his knees, hands clasped tight together. He looks a little nervous. It may just be sorting through some clothes, but to Luke it's a seriously big deal. It's another step to freeing himself from his wife.

She rubs her hands together and turns to face him. 'First things first. Are you happy with what you have on?'

'Well, yeah, I guess. I just threw a few things into my bag last night before I came over to your place.'

'You have no idea how irritating that is.'

'Irritating? Why?'

'Because, I know you did exactly what you just said you did. You literally grabbed the first thing you saw yet, somehow, you still manage to look like that.'

Luke frowns and looks down at his black Reebok hi-tops, black joggers, and grey-t-shirt. 'Look like what?'

'Seriously hot. As in yummy hot, not temperature hot.'

'Really?'

She nods enthusiastically. 'Oh yeah. Seriously really.'

'But it's my messing around clothes.'

'Exactly. You're comfortable wearing them which, in turn, means you're relaxed. And did I mention seriously hot?'

He blushes and looks down at the ground.

Maeve laughs and turns around to face his enormous wardrobes. 'I so love how you don't know how hot you really are. Makes you so much hotter. Right, no time for that now. Let's get this started.'

Maeve shoves everything to one side and takes out a pair of beige slacks. She holds them up to him. 'Now five seconds remember. Yes or no?'

Luke takes a deep breath and, for the briefest of moments, she wonders if five seconds might be pushing it a bit, but he surprises her by shaking his head. 'No.'

She pulls the slacks off the hanger, then throws them on the floor beside his bed. 'One down.' She takes out a pair of well worn ripped jeans, already knowing what his answer will be.

'Yes.'

She smiles at him. 'That was quick.' She hands them to Luke and he puts them on the bed behind him. Less than an hour later the wardrobes are empty and there's an impressive mound of unwanted clothes on the floor.

Luke peers down at them from the bed. 'That's a lot of clothes.'

'You think? That's a ridiculous amount of clothes.'

He turns and examines the much smaller pile behind him. Everything on the bed is Luke. They are items she can picture him in no problem. He'd dismissed all but a few of the formal items, keeping two suits and a handful of shirts. Along with the outfits he wears in public with the band, he'd kept a few leather jackets, jeans, combats, joggers, fitted shirts, hoodies, and t-shirts. Everything else was on the floor.

'I didn't think it would be that much,' he says quietly. 'Did I keep enough?'

'It's the whole quality over quantity thing. You kept what you wanted to keep,' Maeve replies. 'Everything on the bed is you. That pile on the floor isn't. Easy.'

He smiles a little and nods. 'Will a charity shop take it all?'

'Are you kidding? They'll bite your hand off. Do you have any black sacks we can pack them in to?'

'Yeah. In the kitchen. Top drawer under the counter.'

When Maeve comes back in with the roll of sacks, he's staring into a drawer filled with jewellery. 'Most of this can go too.'

Her eyes open wide as she looks at the rows of expensive watches, chains, and bracelets. 'Seriously?'

He nods and holds out his wrist showing her the watch, bandanna, and leather cuff he always wears. 'This is all I want. And some of the rings, but that's it. I don't like yellow gold.'

He laughs and shakes his head. 'I really hate yellow gold. They are all presents she gave me, but I paid her credit card. So I bought myself jewellery I don't like. How messed up is that?'

She hugs him to her side, as he stares down at thousands of Euro worth of gold. Tens of thousands probably. But she agrees with him. Very few pieces in the drawer are him. A lot of the pieces are far too bling for Luke.

She runs her hand over the bandanna tied around his wrist. 'Do you wear this and the cuff because you like them, or to cover the scars?'

'Initially I wore them to hide the marks. While she was still... when we were together and she was still using the restraints... the wounds were raw. I didn't want the guys to see them.'

Maeve slowly unwraps the bandanna from around his wrist, and examines the pale pink scars circling his wrist. It's not just one ring around his wrist. There are so many scars overlapping each other, that they combine to create a thick mark about an inch wide.

Maeve lifts his arm, placing a kiss over the scar before wrapping it again. 'You don't need to hide them. You know that, right?'

He nods and swallows thickly. 'I don't like seeing them. Not yet.'

'I understand that. Besides, the bandanna and cuff look good on you. Have you only got these two? I haven't seen you wear anything else.'

'Yeah. I used what I had at the time. I didn't really put much thought into it.'

'Well if you want to keep them hidden, you could always get more bracelets and cuffs to cover them. Make it part of your wardrobe. Think of it more as adding to your look, rather than hiding something.'

Luke smiles at that suggestion. 'Yeah. I might do that. But what about all this jewellery?'

'There are loads of jewellers who would take this off your hands. It's got to be worth quite a bit. Why don't you pack away what you don't want, then we'll see if we can get a few appointments set up with jewellers.'

'Okay. Do you want to order some lunch while I do this? You missed out on brunch because of the carvings.' He takes out his wallet and hands her his credit card. 'There are loads of menus in the kitchen by the fridge.'

'Sounds like a plan. But I'll get lunch. It's my turn.'

He looks down at his credit card, then back at her, clearly surprised she's not letting him pay. 'Are you sure?'

'Luke, this is a fifty/fifty thing. You paid last time. I'll pay this time. What do you fancy?'

She's sure he'll flip the question back to her, but it seems he's in a decision making mood today. 'I wouldn't mind a baguette meal from the sandwich place. Their curly fries are so good.'

'Oooh - I like the sound of that. I'm on the case.'

He puts his credit card back in his wallet, then turns back to the most expensive drawer she's ever seen. 'Right. Time to get rid of all this.'

Maeve smiles as she goes back down the corridor to his kitchen, selecting the right menu and scanning the options. 'What sandwich?' she shouts while she digs out her phone.

'Chicken. The Cajun one!'

She rings in their order as she looks out the huge window overlooking the Liffey. This is a good day. She loves being with him, doing normal everyday things like this.

He's slowly coming out of himself. It's not a fast process, but she didn't expect it to be. It was never going to happen overnight. More of his personality is breaking free each time she sees him, and she can't get enough of it.

Maeve searches through his cupboards, finding plates and cutlery, then places them on the counter. Her attention is drawn to the noticeboard and a picture of Luke with the band. The smile on his face - on all their faces, is massive.

'What are you looking at?'

He surprises her by wrapping his arms around her waist, holding her against his chest. 'This photo. I love seeing you so happy.'

He rests his chin on her shoulder. 'I always am when I perform. It was the one place she had no control. The one place I could be the real me.'

Maeve places her hands over his, squeezing them. 'And now?'

She can feel him smile against the side of her face. 'Now I'm me... well, getting there.'

The intercom sounds, so Luke kisses her quickly on the neck, before letting go and getting their lunch.

'That was fast!' Maeve says as he unpacks their food.

'I might order from them a lot,' he admits with the grin. 'I haven't really got the hang of cooking for myself yet.'

'I'll have to show you. I can make a killer beans on toast.'

Luke looks up at her, laughing when she winks at him.

Maeve packs the last of his old and ridiculously expensive clothes into a black sack and shuts his wardrobe. Luke rejoins her in his bedroom and nods to the bag on the floor. 'Is that the last one?'

Maeve nods. 'Yep. It is all fitting in your car?'

'I had to put the back seats down but yeah, I'm squashing it all in.'

Maeve wraps her arms around him and smiles up at him. 'I'm so proud of you for wanting to do this.'

'It's no big deal.'

'Don't talk down what you just did. It was a big step. Everything hanging in there is you. It's the wardrobe of Luke Daly, musician and international superstar.' Maeve reaches up and kisses him. 'And did I say how much I love the way Luke Daly, musician and international superstar dresses?'

He grins at her. 'I think you might have mentioned it.'

Maeve pushes back from him. 'Okay. Time to put a bit of distance between us. You're getting me all hot and bothered. Your tongue is dangerous.'

'My tongue?'

'Well the piercing in your tongue, to be precise.'

'You really like it?'

She snorts in an incredibly attractive way. 'Are you kidding? Of course. You kiss me and my mind goes off on a tangent.'

'What tangent?'

'You know. The piercing. How it would feel... well... You know.' She watches the confusion on his face. 'You don't know?'

'I'm lost.'

Maeve wants out of this conversation she's somehow found herself in, but a part of her wants him to know what she's thinking. You never know, he might oblige. 'I might have been wondering what it would be like if you... you know... oral sex with your tongue pierced like that.'

'It would make a difference?'

It hits her in that moment. He's never done it before. But that doesn't make sense. He was with Pippa for years. He must have licked her out at least once. 'You haven't before, have you?'

He looks away and shakes his head.

'Okay.' Maeve isn't sure where to go with that one. Maybe he needs a demonstration. 'Come here.' She unzips her jeans and takes his hand. Maeve slides it down the front of her jeans and under her panties. His fingers brush against her and she gasps. 'You feel how wet I am? That's from me thinking about what you could do to me with that piercing.'

Luke swallows deeply and nods. Maeve groans as he pushes his fingers further inside her. 'Okay, so now I'm getting seriously turned on.'

'Would you mind if I undress you?'

'Of course not.'

He slowly pulls his fingers out from under her underwear and lifts up her t-shirt. Then he unfastens her bra and pushes her jeans down her legs. He takes her hand and brings her over to his bed. Maeve lies down so he can pull off her jeans, his hands caressing her legs as he moves down them.

Luke swallows thickly as he takes the band of her underwear in his hand. 'Can I take them off?'

'Oh go for it,' she says with a grin. Maeve lifts her hips off the bed as he takes care of her underwear, then lies still. The way he's looking at her, admiring her, is giving her goosebumps and driving her crazy.

Then he pulls off his own t-shirt and Maeve's heart races in her chest. Every breath he takes makes it seem like the dragon climbing over his shoulder is moving, and she loves it. She's desperate to kiss and suck his pierced nipples, but she keeps her hands to herself. For now at least. She has no idea what he wants to do, but she does know she's going to lie still and not scare him away.

Luke leans over her and kisses her again. In spite of her best efforts, she runs her hands through his hair as he kisses her. He feels so good she can't help herself, but Luke doesn't seem to mind.

He kisses the side of her neck., his breath warm on her skin. 'What do you want me to do?'

'Whatever you want.'

'Add another page to my notebook?'

Maeve laughs and when he looks at her again, he's smiling. 'What are you waiting for?' She closes her eyes as he works his way down her body. If she looks at him while he's kissing her, tasting her, she'll probably orgasm before he's even touched her pussy.

Then his hands are on her legs, gently pushing them apart. His fingers brush over her entrance and she moans in pleasure.

Then he does exactly what she's been hoping and imagining him doing. He slowly licks her. Then there's a slight pause before his fingers dig into her legs, holding them open. Luke slides his tongue into her and she gasps.

If this is him giving oral sex for the first time, she can't wait to see what else he can do. As if in tune with her body, he quickly learns what she likes and takes full advantage.

The hard stud in his tongue makes it all the more intense. It doesn't take him long to figure out exactly how to use that incredible addition. He presses it against her as he licks and she honestly can't get enough.

'Holy shit, Luke!'

He stops, then peers up at her. 'Did I hurt you?'

She shakes her head. 'No! Exact opposite. Keep going! Please!'

Maeve presses her head back against the pillow as his tongue drives her insane. His hands grip her thighs, the tips of his fingers rough from hours of playing guitar. And it's so much more mind-blowing than she could have ever imagined.

## *Luke*

The moans and gasps coming from Maeve are incredible. She seems to be enjoying what he's doing. He loves every single sound, every move of her hips as she rubs herself against him. Loves it all.

Maeve is hanging onto the headboard, her arms straining as she writhes on the covers. 'Oh Luke. That's amazing!'

He thought he'd be terrible at this. That he wouldn't have the first idea what to do. But Maeve, as usual, makes things so easy for him. There's no judging. No laughing at his inexperience. She has never once made him feel stupid or foolish. And that helps to give him a confidence he's not used to.

Maeve sucks in a long breath and arches back. 'Keep going! So close Luke!'

He swirls his tongue around her clit, massaging it with the piecing in his tongue which seems to drive her crazy.

'Oh fuck! Oh fuck! Oh fuck!'

Her words fade away as she comes, shouting aloud as she grabs at his hair with one hand. Luke takes that to mean she wants him to continue.

Her beautiful body trembles as she comes, but Luke keeps going with what he's doing until she lets go of his hair and sighs contentedly.

He kisses her pussy then crawls up the bed and lies down beside her, watching as she comes down from the orgasm he gave her.

Him.

He was able to pleasure her and he's so damn proud of himself. Most people wouldn't consider it an achievement, but he does.

He smiles as he looks down at her. She is stunning. Her eyes are closed, her cheeks flushed, her lips parted as she catches her breath.

When she opens her eyes and smiles at him, his stomach clenches. 'Hey there sexy.'

'Are you all right?'

'Fuck yes! Did you not hear me? Wow!'

He laughs and lies down beside her. 'I'm glad it was okay for you.'

Maeve turns onto her side and strokes the side of his face. 'That, my dear Luke, was not okay. *Okay* doesn't even come close. There's still a dance going on in my pussy after what you and that magical tongue of yours did to me. That was absolutely fucking fantastic! Thank you!' She kisses him and grins. 'And you taste of me, which is so hot.'

He can't stop smiling. It's like he's pushed past a barrier he didn't know existed. And he did a pretty decent job at it too.

Maeve kisses his chest before snuggling against him. Luke holds her, tucking her head under his chin as he smiles. He can't stop, and he doesn't want to.

For the first time in as long as he can remember, he doesn't feel like he's a worthless partner. He can bring something to this relationship. Give something to Maeve that she enjoys. And that makes him feel like he's ten feet tall.

# 28

## Dillon

The hotel shampoo and shower gel smells like rosewater which he fucking hates, but it's better than nothing. He angrily scrubs his hair and skin, but nothing is going to erase what he just did. What he keeps doing.

Once again, he'd used a fantasy of Luke to help himself get off.

He can't stop himself and he's tried so fucking hard. He's watched hours of porn - too much even for him, worked with a few new subs, even tried not having sex, or jerking off.

Nothing worked. He *needs* sex. It's how he's built. He needs it, but he can't come unless he's thinking about Luke.

It guarantees him one hell of an orgasm. But the crippling pain after is nearly too much for him. He's hurting himself over and over again. Slowly torturing himself.

Which is so unbelievably fucked up. He laughs to himself as the rosewater shampoo washes down the drain. He's fucked up. Always has been. There's something wired wrong in him, but he can't figure out how to fix himself.

It doesn't matter how hard he tries, he can't pull himself out of his messed up routine.

When he went out tonight, he wasn't expecting to have sex. It usually happened, but with his mood so dark, he thought it might be best not to actively look for someone to fuck.

So how he ended up in a hotel room with not just a guy, but a girl too, he's not quite sure. But who is he to complain? He's sure they were talking for a few hours, but he's also got a few hours worth of whiskey in him, so he's not sure about that either.

What he does know, is that he silenced Jace's constant calls a few hours ago. Turned his phone off. Let the bastard try to find him now.

He's also pretty convinced the couple haven't got a clue who he is. He'd done his usual trick of using his surname as his first name. Add a pair of clear lens glasses and he's suddenly incognito. It's fucking ridiculous.

He wishes he could remember the conversation that ended up with the three of them in a cheap hotel room. It must have been interesting.

They seemed to know each other but he couldn't care less if they're friends, or a couple, or whatever. They wanted him to join them, so what the hell. He remembers that much.

And it's not like he's scraping the bottom of the barrel with either of them. Blond, well built guy and brunette pretty hot woman. Actually, they're both pretty hot, so he's got no complaints there.

His go to position would always be the one in charge. The one calling the shots. But, right now, he's pissed off at the world. He's tired of having to think, or plan, or make sure the other party is enjoying themselves. He just wanted to be fucked.

How pathetic is that? He's worth millions. Fans all over the world. Hugely popular, yet massively lonely. Desperate for any attention, even if it means bunking in with a couple for a threesome. Not exactly what he signed up for with all this fame and fortune crap.

It's the way his life keeps playing out. One shitty situation after the next. Fair enough, most of the shitty situations were created by him. Well, him combined with drink and drugs.

Like right now.

But it's done. Not a lot he can do about it. The guy had fucked his girlfriend, then Dillon had fucked the guy while she watched. Whatever floats your boat. He's hardly one to judge. At least the two of them are in a relationship in the first place.

He's loved two people in his life. Really fucking loved, like in the deep kind of love. But one left him because... well, he has no fucking clue why she left him. The other one he can't have, because he stupidly fell in love with a straight guy. Fucking joke.

Gregg once said he envied him, because he has guys and girls to pick from. But all being bisexual means, is that there seems to be more people who can walk away from him.

He grabs a towel from the rack, brushes his fingers through his hair, then opens the door. The couple are still sprawled out on the bed. Both of them smile lazily at him, as he walks around the end of the bed.

'That was incredible,' she says, patting the bed beside them.

'Yeah. Fuck, that was intense.' Her boyfriend rolls over and wraps his arms around her.

'Glad you enjoyed it,' Dillon says as he pulls on his boxers.

She sits up and watches him get dressed. 'You're leaving?'

He puts on his t-shirt then picks up his bottle of whiskey. 'Yeah. Thanks for the fuck.'

Before they can say anything else, he's out the door and down the stairs. He hurries past the reception then down the steps leading outside, looking around to get his bearings.

Like that's going to help him in the slightest. He hasn't got a fucking clue where he is. It's certainly not a part of Dublin he's been in before.

Technically he should call Jace, but after giving him the slip a few hours ago, he's not about to open that can of worms. His bodyguard has staying power, he'll give him that. It's probably down to pure stubbornness that he's still agreeing to look out for him. It's not like he's an easy client.

Wandering around an unknown area of Dublin isn't the smartest idea he's had, but he's running on leftover whiskey, a few painkillers, and post sex buzz so he's not quite thinking straight.

He pulls out his phone to call Luke, but comes to his senses enough to have second thoughts. It's four in the morning. Luke wouldn't be happy if he dragged him out of bed. He's probably tucked up with Maeve.

Dillon curses as that image plays out in his mind. He slams the heel of his hand against his forehead, stumbling against the wall, scraping his arm.

He is so fucked it's not even funny. There's no choice. He has to call Jace. It's either that, or he'll find himself all over social for the wrong reasons - yet again.

It takes three attempts to find Jace's number, and another two to get his finger on the right icon. This is going to be a fun call.

'Well, well, well! About bloody time!'

Yeah. Jace is pissed. 'Hey.'

'You blow me off for hours, turn off your phone, then go for a hey. Why am I not surprised.'

'I get you're pissed, okay. But...' I need help.

He closes his eyes, resting his forehead against the grimy wall. God he needs help so badly.

'Where are you, Dillon?'

'I don't know.' Isn't that the story of his fucking life.

'I'll track your phone. Stay put and keep your head down. I'll be with you as fast as I can.'

He nods, strangely grateful for Jace.

'Dillon? You hear me?'

'Yeah. I hear you. Thank you.'

Jace pauses for a minute before responding. 'You're welcome.'

## Luke

He blindly gropes for his mobile, as the alarm drags him out of a dreamless sleep. He turns it off, tucks his head under the duvet, then reaches out to grab his phone again and checks the time.

He slept all night! He can't remember the last time he slept through, especially without any nightmares waking him up.

For the first time in months he feels rested. He knows it's thanks to Maeve, and everything she's doing for him. He'd lost his identity and honestly didn't think he'd get it back again.

He stretches, then frowns when another part of his body wakes up. It's been a long time since his dick has been interested in anything first thing in the morning. Or at any time of the day.

But the more he tries to ignore it, the harder it gets. Thinking about Maeve isn't helping get control of it one little bit. It's having the opposite effect on him.

He's going to ignore it and hope it calms down. But he stops himself from getting out of bed. This is normal. Getting turned on because he's thinking about someone he's attracted to, is absolutely normal. Why is he trying to dismiss it?

Luke pushes his boxers down his legs and kicks them off. He looks down at his dick for a long time, half wishing it would calm down. But it wants attention and he wants to give it attention.

He slowly reaches out and touches his dick, closing his eyes as he wraps his hand around it. Even holding it feels so good. He slowly runs his hand along it, brushing his fingers against his balls. The groan that comes out is genuine.

Feeling a little braver, he takes the bottle of lube that Maeve gave him, from his drawer, squirting some onto his hand before gripping his dick. He closes his eyes and Maeve's face instantly comes to mind. And her body. Then he's back in her bedroom, watching as she plays with herself, her fingers pushing into her pussy.

He moves his hand faster, using his other hand to massage his balls. He glances down, watching the head of his dick sliding through his fist. His dick is seriously hard and this feels so damn amazing. His balls tighten, his breath coming faster as the orgasm builds.

Luke shouts out as he comes, but he doesn't stop. It feels too damn good to stop. He keeps working himself until he's completely spent, then lets go of his dick and drops his hand to the bed. He kicks off the duvet, and laughs when he sees the mess he's made of his bed. But he couldn't care less.

That was better than he remembered. So much better. He can count on one hand the number of times he's had an orgasm over the last year or so, and now he's had two epic ones in the space of two days. This is definitely something he can get used to.

Still smiling to himself, he gets up and strips his bed. Then he turns some music on loud and has a shower, before getting into a pair of black combats and a sleeveless black t-shirt.

He's still smiling like some kind of idiot, as he examines the small boxes of cereal in his cupboard. It's not exactly healthy, but he reaches for a box of Coco Pops, and empties the contents into a bowl.

As he's eating, his phone vibrates as a message comes in from Maeve.

*Morning gorgeous. How'd you sleep?*

His chest tightens as he reads the message again. Five words. That's it, but they lift him so much. He's still smiling as he writes the reply.

*Morning. Slept all night. Woke up thinking of you. Had to take care of myself. Made a mess all over my bed.*

He frowns at the words, not sure if he should send them to her. Before he can talk himself into deleting the words, he sends it. Luke stares at the screen in horror. What if she—

Her reply comes back faster than he expected.

*Glad to hear it! I woke up thinking of you and had to take care of myself too. What are we like!*

He takes a mouthful of coffee before he replies. This is all new to him, and he's terrified of saying the wrong thing.

*Can I see you after work?*

*Of course. I'm on till eleven. It's going to be a looooooong day.*

*I'll pick you up from the bar if you want?*

*I'd like that. Have fun at rehearsals. Damn! And now I'm thinking of you being all sexy playing your guitar. Yeah, it's going to be a looooooong day x*

Luke grins widely as he reads the message. He's never been called sexy before. It's been mentioned in magazines and on social media or whatever, but he didn't take any of it seriously. He's famous. It sort of comes with the territory. But, this feels so much different. And he likes it.

Then he notices the kiss at the end of her message. He quickly writes his reply, ending with a kiss of his own.

*Can't wait to see you x*

He sends the message and puts down the phone. Today will be a good day. He's got rehearsals in about an hour, then he'll see Maeve later.

He's still smiling as he cleans his teeth, then grabs his coat and keys to his car.

Tate opens the door to his studio and frowns at him. 'What are you smiling about?'

'Nothing.'

Tate steps aside letting Luke inside. 'You want a drink?'

'Coffee would be great.' Tate hands him a cup and he fills it with coffee from the machine. 'Are Dillon and Gregg here?'

Tate shakes his head, as he hands him the milk. 'Nope. You're the first.' Tate leans against the closed fridge and smirks at him. 'You good?'

'Yeah. I am.'

'You look it. Did something happen last night with Maeve?'

'No, well, not exactly. Maybe.'

Tate leans on the counter and frowns at him. 'What do you mean by not exactly, maybe?'

'I was alone, and it was this morning.'

Tate grins widely. 'I'm taking it you haven't done that for a while, huh?'

Luke shakes his head. He used to feel embarrassed talking about stuff like this with the guys. They'd always been open with each other, but he just nodded along in the background, too afraid or embarrassed to get involved. He's still not overly comfortable, but it's getting easier. 'No. Pippa wouldn't let me.'

Tate's blue eyes harden as he sips his coffee. Luke knows he's taking time to calm down. He hates talking about her and what she did, but he needs to. Maeve is right. He's got nothing to be embarrassed or ashamed about.

Tate places his coffee down on the table and does the last thing Luke ever thought he'd do. Tate pulls him into a hug.

Tate has hugged him before, but it tended to be a quick slap on the back kind of hug. This is different. He's not letting Luke go. When Tate is still hugging him a few seconds later, he hugs him back.

Eventually, he's released, and Tate turns away from him. Luke could swear he rubs his face, but dismisses that thought. Tate doesn't cry. Then again, he's not usually one for hugging people either.

'How are Chloe and Brandon,' he asks, trying to take the attention away from whatever is going on with Tate.

'Yeah. All good. Her sister is visiting for a few days so I'm keeping out of the way.'

When he turns around again, he holds out a packet of biscuits to Luke. 'Thanks.' He takes one and sits on the couch beside Tate. 'I was thinking of getting a camper.'

Tate slowly lowers his cup and frowns at him. 'You what?'

'A camper. Maeve got me thinking. I used to go camping a lot when I was a kid. I just thought it might be nice to do it again. Maybe with Maeve. I don't know. It was just an idea.'

Tate nods slowly. 'Why the hell not? If it's something you want, then fuck it! Go for it!'

'You don't think it's a stupid idea?'

Tate places his cup on the table and turns around to face him. 'No! Of course not! Sounds like a fucking great idea to be honest. It would probably do you the world of good to get away from everything, even for a few days. And I think it's finally time you spent some of your hard earned Euro on you.'

'You're right. I'll do it!'

250

'Good.' He stands up and grabs his jacket.

''Where are you going?'

'We are going camper shopping.'

'What? I didn't mean now. We're meant to be rehearsing.'

'Ah fuck that! We've got that in the bag. A few hours off won't kill us.'

'But what about Dillon and Gregg?'

'They can come too.' He pours Luke's coffee into a travel mug and hands it back to him. 'Road trip time!'

# Maeve

'You know I'm placing my life in your hands. If I fall, I'm going to be seriously unimpressed.'

Luke turns her to the left, his grip on her hand tightening. 'I promise I won't let you fall. We're nearly there. No peeking.'

She lets him guide her out of the elevator to what sounds like the garage of his apartment. Luke grips her shoulders, pulling her to a stop. 'Okay. Stand there for a second and no peeking.'

'I'm not peeking. What am I not peeking at?'

He laughs and pulls off the blindfold. 'Well, what do you think?'

Maeve screeches when she sees the shiny blue VW camper in front of them. 'Oh! My! God! What did you do?'

'I bought a camper. '

'You bought it! It's yours?'

He nods, looking adorably pleased with himself. 'I couldn't stop thinking about our conversation on the beach. I hate talking about money and stuff like that, but I can afford it, and it's not like I spend anything on myself really. I tend to invest, instead of going mad on my spending. I wasn't going to do it, but I mentioned it to Tate a few days ago, and he dragged me out with the guys to look at them.'

'It's beautiful. Oh I'm so excited for you!'

'Thanks. It was actually really nice to treat myself like this. I can't remember the last time I did that. It's not new, but it's in great condition.'

Maeve slides open the side door and climbs inside the van. It's immaculate. 'It looks brand new. You should never buy new cars anyway. You lose a fortune as soon as you drive it out of the garage.'

Luke leans on the open door and laughs. 'You know, that's pretty much exactly what Dillon always says.'

'Well he's right. Damn, that felt weird saying that! Didn't think I'd agree with Dillon.'

'I know what you mean, but he does have good ideas from time to time.'

'How about we don't tell him that? I think his head is big enough! So, when are you going to try this baby out?'

He climbs in and sits on the bench seat beside her. 'Well, I was kind of hoping to give it a go next time you have a few days off? If you want to?'

'Me? You want me to come too?'

'Of course! I don't think I would have even considered getting one until you mentioned it. I'd like you to help me christen it. I mean by taking it out!' he adds quickly, his cheeks reddening. 'I wasn't implying anything else.'

'Hey! I get what you're saying. It's okay. And I'd love to christen it with you. I'm off Wednesday til Friday.'

'As in tomorrow?'

'Bit too soon? We could do next week if that's better for you.'

He shakes his head. 'No. You know what? Tomorrow sounds perfect. If you're sure?'

'Of course I am. Ooh - this is so exciting! Where are you thinking of going?'

He pauses and leans back in the seat. 'Ah. Didn't think of that part. We're not going to have many options this time of year and at such short notice.'

She shuffles up beside him and lifts his arm so she can lean against him. 'Okay, so where did you go when you were a kid?'

'Galway mainly. Do you fancy going there? I can try a few places to see if they can fit us in last minute.'

'That sounds perfect, Luke.' She takes his hand and gets out of the camper, pulling him back towards the elevator. 'What are you doing?'

'Time's ticking by, Luke. We have a lot of packing to do!'

## Luke

After walking through the apartment one last time, Luke turns on the alarm and locks the door. He barely slept a wink last night, but it had nothing to do with nightmares. It was excitement. Pure childlike excitement.

After a few phone calls, he'd found a campsite in Connemara that was willing to let them stay for a few days.

Just Maeve and him, at the beach, in his camper. Who needs posh hotels and exotic countries. This is what he loves, what he's wanted for so long. No fuss. No fancy outfits, or stifling restaurants.

And he can't wait!

There's barely any traffic, so he gets to the pub in about twenty minutes. He drives under the bridge and rounds the corner, instantly spotting Maeve in the pub car park. She waves at him, jumping excitedly as he pulls in beside her.

Luke gets out to open the door for her, but she's already in and strapped in before he gets around the front.

'You couldn't wait for me to open the door for you?'

She grins as she slips on her sunglasses. 'Don't have time for that. Hit the road, rock star!'

'Whatever you say.' He pulls out of the car park, then glances over at her as she taps her fingers on her legs. 'Are you okay? You seem jumpy?'

'Caffeine my dear Luke. Couldn't sleep a wink, so I may have had two large mugs of coffee. Which has woken me up, but just to warn you, there will be quite a few unscheduled toilet stops as a result.'

'Why couldn't you sleep?'

'Okay, don't laugh, but I'm really freaking excited! It's ridiculous, I know.'

'Can I let you to a secret? I didn't sleep either. I was too excited.'

She reaches across and squeezes his hand. 'Well I have to say that's a pretty good sign. It would put a downer on the whole trip if one of us was dreading it.'

'Yeah, I think it would. Thanks for doing this with me. It's been a dream of mine for years. I can't believe I'm finally doing it.'

'Another page in the notebook filled?'

'A page? No, this is more than just a page. This trip will fill a lot of pages. Getting the camper, going away in it... with you.'

'Well if I had a notebook, this trip would be in it too. I'm really looking forward to a few days just you and me.'

He couldn't agree more. Going to the UK was great, but that was work. He was surrounded by assistants, security, the rest of the band. This is just the two of them, and that's the part he's looking forward to more than anything.

'Can I ask you something strange?'

'Of course.'

'I know in the UK it was a given you'd be recognised and fans would be falling at your feet - rightly so. But what happens on a day to day basis? Up to now, we haven't had any fan encounters.'

'Yeah well I've been avoiding bringing you places where I'd be with loads of people. Being recognised is part of what I do, but it's a part I'm not entirely comfortable about. I'd prefer to keep hidden as much as I can instead of having to meet people.

'I'm not being rude to my fans. They're the reason I can do what I love. It's the intense screaming ones I try to avoid.'

'Ah. Yeah, I get that. I've seen it at concerts from time to time. The *knicker throwing screamers*. Downright terrifying.'

'Yeah, definitely terrifying,' he admits, laughing. 'I can't handle that. But if I am spotted, I'll deal with it. I think I'm actually being avoided a bit since the whole Pippa issue.'

'Well, if it helps, I'll be the face of our camping party. This is about you getting away and relaxing. Stay hidden if that makes you more comfortable.'

'Thanks, but I don't think there's going to be a hoard of Broken fans at a campsite in Connemara on the off chance one of us shows up. I think we'll be safe enough.'

# 30

## Maeve

Luke passes Maeve a plate, then she helps herself to a sausage from the barbecue and places it in the bread roll. After smothering it with ketchup and grilled onions, she takes a bite and groans. 'That's the best damn thing I've ever tasted,' she mutters with her mouth full.

Luke grins and takes a drink of beer before tucking into his own dinner. This is probably the most relaxed she's seen him... well, ever. Getting away like this was absolutely the best thing they could have done.

It's the end of the camping season so most of the tourists have headed home. Apart from an elderly couple in a caravan, and a few tents, they have the place to themselves.

It couldn't be more perfect. She has no problem with people recognising Luke, but she wanted him all to herself for this trip.

Selfish yes, especially considering he's a celebrity. But she wanted this to be about them. About Luke doing something he's wanted to do for a long time, but was unable to.

And so far, so good.

Since the minute he picked her up from the pub, he's been smiling. Not his reserved smile, but a truly beautiful smile she could never tire of seeing. He's genuinely happy and she loves it.

Rock star Luke Daly is in old combats, trainers, and a hoody, sitting on the grass cooking sausages on a barbecue. Fucking stunning rock star Luke Daly!

She thought the *oh my God, would you look at him* level of attraction would wear off at some stage, but nope! If anything, it's growing in intensity. As more and more of the *real* Luke breaks out, her attraction to him grows.

She's in serious trouble. She's fallen for him - hook, line, and sinker. She's a goner. Completely head over heels in love with this incredible man.

Which is amazing apart from one small but vital detail.

How does she tell him?

When does she tell him?

This trip would have been the perfect time, but she's having second thoughts. Their relationship is going from strength to strength. She was even invited to Tate and Chloe's wedding next week, and not as a plus one. She saw the invitation. It was addressed to Luke and Maeve.

Seeing their names side by side like that on the invitation, to the wedding of one of his close friends, had been a bit of a moment for her. A major one.

She knew they were a couple, but seeing the invitation had brought it home to her. After everything Luke had been through over the last few years, he was finally healing. Finally at a place where he could trust someone again and let them into his life. And she could not be more over the moon that he picked her.

He looks over at her and smiles as he points to the corner of his mouth. 'You got a bit of ketchup on your face.'

She wipes it away, then licks it off her finger. It wasn't meant in a seductive way, but his eyes lock on to what she's doing, his lips parting ever so slightly, before he turns his attention back to the fire.

'How many more of those have you got?' she asks, nodding to the packet of sausages.

She knows Luke wants to have sex with her, but he's holding himself back. As much as she wants to initiate things with him, she's not going to. She may have given him a nudge previously, but it feels wrong doing it in this circumstance.

She knows it wouldn't be anything like what happened with Pippa. Not in any universe. But she's not going to nudge him towards having sex with her.

Pippa had used him in the worst possible way. Every single part of sex was out of his control. It was something he was forced to endure to keep his wife happy.

She wants to be with him. Wants to take that step with him. But it has to be taken *with* him when he decides he's ready, and not a moment before.

Luke checks the bag beside him. 'I've got about a dozen or so bread rolls and about twice that many sausages. Why? You planning on polishing off the lot?'

She shrugs and takes another bite before answering. 'Might do. Why? You got a problem with that?'

He shakes his head. 'No. Not at all. No way I'm getting in between you and food!'

'Right answer.'

Luke finishes his dinner and disappears into the camper, returning with a large cheesecake, some clean plates and a couple of forks. 'Should I bother cutting it up, or give it to you like this with a fork?'

Maeve sticks out her tongue, then takes the cake from him and pats the ground beside her. 'Smart arse! But we can dig into it like this. Less washing up.'

Luke sits beside her, and they help themselves to forkfuls of strawberry cheesecake, as they listen to the waves lapping gently on the sand at the other side of the grassy bank.

'This place is amazing, Luke. Thanks for inviting me along.'

He grins at her and scoops more cheesecake onto his fork. 'Thanks for agreeing to come. I wasn't sure if you'd be interested. To be honest, I thought you'd think it was a silly idea.'

'Silly? Why?'

He shrugs, and when his shoulders drop a little, she knows why. 'We're not all like that, Luke. Some girls actually do like getting back to nature like this. And luckily for me, I am one of those girls.'

Maeve shuffles closer to him, relieved when he doesn't tense at the contact or, even worse, move away. 'I used to go camping a lot when I was a kid. We'd stay near the beach like this and stay up till all hours reading and playing.'

'And eating.'

She elbows him in the ribs and laughs. 'Yes. It's the sea air. Makes me hungry.'

'Me too,' he says, helping himself to more cake. He pushes the plate away when he's eaten it. 'But no more. I'll be sick.'

Maeve moves it to the other side of her, then lies against his arm. Luke tucks her in beside him, holding her close. He slowly traces his fingers along her arm, following the lines of her tattoo.

'Do you want to go for a walk before we head to bed?' he asks, as he continues to trace his fingers along her arm.

'That's a great idea. If I sit here much longer, I'll be asleep on you in no time at all.'

He gets up, then helps her to her feet, but keeps hold of her hand as they walk down to the beach. Maeve kicks off her shoes so she can paddle in the sea.

Then she gets an idea.

She holds out her hand. 'You going to join me or what?'

'In the sea?'

'Oh yeah. In the sea. I want to dance with you.'

Luke looks around, but there's no one else there. The other campers are tucked in for the night. It's just them and an empty beach.

She turns to face the horizon and holds out her hand, hoping he won't leave her out here like a twit.

But she should have known better than to even think he'd do that. Luke takes her hand and turns her to face him. His trainers are on the beach with his hoody, leaving him in his combats and a tank top. Not in any way sexy. 'Can you dance with no music?'

His smile is sure and confident, and really fucking gorgeous. 'I've always got music in my head.'

'Is that right!' This may have been her idea, but now she's standing in the sea with Luke, the waves lapping around their legs, she's not so sure she remembers the steps. He surprises her by spinning her around, then pulls her against him, pressing her back to his chest.

This is ridiculous. It's her choreography. She should know what to do, but it's all gone. He rests his hand on her hip and the other grips her hand.

When he sings she could have come right then and there. He's singing right in her ear, his deep voice sending goosebumps scattering over her skin. He stops singing, his lips brushing against her ear. 'Please dance with me.'

'Any time.' It's all the reply she can get out. She's so unbelievably turned on she can't think straight.

He continues singing and something in her brain clicks on again. She wants to dance with him like this. Luke fares better than she does as they dance together in the shallows. His movements are fluid, every single step made perfectly.

She, on the other hand, is like a love struck teenager drooling over the sexy rock star. He effortlessly lifts her out of the water, his powerful body holding her high above him, before slowly lowering her again.

But instead of the usual finish, he doesn't put her back on the ground. He keeps her at eye level so he can kiss her. 'Are you cold? You've got goosebumps?'

She shakes her head. 'No, not at all.' What she is, is very turned on.

He opens his mouth to say something, but stops himself, frowning deeply.

'What is it?'

Whatever he was going to say gets turfed aside. 'Nothing.'

He takes her hand and leads her out of the water back to their shoes.

She wishes he'd stop holding back like he is. He's so close. She knows he is. All he needs to do is say the words and she'll take care of the rest. Or at least guide him. Help him. Whatever he needs. All he has to do is tell her that's what he wants.

But something tells her that might not happen. He could spend the next who knows how long talking himself out of it.

## Luke

He's nervous. Excited mainly, but nerves are always hiding under the surface. Part of the nerves are his fault. He's overthinking things again. What he needs to do is take a deep breath and calm down.

Easier said than done.

He wants to have sex with Maeve tonight. He really, really, wants to. When he was dancing in the sea with her, he'd been tempted to tell her, to at least give her some sign that's what he wants. But he froze.

Chickened out.

And he doesn't know why. It's Maeve. She cares about him and he's in love with her. There's nothing to be scared about.

He wants to do this for her. With her. And he wants it for himself.

But it has to be amazing for her. It's not like she hasn't waited long enough for him to get to this stage. She's been nothing but patient and encouraging. She's never forced him to do anything he wasn't comfortable with.

He scrubs his hand over his face and groans aloud. If he's not careful he's going to think himself out of the mood. Maeve will be back any minute. She went over to the toilet block for a shower, then she'll be back to spend the night with him.

He pushes open the door of the camper and climbs out, suddenly feeling like he's suffocating in there. Only wearing his boxers, Luke paces the grass beside the van, concentrating on breathing in and out, without throwing up.

He's being downright pathetic. He knows that, but it doesn't help relax him. It's sex. People have sex all the time. It's a perfectly normal part of life.

A part of life he's terrified of.

Maeve hasn't done anything to hurt him. And it's not like they haven't explored each other's bodies. So why is he getting hung up about this part?

Before he can stop himself, his attention goes to the leather bands around his wrists. He unbuckles both and looks at the thick scars around his wrists.

That's why.

But Maeve isn't Pippa. She's nothing like her. Every other time she's touched him he's loved it. Why would this be any different?'

Maybe because he's going to initiate it. He's going to make the first move, to show her what she means to him.

To show her how much he loves her.

He's not going to tell her how he feels about her. Not yet. It's too soon for him to get carried away.

'Hey. What are you doing?'

He smiles at her as she walks over to the van, wearing a pair of shorts and a strappy top. 'You're beautiful.'

He could kick himself for saying those words. Talk about corny, but his mouth just ran away, without any thought for his embarrassment levels.

But instead of laughing at him, Maeve smiles widely and kisses him on the cheek. 'Thank you.' She tucks herself under his arm and sighs contentedly, as she looks out at the sea. 'It's stunning here, Luke.'

'I wouldn't want to be here with anyone else.' His mouth is well and truly taking control of him tonight. But Maeve doesn't seem to mind. Quite the opposite in fact. She hugs him close, wrapping her arms around his waist.

'Maeve?'

When she lifts her head to look up at him, Luke kisses her. He combs his fingers through her hair as his confidence grows, any doubt quickly disappearing when his tongue finds hers and she moans against his mouth.

He stops thinking and lets his body take control. He lifts her, loving the way she wraps her legs around his waist as their kiss picks up pace. He carries her back to the van, and lies her on the bed, before closing and locking the door behind them.

He kisses her again, but instead of keeping his body away from hers, he lowers against her, propping himself up on one arm so he doesn't hurt her. Maeve cups the side of his face, her thumb stroking his cheek as they kiss.

'Maeve?'

She looks him in the eye, the flush to her cheeks and swollen lips so stunning.

'I'd like to...' The words fade away, but he forces himself to continue and meets her eyes again. 'I want to be with you Maeve. I mean properly with you. If that's what you want?'

Her smile lights up the small space inside the van. 'I'd really like that. Do you want me to do anything or...'

'Just do what you want. I trust you.'

## 31

*Maeve*

*Oh my God! This is really happening!*

Hearing that he wants to have sex with her is one thing, but when he said he trusts her, that nearly meant more to her. She's wanted this for so long, but now it's happening she's suddenly unsure of herself.

Before she met Luke, sex hadn't meant too much to her. If she had sex with someone she didn't tend to dwell on it for long afterwards. She can't remember even having to think too much about it beforehand.

This is so very different in every way. It's more than sex. This is Luke giving her a piece of himself. A piece he's kept protected. A piece that was hurt and abused instead of being loved and cherished.

And now he wants to share that piece of himself with her.

Her magnificent boyfriend lies back on the bed in the van and gives her a look that had goosebumps scattering across her skin. The bars piercing his nipples catch the moonlight streaming through the skylight as he breaths steadily.

'Are you all right?'

She smiles at him and nods. 'Me? Yes. Absolutely! Why?'

'You look nervous.'

She lies down beside him, her hand running over his chest. 'There's a chance I might be. But it's a good nervous. A really good one.'

'Me too. But it's a good nervous. I want this Maeve.' He pushes to his elbow and smiles down at her. 'I want you.'

When Luke kisses her, Maeve groans to herself. He is hands down the sexiest man she's ever met without even having to try. Just being himself he manages to take her breath away.

His hand combs through her hair, brushing it back from her face, then moving down her body as his kiss growing in confidence.

The air inside the van grows heavy as their bodies move against each other. Luke's hips grind against her, his dick rubbing along her stomach as he moves hypnotically on top of her.

Any of the nerves she may have felt initially, quickly dissipate. She wants more of Luke. She needs more of him. Instincts take over, the raw sexual energy too difficult to hold back or ignore.

Maeve rolls over, kissing Luke as she straddles him. It takes less than a second to realise the enormity of her mistake. She didn't mean it. Far from it, but she just got carried away in the moment.

Luke turns to stone beneath her, his breathing quickening, but not in a good way. Far from it.

She quickly scrambles off him, but it's too late. She's scared him. More than that. He's absolutely terrified. His eyes are wide and his face has lost all colour.

'I'm sorry, Luke! I'm so sorry. I didn't mean to... I'm sorry.'

He sits up and shuffles back from her. 'It wasn't your fault. I'm sorry. I just… it was…' In a move that's completely out of character, he slams his fist against the side of the van, before burying his face in his hands. 'Fuck!'

'Hey. Look at me. Luke, please look at me.'

He drops his hands to his knees and looks at her. 'This is why I've been talking myself out of doing this for ages. I can't, Maeve. I'm fucked up!'

Two curses in the space of as many minutes, but she doesn't mind. She'd prefer he was angry than timid and withdrawn. 'You're far from fucked up, Luke. I shouldn't have done what I did.'

'You straddled me. It's not like you were doing anything wrong. This is me, Maeve. My issue, not yours.'

She takes his hand, hanging on when he tries to pull it away. 'It's not your issue, Luke. It's ours, okay. You and me. I want this to happen between us. I got carried away and I shouldn't have.'

'You shouldn't have to plan every move, think about everything you're doing in case I freak out. I don't know much about how it should be, but I know it shouldn't be like that.'

'It's about making sure the person you're with enjoys it as much as possible. And I want you to enjoy it. You said you trust me, right?'

'Of course I do.'

'So will you let me try again? Will you let me show you how it should be?'

He frowns at her. 'You really want to try again?'

'Of course I do, silly! Please. I promise I won't get too carried away this time.'

'Do you not think I've ruined the moment?'

Maeve shuffles closer to him, cupping the side of his face in her hand. 'The thing with moments is, there's always another one.' She kisses him. 'And another after that.'

'How did I manage to find someone like you?'

'I am quite a find, true. But so are you, Luke.'

She waits, leaving him to his thoughts for a minute. She'll never forgive herself for messing this up for him, or for them. All she can do is hope he can trust her enough to try again.

Something changes in his face as he looks at her. Something that says she hasn't blown this for good.

He wraps his hand around the back of her head, pulling her closer to kiss her. But this time he lowers her onto the bed as he kisses her.

Terrified of taking things too fast again, she tries keep her hands to herself, but it doesn't feel right. It's too impersonal.

'You can touch me. I promise I won't freak out again.'

When he groans as she wraps her arms around him, she relaxes into it again.

His naked body presses against hers, his arousal back and digging into her thigh. Her hands run down his back to his ass, squeezing the firm flesh as she lifts her hips, slowly grinding against him.

He stops kissing her, then sucks in a breath. His face is inches from hers. His focus is on her eyes as she moves against him, rubbing his dick against her leg.

His hard body moves, rubbing against her in the best way. They keep that up for a few minutes, just rubbing against each other, their sweat soaked skin creating an amazing friction she can't get enough of.

Maeve moans as Luke adjusts his hips, lifting and repositioning so he's resting over her pussy.

'Are you okay?'

God this man is incredible! She should be asking him that, not the other way around. 'I'm more than okay. That feels amazing, Luke. Kiss me.'

He lowers again, his kiss a little more sure and confident than before. His pierced tongue pushes into her mouth, followed by the tip of his dick in her pussy. Maeve gasps against his mouth, as he holds his position. He's barely in her, but it feels so good.

Encouraging him, she squeezes his ass, but doesn't move herself. She'll stick to his pace, even if it's driving her crazy. She wants to feel all of him in her. Needs to feel it.

Luke takes the hint, moving his hips forwards then pulling back, and pushing forward again. Each push of his hips drives his dick deeper, then out again, before going deeper still.

He stops moving and looks at her. 'Still okay?'

'Oh I'm very okay. You feel incredible, Luke. Are you okay?'

He nods, then smiles. 'Oh I'm very okay,' he says, repeating her words.

In the dim interior of the camper she can't make out a lot of his face, but she does know his eyes are watering. She wipes her thumb under his eye, feeling dampness.

'What's wrong?'

'Sorry. I never thought I'd get to this stage again, you know. And I'm glad it's with you. I wouldn't want to be here with anyone else.'

Maeve rubs her thumb along his cheek. 'I wouldn't want to be here with anyone other than you, Luke. Be with me Luke. Just you and me, here and now.'

He flashes her one hell of a sexy smile before kissing her. She has no idea whether it's the dancer in him, or his natural rhythm, but his hips are downright dangerous.

Each time he thrusts into her, he seems to hit somewhere new, each sensation mixing with the next, until Maeve has no idea what he's doing. All she knows is that she never wants him to stop.

The fresh scent of his cologne and his sweat is intoxicating. His tight muscles relaxing and contracting against her feels better than she imagined it would. Everything about this moment is perfect.

Luke straightens his arms, pushing himself upright over her. Maeve nearly comes when he looks down, watching his dick sliding into her pussy. Holy shit, that's hot! 'Keep going Luke. I'm so close.'

Clearly turned on by the sight of his dick pushing into her, his pace quickens. He places his hand on her waist, slowly moving down towards her pussy.

She wants him to touch her, to play with her, but he's way ahead of her. His thumb circles her clit, rubbing against her in perfect rhythm with his hips.

The air inside the camper is heavy with the scent of their sweat, the sound of their slick flesh slapping together mixed with their panted breaths.

Maeve's orgasm hits like a punch, tearing the breath from her lungs as the sensations explode through her body. She has no idea if she screams, or if there's any air left to scream. Every touch, every thrust is amplified as the pleasure takes over.

Maeve opens her eyes, desperate to see him come. Wanting to see this stunning man fall apart for the first time in too long.

He doesn't hang on for long, falling forward, barely catching himself before he lands on her. The orgasm rolls through him, his muscles tensing as he comes. Luke's groan of pleasure is the sexiest thing she's heard.

He pulses inside her, again and again, until he stills and shudders. 'Fuck!'

Maeve laughs and rubs his arms. 'I hope that's a good fuck.'

He lifts his head and grins at her. 'Yeah. So good.' He slowly pulls out of her, watching as he slides out of her. She's just come, but seeing him do that has her wanting to go again.

Luke collapses beside her then grabs her, pulling her onto his chest. 'What are you doing?'

'I want you to lie on me.'

'But what about before?'

'Like you said, that was a moment. This is another one. I want to feel you lying on me.'

Maeve rests her head on his chest, listening to the rapid beat of his heart. Now she's the one crying.

'Thank you Maeve.'

'For what?' She doesn't want him to know she's being emotional about all this, mainly because she doesn't know why she's being emotional.

'For the best orgasm I've ever had.'

'Oh you're more than welcome for that.'

'Look at me.' She lifts her head off his chest and looks at him. 'I'm the emotional crier in this relationship.'

'I'm sorry. I thought I'd blown it when I lay on you before. Now we're doing this and I... well, it means a lot Luke.'

He wipes her eyes. '*You* mean a lot Maeve. I'm sorry I freaked out earlier. It wasn't you. My head just went back there for a few seconds. I'm here with you, Maeve. Only you. I hope you know that.'

'Of course I do.'

'Good.' He kisses her forehead, then hugs her again. 'Was I... was it okay? For you.'

'Are you freaking kidding me! Yes, Luke. Abso-fucking-lutely yes!'

His chest rises as he takes a deep breath. 'Can I hold you like this for a bit?'

Maeve kisses his chest before lying back down on him. 'You never have to ask.'

# 32

Luke

'Fuck me!' He doesn't curse, or at least hardly ever does. Tate and Dillon do enough of that to more than compensate for Gregg and himself. But at this moment he can't find anything else to say.

Maeve is waiting for him, propped up against the bar talking to Mike as he restocks the bottles. She's so beautiful. Luke has always thought that. She caught his eye in school, but the woman she's become today takes his breath away.

She turns to face him, and when she smiles he is nearly brought to tears. Which is pathetic, but he'd challenge anyone not to be floored by her.

The long flowing halter neck dress is the exact same shade of purple as in her hair, which hangs in soft curls over one shoulder.

'Did you just curse Mr Daly?'

'I think I did,' he says, finally reconnecting with his feet again. Luke stands in front of her and smiles like some giddy teenager. 'You are beautiful.'

'I hope so. A lot of work went into this,' she says, holding her arms to the side and spinning. 'I'm glad you approve.'

He takes her hand, rubbing his thumb over the back of it. 'I'm one lucky man.'

She pulls him closer to whisper in his ear. 'I'd appreciate if you showed me exactly how lucky you are later.'

'Enough!' Mike shouts, covering his ears. 'I don't need to hear this.'

She reaches across the bar and smacks him on the arm. 'Idiot. So are you ready to go?'

Luke nods. 'The car is outside.'

'You're not driving?'

'No. Tate booked cars for everyone. I don't think he wants a few dozen cars messing up his driveway.'

'Ah. That makes sense.'

Andy opens the door of the SUV for Maeve, then Luke slides in beside her and takes her hand. 'Did I tell you how stunning you are?'

'I think you might have. Thank you. Between you and me I'm a little nervous about this.'

'You don't get nervous about anything.'

'Yeah, but this is a big deal. Like an epic deal. I want to do you proud.'

'Hey, you never have to worry about that. And it's not like it's the first time you've done something with the band. You went to the UK with us. This is nothing like that.'

'It's Tate and Chloe's wedding. The guys are your family, Luke. I can handle all the fame and celebrity stuff. No problem there. But I never expected to be invited to Tate's wedding.'

'He likes you. Of course you'd be invited. And it's not going to be a mad big wedding. They're not like that. It's his family, Chloe's family and a few close friends. That's it. I mean one of the guests is his horse! You can't get less formal than that.'

She turns her head slowly towards him. 'Did you say horse?'

'Yep. Jove will be there.'

'Well I have to say this will be the first wedding I've been to with a horse as a guest.'

## Maeve

She wasn't kidding when she said she's nervous about today. It's the intimacy of the event that's making her nervous.

The band are international superstars. Being a guest at the lead singer's wedding is a big deal. She knows it's closed off to the press, but it's not the world she's worried about messing up in front of. It's Luke.

But judging by his reaction when he walked into the bar, she's off to a really good start.

But he's not letting the side down himself. It may be a casual wedding as far as a celebrity wedding is concerned, but that didn't mean Chloe was going to go too casual. The four guys are all wearing navy suits which, according to Chloe, is her favourite thing to see Tate wearing.

And the woman has good taste. Luke and the suit are a match made in sex heaven. It's going to be a long day waiting to slowly undress him. She has to stop herself from unbuttoning the waistcoat to uncover that hard chest underneath. To free his thick dick from the trousers.

'Stop it!'

'What's wrong?'

She squirms in the seat. 'Oh nothing. I'm mentally undressing you and now I'm really horny.' The look he gives her has her laughing out loud. 'What? You asked.'

'Yeah. I guess I did.'

'What do you expect? Look at you being all handsome. I'm only human.'

'Are you going to be able to hang on until later?'

'It depends.'

'On what?'

'On whether you have time to deal with the situation before we get there.'

She says it as a joke, expecting him to laugh and for nothing to happen. But yet again, he manages to surprise her.

'Pull in Andy.'

'What?'

'Pull the car in somewhere private.'

Andy turns around in the passenger seat and frowns at the two of them. 'Ah. I get you.' He nods to the driver. 'You heard him.'

'What are you doing?' Maeve hisses, as the SUV moves off the main road to a forest path, winding through the trees until they're hidden from the road.

'Dealing with it,' he says with a seriously sexy grin.

'Here?'

Without having to be asked, Andy and the driver get out, walking away from the car.

Maeve is still trying to process the fact he's considering doing something like this - especially in the car, with Andy and a random driver outside.

'You better take your dress off or push it up.'

'Are you seriously going to do this now?'

'You don't want me to?'

'No! I mean yes! I do. Fuck, I really, really, do.'

'Well how about you stop talking and let me sort you out.'

'Whatever you say.' Maeve carefully lifts the bottom of her dress up and out of the way.

She has no idea where this assertive Luke is coming from, but she likes it a lot. She likes it so much, she actually does need him to deal with her, before they go to the wedding.

Maeve slides back against the door and shrugs her panties down her legs, kicking them off. But instead of using his fingers, Luke leans over and licks her.

'Holy shit, Luke!'

He looks at her from between her legs and grins. 'I know we've got company outside anyway, but maybe keep it down a bit.'

'Easier said than done. And why are you stopping?'

Luke licks her again, his pierced tongue sending shivers through her, over and over again, as it rubs against her clit.

To stop herself from grabbing his hair and messing it up before the wedding, she holds onto the handle over the door, hanging on tight.

All men should have their tongues pierced, if this is what it feels like when they lick you out. 'Oh God Luke! Press harder there. Please...'

He does, sending her rearing back off the car seat. His hand slides up her leg, holding it to the side so he can get his tongue in deeper, pressing the stud in his tongue against her, driving her closer to the edge.

His deep brown eyes look up at her from between her legs, and it's so unbelievably sexy. Then he fucks her faster, his tongue deep in her pussy, while his thumb slides over her clit.

'I'm so close. Don't stop!'

She writhes on the seat, gripping the handle above her head so tight she's surprised it doesn't break off in her hand.

Then he swaps over, his fingers in her pussy, and that amazing tongue teasing her clit, massaging it until she's breathless.

She tries to stay quiet as she comes, she really does, but some things are impossible. Luke can hold himself responsible for the loud and very unladylike *FUCK* that tears from her as she comes.

When she opens her eyes, Luke is leaning over her, smiling. 'That wasn't quiet.'

She licks her lips and uncurls her fingers from around the handle. 'Totally your fault. Oh fuck! Wow!'

'So did I manage to deal with it okay?'

'Eh, yeah. And don't ever use the word *okay* with what you just did. And for the record, that tongue piercing needs a health warning with it.'

He laughs, coming across a little embarrassed. 'So that dare paid off then?'

'Oh yeah. Best dare ever. Remind me to thank the guys for that.'

He tilts his head to the side, but doesn't say anything for a few seconds. 'I love when you're like this.'

'Like what?'

'After I've been with you. Your cheeks are flushed, and you get this sort of dazed look in your eyes. And I really like hearing you come.

'I know it's going to come across so big-headed, but knowing that I did that to you. That I was able to make you come like that... I don't know, maybe it's pride or something like that. But it makes me happy.'

Maeve cups the side of his face, running her thumb along his cheek. 'Only you have been able to do that for me. That intensity is totally down to you.

'And knowing you can pleasure someone else, isn't big headed. It's sweet to know you care about that. A lot of people want to sort themselves out, and don't care about the other person. You do, and that's such an amazing thing. So, do you want me to deal with you now?'

'I'd love you to, but if I'm late Tate will kill me. Besides, I didn't do that so you could return the favour. I wanted to do that for you. And it's not like I didn't enjoy it. I did, a lot. Every time I look at you today I'm going to remember being in between your legs, tasting you.'

Maeve groans. 'I mean what exactly are you trying to do to me? We have to go and mingle with Tate's family and you're saying stuff like that to me.'

The smile he gives her is more mischievous than she's seen before. 'I could say I'm sorry, but I wouldn't mean it.'

'You know what? I'm liking this cocky Luke that's come out to play today. Where's he been up to now?'

He shrugs. 'Hiding. Scared. Not anymore though.'

Maeve pulls him into a hug. 'No more hiding and definitely no more being scared.

'I love you, Maeve.'

It's probably only a few seconds, but when Maeve pushes back from him it feels like minutes have passed. She looks at his face, searching for some hint that she might have misheard.

But she knows she didn't.

Firstly, Luke would never say something he didn't mean. That's not how he is. And second, he looks downright terrified.

'You love me?'

He nods, but doesn't say anything.

'Are you sure?' It's a ridiculous thing to say, but she never expected him to say that to her. Hoped that maybe one day he would, but not yet. Years down the line, but certainly not yet.

'I wouldn't say it if I wasn't sure. You don't have to say it back, that's not why I told you. I just wanted you to know. Anyway, you better get dressed again. We probably should go.'

He picks her panties off the floor of the SUV, but instead of taking them, she stares at them in his hand for a minute before looking at him. 'I love you.'

'You do?'

'Yeah. I do. I've been in love with you for weeks, but I didn't think you felt the same, so I kept it to myself. I wanted you to get there in your own time.'

'I've felt this way for weeks too, but I didn't want to scare you off.'

'Seriously!'

He nods, then kisses her, and it's so different to every other time he's kissed her. There's no hesitation. No second guessing, or holding himself back. This is confident Luke kissing the woman he loves. Her.

Ignoring her previous efforts not to mess his hair before the wedding, she drags her fingers through the thick locks, pulling him closer.

Both gasping for breath, they break the kiss and look at each other. 'I love you, Maeve.'

She smiles, her whole face hurting from the enormity of the smile. 'I love you, Luke.'

'As much as I want to stay here, or actually go somewhere more comfortable with you, we really better go.'

'Yeah. We probably should. There's just one small issue?'

'What?'

'You're going to have to give me back my underwear.'

*Luke*

He thought today would be difficult. He hoped it wouldn't, but the last wedding he went to was his own. All the signs were already waving in his face at that stage.

That day had been stressful and horrible from the minute he woke up. You should enjoy your wedding, but he'd hated every minute of his.

This wedding had been completely different, so relaxing and beautiful, from the minute they arrived. The ceremony took place on the beach, surrounded by Tate and Chloe's families, then everyone moved up to a marquee in the back garden, for an *all you can eat* buffet consisting of all Tate and Chloe's favourite foods - including pizza for Gregg. It was informal and comfortable, but that's what the newly weds wanted.

Dillon sits down beside him, and helps himself to another slice of cake from the plate in the centre of the table. 'Okay?'

He nods. 'Yeah. I really am. I enjoyed the wedding.'

'You know what? So did I. I'm not usually a fan of weddings, but they made this one fun. Gotta say our boy looks happy too.'

Luke couldn't agree more. Tate is sitting on the steps of his new house, shirt sleeves rolled up and tie loosened, rocking his son in his arms, while he talks to his brother, Shane.

But his attention isn't fully on his brother. It's on his new wife, dancing with his sister.

Chloe's dress is simple yet elegant, and judging by the look on Tate's face he approves.

'He's madly in love with her, isn't he?'

'Yeah, he is.' Dillon lounges back in the chair and unbuttons his waistcoat. 'We nearly lost him to heroin last year, and now look at him. Married with a kid. Sickeningly happy too,' he adds with a grin. 'It's enough to turn me off my cake.'

'Oh knock it off! You're a romantic at heart.'

'Fuck off!'

They laugh, then someone else catches Luke's attention. Maeve glides down the steps with Chloe's sister. She stops and speaks to Tate, before joining Chloe and Bria on the dance floor.

'I got to say, she looks beautiful tonight, mate.'

Luke nods and smiles at Dillon. 'I know. She told me she loves me.' Dillon slaps him on the shoulder so hard it sends him flying forward. He manages to get his hand out in time to stop himself whacking against the table. 'Ouch!'

The bear hug his friend gives him, isn't any more gentle. Luke extricates himself, then freezes when he gets a proper look at Dillon. 'Are you... Are you crying?'

Dillon quickly wipes his face. 'If you tell anyone, I swear I will deny all knowledge. What did you say to her?'

'I told her I love her too. Actually I said it first. It felt right. I love her Dillon. Since I threw up in her apartment, things have felt... different. I know you guys helped me so much since I got back, but being with Maeve... I don't know. I love her. I really do.'

'And that's why I may possibly have cried a little. I am so fucking happy for both of you! You deserve this Luke. You deserve her and... fuck! This is great!'

'What is?' Gregg asks coming up behind them, startling Luke.

'Maeve said she loves me.'

'Wehey! That's awesome buddy!'

Luke winces when Gregg tackles him, squeezing him tight. 'Thanks. You can let go now. I'm bruised enough from Dillon hugging me.'

'Why are you guys being all touchy feely?' Tate sits on the seat next to Dillon, looking at the three of them like they've lost their minds. 'You sneak some alcohol in or something?'

Gregg snorts loudly. 'As if buddy! And personally, I take offence with the fact you immediately get suspicious when we're smiling. It does happen from time to time.'

Tate takes a drink of cola, then smirks. 'It's not really our thing.'

'Fair point, but in this case there's a lot to smile about. Like the grumpy lead singer tying the knot with someone who clearly must be slightly crazy, if she agreed to marry you in the first place.'

'Fuck you!' Tate replies. 'I'm fucking irresistible, that's why she married me.'

'Whatever you say buddy,' Gregg says, laughing loudly. 'But Luke has something to smile about too.'

'Is that right?'

'Maeve said she's in love with me. And I'm in love with her.'

He manages to get his hands up in front of him before Tate hugs him, keeping Tate from crushing him. The guy is a giant and his hugs are powerful.

'Stop crushing my boyfriend!'

Maeve pushes past the band and slides on to Luke's knee, kissing him in front of the guys. She gets to her feet and holds out her hand. 'Fancy a dance, sexy?'

'Yeah. I do.' He stands up and turns back to the guys as he's being lead away. 'I'm off to dance with my girlfriend.'

It's so amazing to be able to say that, but when he steps onto the dance floor and Maeve dances with him, he swears he's going to burst.

'I take it you told the guys? Either that, or all this wedding stuff is making them go soft.'

'No, I told them. Should have braced for the hugs. My ribs are sore.'

She holds him closer as they move around the dance floor. 'And are they okay with it?'

'Yeah, they're really happy for us.'

'And so they should be. Are you enjoying yourself?'

'I am. The whole day has been amazing. Everything about it, is Tate and Chloe. It's personal to them. I love that.'

'You didn't have that for your wedding? Sorry, I shouldn't have brought that up.'

'No. It's fine. But I didn't. I mean Pippa went to town, but this is more me. I'm all about quiet and understated.'

'Oh there's nothing understated about you, Mr. Daly. Nothing at all. Me on the other hand. Well, I'm usually one for blending into the background.'

He laughs at that. 'Yeah? If it's one thing you don't do, it's blending! And that's why I love you. You're never afraid to live your life the way you want to. And I can't wait to see what trouble you can get me into.'

'I'll do my best not to lead you astray... well, not too much at least.'

As they hold onto each other, surrounded by his closest friends, he realises for the first time in so long, he can't wait to see what tomorrow brings.

'I'll do my best not to lead you astray... well, not too much at least.'

As they hold onto each other, surrounded by his closest friends, he realises for the first time in so long, he can't wait to see what tomorrow brings.

# Maeve

She grins widely when Bria walks over to Tate and hands him a fiddle. 'Come on big bro. Time for a bit of music.'

'It's my fucking wedding!'

'Exactly,' she says, holding the instrument right up to his face. 'If we don't have an Archer family singalong at your own fucking wedding, as you put it, when will we. Move it, Tate.'

He looks to Chloe for a bit of backup, but she nods towards the fiddle. 'My first request as your new wife is to do exactly what your sister wants. You know you want to. I can see it in your face.'

'What's going on,' Maeve asks as Tate looks between his brother and his sister.

'It's kind of a thing we do when we get together like this,' Luke explains. 'We have a session. It's a bit different to our usual style.'

'Please tell me you're talking about a trad session. Like a proper Irish sing song.'

He grins as he nods. 'Oh yeah. Bria and Shane are amazing singers and musicians too. It's a big family thing. The rest of the band gets pulled in too.'

'Oh my God! This is amazing! I didn't know you did music like this.'

'It's not something we'd ever release. It would be a bit confusing given the heavier rock style we usually do, but it's good fun. A great way to let our hair down and have crazy fun.'

'Come on then guys,' Tate says as he gets to his feet. 'Time to do our thing. It appears I'm not getting a night off.' He smiles and kisses Chloe before leading them over to the steps of his house.

Maeve sits at a table with Chloe as instruments are handed out to Tate, Gregg, Shane, Dillon, and Luke. 'Do you not get involved?'

Chloe laughs, shaking her head. 'Oh no. I leave this part to the experts.' She leans closer to Maeve. 'Besides, I wouldn't miss watching Tate for the world. That's half the fun.'

Tate starts them off on the fiddle, which Maeve loves. She's seen him play the guitar and piano when they perform, but this is so different. Then Bria sings and Maeve is struck silent. They may not be related by blood, but Bria 's voice is just as powerful as Tate's.

'I didn't know she could do that!'

'Oh yes,' Chloe agrees. 'She's an incredible singer.'

As more and more family and friends join in the singing, Maeve's attention is drawn to Luke. He's beaming as he plays his guitar, his movements lively as he really gets into the music.

And she can't blame him. It's impossible not to get carried away. Here she is at Tate Archer's wedding, watching the massively famous band playing traditional Irish music. It's the most fun she's ever had at a wedding. Her brother's pub could use something like this on a weekend.

Completely drawn in by the atmosphere and the music, Maeve joins in the singing and clapping, her attention never leaving Luke. He's singing along with everyone, the smile taking over his face.

He looks over at her, then nods to the dancefloor.

It takes her a few seconds to get what he's hinting at. She is not getting up and dancing in front of everyone. He can gesture to the dancefloor as much as he wants.

He lifts his hand from his guitar and points to the dancefloor. She shakes her head, but he's not taking no for an answer. He rests his guitar on his knees and just looks at her, his arms crossed.

'I think he wants you to dance,' Chloe says from beside her.

'Oh, you think!'

'Go on. You'll get everyone else going.'

She wants to dance. The longer the music continues, the more the urge to move takes hold. 'Would you mind?'

'Why would I mind? I've heard you're an incredible dancer. Why don't you show all of us how it's done.'

Maeve slips off her high hells and stands, earning herself a huge grin from Luke. He picks up his guitar again, his eyes never leaving her as she walks over to the dance floor. Chloe shouts out her name and claps which encourages her.

But it's Luke's attention that really spurs her on. Once she begins to dance, the wedding guests join in the cheering and clapping, some even joining her on the dancefloor.

As she dances, Luke's attention doesn't move from her for a single second. She's dancing for him and he's playing for her.

And it couldn't be more perfect.

## 33

*Dillon*

He shouts out and sits up in bed, lashing out at whoever woke him.

Gregg jumps off the bed before he can deck him, stepping back and holding his hands up in front of him. 'It's me! Sorry, buddy.'

'What the fuck are you doing?'

'I didn't mean to startle you.'

Dillon wipes a hand over his face. His fucking heart is going nuts. 'Well you did! What the fuck are you doing in my house in the middle of the night?'

'I needed to see you.'

'Really? How romantic. You couldn't wait until the morning maybe?'

Gregg passes him a piece of paper. 'Thought you should have company when you read this?'

Dillon frowns at Gregg as he reaches out and takes the paper from his hand. He scans through the document, his temper rising as he reads the words. 'What the fuck is this?'

'A statement Pippa released a few hours ago. It's all over social. I'm guessing she saw the few photos of Tate and Chloe's wedding that they released to the press. There's one with Luke and Maeve. Presumably it got dear Pippa's hackles up. Might be her last ditch attempt at smearing Luke's name, or something like that.'

Dillon has to hand it to Pippa. For a final blow, it's a good one. She's claiming Luke was cheating on her for years with Maeve. And with him. She's given the press a vivid picture of some sordid, fucked up threesome.

But it gets worse. Apparently she was pregnant at the time, but was so distraught when she found out about the affair, she lost the baby. Pippa was never pregnant. He's fucking positive about that. But it's a low and seriously fucked up blow considering the vasectomy she forced him to get.

Having Maeve's name smeared all over the press in relation to a phantom miscarriage and affair, is going to be devastating to Luke.

Dillon climbs out of bed, not caring that he's butt naked in front of Gregg. He grabs a pair of jeans, quickly putting them on before heading to the door of his room.

'Where the hell are you going?'

'To talk to the bitch!'

Gregg grabs him by the arm, spinning him around. 'No you're not! You're going to sit down and take a few minutes.'

'Let me go!'

'Not happening. What exactly do you think you can achieve, by storming up to a prison and demanding to see her, huh? I'll give you a hint. Absolutely nothing!'

Dillon squares up to Gregg. 'Won't know until I try. Now, move!' He's taller and heavier, so he could easily shove him aside.

Gregg smirks at him. 'Don't think about it. I'm trained to take down hefty arseholes like you. I've taken Tate down before. I'm confident I can do the same to you.'

Unfortunately, he's not in the mood for seeing sense. He pushes Gregg to the side, but doesn't get far.

Gregg moves faster than he was expecting, sending him crashing to the ground as he tackles him. Dillon grunts when Gregg flips him onto his front and twists his arm behind his back. 'Fuck Gregg!'

'I told you, buddy. You may be bigger, but I'm a hell of a lot faster. Now how about you take a minute, get your shit together, and we'll try this again.'

'Get the fuck off me!'

'Nope.'

Dillon tries to lift himself off the ground with Gregg attached, but whatever way Gregg is holding his arms, is seriously screwing with him.

'Get off me, or I swear I'm going to fucking kill you!'

Gregg presses his knee into the centre of Dillon's back and takes a long breath. 'I'm completely immune to threats. It's one of my superpowers! That, and being a total drumming God, of course.

'Now, while we're both here relaxing, why don't you maybe try to calm the fuck down. And now you've made me curse, and I don't like that.'

He shouts into the floor, no nearer to calming down. 'I'm going to kill you, then her. Get off! Gregg! You're going to break my fucking arm. Gregg!'

But he's ignoring him, and that pisses off Dillon even more. He rests his forehead against the floor and tries to calm down. Gregg won't move unless he does, and the fucker can be irritatingly persistent.

Dillon finally runs out of steam, closing his eyes as he lies on the floor. How the hell is he going to make this better for Luke? 'This is going to destroy him, Gregg.'

'I know.'

'And dragging Maeve into it is fucking low.' Luke was just getting his life back on track again. He was smiling. Laughing. Having fun like he did years ago. This is going to open that fucking shite wound again. He doesn't care that he's mentioned. It's the threat to Maeve and Luke that's fucking with him.

'If I let you up, are you going to sit down and talk about this calmly?'

'Yeah.'

'Dillon...'

'I said I would, now get the fuck off me!'

Gregg pushes off his back, and holds out his hand to help him up. In a seriously foul mood, Dillon ignores Gregg's gesture, swatting his hand aside and dragging his own ass off the floor.

He slumps into the chair and glares over at Gregg. It's not his fault. He's pissed off at everything, and Gregg is going to get the brunt of it.

Which is probably why he was picked to show him the statement. He's level headed and, like he said, thanks to his stint as a Garda, he's trained to handle unruly people.

'Luke is going to need you to be calm, Dillon. You can't help him if you're blowing up like this.'

'Help him? Are you fucking serious? How exactly can we help him with this? They've got her on one count of assault, Gregg. One! She beat and raped him for most of their relationship, and all she got was a few years. That's it.

'He'll never be free from her and, after that crap she's released, his credibility will be shot. You know what she's like! She'll have the world believing she was the poor neglected wife. That her husband was off fooling around with an old school friend and a band mate, at the same time. That he was having a threesome, fucking me, and Maeve!

289

'Or maybe I was fucking the two of them? Who knows? I mean it's not like I don't have form.'

'It's a colourful picture she's painted all right.'

'Colourful? It's fucking sordid - even for me. Fuck, Gregg! Does he know yet?'

'Yeah. Ellen was on her way to tell him. She was going to give Alex a call. See if he would meet her at Luke's place.'

'I should have stayed at my apartment last night. The one fucking time he needs me, and I'm an hour away.'

'Oh come on, Dillon! You've been keeping an eye on him for months. You can't put your life on hold because of Luke. He wouldn't want you to do that.'

He's not got much of a life to put on hold either way, but there's nothing he wouldn't do for Luke. It's partly down to his feelings, but it's not just that. He'd do the same for his sisters, Tate, or Gregg. 'What can we do?'

'Honestly, I don't know. There's only one thing that can help Luke. Shutting Pippa up, and I don't mean the way you want to shut her up, so don't even go there. I mean her credibility. As it stands, she's been put inside for hitting Luke that one time. If he... I don't know.'

'If he told everyone that she raped him for years, it would shut her up.'

Gregg nods. 'He's already said he can't, or won't, do that. And unfortunately it's his call. Besides, even if he did make a statement about what she really did to him, it would be her word against his.'

'He's got old fractures from her hitting him.'

'Or falling off his motorbike? Or tripping? Or falling somewhere? She can explain it all away. And Luke didn't exactly help by covering for her for years. And I get why, so stop glaring at me like you want to tear my throat out! I'm just saying.'

Dillon stands up, a little more relaxed, but still itching for a fight. Gregg is right, which is seriously messing with his calm. 'She can't have begun this controlling shit with Luke.'

'What do you mean?'

'The bitch must have pulled this with another of her exes. She must have hit, or abused, or done something fucked up with someone else.'

'You thinking we could get one of them in to corroborate Luke's statement?'

'Maybe. She's mentioned at least one guy she was with, before Luke. You know what she's like. All the details are on social somewhere. We need to find him.'

'Dillon...'

'Come on, Gregg! You worked as a Garda for years. You really going to sit there and tell me that she started with Luke? There's no way she found him and decided to control him. There had to be someone before him.'

Gregg plays with his leather cuff, as he thinks about that one. Dillon has spent enough time up close and personal with the legal system to know Gregg still has connections. Connections they can use to help Luke.

'Fair enough. It's doubtful she went into full blown psycho wife mode with Luke for starters.'

'Exactly! We need to track down her ex. Jimmy? Jack. Fuck, I'm shite with names!'

'Joe,' Gregg offers.

'That's the one! We need to find him and have a chat with him.'

Gregg sits up and shakes his head. 'Ah now hang on one minute. I know you and your chats. It usually ends up with someone bleeding.'

'I'm not going to beat him up. I just want to talk to him.'

'That's what I said. You talk with your fists. Getting you locked up again won't help anyone. And what makes you think we can find this Joe bloke? Or that Pippa did anything to him? Or that he'll talk to us, with, or without, getting your fists involved?'

'Because right now, the fucking bitch is still controlling Luke. He's too scared to break away from her for good. She's got him fucking terrified to do anything to hurt her. She's inside for beating the shite out of him, yet he's the one ashamed. That's not right.

'I'm thinking that maybe if this Joe guy went through something similar with Pippa, Luke might just get the courage to go public with what's been going on? And vice versa. Maybe Joe is thinking no one will believe him if he tells the truth?'

'Hang on! You want Luke to go public about the abuse?'

'I don't think there's any other way of escaping her once and for all.' Dillon would give anything to spare Luke the pain of doing that but, unless he stands up to her, she'll keep that hold on him forever.

Gregg lies back in the chair, brushing his hand over his crazy hair as he thinks. 'Do you think he's strong enough to do that? And I absolutely don't mean that in an asshole way. He's been through a lot Dillon. He may not have enough left to stand up to her.'

'He survived being married to her. He survived an overdose that was meant to kill him. He made it through rehab and months of therapy. He's the strongest person I know. He can do it.'

'Fuck,' Gregg mutters under his breath. 'So I'm guessing you want me to have a chat with Max? Convince my old Garda buddy to find out where Joe is?'

'I'd ask him, but every time I see him I get arrested. I'm done with that.'

Gregg snorts, sitting up to smirk at Dillon. 'We're all done with that, thanks all the same! I don't think third time is the charm in this instance. Okay, I'll give him a buzz. See if he can track him down. But I don't want you to get your hopes up. He might not be willing to help, and even if he does, there's nothing to say Joe will be overly chatty.'

'I'll convince him.'

Gregg stands and points a finger at Dillon as he walks past. 'That's exactly what I'm afraid of. I'll ring Max from the spare room. I don't want you yelling in my ear, as I try to sweet talk him around to helping us.'

Dillon slouches back in the chair and stares up at the light fitting over his head. It's a long shot, but it's worth trying. He'll do whatever he needs to do, to get Luke away from Pippa, once and for all.

## Luke

He takes the cup of coffee from Alex, placing it on the table in front of him. He doesn't want it. Doesn't want anything. The queasiness he'd been free from for the last few months is back, churning his stomach so violently he's struggling not to throw up.

Alex and Ellen are talking, but he's not paying attention to what they're saying. All he can focus on is the statement from Pippa.

An affair

A miscarriage

A disloyal husband who hurt his wife so much, she lost their baby.

That's the part of her lie that hits him the hardest. She knew he wanted to be a father. Knew how much it meant to him, and for her to use that to hurt him, or whatever she's trying to do, sickens him.

And as for dragging Maeve into their marriage... that's not fair on her. She never asked to be involved, or to be implicated as a member of this imaginary threesome.

The problem is, it's not going to stop. Once Pippa sets her mind on something, there's no going back. It happened with their house, with her car, with every holiday they had. Everything she wants, she gets.

That's his fault - he knows that. He's the one who paid for everything. Who went along with everything she wanted. But if she knows about Maeve, and wants to drag her name through the press, she'll do it. This is only the tip of the iceberg. It's only going to get so much worse for Maeve.

Being with him will make her life so much worse.

He blinks when Alex nudges him in the arm. 'Hey? Are you with us?'

'What?'

'Ellen was talking to you.'

'I'm sorry. What were you saying?'

'No need to apologise,' Ellen says in her no nonsense tone. 'I know this is an incredibly shit thing for Pippa to do, but I need to get some facts if I'm going to go up against her. First, is anything she said true?'

Luke shakes his head, but doesn't look up.

'I'm sorry I had to ask. And when did you meet Maeve?'

'In secondary school.' Luke still can't bring himself to look at her. 'But we only met again a few months ago. I didn't cheat on Pippa. I'd never cheat on anyone.'

'I know, Luke,' she says. 'Well, I'll put out the usual statement. Your private life is just that etc., etc. Hope the comments are forgotten.'

'No!'

Luke can feel them both looking at him.

'What exactly do you mean by no?' Alex asks. 'You need to make a statement, Luke. Shut her down!'

'If we use the same line we've been using since I overdosed, how is that going to help Maeve?'

'Maeve will be fine,' Ellen says.

'How can you say that? You both know what Pippa is like. She saw her husband at a wedding with another woman.' That thought suddenly strikes home. 'I am cheating on her!'

'Jesus, Luke! You're separated. And she beat you, so fuck your marriage!'

'It's not that simple, Alex. I'm still married to her. I'm seeing someone else. I did that. I brought Maeve into this. I need to get her out of it again.'

Ellen shuffles forward in her seat, clasping her hands on top of the file on her knee. 'So, how would you like us to handle this? It's your call.'

'This won't end. She'll only come back with something else. Until we're divorced, I can't do anything that will upset her. So much of my life is linked to her. I can't afford to give her more ammunition.'

Alex snorts loudly. 'Ammunition? Are you fucking kidding me? You're the victim here, Luke!'

'I know that! I've heard that enough times over the last year, okay. I get it! But that isn't the way Pippa sees it. You both know she's been telling anyone who listens, that she didn't do anything wrong.

'She was only convicted on dumb luck. I'm not having Maeve targeted by her. Not like that. I need to do what I can to separate her from me. It's the only way.'

His stomach spins, and he retches, barely making it into the kitchen before he vomits in the sink. Alex hands him a glass of water, then pulls one of the stools over so he can sit.

'Better?'

'Yeah. Thanks.'

Alex pulls up another chair beside him. 'Look at me.'

When he doesn't, his brother raises his voice a little. 'For God's sake, Luke! Can you look at me?'

He forces himself to look at Alex. 'You can't mean what you told Ellen in there?'

'I can't win.'

'Don't give me that. Of course you can! You need to fight. You'll never break free from her, if you let her do this to you and Maeve. You are the most sincere, loyal, honest person I have ever met, and you're going to stand by and let her label you a cheat? You're going to let her drive a wedge between yourself and Maeve?'

'I'm doing this for Maeve. Pippa isn't someone you mess with, Alex. She terrifies me, okay! I'm scared of her, and scared of what she's capable of. I'm not going to give her any reason to target Maeve more than she already has. I love her and I won't let that happen.'

'Pippa can't touch you. There's a barring order—'

'Come on Alex! You really think that can stop her? She kicked my leg until it snapped in two! You really think a barring order will stop her if she really wants to get to Maeve?'

'So, you give her what she wants? Roll over and let her label you an adulterer and shitty husband for the rest of your life? Then when she gets out, she can live happily ever after, in a house *you* paid for, spending money *you* worked fucking hard for! Please tell me you see why I have a problem? And what about Dillon?'

'What about him?'

'She's clearly got it in for him. There's already a restraining order against him, from when he attacked her in the hospital, right?'

Luke nods.

'What's to stop her calling it in? Making something up about him coming too close or whatever? Then, it's goodbye Dillon.'

'She wouldn't—'

'Oh come on, Luke! You have to know she would. She called the Garda in during your wedding. Got Dillon arrested right after the dinner. She's pulled all this bullshit out to destroy your name. Why would she stop there? Anyone with half a brain would expect Dillon to react to this. You really think the Garda would believe he wouldn't go after her at some stage?'

He's right. Luke knows he's right. But would Pippa really do that? Then again, bringing Dillon into the whole mess is confusing him. Having her husband cheat on her with another man is horrible.

But surely that would embarrass Pippa as much as him? She always wanted to look perfect to the rest of the world. Telling everyone her husband slept with a man would tarnish that. He was with her long enough to know that much for sure.

'Please, Luke! Please fight.'

'I've made my decision, Alex. I need my brother to support me. Please.'

Alex curses, pacing the kitchen, as he scrubs his hand over his hair. Luke has only seen him this angry once before, and that was when he admitted what Pippa had done to him.

Alex has always protected him. Always stood up for him. But he doesn't need that right now. All he wants, is for him to accept his decision, and support him.

But that would be like asking Maeve and Dillon to accept his decision. Deep down he knows it's probably asking too much.

'Fuck that! I know the truth, and so does everyone who gives a damn about you. The only person not accepting that, is you.'

'I get what you're saying. And what Ellen is saying. I hear you, but I want to do this my way. The more I fight, the more she'll attack. That's what she does. This is my problem. I created it. I was weak and scared and brought all this on myself. Let me end it, please.'

Alex stares at him for a long few minutes without saying anything. 'You believe you brought it all on yourself?'

'Of course I did! Something about me made her do all that.'

Alex takes a step closer to him, but he backs away, shaking his head. He doesn't want him, or anyone near him right now.

'Please, Alex. Can you go?'

'I'm not leaving you.'

'Just go!' he shouts louder than he meant to. When he doesn't move, Luke opens his door and stares over at his brother. 'Go, Alex!'

He grabs his keys off the counter and marches towards the door. 'You're not pushing me away, Luke. Not ever!'

Luke slams the door after him, and leans against it as he catches his breath. That could have gone so much better. He doesn't need to lose any more people from his life. Not now.

He looks up as Ellen walks over to him. 'I should go.'

'Make the statement, Ellen.'

'Are you absolutely sure, Luke?'

'I'm sure.'

## Maeve

She reads the words on the page a few times, the knot in her stomach hardening each time she reads it. *She's just a friend. She means nothing to me.*

Maeve sniffs, hating that the tears won't stop pouring down her face.

Reading Luke's statement in black and white is a killer. Less than forty-eight hours after declaring their love for each other, he decides to tell the world it was what? A lie?

Mike steps up behind her and pulls her into a hug.

'I'm sorry. Maeve. Have you tried to talk to him? Maybe this is a publicity thing or something? His wife sounds like a total nutcase. She blames your *affair* with Luke and Dillon for everything.

'Seriously, that woman is scaring me, and not many people do. I don't know how all this celebrity stuff works. It could be nothing. Talk to him.'

'Is there any point?' she asks. 'He just told the whole world I mean nothing to him. It doesn't matter if he meant what he said, or not. The fact that he said it, that he felt he had to play down what we have, to keep her happy. That's the part I'm upset about.'

She slumps onto her couch and lets the tears out. There's no point holding them back either. This is worth crying over. The man she loves told everyone he doesn't love her. Just likes her as a friend. All to keep his abusive wife happy.

Mike sits beside her, draping his arm across her shoulders. 'I get why you're upset, but you don't do this.'

'What?'

'Cry.'

'I know, but I care about him Mike. Fuck it! I love him. I'm crazy in love with him and it's... it's all gone. He couldn't even tell me, Mike.'

He turns her to face him and takes her shoulders in his hands. 'Where is my stubborn sister gone? The Maeve I love, would get on to him straight away and ask what the fuck is going on.'

'I can't do that.'

'Why not?'

'Because it's Luke. He's got so much going—'

'Stop it!' She jumps when Mike shouts at her.

'Stop what?'

'Why are you treating this situation differently to any other situation you've been in? What this boils down to, is the relationship between you and Luke right now. That's it.

'Forget his ex. Forget who he is and all that messed up shit that happened to him. This is you and him, so deal with it that way. He's just a guy who's messed up. He's made a mistake. You need to find out why.'

She gets to her feet and wipes her face. He's right. Why is she slinking away with her tail between her legs. She doesn't do that.

Whatever happens in the long run, she needs to face Luke and find out what he's playing at.

'You're right. I've done nothing wrong, Mike. Nothing. I did everything I could to support him. To help him deal with what his wife did to him.'

'Couldn't agree more,' Mike says.

'I'm not saying it'll do any good, but I need to know for sure. Maybe it's a lost cause. Maybe, deep down, he's not over her. No matter how much I wish otherwise, she's still got a hold on him - even from prison. There's a chance I won't be able to break that connection.'

Mike nods slowly. 'It's a possibility, but at least you'll know you tried, that you fought.'

'I'm just afraid I might have met the right person at the wrong time.'

She breaks down, the tears flowing freely again as her brother holds her.

She's been fighting Pippa since the first day she met with Luke again. Fighting with a bitch who hurt, manipulated, and abused him for years.

Until he's ready to stand up to her, she's fighting a losing battle.

## Luke

He opens the door, not surprised when Maeve storms past him and stands in his living room.

She's angry with him. Or maybe disappointed in him. He thought he'd got past all that. But he's done it all over again.

'You read it.'

'Oh I read it.' She sniffs and wipes her nose. 'What's going on?'

Luke sits on the arm of the chair and wrings his hands together.

'Pippa was dragging you into our marriage. I didn't want that.'

'So you decide to help the situation, by telling the world I don't mean anything to you?'

'I didn't mean it like that. I just wanted her to leave you alone.'

She wipes her nose again, then laughs harshly. 'And that was your answer, huh? To embarrass me like that!'

'That's not what I want! I thought if I took the attention off you, it would—'

'Well you didn't do what you set out to do. There's a hoard of reporters outside the pub. They're all asking for an interview with the woman who is chasing after Luke Daly. How do you think that makes me feel?'

'I didn't want that. I swear.'

Maeve inhales deeply and shakes her head. 'I know, Luke. But that's what is happening. I don't understand why you said what you did? I don't get why you thought that would work?'

'Pippa is mean. She'll just keep coming after you.'

'Physically?'

'What?'

'Are you worried she'll try to hurt me, physically?'

'Of course not. She can't get anywhere near you.'

'Okay, so what are we left with? Throwing a bit of mud at me? Is that it?'

'Well, yeah...'

'Who gives a fuck, Luke! Seriously! Cause I don't, and I think I'm a fairly important part of the situation. You should know me well enough by now, to know I couldn't care less what other people think, or say about me. I can take care of myself.'

'I know you can. I just—'

'You just thought you'd do this alone, huh? You didn't think to involve me in your decision? To maybe ask what I wanted to do, before you publicly ended our relationship? Not that we had a relationship. I was a what? A stalker or something.'

'Of course not—'

'You told the world I didn't matter to you. And if that's true, I'll have to accept that. But why wouldn't you have the decency to tell me, before every other fucking person on the planet? Why would you do that to me?'

'I didn't mean for it to come across that way.'

Maeve angrily wipes her face, brushing the tears away. 'What other way would it come across, Luke?'

He opens his mouth to reply, but what can he say? She's absolutely right. He told the world she was nothing to him, when in fact, she's the most important person in his life.

What the hell did he do?

He thought he was doing the right thing by keeping Pippa away from Maeve. By protecting her. By not giving Pippa any reason to think Maeve was a problem.

But all he did was make her think he doesn't care. 'How can I make this right? What can I do to fix it, Maeve? Tell me.'

She sniffs and shakes her head, looking out the window as she thinks about that. But he knows the answer. He can see it in her face. He's blown it.

'It's not up to me to tell you how to fix this, Luke. To be honest, I'm not even sure it is fixable.' She wipes her face again, then looks back at him. 'I thought we had something special. I thought I could...' She shakes her head again. 'I don't know if there's anything you can say that will make this right. I have to go.'

He reaches out for her, but she pulls her arm out of his grip. 'Please Luke. I need to go.'

'I don't want to lose you, Maeve.'

'Yeah, well you should have thought about that before you made that statement.'

Luke watches, helpless and frozen to the spot as she walks out of his apartment.

And out of his life.

## 35

### Dillon

He pulls up outside the address Max gave them and looks out at the bungalow behind the pristine white gate. 'You want to stay in the car?'

Gregg slowly turns his head to look at him. 'You're hilarious, you know that! You honestly think I'm going to sit here and let you talk to this guy all on your lonesome? Really?'

Dillon blows out a breath, resigned to the fact he's going to have to behave himself, or Gregg is going to send him back on his ass with another of his flashy Garda moves. 'You really don't trust me, huh?'

Gregg grins widely. 'Honestly? Nope! Not in the slightest.'

Dillon holds up his middle finger as Gregg opens the door and climbs out of the Mustang. Cursing to himself, Dillon pulls the keys out of the ignition and follows after Gregg, making sure to lock his car.

Gregg waits for him to join him on the doorstep, before jabbing him in the chest with his finger. 'Behave! Let me talk, okay?' He rings the doorbell. 'You button it!'

'I'm so fucking close to decking you, you know that?'

'Love you too. Hey,' Gregg says as a blond haired man opens the door. 'How are you? I'm looking for Joe?'

The guy looks them both over a few times, before he answers. 'I'm Joe.'

Gregg holds out his hand and Joe shakes it. 'I'm Gregg and this is—'

'Dillon,' Joe finishes before Gregg can speak, surprising the two of them.

Dillon grunts, when Gregg elbows him in the gut. 'What did you do? Have you been here before?'

'Fuck off Gregg! Of course not!'

'Stop glaring at the guy.'

'I'm not!'

'Are too. You're giving him the *I want to fuck you over* face. You're freaking him out.'

'I wasn't expecting it to be someone from the band,' Joe says, silencing their squabbling.

Gregg turns back to Joe. 'I'm sorry?'

He stuffs his hands into the back pockets of his jeans, and drops his gaze to the floor, in a move that reminds Dillon so much of Luke. 'I was kind of expecting someone to come and talk to me at some stage, but not someone from Broken Chords.'

'You were?' Dillon shoves Gregg aside, ignoring his protest. 'Why?'

Joe shrugs and looks up at them again. 'I saw all the reports on TV about what happened to Luke. You're here to talk about Pippa, right?'

Dillon glances at Gregg, before they both focus on Joe again. 'Yeah. We are.'

Joe steps aside and opens the door fully. 'You better come in then.'

# Maeve

Mike lifts her bags onto the back of her bike, securing them with the straps while she locks up her flat.

She's going to miss living here. Having the sea right outside her door is something she's going to deeply miss. Among many other things. She shakes herself out of her thoughts and joins Mike in the car park.

'Stop looking at me like that. Mike...'

He leans against the wall, his arms crossed as he glares at her. 'What? You expect me to be happy about this? I've just got used to you being around. You're a pain in the butt, but I'm going to miss you.'

'I know. And I'll miss you too. But I need to get away for a while. Please. I need to go somewhere there are no rock stars.'

'Really? I'm fairly sure there are a few of them in Wales.'

'The dance school is the perfect distraction I need. It's an amazing opportunity. I've always wanted to choreograph a show. You know that.'

'Would you have taken the job if you and Luke were still together?'

He's got her there. 'Please, Mike. Just be happy for me.'

'I'd prefer to deck Luke Daly, but yeah, I am happy for you. You know I am. Please promise you'll stay in touch.'

'Of course I will.' She hugs him tight, holding on to him for a long time. 'I'll text you from the port, from the ferry, when I dock, and when I get to the room I'm renting.'

'You damn well better. You got all your bike documents?'

'Would you stop worrying! I've travelled all over the world on my own. I think I can handle a teeny road trip to Wales.'

He nods, then pulls her close for another bear hug. 'Oh I know you can more than handle yourself. What should I tell him, if he gets in touch?'

She'd thought about that one non stop since she made the decision to leave a few days ago. She'd blocked his number, but that wasn't because she hates him. It's a self-preservation thing. She can't deal with seeing or talking to him. Not yet. Maybe not ever.

'He won't, but in case he does, tell him the truth. I've left.'

'I presume you don't want him to know where?'

'I think it's best he doesn't know.'

Mike nods. 'Yeah. Got it. You'd better go. Don't want to miss your ferry.'

'I love you, Mike.'

'Love you too. Drive safe.'

She climbs onto her bike and fastens her helmet. Maeve beeps her horn, waving at Mike as she pulls out of the car park and heads towards Dublin Port.

As she rides, she can't help but look around, a part of her hoping to see Luke's car somewhere along the road. But there's no sign.

Time to put him behind her, to move on with her life away from the spotlights that have turned in her direction since he made his announcement.

With her helmet on, there's no way to wipe away the tears that continue to pour down her face. She thought she had a future with Luke, hoped for one of those soppy happily-ever-afters you see on TV.

Instead she's leaving everything she knows and loves, taking a broken heart to another country, to try and get on with her life. Alone.

*Luke*

He follows Dillon into the living room, and sits on the couch facing the huge window. His penthouse apartment has a stunning view, but it's not something he can enjoy at the moment.

He'd spent the last hour with his therapist, talking about the darkness that's threatening to drag him under again.

He's okay. Well he's not really okay, but he's better than he was an hour ago. Dillon sits on the couch beside him, chewing on his lip ring while he glares out the window, deep in his head somewhere.

'Are you okay?'

Dillon nods, but keeps his attention on the window.

'There's something wrong.'

His friend finally turns towards him. 'You really want to know? Cause I'll tell you, but you might not like what you hear.'

'Of course I want to know.'

Dillon shuffles around on the couch and hits him with an intense glare. 'Why the fuck did you make that fucking ridiculous statement?'

He knew Dillon probably wouldn't be happy about what he said, but he wasn't expecting this level of anger from him.

'I had no choice. I don't want Pippa saying those things about Maeve. I should have said something about you too. I'm sorry. I was so focused on Maeve, I forgot about what Pippa said we did.'

'Fuck that! All you have to do is stick my name online and you'll get a few dozen stories about who I fucked. Do you really think I care if she's saying we had a threesome? It wouldn't be the first time I've had one, and I hope it won't be the last.

'Adding you and Maeve to that list doesn't bother me. We all know it didn't happen, and so does everyone we give a fuck about. End of subject.

'The bit I'm pissed off about, is you telling the world Maeve means nothing to you. You turned your back on her and let her go!'

Luke nods, not able to bring himself to look at Dillon. This is so much worse than anything Pippa did to him. Probably because he did this to himself.

He fucked himself over, and now he's alone again. Not only that, he's managed to hurt Maeve, and that's the part that's sickening him.

He's deeply in love with her. But instead of telling her, he told the world she didn't matter to him.

'Hey! You got nothing to say?'

'What do you want me to say, Dillon?' Dillon curses under his breath as he focuses his attention out the window instead. 'You're cross with me.'

'Fuck, Luke! I'm not cross with you. You have to stop thinking that.'

'Sorry.'

'Stop that too!' Dillon gets up and paces in front of the large window, his hands on his hips as he marches back and forth. Luke hasn't seen him this worked up for ages. 'Sorry for shouting at you.'

'I probably deserve it.'

Dillon stops and the look he throws at him has Luke shuffling back in the seat. 'Actually, screw it! In this case yeah, I reckon you do deserve it. You've just thrown away a fucking amazing relationship, to keep that *bitch* of an ex of yours happy!

'You are hands down the smartest person I know, but this is the dumbest move you've ever made. As in seriously fucking dumb. I just... you need to...' Dillon shakes his head and turns back to face the window.

'We've spent the last year trying to help you see what a fucking amazing person you are. We've encouraged you, without pushing you. Done what we can to draw you out of your shell, to give you a nudge when needed. And you've come a hell of a way Luke.'

He turns to look at him, leaning back against the wall with his arms crossed. 'But you're still under her thumb. I'm not trying to guilt you, or be a dick. I'm really not, but what the fuck have you been doing for the last year if you're right back here again?'

'I'm not—'

'Yes! Actually you are. You're protecting that cow, dancing to her fucking dance, as per usual.'

'That's not what I'm doing. I don't want Maeve to be dragged into my marriage.'

'Marriage? Give me a fucking break! What you had with that bitch wasn't a marriage. She abused you, Luke!'

'I know that, Dillon.'

'Then why do you give the slightest fuck what she thinks?'

'I don't. I just...'

'Do you love Maeve?'

Luke pauses, thrown off by Dillon's interruption. 'Well, yes. Of course I do.'

'So why didn't you say that to the press? Why didn't you stand up in front of everyone and tell them how much she means to you? Why did you shove her away like you did?'

'I didn't shove her away. I was trying to keep her out of it. If Pippa thought she didn't mean anything to me, then she'd leave her alone.'

Luke cowers when Dillon slams his fist in the wall, but he's in such a rage he doesn't notice. 'That there is my whole fucking point! Why didn't you stick two fingers up at Pippa and tell her to mind her own fucking business?'

'I—'

'Why didn't you tell that abusive rapist wife of yours that you care about Maeve, and you don't give a flying fuck what she thinks about it? Or even what she writes about it.

'I don't know much about Maeve, but I know she wouldn't have given a damn what Pippa was saying about her. So why did you?'

'Because...' Why did he? It was a spur of the moment reaction. Pippa questioned their relationship and Luke... He closes his eyes, burying his face in his hands.

He fell straight back into the old way of doing things by nodding and smiling like a trained puppet. Like Pippa's trained puppet.

She didn't like Maeve so he dismissed her. Just like he'd dismissed his relationship with Dillon. He did that to spare Pippa's feelings. But at what cost to Dillon and Maeve?

And Dillon's right. What does it matter if Pippa is hurt by him being with Maeve? It's got nothing to do with her.

'You going to sit there and say nothing? This is your life Luke. Own it!'

'I'm trying. It's not that easy.'

'Stop making excuses!'

'I'm not! I just... I don't know how to stop being like this. I'm trying, but I keep going back to this. I don't want to, believe me, but I can't help it.'

Dillon sighs and rubs the back of his neck, leaving the silence hanging as the two of them calm down. 'You know you're not the only one she's done this to.'

'What do you mean?'

Dillon rubs his hands together as he looks out across Dublin. 'Myself and Gregg spoke to one of Pippa's exes, Joe.'

'Why... why would you do that?' Pippa spoke of Joe a few times, but Luke doesn't know much about him.

'Okay, so we figured Pippa must have been a bitch to someone else, other than you. There's no way she would have gone from a nice girlfriend to a controlling bitch with you. She must have at least tried some of that shit before you.'

'So you tracked him down to interrogate the guy? Why? If she did do it to him too, maybe he wants to forget? Maybe she messed him up so much, he doesn't want to talk about it? Why didn't you just leave him alone?'

'Because this all needs to end, Luke. All the fear. All the worrying. All the fucking covering up for this woman. She did the same shit to Joe that she did to you. Not to the same extent, but he's had a rough

312

time because of her.'

Luke takes a long time to process what Dillon just said. She did the same thing to Joe? He thought she was the way she was with him, because of something *he* was doing wrong. That's what she always said.

Every time she shouted at him or hit him, he had *brought it on himself.* Pushed her to react. Forced her to punish him for saying or doing something that angered her.

But if she'd treated her ex the same...

'He wants to talk to you, Luke.'

'To me? Why?'

'Because like you, he's been covering up for Pippa. He didn't think anyone would believe him. But now there's two of you. Two of you to stand up to her together.'

Luke pushes to his feet, needing to put some space between himself and Dillon. He can't breathe, the air in the vast apartment suddenly too hot and heavy, threatening to suffocate him.

He doesn't want to talk to Joe. Doesn't want to hear about everything Pippa did to him. Compare notes on how she had torn them apart. All he wants to do is forget about it. Move on with his life, such as it is.

And as for standing up to Pippa... that's not happening! What good could that do? She's in prison and should be there for another while. If he makes any more trouble for her, it would only make more trouble for him.

He wants to divorce her. Wants to get away from her once and for all. But she could contest, or make it difficult for him in so many inventive ways.

Without a word, he backs out of the room, slamming Dillon's apartment door behind him. He needs to get away from here. Get away from Dillon and any talk of standing up to Pippa.

He should have known it wouldn't be that easy. He's barely made it to the elevator when he hears Dillon's heavy footsteps behind him. 'Hey! Luke! What the fuck was that?'

'I just want to go home.'

Dillon braces his arm across the lift entrance as the doors open, blocking Luke's escape. He levels his green eyes on Luke, but doesn't say anything. And for some reason that pisses Luke off.

'Can you move your arm please?'

'What's wrong?'

'Please, Dillon! Move your arm. I have to go.'

'Not until you tell me what the hell happened back there. I'm having a conversation with you and you make a run for it. What's wrong?'

'You!' Luke doesn't realise what he said, until Dillon frowns at him. Luke has been pissed off with Dillon more times than he can remember. It's a regular occurrence when it comes to being friends with him.

But this is going way beyond pissed off. In that moment, Dillon is the embodiment of everything shitty that's happening in his life.

'Me what?'

'You're what's wrong.'

Dillon narrows his eyes. 'Really? How'd you figure that out?'

'Because you just can't help yourself, can you?'

Dillon crosses his arms. 'Go on.'

'Leave me alone!'

'Not a fucking chance! What the fuck is wrong with you? Well, apart from me of course.'

Luke tries to get around Dillon but he's too big and blocks his escape. 'Why are you always like this? Why do you have to be the one controlling every single thing.'

He flashes him a tight smile. 'That a trick question?'

'I'm being serious! Stop taking the piss out of me.'

Dillon's face hardens. 'Watch it! I've never once taken the piss out of you. What the hell is going on here?'

'I'm sick and tired of everyone else running my life. Making decisions for me. Just for once, I want to be in control of something in my life. One thing. Is that too much to ask?'

'Of course not. No one is trying to control anything. I just want you to talk to Joe for five fucking minutes. That's it.'

'That's it? What makes you think I need to hear anything he has to say?'

'Because you do! You're not alone in this Luke.'

'Yes I am! Every single day I wake up, the first thing that comes into my mind, is that my wife saw how much of a loser I am, and took advantage of that. I was such a pathetic man she felt she had beat me, to hurt me, to humiliate me. I meant nothing to her, Dillon! Nothing. I was someone she could take out her anger on, or put down whenever she felt like it.'

'Luke—'

He holds his wrist up and pulls the bandanna from around it. 'She chained me to the bed every single day! She couldn't even have sex with me like any other normal couples do. That was because of me!'

'No it fucking wasn't. And you're not pathetic—'

'I am! You all think that, so don't lie to me! I may be many things, but I'm not an idiot. I can see it in your faces. You all feel sorry for me. Look at me with pity. Walk on eggshells around me.'

'Hey! We don't do that. You're family, so we look out for you. But that's what we do. We all look out for each other. It was no different when Tate was on drugs, or Gregg was recovering from that stalker cow. It's what we do.'

'This isn't looking out for me! Just back off, please, and let me go back to my apartment.'

For the briefest of seconds, Luke thinks he's won this round. But he should have known better. Dillon never backs down.

'No.'

'Please.'

Dillon takes a step closer, well and truly invading his personal space. Dillon has a few inches on him and uses it to his advantage. 'I said no.'

Luke has never once reacted physically to anything Dillon has said or done. He can't ever remember lashing out at anyone, which is probably part of his problem. He's too weak. Too much of a pushover.

But he's been pushed too far.

Luke shoves Dillon back. Or at least tries to. It's like moving a tank.

Dillon smirks at him. 'Okay. What exactly was that?'

Luke shouts and shoves Dillon, harder this time, driving him back a step. But his infuriating friend laughs as if Luke didn't do anything to him. 'Stop laughing at me!'

'What do you expect? I mean what the fuck are you trying to do?'

'Stop!'

'Then stop flirting with me, and give me a reason to take whatever this is seriously.'

Luke shouts, throwing himself at Dillon. He lands on top of him, his friend taking the brunt of the impact when they hit the floor. Luke straddles him, aiming his fist at Dillon's face. Landing blow after blow anywhere he can make contact.

Dillon rolls to the side, dislodging Luke, but that opens up his torso. So Luke takes advantage.

Dillon groans when Luke's thumps him in the gut, driving the air from his lungs. While he's distracted, Luke gets him in the jaw, followed by the side of his face.

Dillon curses as his lip splits, but Luke doesn't hold back. Dillon is getting the brunt of his frustration. Years of pain and frustration. Years of feeling worthless and defenceless.

It takes him longer than it should, to realise Dillon isn't fighting back. He's lying on the floor, taking everything Luke is throwing at him.

He's the best fighter out of the four of them. It's part of the reason he gets in trouble as much as he does, so he should easily be able to put an end to this. But he doesn't. He lies on the floor of the expensive building he owns, and lets Luke beat the shit out of him.

He doesn't know when the tears start, when he finally breaks down. One minute he's hitting his friend, who is irritatingly lying there and taking it, and the next he's crying uncontrollably.

Dillon's face blurs as the tears flow, but he can't stop. Even though he has no idea where he's hitting Dillon, he keeps lashing out, his fists making contact with his friend, over and over again.

He has no idea how long he keeps it up for. No idea how long Dillon lies on the ground doing nothing. But eventually his friend pulls him close, holding him as he cries out, releasing years of pent up emotions.

He's cried over what happened, cried too many times to count, but not like this. Nothing like this.

And now he's released it, he can't stop.

## Luke

He rubs his eyes and looks around him. He must have dropped off for a bit after his epic breakdown. He's still on the floor outside Dillon's apartment and he's not alone. Dillon is lying in front of him, his arm draped over Luke's waist.

His eyes are closed but Luke doesn't think he's asleep. At least it's just the two of them. With Dillon owning the building, he's the only one with access to the penthouse level. No one else would have seen what he did, and for that he couldn't be more grateful.

The evidence of his attack on his friend is all over Dillon's face. As well as a split lip, Dillon's nose is bleeding, there are red marks on his cheek, around his eye, along his jaw, and the side of his neck. He's also hugging his other arm to his chest so Luke probably got him there too.

'Oh God! Dillon... I'm sorry.'

Dillon opens his uninjured eye, and winces. 'That good, huh?'

'I'm so sorry. I didn't mean to hurt you. I just ... I don't know what happened.'

Dillon grins, wincing when his lip protests. 'It's grand.'

'How is this grand? I hurt you. Your face is a mess. Where else did I hit you?'

'Just my gut, arms, and my ribs are fucking sore. Think that's it.'

'We should get you to hospital.'

'Forget that. How do you feel?'

'Terrible—'

'I don't mean about that. I mean how do you feel after getting all that out of your system, at long fucking last?'

Luke looks at the floor between them and thinks about that one. He actually feels a hell of a lot better. Almost like the heavy weight he's been carrying around for the last year has finally been lifted from his shoulders.

'Yeah. Pretty good actually. My hands hurt, but I guess I deserve that. But it felt good to blow it all out like that.'

'That was my grand plan,' Dillon says, smiling at him. 'It's therapeutic to beat the shit out of something every now and again. I've done it enough times.'

'It didn't have to be you I lost it with, though.'

He shrugs, wincing again. 'Wasn't part of my grand plan, believe me. I was kind of hoping to get you as far as my gym and the punching bag I use, but fuck it! It worked.'

'I really should bring you to hospital to get you checked out.'

'It's only blood and a few bruises. Don't worry about it. So,' he says, propping his head up in his hand. 'What's the plan now?'

'What do you mean?'

'Maeve.'

'I'm not sure there is anything I can do. I've blown it big time.'

Dillon's hand moves from Luke's waist to the side of his face. 'Do you want to get her back?'

'Of course I do. I love her, Dillon.'

Dillon smiles, and Luke realises, for the first time in years, it's genuine.

'Then there's only one thing you can do. You've got to fight for her. Prove to her that she's the most important thing in your world. Tell her you were stupid or an idiot. Whatever you need to say to show her how you feel.'

He doesn't know much about that one woman Dillon gave his heart to, but he knows losing her had eaten away at his friend, every single day since then.

'Why didn't you fight for her Dillon, all those years ago?'

'Dumb fucking pride.' Dillon shakes his head. 'I was so in love with her. I mean crazy in love. But she left and I let her go. Just got angry and brooded. Probably cursed her out a fair bit. I never went after her though. Never found out why she left. And that was a fucking epic mistake I've been paying for ever since.

'Don't make the same mistake. You don't want to end up an angry bachelor like me. Believe me. Fight for her.'

Dillon's thumb rubs against the side of his face, but he doesn't move away. Dillon has always been a bit hands on with him, but he doesn't mind.

'You are an incredible man, Luke. You're the strongest person I know. I have so much admiration and respect for you. Fuck, you're the only person I admire or respect for the most part.

'You didn't deserve what happened to you. None of it. Be happy, please. Move on from what that bitch did and live your life. Don't let her take Maeve from you.'

He doesn't know why he does what he does next, but he acts on impulse and kisses Dillon. There's nothing sexual about it like the last time. It's just a kiss, but when Dillon kisses him back, he lets him.

Dillon's hand slides back from his cheek, his fingers combing through Luke's hair, as their tongues meet. Neither one of them takes it any further, but Dillon does hang on to him after they break the kiss, resting his forehead against Luke's.

He releases him and leans back, licking his lip ring. 'This isn't a complaint, but what was that for?'

'It felt right. I'm sorry.'

Dillon smirks at him. 'Never apologise for kissing me.'

'Yeah, but did I just make things awkward between us? Because that's not what I wanted. I don't really know what I wanted to be honest, but I don't want there to be any weirdness.'

'No weirdness, Luke. It was just a kiss. I'm not going to get down on one knee and fucking propose to you or anything. But thank you. I liked it.'

Dillon sighs and rolls onto his back. 'What the fuck are we like? You're still worried about what your ex thinks of you, and I'm still hung up on you.'

'You are?'

Dillon glances at him, before focusing on the ceiling again. 'It's not going to disappear overnight, no matter how much I want it to. It's getting kind of annoying at this stage,' he says, winking at him.

'I'm sorry. I shouldn't have kissed you.'

'You apologise for doing that one more time, and I'll be forced to deck you. I'm seeing it as a *cop on to yourself* kiss. Reckon it's about time we both got our shit together and started living our fucking lives, before we're old men still going around the same circles.'

'You think we'll still be friends when we're old men?'

Dillon turns his head to look at him. 'Well, if you keep kissing me like that I'll think about it. That was a joke!'

He laughs then touches his lip. 'Fucking lip ring is like a target. Why do people keep hitting that one spot when they punch me? I've got a whole fucking face to hit. No need to target one side of my lip.'

'Sorry, but it's kind of hard to avoid.'

'Clearly.' He lies back on the floor and massages his ribs. 'So, back to your grand plan.'

Luke looks up at the ceiling as he thinks about that one. It takes less than a few seconds. 'I'm going to fight for her.'

'Too fucking right you are!' Dillon gets up, groaning as he straightens. 'Ouch! You fucked me over pretty good.'

'Sorry.'

'Don't be.'

Luke pulls Dillon into a hug. 'Thank you. I needed that kick you just gave me.'

'I think I was the one getting the kicks.'

'C'mon,' Luke says, draping Dillon's arm across his shoulders. 'Time to access the damage.'

Damage is the perfect way to describe what he did to Dillon's body. After taking a long time to drag his friend off the ground, Luke manages to deposit him on the end of his bed so he can get some first aid supplies, which thankfully, Dillon always has plenty of.

When he comes back out of the bathroom, Dillon is struggling to pull off his t-shirt. 'Shit. I'm sorry.'

'Don't keep apologising. Just help me get this fucking thing off.' Once he manages to extract him from the t-shirt, Luke pulls a chair closer and starts with Dillon's face, gently dabbing the blood from around his lip piercing.

Not only is his face a mess, but the more Luke examines him, the more he realises Dillon doesn't look well. His skin is pale and the rings under his eyes are impressive. 'You sleeping okay?'

Dillon shrugs and that's as far as the answer goes. He was never a great sleeper, usually depending on drink or drugs to knock him out.

Sometimes on tour he would stay up for a few days in a row, which was far from healthy. But there's no talking to him.

Dillon's eyes drift closed as he cleans his face, but the stubborn fool forces them open again. He's far too proud for his own good.

'I need to tell you something, Dillon.'

'Yeah? What?'

'Okay so don't get mad, but I had a vasectomy before my wedding.'

Dillon frowns for a few seconds, then laughs harshly. 'The guy who adores kids had a vasectomy? I'm taking it the *Bitch* made the decision for you, right?'

'Yes.'

'Fucking manipulative bitch!' So much for not getting mad. Dillon climbs off the bed and paces his room, his fists clenched by his side. 'As if she didn't do enough to you. What the fuck is wrong with her?'

'Please calm down, Dillon. It's okay.'

'Are you fucking kidding me! It's not okay, Luke. It's your fucking body. She had no right to make that decision for you.'

'I know, Dillon! I know, honestly. But I'm going to talk to my doctor about a reversal. I want kids. I want to be a dad, and I know it might not work, but I have to give it a shot.'

Dillon takes a few deep breaths, clearly doing what he can to control his temper. 'Maeve have a hand in this? The reversal idea I mean?'

'It kind of came up in conversation a while ago and she mentioned a reversal. I hadn't thought about it until then.'

'Why the fuck didn't you tell me?'

Luke drops the bloody cloth into the bowl. 'I don't know. I was embarrassed I guess. Just like with everything else she was doing to me. It was just another way she was controlling me. I was hardly going to come out to you guys and tell you about it.'

Dillon sighs and sits beside him. 'I get that. And it probably doesn't help that I fly off the handle every time you talk about her. I'm sorry.

That's not helping.'

'No, I get why you do and I don't mind.'

'Don't humour me. I can be a dick. I know I can. Enough people tell me,' he says with a small smile.

'Would you come with me? It should only be a day thing.'

'Of course I will. I'll do anything for you, you know that.'

'Thank you.' He wrings out the cloth and gets back to Dillon's face. 'Can I ask you something else?'

Dillon slowly lifts his eyes to look at him. 'What?'

'What are you taking?'

Dillon drops his gaze again, rubbing his bruised side as he glares at the floor.

'Dillon...'

'Back off, Luke.'

'I can't. I'm worried about you.'

Clearly done with the conversation, Dillon gets up and brings the bowl of water into the bathroom.

'I'm not finished with your face.'

'It's fine,' he says from the bathroom.

'You look...well, you don't look the best.'

Dillon leans against the door frame and crosses his arms. 'What the fuck do you expect? You just beat the crap out of me.'

He may smile a little to ease the harshness of his words, but Luke isn't buying it for a second. Dillon is really pale and, now the adrenaline of the fight has worn off, he appears really drowsy.

'When was the last time you took something?'

'I took a painkiller an hour ago. Happy? Can I get some fucking clothes on now?'

Luke gets up, frustration building again. Dillon has to be one of the most infuriating people he knows.

'Can you take this seriously for one minute! I'm not talking about a paracetamol.'

'Neither am I.'

Luke stares at his friend's bruised face, his words taking a minute to register with him. 'Jesus, Dillon! Painkillers?'

'Stop looking at me like that.' He pushes off the door frame, wincing when he straightens. 'I told you to drop it, okay. You should go. You need to talk to Maeve.'

'Don't do that.'

'Do what?'

'Push me away like you always do. You're taking painkillers. That's really serious. How bad is it?'

'What makes you think it's bad? I'm in control of it.'

'Daily? More than once a day? You've already told me what you're taking. You might as well keep going. It's not like it'll make the slightest bit of difference. You'll do what you want, like you always do.'

'Daily. Maybe more.'

'Jesus. What is it?'

'Whatever I can get at the time.'

Luke knew Dillon was using, but not to this extent. 'This is getting better and better. What about drink? Have you given it up, or are you still drinking whiskey like it's water?'

'What the fuck is this? I let you hit me. That's as far as this is going, so drop it. I'm fine, Luke. I don't need you to come in here and try to fix me. Concentrate on yourself.'

He doesn't want to leave it, but he also knows it would be like arguing with a rock. He's not going to get anywhere with him. It's a complete waste of breath.

'Get into bed.'

Dillon stops at his wardrobe and looks at him over his shoulder. 'You what?'

Luke takes off his boots, then pulls down the duvet on Dillon's bed. He lies down and pats the mattress beside him. 'I said get into bed.'

Dillon faces him, clearly not having a clue what's going on.

'I'm just talking about sleeping. You look exhausted, and I could do with some sleep before I decide what my next move is. Please, Dillon. I'm tired.'

Luke then turns over and closes his eyes. Dillon needs to sleep, but so does he. He wasn't lying about that part. Everything that's happened the last few days had worn him out.

The best thing he can do right now is get a few hours decent sleep, then he can decide how he's going to claim back his life and, hopefully, in turn, Maeve.

It takes Dillon longer than he thought it would, to give in. But he does. Luke hides the smile as the bed dips when Dillon lies down beside him, then covers them both with the duvet.

'Goodnight Dillon.'

'Yeah. Night.'

Luke smiles to himself as Dillon turns his back to him. Stubborn to the last.

Over the last few months, Dillon has spent a lot of his time looking after him. Making sure he was all right. Staying with him when he couldn't sleep or had nightmares. Whenever Luke needed him, Dillon would be there without question.

Now it's his turn.

Dillon won't talk to him, but it's not personal. Dillon doesn't talk to anyone. Never has. He's notoriously closed off. This is the best he can do for him, so he's going to do it.

Luke rolls over and wraps his arm around Dillon's waist, then closes his eyes again. Dillon holds his breath for a second and tenses.

'Go to sleep, Dillon.'

It takes another minute before he relaxes again and less than five minutes later he's asleep.

## Luke

'We've got you, Luke.'

He nods at Gregg, but doesn't feel any better hearing his statement. He's on the verge of either bolting from the car, or throwing up all over it. The only thing holding him back is the fact that Dillon would kill him if he did. He loves his Mustang more than most other things in his life.

Dillon takes the key out of the ignition, a silent confirmation that they're staying put until he does this. 'He's a nice bloke.'

He's sure Joe is a nice bloke. But that doesn't mean he wants to talk to him. Or even see him. He's Pippa's ex.

But Luke is Pippa's ex too now. An ex boyfriend and an ex husband - both terrified of the woman they were in love with. Sounds like an amazing way to spend the afternoon.

Dillon and Gregg don't say anything, which in itself is really weird. Gregg doesn't usually do quiet. Dillon is even sparing him his usual deep glare, keeping his attention on the dashboard in front of him.

They're giving him space and time to psyche himself up to meeting another of Pippa's victims. A victim just like him.

He needs to speak to Joe. He knows that. But knowing something, and actually getting his body out of the car, are two completely separate things.

He glances over at Dillon. The bruising around his eye darkened overnight and is clearly visible under his sunglasses. They'd both slept a good twelve hours, and he feels so much better because of it. Dillon has lost some of the greyness to his skin, but the bruising he caused is so much worse.

When they woke up, Luke had decided against confronting Dillon again about the painkillers. His back was up and any discussion would result in a blazing row he wouldn't win. The only thing Luke can do is wait and hope Dillon talks to him soon.

But not today.

Dillon didn't push him to breaking point so he can chicken out yet again and hide, like he's been doing for years.

'Will you both come in with me?'

'Don't have to ask,' Dillon says, smiling at him. 'Like Gregg said, we've got you.'

'Thanks.' He takes a deep breath and opens the car door. 'Let's go now before I change my mind.'

He follows Dillon up the driveway, just concentrating on breathing as he waits for Joe to answer the door - which he does far too fast.

The blond haired man glances at Dillon and Gregg, before looking at Luke. 'I wasn't sure you'd come.'

'I wasn't sure I would either.'

Joe steps aside. 'Come in.'

The walk into Joe's small but modern living room. Joe gestures to the two couches and they all sit, Gregg and Dillon taking the one to the far side, leaving Luke and Joe sitting opposite each other.

'I hope you don't mind Gregg and Dillon being here?'

Joe smiles and shakes his head. 'No problem at all. I'm all for strength in numbers too.'

'Dillon mentioned you weren't surprised when they called around?'

Joe shakes his head again. 'When the report went out about Pippa hitting you and being arrested, I knew it was only a matter of time before someone would come looking for me. To be honest, I wasn't going to answer the door if that happened, but I changed my mind.'

'Why?'

Joe fidgets with the sleeve of his shirt. 'I've been embarrassed and ashamed for too long. What she did... she killed my confidence, big time.'

He laughs nervously. 'She killed a lot of what made me, me. But when I heard that she was arrested for what she did to you, it gave me some of that confidence back. I thought nothing would ever be able to touch her. That no one would believe what she had done, had I come clean. But when you pressed charges like you did, I realised that it can't have been my fault.'

Luke knows exactly what Joe means. It's something he'd been living with himself. The blame. 'I felt the same.'

Joe smiles. 'You have no idea how much of a relief it is to hear that from someone else. Knowing that she did the same to you, is like a weight off my shoulders. I know that sounds harsh, and I don't mean it to be. But, I'm not alone anymore.'

'Yeah. I get that.'

'Are you okay to talk to me about it? I think it might help both of us. No pressure though. If you don't want—'

'No. I think you're right.'

Joe smiles as he gets to his feet. 'Great. Do you want a drink? We

329

could both probably do with the caffeine hit.'

'That would be great. Thanks.'

Not for the first time in the last few years, Luke wishes time travel were possible. He'd give anything to go back in time and walk away from Pippa the first night he met her. To have politely chatted, then turned and left. Or maybe stood up to her the first time she put him down? Not that he can remember the first time. He can't pinpoint the moment it began.

But he can decide on the moment it stops.

Today.

He lost himself to her. Nearly lost his life. And now he's lost Maeve. Lost the only woman he's truly loved. The only woman who liked him for being himself - faults and all.

But enough is enough.

He may never get Maeve back, and that's something he has to accept.

Luke looks down at his bare chest and stares at the scar on his side. When Pippa threw her expensive jewellery box at him, it had left a mark. The scar is hidden by the tattoo, but up close you can see it clearly enough.

He's got another in his hairline. One on his back. A few on his legs, along with the large surgical scar from when his leg was put back together, after she kicked it so hard it broke.

He takes the bandanna and cuff from his wrist. He likes wearing bracelets and cuffs, but he wears these ones to hide what she did.

As he stares at the scars he realises something. Something he should have realised a long time ago.

He's still protecting her.

After everything she's done to him over the years, he's still watching out for her. Still covering up for her. Still letting her control his life. Still coming between him and his friends. Still hurting the people he loves.

Still letting her hurt him.

He looks at the shelves on the wall behind the couch, lined with dozens of awards he's received as part of Broken Chords. He worked so hard for every single one of them. He'd worked long days and even longer nights. Stayed in some shit holes and lived off baked beans for weeks, when they were first starting the band. That was his achievement, not hers. If anything, she'd tried to hold him back.

She wouldn't even let him put the awards on display. Didn't like that he was more popular, or more successful, than she was.

It's time he stepped out of her shadow and took back some of the limelight she didn't want him to have.

It's time to take back his life.

He'd barely slept a wink last night, but for the first time, it had nothing to do with nightmares. His conversation with Joe had kept going over and over in his mind. Speaking to Joe was the best thing he's done. He no longer feels alone.

His family and friends will always support him, he knows that. But having someone else out there who went through more or less the same thing he did, makes him feel stronger.

It's no longer him against Pippa. It's now two against one, and however petty that may sound, it gives him the courage to take the next step.

He goes back to his wardrobe and takes out a pair of black jeans and a long sleeve black top. After pulling on his boots, Luke completes his outfit with the leather bracelets his nephews bought him for Christmas last year, smiling as he buckles them around his wrist. Pippa had never let him wear them. They're not thick enough to cover the scars, but he doesn't care.

Luke stands straight and examines his reflection. He runs a hand over his hair, ruffling the short spikes, then slips on a baseball cap backwards.

It's stage ready Luke facing him, but that's who he is. It's who he's always been. For as long as he can remember, Pippa had been trying to turn him into something he's not.

Being on stage, performing in general had made him happy. Being Luke Daly from Broken Chords makes him happy. Being Luke Daly, Pippa's husband had brought him nothing but misery. And a lot of pain.

He smiles to himself and grabs the keys to his bike from the drawer in the hall. Time to end this on his terms.

'Well, this is a different Luke,' Sam says as she looks him up and down. 'You look... different somehow. Is everything all right?'

'Is Ellen free? It's kind of important.'

'Please don't say you're leaving the band!'

'No! Definitely not.'

'Okay. I might have got a little freaked out there. Go straight in.'

Ellen closes her laptop and leans back in her leather chair when he closes the door behind him. 'Luke. Have a seat. Do you want something to drink?'

He sits in one of the chairs opposite her desk, then shakes his head. 'No thanks.'

She looks him over. 'I have to say, you look really well. How are you?'

'I'm good. And this is the real me. The one who is done taking shit,' he replies.

Ellen raises her eyebrows and nods approvingly. 'Well, I have to say I'm incredibly pleased to hear that. My dislike for your wife is reaching all new levels. I thought that would be near on impossible, but there we go. So, I'm presuming there's a plan of sorts you'd like to discuss?'

He hasn't rehearsed this at all, so just comes out and says it. 'I want to go public about Pippa. About what she did to me.'

Ellen doesn't say anything for a long time, so he waits. Who knows what sort of publicity issues will be going through her head.

After a long wait, she gets to her feet, then walks around her desk to give him a tight hug. Ellen doesn't hug, ever, really. She's all business. Always has been.

When she eventually pulls away, she wipes her face and smiles apologetically. 'Sorry about that. Just had the sudden urge.'

'It's fine, really.'

She sits back on her chair and straightens her hair. 'Okay, so needless to say I fully support your decision.'

'You do? Will Vox feel the same?'

She waves her hand dismissively. 'Between you and me, who cares, but yes, I'm sure they will. This is about you Luke. No one else. May I ask what's brought on this decision?'

'I'm done being embarrassed and ashamed of what happened. I didn't do anything wrong, well, unless you include protecting her, by keeping quiet.

'I want everyone to know what she did, and the real reason I was in the centre. I want to finally be free from her. I don't think I can do that, unless I come clean about what she did.'

'Of course. What about Pippa's last statement?'

'I want to talk about that too. This is between Pippa and myself. Dillon and Maeve shouldn't have been dragged into it.'

'Okay, so would you like to make a statement, or do a press conference?'

He hadn't thought that far ahead, but the thought of doing a press conference in front of all those cameras absolutely terrifies him.

'I don't think I can get up in front of everyone, but a statement isn't personal enough. Knowing her, she'll say Vox wrote it, or made it all up.'

'Good point.' She taps her pen against the desk for a few minutes, before smiling.

'You have an idea?'

'I have an idea. How does this sound? We set you up in front of a camera - just you in the room. Or maybe Dillon? Tate and Gregg too if you want, then you make the statement. It's personal, but you won't have to deal with strangers, or all the cameras. It could be a good compromise? I will personally walk you through this. I'll help you prepare a statement, or you can ad lib, if you'd prefer.'

'I want to write it myself — if that's okay? I think it has to be from me, or it won't mean anything. I don't want there to be any doubt that it's my words.'

'Of course, Luke. I think that's a good idea.' She pauses, then shuffles the files on her desk. 'How much do you want to say?'

'Everything. I've been covering for her for too long. I've always hated admitting what she did to me out loud.' He laughs without humour.

'I'm a six-foot-one guy, I work out regularly, and I was being controlled by a woman half my size. I couldn't say it, Ellen. I felt embarrassed. But I shouldn't be ashamed that she hit, beat, and raped me. She's the one who should be hiding - not me.'

She reaches across the desk to take his hand. 'Well, you are more than making up for that now. Whatever she decides, you've taken back control, by standing up to her.'

He smiles and nods. 'Yeah. It feels good, to feel good.'

'And it damn well should! You should be incredibly proud of yourself, Luke. I know I am.'

'Thanks.'

'So, when would you like to do this?'

'Now? Or today at least. If I go home, I'll just talk myself out of it.

I've lost too much of my life to her. Lost someone I care about, because I didn't do this a long time ago. It needs to happen today.'

## Luke

Over the last year of his life, he's been so close to freaking out too many times to count. Being with Pippa meant he was living in constant fear of upsetting her, leaving him on edge all the time.

But when he woke up this morning and decided to take back control of his life, he wasn't scared. For the first time in so long, he's absolutely sure of his decision and what he has to do.

Fair enough, actually doing the deed itself is another thing, but he can do it. Making the decision was the hardest part. He can absolutely do this!

He has to. If he's to stand a chance of breaking free from his past once and for all, he has to do it. Only then can he even consider anything with Maeve. He's messed her around enough over the last few months. Until he's baggage free, he won't go near her. It's not fair on her.

Dillon crouches down in front of his chair and rests his arms on Luke's legs.

'I'm not usually one for soppy speeches or anything like that. I want to say how fucking proud of you I am. This is... I think...'

Luke has never, ever seen Dillon lost for words. 'Do you need a hug?'

Dillon smirks at him as he pushes to his feet. 'Cocky shit! But yeah. I do actually.'

Luke stands and wraps his arms around Dillon's shoulders.

'Group hug!' Gregg launches himself at the pair, quickly followed by Tate.

His three friends hold him, offering their support as they have since he woke up in the hospital last year. He doubts he would have made it this far without them.

His brother clears his throat behind him. 'Fuck off you lot! I want a second with Luke.'

They unwrap him from their arms, leaving him alone with Alex. 'How are you holding up?'

Luke nods. 'Yeah. Okay I think. It's terrifying, but in a good way.'

'Of course it's terrifying. This is a big deal Luke. A massive deal.'

'Do you think I'm doing the right thing? I mean really believe that?'

Alex takes hold of his shoulders and looks him in the eye. 'One hundred percent, yes.'

'What about Mum and Dad?'

'Luke, we're all with you on this. Why should you be the one hiding? Why are you the one living in shame? Time to throw the spotlight on her. Show the world what an absolute fucking bitch she is.'

'Wow! Don't hold back there.'

Alex shrugs and grins. 'I think we all held back too long, in relation to Pippa. That ends today though. Have you heard anything from

Joe?'

'Not yet. He was due to meet with Max about an hour ago. It might take a while to make his statement.'

'Dillon can be a right pain in the ass at times but finding Joe was a stroke of genius on his part. Although don't tell him I said that. His ego doesn't need any help.'

'Do you think it'll make a difference though?'

'Joe telling the Garda what she did? Of course! If nothing else, it will make a difference to both you and Joe. That's the most important part. Whatever else happens after that is a bonus.'

He pauses and rubs the back of his neck. 'I wasn't going to bring it up, but what are you going to do about Maeve?

'I put Pippa before her for the last time. I need to sort this situation first. Put a full stop to my messed up time with her, well, until our divorce, but I'll deal with that later. For now, I just want to stop being ashamed of what I went through. Once I've done that, I'll get down on my knees and beg Maeve to give me another chance.'

'Sorry to interrupt,' Ellen says, coming up behind them. 'We're ready whenever you are.'

As the room clears of the camera and sound crew, Luke keeps his attention on the floor in front of the chair that's supporting him. He doesn't think he'd be able to stand right now if he tried. His body is like jelly. His stomach is churning so badly the only thing keeping him from throwing up is the fact there's a camera pointing at him.

It's already recording, but that's part of the deal. There's no one operating it from this room. The tech is outside making sure the camera keeps recording. He's not going to be able to do this again. It's a one off *bare his soul to the world* deal. No second take or redo.

If he gets through this without falling apart he'll be grateful.

But he's not going to back out. Not now. As terrifying as this is, it's the first major step in taking back control of his life.

Everything else he's done up to now - the months in the centre, all the hours of therapy, the constant talking - it was all to keep him alive. To stop him from attempting to take his own life again. But until recently, he hadn't felt like his life was his. That he was in control of it.

Maeve helped him so much. Helped him to gain a little of that control back.

But Pippa still has a hold on him. And that's *his fault*. The weak, obedient man she married is still protecting her.

Luke uncurls, sitting back against the chair. Time to stop being *that* man. Time to channel some of the Luke Daly who gets up on stage and plays to thousands of fans.

Time to own his life.

He looks to his left. Dillon, Tate, Gregg, and Alex, are sitting on the couch against the far wall. They're all here to support him. To have his back while he does this.

Time to end her control - of both himself and of Joe.

He takes a steadying breath, then looks at the camera.

'I know there has been a lot of speculation about what happened between Pippa and I last year. And I know I probably should have make this statement a long time ago. But I didn't fully understand the situation myself until recently. I probably wasn't brave enough to make it before now either.

'I'm going to do this in one take. No edits. No script, no retakes of it in any way.'

He pauses, suddenly unable to get the words out. But then the scars around his wrists catch his attention. He has them because of Pippa. Seeing them spurs him on.

'I fell in love with Pippa within a few weeks of meeting her. She was smart, beautiful, great fun to be with.

'After a few months, Pippa started making small digs. It might have been a comment about my clothes, or that I was neglecting her. That maybe I could make more of an effort with her. Nothing major, but enough to have me doubting myself.

'Over time, I pulled away from my friends and family. Gave up things I enjoyed doing, so I wouldn't upset her. I was in love with her. All I wanted to do was make her happy.

'Then she started hitting me. A tap first time, then a slap, then a full force kick. It was all my fault though, apparently. I had done, or said something, to upset her, or neglected her in some way. And I believed her. I thought I *deserved* it. I'd apologise and beg her to forgive me. Tell her I'd try better. I'd be a better boyfriend. A better husband. But it was never enough.'

He pauses and wipes his hands on his legs. 'She... she raped me. Pippa used to handcuff me to the bed and rape me.' As he's speaking, he uncovers his wrists, showing the world the marks he's most embarrassed by. 'It didn't happen once or even twice. It was repeatedly over a year or so.

'I accepted everything she was doing to me. I honestly believed I'd done something to justify that treatment. And then she told me I had to leave the band. She told me that I couldn't be part of Broken Chords any longer.

'But I couldn't do it. So she retaliated. Pippa beat me with her hairbrush, nearly knocked me out,' he says, moving his hair aside to show the deep scar. 'When I was on the ground she kicked me until my knee cap shattered, and stamped all over my legs with her stiletto's.

'Then she locked me in the room with a broken leg, no food, no phone, no way of helping myself, and went out to lunch. I didn't know what to do. I was so low, so convinced *I* was the problem. So I swallowed her entire bottle of sleeping pills. I thought if I wasn't alive, her life would be so much better.

'Dillon found me in time and called for help. But Pippa blamed Dillon for my injuries, and he was arrested. I had no choice but to admit what she was doing to me. I couldn't let Dillon spend even a day in prison because of me.

'Pippa has been trying to blame me for the fact she's in prison. Through her contacts, she's been doing what she can to slander me. To shift the focus on to me.

'But she's right. I am the reason she's in prison. Pippa verbally, physically, emotionally, and sexually abused me for years. That's where she belongs. I've been living in fear, in shame, in embarrassment, but I'm not going to do it any more. I didn't do anything wrong. All I did was try to love her.

'Pippa was never pregnant either. She booked me in for a vasectomy a few weeks before we were married, and I have medical documents to prove that it was successful. There was no baby, and there was no miscarriage.

'And in spite of everything she was doing to me, I never cheated on her while we were together. Never even considered it.

'I met an old school friend during the summer and have been spending a lot of time with her. I actually fell in love with her. She made me happy, made me feel like I was someone special. I haven't felt like that in years.

'But I let this fear of Pippa come between us and I drove her away. I hope I can repair what I did, but that's my private business.'

Luke stops, rubbing the scars around his wrist for a minute before he continues, looking directly at the camera for the next part. 'Since the moment I met Pippa, she's wanted the spotlight. Wanted all the fame, the attention, the social following that came with dating someone in a band like Broken Chords.

'Well, I'm more than happy to give her all that. It's time now to direct the spotlight on Pippa. It's no less than my wife deserves.

'I'm going to continue figuring my life out, with the help of my family and friends. I'm going to keep performing with the band. Keep doing what I love. Take it day by day for now. That's all I can do.

'I'll leave it at that for now. Thanks for taking the time to watch this. I hope it helps to clear some things up.'

Luke nods at the camera and the light above the lens goes out.

'Not a fucking chance in hell! Leave my bar now, before I kick your celebrity ass out the door!'

Luke follows Mike down to the other side of the bar, ignoring the looks he's drawing from the people drinking in the pub. He knew Mike would go into protective brother mode, but he's nearly hostile with him.

'Mike, please! I need to talk to her.'

Mike shakes his head. 'Oh, you had your chance to talk mate. And you blew it. Big time. Now, please fuck off and let me get back to work! I've lost my best bartender because of you.'

Lost? Luke's stomach sinks at the word. 'What do you mean lost?'

Mike slams his palm onto the bar top. 'What the fuck do you think I mean by lost? She's gone Luke. Left the fucking country actually. So, big thanks for that!'

'Left? Where? When?'

Mike laughs loudly, as he passes a bottle to beer to one of his customers. 'Yeah right. Like I'm going to tell you that?'

He turns away, dismissing Luke and walking to the far side of the room to collect glasses.

Maeve is gone. Left Ireland to get away from him. Did she really hate him that much?

That's not right. She shouldn't have to leave everything she loves, leave her home because he was too much of an idiot to stand up for her. Never again!

He storms back over to Mike and stands in front of him, blocking his way. 'Move, Luke!'

'No! Tell me where she is.'

'No way! Unlike you, I actually give a fuck about her and her happiness. She left to get away from you. Why do you think I'd tell you where she is?'

'Because I fucking love her, that's why!'

It takes Luke a few seconds to realise the entire bar has turned their attention to him. But in that moment, he couldn't care less. He got Mike's attention and that's all that matters.

'Listen, I know I fucked up. I know I dismissed her like she meant nothing to me. But I did that to protect her. My wife is a unpredictable. She's cruel and I don't trust her for a second. I didn't want her to have any reason to come after, or target Maeve.

'I get the way I did that was wrong. But I can't apologise to her, can't tell her how much I love her, if I don't know where she is.'

All the patrons keep their attention on Mike, as he mulls it over in his mind for a hell of a long time.

He has no idea where all this confidence is coming from, but he's not completely against it. It's about time he stood up for himself. It probably would have been best if he didn't start with Dillon, then move on to Mike, but if it works, he won't be complaining. He needs to find Maeve.

Mike takes a step closer to him. They're the same height, but Mike is broader than him. He's learned enough from Dillon over the years to know you never let on if you're intimidated. Which he absolutely is.

Mike looks around at the patrons before sighing, then turning back to Luke. 'You're a persistent fucker, you know that?'

'I'm trying to be.'

Mike laughs and slaps him on the back. 'Come on. I'll get you her address.'

Luke grabs a bag from the top shelf of his wardrobe and throws it on his bed.

'Are you sure you don't want me to come with you?'

He looks over at Dillon, sitting in the chair beside the bed. His friend is dubious about the entire plan. Not that it's a plan as such. He's reacting and going with it.

'I have to do this alone, Dillon. I fucked it up alone, and I'm going to fix it alone. Or try to. Hopefully.'

If he allows himself to think about the possibility Maeve will slam the door in his face, he's going to have second thoughts about going after her. He loves her. All he can do is hope she still loves him, even after he was such an idiot.

Dillon nods, but he's chewing on his lip ring which doesn't help Luke and his confidence levels. Ignoring his friend, he throws a few days worth of clothes in the bag and zips it up.

'I'll be fine, Dillon. I'm a big boy. I can go off on my own.'

Dillon nods again, but if he keeps chewing his lip ring he's going to pull the piercing out.

He sits on the edge of the bed, facing Dillon. 'Hey, I will be fine. I swear. I need to do this, Dillon.'

'I know you do. Fuck, Luke, I'm fully behind you, you know that. It's the alone part I'm struggling with.'

'I'm going to drive from here to the port, get on the ferry, then drive to the dance studio to find Maeve. How many fans do you think will be looking out for me in a camper van in Dublin Port?'

Dillon smiles. 'Yeah, you might have a point. I really need to let go, don't I? This over-protective shit is beginning to piss me off.'

'I have no problem with you being protective of me, but I'm not afraid anymore, Dillon. I'm stronger than you all think I am.'

Dillon pushes up in the chair. 'Hey! I know that. You've shown that again and again over the last few months. This is me being a dick. You need to go and get her back.'

344

'If she'll have me?'

Dillon takes his hand and squeezes it. 'If she's got even an ounce of common sense, she'll want you. Just be honest with her. Lay it all out and she'll see how much you love her.'

Luke grabs Dillon, pulling him in to a hug. He hates how sad Dillon is lately. Hates that a part of that is down to him, and there's nothing he can do about it. It's something Dillon is going to have to get over on his own, in his own time.

'I love you.'

Dillon tightens his hold for a second, before releasing him. 'I love you too.' He smiles, then gestures to the bag of clothes. 'What the fuck are you still doing here? Go get her back.'

Dillon walks with him down to the garage and waits while he loads his bag into the back of his camper. He's thirty-eight years old and heading out on his first solo road trip. It's equal parts exciting and downright terrifying.

If the end result is having Maeve in his life again, he'll do it.

'Keep in touch, okay?'

'Of course I will. And you behave while I'm gone.'

Dillon laughs loudly. 'Yeah right! When have I ever done that? Seriously though, you know where I am if you need anything. Tate and Gregg too. We're all here for you.'

'I'm not going forever. We're performing in two weeks. I'm not missing that for anything.'

'Broken Chords will always be there. This is your time, Luke. Fuck everything else.'

Dillon grabs him by the back of the head and pulls him close, kissing him on the forehead. 'Now, go!'

Luke climbs into the driver's seat and starts the engine. With one last wave at Dillon, he pulls out of the car park and heads towards the port.

As he joins the heavy line of traffic, the terror he was feeling at the thought of doing this alone, dissipates a little. Possibly seeing Maeve again helped to turn it to excitement.

He's got a lot of grovelling to do — he knows that. But he's not going to walk away from her. Dillon always said he regrets not fighting for the woman he was with. Luke isn't going to make the same mistake. However long it takes, he will win Maeve back. He has to.

## 39

*Luke*

He checks the address on the piece of paper Mike gave him. The dance studio is quite a bit larger than the studio she taught in back in Ireland.

The problem is, it seems there's a show on tonight and, judging by the number of people queuing outside, it's going to start in a while. Landing on her while she's putting on a show, wasn't part of his plan. He didn't actually have a plan beyond finding her.

He probably should leave her for tonight. Try to meet up with her tomorrow. But he doesn't want to.

He's already left it long enough. He needs to grow a set and do this now.

Luke looks out at the queue of people. 'Fuck it!' He pulls the keys out of the ignition, then gets out of the car and faces the building. Now what?

He could buy a ticket and go in the front door, but that would mean standing in the ever-growing queue with all those people. The odds of at least one person recognising him is fairly high.

That leaves the only other option.

He'll have to try the back door first. He veers around the left side of the building and knocks on the heavy metal door. He's about to give up when a really pissed off guy yanks it open and glares at him.

Luke opens his mouth to begin pleading to see Maeve, but that's as far as he gets. The man screeches like a banshee, then launches himself on top of Luke.

Luke freezes as the man attaches himself around his body, screeching in his ear.

'Oh my God! It's you! I love you! I've been to all your concerts. Well, the ones in the UK. I tried to go to other ones, but you know yourself. Busy. Busy. But you're here! Yay! I can't believe it! Pinch me!'

The man holds out his arm, but Luke stares at it in stunned silence. The man doesn't seem to notice his confusion, lowering his arm again. 'This is so exciting!'

Luke manages to peel the guy off him, then smiles at him as he straightens his t-shirt. 'Hi.'

The guy waves wildly. 'Luke Daly said hi to me!'

'Eh, yeah I did. I need to speak to Maeve Doyle. Do you know her?'

The man holds out his hand and Luke takes it, a little confused about a lot of things that are going on right now. 'I'm Dessie. I knew you'd come!'

'Nice to meet you. What do you mean, you knew I'd come?'

'For Maeve of course! True love always prevails. I'm an old romantic like that. You two are madly in love and you've come to get her back. It's like one of those romance films. I love it!'

Dessie turns and walks back into the building, pausing at the door to gesture to him. 'Come on then. Inside fast, before some crazy fan spots you.'

Luke follows after Dessie as he leads him through the building, down countless corridors and up a level, before he stops at a large dressing room. The entire room is packed full of dancers wearing colourful outfits, practising or chatting amongst themselves.

'She's in there... somewhere.' Dessie says, peering into the room. 'I have to get ready myself. Good luck.'

He embraces Luke again, before he hurries back the way they came, and disappears around the corner.

Luke takes a deep breath, then steps into the room, immediately being hit by so many perfumes, hairsprays, and deodorants. The further he ventures into the room, the more people recognise him. When the dancers move aside, clearing the way for him, Luke is left alone in the middle of the dressing room, looking at Maeve.

Engrossed in running through a bit of the routine with one of the dancers, she doesn't notice him, until the woman in front of her nods towards him. Maeve turns and stares at him for a long time, nothing showing on her face, which doesn't help him gauge if she's happy to see him.

'Hi Maeve.'

'Luke, what are you doing?' she hisses, smiling at the dancers gathering around her. 'There are quite a few people watching.'

'I don't care. I need to talk to you.'

'I can't talk right now. The show is about to begin.'

'Please. It will only take a minute.'

'Okay, but can we maybe go somewhere more private?'

Luke shakes his head. He needs to do this now, and he honestly doesn't care how many people are watching or not watching. It's all about Maeve in this moment. 'I messed up.'

'Luke...'

'No! Shut up and let me talk.'

Maeve blinks and presses her lips together. She's as shocked by his outburst as he is.

The entire room of dancers, waiting to go on stage are focusing on them, but he blocks them out. And the phones that have appeared in some hands to record or photograph what's happening, but he doesn't care.

'Like I said, I messed up. You were right. I was protecting her. After everything she did, I was still putting her first and that was a fucking massive mistake.'

'Did you just curse?'

'Yeah. I did.' He unbuckles the bands from his wrists and looks down at the scars. 'I've been ashamed and embarrassed about what happened. I did everything I could to keep the spotlight off her and what she did. But I'm done protecting her. I've made a statement, which has probably just gone out. I was open and honest about what she did. Every single bit of it. I'm done hiding, and I'm done protecting her.'

'I'm glad to hear it.'

'I'm not finished.'

'Right. Have you been taking lessons from Dillon?'

'Maybe? Just let me finish.'

'Sorry.'

'I was living from hour to hour before you came into my life. I think I was pretending to be okay. But I wasn't. Not until you. Maeve... you've turned my life upside down in the best possible way. You've helped me figure out who I am. I'm not afraid anymore.'

He pauses, when a tear rolls down her cheek.

'I honestly thought I was protecting you, when I pushed you away. But that's not how it works. I should have known that, after the last year.

'You don't protect someone by pushing them away. You do that by keeping them close. I should never have said what I did about you to the press. I thought I was doing the right thing, but I wasn't and I'm so, so, sorry.'

'You really hurt me, Luke.'

He nods. God, he wishes he could go back and never make that statement. But it's done. No going back. He glances over his shoulder, wincing when he spots the crowd he's pulling. It's a little late to worry about that.

'I'm so deeply in love with you, Maeve. I love your spontaneity, your enthusiasm. Love your mischievous, seriously sexy smile. The way your body moves when you dance. The way your eyes light up when I sing to you. I even love watching you stuff Coco Pops into your mouth!

'I don't want to think of my life without you in it. When I'm with you, I feel like I do on stage. I'm happier than I ever remember being. I'm safe. I'm free. I'm confident. I never thought I could feel that way, except on stage. But I do when I'm with you.'

'That's a lot to process.' She wipes her face. 'And I'm crying. Don't do that often. You're really in love with me?'

'Oh yeah,' he says, smiling at her. 'So much. Do you still feel the same, or have I ruined that forever?'

'You realise everyone here is listening?'

He looks over his shoulder again. She's right. They've got the full attention of the dancers, a few extra performers, and back stage staff, everyone silent as they look at the couple. 'Ignore them.'

'Where has this confident Luke come from? That's not a complaint. I kind of like it.'

'I think he was there all along. Just buried under a hell of a lot of doubt. He needed you to help dig him out.'

'Answer him!'

They laugh, when someone shouts out from the back of the crowd.

Luke is on the verge of throwing up. He's trying to remain composed, but this is the single most terrifying thing he's done. And it's got nothing to do with the audience watching him pour out his heart and soul to Maeve. It's all down to what her answer is going to be.

Then the corner of her mouth curls into a small smile.

'Luke Daly?'

'Yeah?'

'Of course I'm madly in love with you!'

'You are?'

'Oh hell yeah I am!'

Luke picks her up, holding her tight against him, as he kisses her. Behind him the onlookers cheer and shout, but he couldn't give a damn. She wraps her legs around his waist and grins widely at him. 'So you're all mine, Maeve?'

'Completely. But as much as I love you, I really have to go on stage. Will you watch me?'

'You never have to ask me that. The answer will always be yes.'

'Hey, that's my line!'

# Maeve

She grabs a bottle of water from the cooler, then sits down at the edge of the stage. The performance went without a hitch and the audience thoroughly enjoyed it from the standing ovation they received.

And she's not surprised. The dancers are the best she's ever worked with. She doesn't think she could ever get bored watching them perform her routine night after night in front of hundreds of members of the public. She honestly doesn't think anything could feel as amazing.

Or didn't, until *he* walked back into her life.

Luke Daly is standing at the far side of the stage talking to Dessie. She lost count of the number of times during the evening she had to keep checking to make sure he was real.

When she left Ireland, she had really thought that was it for their relationship. She wasn't blaming him. Not really. Luke had so much to get through. So much to try and understand about himself and what his wife did to him. He was bound to make mistakes, and she understands why he did what he did. It didn't help it hurt any less, but she understood.

Walking away from him had been the most difficult thing she's ever done. It tore her to pieces, but it was the right thing to do - for both of them. He needed to figure out what he wanted for himself. Needed to find out who the real Luke Daly is after all the abuse.

But she needed to protect herself too. Distancing herself from him was the only solution to help herself.

When she saw him standing in the dressing room, looking like the confident rock star she had hoped to see more of, it was like a dream come true.

He hadn't needed to say that he was ready to move on. She could tell that much about him from one look. He was standing straighter, taller, the lines from around his eyes and mouth gone.

She hadn't expected him to come for her like he did - especially alone. Driving from Ireland to Wales to get her back, was hands down the most romantic thing anyone has ever done for her. The confident rock star had come across the Irish Sea to get her back. She wasn't one for soppy movies, but what he did absolutely deserved to be in one.

She smiles when he laughs with Dessie. She hasn't seen him like this before. So relaxed and sure of himself. Making that statement was the best thing he could have done. She took a few minutes to herself to watch it while the cast was performing. The tears had poured down her face as she watched him tell the world what he'd been through. It was heartbreaking, but she could not be more proud of him.

His words. His truth.

It was absolutely the best way he could have made that statement. It was the perfect way to stick a finger up at the bitch of a wife. Let her talk her way out of that!

He turns to look at her, smiling widely. She crooks her finger at him, calling him over to her. Luke says something to Dessie before walking across the stage, then helping her to her feet.

'Dessie can talk,' he mutters under his breath as he drapes his arm across her shoulders.

'You think! He's a massive Broken Chords fan. I'm actually surprised he's not clinging to you more than he is.'

'Are you nearly done here?'

'Why?' she asks, pulling him closer. 'What do you have planned for me?'

'I was kind of thinking of getting you back to your place as fast as possible.'

'Is that so? Interesting. And why do you want to get me home as fast as possible?'

Maeve screeches when he picks her up, throwing her over his shoulder. 'How about I show you instead.'

# 40

## Dillon

The last time he was here, he was a guest himself. Sitting on the other side of the table doesn't help relax him. He's still on edge, half expecting one of the guards to call him back to his cell. One month inside had been enough of a kick to help him keep his temper in check.

Most of the time. He's on his second punch bag, but it's better than finding himself locked up here again. It had been made perfectly fucking clear, he'd be locked up for years next time he stepped out of line.

This meeting is about to put his carefully restrained temper to the test. Just to be sure he didn't flip out, he'd veered away from taking anything when he woke up. It seemed like a good idea at the time, but now he's not so sure.

He'll never admit he's addicted to any of the many drugs he takes.

That would mean admitting he's not in control of some aspect of his life. Not going to happen. He crosses his arms, shoving his trembling hands under his armpits. It's probably got nothing to do with his body missing the drugs after a few measly fucking hours.

The door opens at the end of the room and the person he's here to meet is led in. She sits on the plastic chair opposite him, her blue eyes boring into him, as the guard walks away to give them a little privacy.

When he got the visitation request from Pippa, his first reaction was to throw it in the bin and forget about it. But curiosity had won out and here he is. Seeing the effect of prison on the once flamboyant woman, was worth the drive alone.

Pippa had used Luke's money to maintain a near perfect image. Her hair was always styled, make-up worthy of any magazine cover, clothes the best Luke's money could buy. Seeing her now in an ill fitting grey tracksuit, hair scraped back into a ponytail, and no make up brings a smile to his face.

'Fuck, you look shite!'

She smiles at him, brushing her blonde ponytail off her shoulders. 'I'm sure you looked equally as good when you were here? We're more alike than you think, Dillon, so don't look down at me like that.'

He leans on the table and smiles, even though his tone is far from cheery. 'We're nothing alike, so don't even go there! Why did you want to see me?'

'How's my husband?'

'Why did you want to see me?'

'Answer my question and I'll answer yours.'

Dillon sighs. ' How do you think he is? He's broken free from you. He's in love with an incredible woman who loves him. He's living the dream - finally.'

Her smile fades, her face hardening as she glares at him. 'Is he now?'

'Oh yeah. He's not afraid of you anymore, but you've probably figured out that part for yourself. What was it like watching him tell the world how fucked up you are?'

'I'm not an idiot Dillon. I know Vox orchestrated that announcement.'

'Luke went to Vox all by himself, and we sat with him while he recorded that message. His words, Pippa. It was all him.'

He gets a kick from the way the corner of her mouth twitches at that news. She believes him. She has no reason not to. Dillon isn't a liar. She knows that.

'Finally sinking in, huh? You've lost him, Pippa.'

'What's it like?'

'What?'

'Being in love with someone who will never love you back? I mean, it must tear you apart every single time you see him with that woman, knowing that you'll never have that? Knowing that you'll die alone. I have money on you overdosing in the next few months.'

'Wow! Okay, that supposed to get me upset or something?'

She shrugs, examining her nails. 'I know you don't do the whole emotion thing, so no, I'm not expecting that to upset you. But maybe it will eat away at you. You see, I know you better than you think Dillon.

'I know there's so much pain inside you, it's slowing devouring you. You drink to excess and as for your drug use, well, that's impressive. You do everything you can to dull your emotions. Fucking, and using, to shut off your brain. It's quite tragic really.'

He smiles, giving himself a few seconds to calm the fuck down. Bitch may have a point, and the victorious smile on her face says she knows she's hit a nerve.

'Yeah, I'm in love with him. But at least I didn't have him and lose him. At least I didn't have to beat and rape him, force him to be with me. At least I didn't make him feel so miserable that he tried to kill himself to get away from me.

'You can give yourself a pat on the back for all that Pippa. You can say what the fuck you want about me, but I'll never top that fucked up shit you did.'

She glares at him for a long time, before the sweet, fake smile she used too often over the years, comes back. 'So, I called you here because I need to tell you something.'

He sits back and crosses his arms again. He's not liking the look in her eyes. The bitch is seriously unstable. He can see it clear as day and it's more than a little unsettling.

Pippa leans over and lowers her voice, the smile still out in full force. 'I wanted to give you a bit of a heads up, Dillon. Like I said, I'm not an idiot. I know the way I handled Luke will be frowned upon by most people.'

'You think?'

'Oh stop being all high and mighty, Dillon! When was the last time you went for a few hours without drinking or using? I bet you can't even remember, can you? You're heading towards forty and need drugs, drink, and endless mindless sex to get through the day. Endless broken relationships. Parents who can't stand you. It's only a matter of time before you're in here with me, or six feet under.'

'Can I have a second? I need to compose myself. You've hurt my feelings so badly, I might cry.'

'I know I will probably be here for a while,' she says, ignoring the interruption. 'I've resigned myself to that fact. But it's not a bad thing really. It gives me plenty of time.'

'For what?' he asks, before he can stop himself.

'Thinking. Planning. You see, there is only one person who is really to blame for all of this. For me losing Luke. For my time in here.' She lifts her eyes, tilting her head as she smiles at him. 'That's you, Dillon. It's all down to you.'

'Is that so? I don't remember being there when you raped him.'

'I didn't rape him. He enjoyed it, but we're getting off the point. If

358

you had kept your fucking nose out of our relationship, out of our marriage, none of this would have happened. So I'm going to use my time in here wisely, Dillon. Every single second is going to be spent thinking about you.'

He swallows thickly, not liking where this is going. 'I'm flattered.' But he's not. He's freaked out and it takes a hell of a lot to freak him out.

'You should be. Because when I get out, you're the first person I want to see. And I'll let you into a little secret,' she says, her voice dropping to just above a whisper. 'I'll be the last person you ever see.' She winks then gets to her feet. 'Guard! We're done.'

Dillon stares after her, as she's led from the room. He plays her last sentence over and over as he walks back to his car.

He's been threatened before. His attitude tended to rub people up the wrong way on nights out, and it usually ended with him in a fight with someone. But this was a whole other level of threat.

Did Pippa just say she's going to kill him when she gets out? He laughs to himself, starting the engine and pulling out of the prison car park. It's fucking ridiculous!

But if it's so ridiculous, why does the laugh die away within a few minutes?

## Luke

He strokes Maeve's side, following the line of her tattoo along her skin. She's still asleep and he's in no rush to wake her. He loves watching her like this. He could never tire of looking at her.

She feels perfect against him. So perfect he never wants to let her go. Never again.

She's still asleep and he's in no rush to wake her up. He loves watching her like this. He could never tire of looking at her.

She smiles and opens one eye. 'You're staring at me.'

He kisses her arm and she shuffles closer to him. 'I can't help it. You're beautiful.'

'And you are going to give me a big head if you keep complimenting me like that. You've got a strange grin on your face. What are you so happy about?'

'I thought I'd lost you.'

She nods, then takes hold of his hand. 'Yeah. I thought I'd lost you too. I watched your statement online. How do you feel now it's all out there in the world?'

'It was the best thing I ever did. My only regret is not doing it sooner. But I don't think I would have done it if not for Joe, Pippa's ex. She didn't go as far with him as she did with me, but he's still been affected by what she did.

'I think hearing that he'd been through the same thing gave me a bit of a kick. Telling the world what happened was like the best therapy I've had. I don't care if everyone believes me or not, I honestly don't. But if even one person sees through Pippa, I'm happy.'

'I can't tell you how fucking proud I am of you! I mean that Luke.'

'Thanks. It felt good to finally stand up to her. I'm not going to let her kick me around anymore.'

'I'm glad to hear that. So what's the plan now? Is she going to get in more well-deserved trouble because of Joe?'

'Max doesn't know. Joe made a statement about the abuse and I did the same. Every detail I could remember from over the years. It should go against her, but I don't know.

'Making that statement wasn't about that as much. It was about cutting that final link to her. Or at least until I have to deal with the divorce.'

'Wow! You've finally escaped, huh?'

He smiles and kisses her. 'About fucking time!'

She laughs. 'You know, I don't know how to take this version of Luke who curses. I have to admit it does add a sexy edge that I can't resist, but it sort of goes against the sweet image I have of you.'

'I can be both. I can be the sweet, polite, well mannered guy until I get you alone. Then the other version can come out.'

Maeve pushes back from him examines his face. 'Interesting prospect. You are breaking out of your cocoon, aren't you. So, until you ravage me in about three minutes, do you have a long term plan? I mean it's amazing you being here, but how long do you have until you have to get back to Ireland?'

He hadn't thought beyond finding Maeve, but now he's here, he's not in any rush to get back. He has a couple of weeks off before they have to perform again so there's nothing to rush back for. 'How long is the show running?'

'Actually, that was the last night. I was thinking of moving on somewhere else. See what else I can find to keep me out of trouble, but now... well, things might be different now.'

'They don't have to be.'

She pushes back from him. 'What do you mean?'

'What if I stayed here? We could go wherever you wanted to go. I've got the camper with me so we could stay in that. I'll get a trailer for your bike, so that's not a problem.'

'Are you serious? You'd stay here with me? Drive around the country, living in the camper, so I can work?'

Until the words popped out of his mouth he hadn't thought about what he's suggesting. But it feels right. Being with Maeve is all he wants.

'I can't think of anything I'd love more than living in the back of the camper for a while - just you and me.

'I might even be able to stretch to a hotel room or Airbnb if you want every now and again if you need a break from the camper? I don't care where we stay or where we go. I want to be with you Maeve. If you'll have me.'

She throws her arms around his neck and screeches. 'Of course I'll have you, you daft, gorgeous, unbelievably sexy, twit! I love you. But what about the band? Do you not have to be in Ireland for work?'

'I've got a few weeks to myself before we head off again. Besides, Wales isn't the other side of the planet. I can get to where I need to be from here. If I need to go back for any reason I'll hop on a flight. It's not a big deal.

'And maybe it wouldn't be a bad idea to have a break from Ireland for a bit, especially after all the Pippa stuff has broken.' He pulls her closer again. 'I don't want to let you go again. I want to be with you, Maeve. If that means being where you need to be, that's where I'll be too.'

She sniffs and Luke realises she's crying.

'Hey, I didn't want to make you cry.'

'Oh these are happy tears, believe me. Wow! So are we going to live together?'

'If you're okay with that?'

'I think I can force myself to live with a celebrity rock star in his camper. It kind of helps that I'm madly in love with you, so that's the real selling point. So we're really doing this? We're moving to Wales and living together.'

'Yeah. We are.'

She throws her arms around his neck again, then kisses him. 'I love you Luke.'

'I love you too, Maeve.'

He smiles widely as he holds her against his chest. His face hurts he's smiling so much, but it's such an amazing feeling. He's truly happy, so happy he could burst.

Not only is he madly in love with an incredible woman, he's in charge of his life for the first time in years and he's not going to let it go again.

He's got so much time to make up for, still has a long way to go, but there's no rush. With Maeve, his friends, and his family by his side, he'll get there. He'll keep adding to his notebook, keep figuring out who he is.

But he's not scared about the future. He's no longer living from day to day, forcing himself to get out of bed and face the day.

He can't wait to live his life and face whatever comes his way.

Bring it on — he's ready.

# Epilogue

## Dillon

He's wet. Absolutely fucking soaked actually, but he's too drunk to consider moving. He'll have no choice soon. The tide is on the way in. He's probably got about twenty minutes until he has to move, or else get his boots wet.

In twenty minutes he'll have finished the bottle of whiskey. At that stage, he might not care about getting his boots wet. It's been raining the whole time he's been sitting on the beach. His jeans and t-shirt are already stuck to his skin. It's not like he can get any wetter.

It's not like he cares either way.

The pills he took made sure of that. The whiskey is making doubly sure.

Dillon finishes the bottle, dropping it onto the sand beside him before lying back, and glaring at the black clouds above him. His phone rings but he ignores it. It's either going to be the band, or one of his sisters. No one else calls him.

He slams the heel of his hand against his forehead, cursing loudly. Fucking pity party yet again. When he vomits, barely turning his head to the side in time, the pity jumps up to fucking pathetic.

He doesn't feel so good. He probably should get up and walk back to his cottage while he still can.

But that would be sensible. Not where his head is, thanks to the pills.

He's not addicted to painkillers. No way. But isn't that what all addicts say? What he's doing isn't the same as Tate. He has no fucking intention of sticking a needle in his arm. No intention of sticking who knows what shit in his veins.

Painkillers are different. They're clean. Easier to take without anyone really noticing.

Or at least that's what he keeps telling himself.

His phone rings again, so this time he picks it up, squinting to try and make out the name on the screen. It's Clara.

His sister seems to have an inbuilt *Dillon-is-fucking-up* sensor. He silences the call. If he speaks to her she'll know he's off his head and will come around. That's the last thing he wants.

Not that he knows what he wants. Hasn't for years. He's drifting from day to day, using drugs, drink, and sex to keep himself going.

He pulls the chain out from under his t-shirt and holds the ring in his hand. He should throw it out. Leaving it hanging around his neck for the last decade is like a noose around him, weighing him down.

It's funny how one person can completely throw your life off track in such an extreme way. He should have expected the relationship with her to fail. Should have known he'd do something to fuck it up.

It's what he does. There's something messed up in him that turns people off, or drives them away.

Since the minute he was born, he's been pushing people away.

How a baby can do that he has no fucking idea, but leave it to him to do it. Maybe he'd seriously fucked up in a previous life.

Whatever the reason, he's been hit with heartache after heartache continuously, for as long as he can remember, and he's about done with the whole thing. Forty years of being hurt is taking its toll on him.

People have always been attracted to him. He's never had any trouble finding companionship. He laughs at that.

Companionship? That's a fucking joke. They want to be fucked by him. That's all they want. They want what he can give them, they don't want him. Not the real him.

He's good looking. He knows that. It's got nothing to do with ego. He wouldn't draw as many people to him unless he was.

But each encounter is selfish - and not on his part. They just want to be able to say they were fucked by Dillon Ryan. That the bad boy of Broken Chords had picked them to have sex with.

It's a fucking joke. Mainly because he does what they expect of him every single time. He doesn't even try to get to know the person. There's no point. They'll get what they want - want a lot more of it because he's fucking good at it - but that's it.

He's got so much baggage, that if he even tried to open up to someone, they'd run screaming from him. So what's the point? It's easier, and less painful, if he treats them the way they think he's going to.

Fuck them, then leave them. It's what he's got a reputation for doing after all. Wouldn't want to ruin that image.

What would they think if they could see the trouble making, sex crazed, bad boy of the band now? Lying on the beach in the rain, crying like a fucking baby would kill that image forever.

He plays with the engagement ring, wondering what his life would have been like had she not left him. They'd probably be married by now. Maybe even have a kid or two. He'd like that. Really would.

Around the guys, he never let on he wanted the whole family thing. He survived by being this hard ass, who didn't give a shit about anything. Biggest fucking joke, considering he's the exact opposite.

He's an emotional mess desperate for someone, for anyone, to love him. He wants what the other guys have.

Seeing Tate with Brandon for the first time, had been like a knife to the gut. Until that moment he didn't realise that's what he wanted too. At the time he'd hidden his feelings by looking after Luke when he broke down, but Luke was holding him, as much as he was holding Luke.

Unfortunately, there's not much chance of a happily ever after for him, while he's still in love with his straight best mate. He has to get over Luke. He's with Maeve now. He's with someone who genuinely appreciates how amazing that man is.

Dillon is happy for them both. It's impossible not to be. Maeve is exactly what Luke needs, helping to bring Luke out of his shell for the first time in years. She's good for him. Better than he would have been.

With his track record he probably would have fucked up anything he had with Luke.

He wishes he knew why he's so unlovable? He can be a total asshole at times, but you'd never find anyone who puts others first more than he does. He's ridiculously protective - probably too much at times, but he can't help it.

When you love someone you should do everything in your power to make them happy, to make sure they're safe, protected. To make sure they feel loved every single minute they're with you.

The waves lap at his knees and he finally convinces himself to move, crawling up the beach, until he's above the high tide mark, before slumping onto his back.

He'll have a nap here, then go home, try to sober up. Maybe tomorrow he'll turn over a new leaf? Try to get through a few hours on coffee and happy thoughts?

Dillon rolls onto his side and curls into a ball, laughing to himself at that idea. Who the fuck is he kidding? This is the way it's going to be for him. Or will, until he accidentally takes himself out, or Pippa gets her hands on him.

That thought has him smiling. He hopes she does come after him. She can take him out, he doesn't really care about that.

But if she thinks she gets to walk away from what she did, and live the rest of her life, she can think again. He'll make sure of that.

He still thinks about what he could do to Pippa given five minutes alone with her. After her very clear death threat, he'd only need one minute with her.

He's not saying he'd kill her. But he's not saying he wouldn't either.

But it's that temper, that anger always bubbling beneath the surface that keeps him alive. It's what he feeds off. Better that, than this fucking misery he's letting get to him now. No good comes of moods like this. His thoughts turn dark, and when he goes that far, it's hard to pull back.

But he made a promise to his sisters a long time ago. He'd stay with them. Keep fighting, even when it's the last thing he wants to do. If it wasn't for that promise, he'd have given into the dark thoughts years ago. But he won't hurt them like that. Not again.

His phone rings again from somewhere nearby. Why didn't he silence the damn thing? He doesn't even know where it is.

A shiver runs through his body. He's so fucking cold, but his house is too far away. It's only up the beach, but it could be in another country the way he feels right now. It's all too difficult.

Everything in his life is difficult. Pretending to be okay is difficult. Not being okay is just as difficult. It's all the same. Every day is a fight to get through to the next morning. Then doing the same thing the next day.

With Luke gone, he has no one. Tate and Gregg have their own lives. So do Clara and Eva. It's just him left alone and he hates it.

Luke is gone.

The reality of that thought hits him like a kick to his gut. He's so happy Luke is safe, and finally living his life. But his heart is breaking, and it hurts so much.

It doesn't matter that Luke could never have loved him back. Not the same way. He fell hard for him and can't seem to pick himself up again.

Luke doesn't need him anymore. He's got Maeve to look out for him. Maeve to love him. From now on, he'll be calling Maeve if he has a nightmare, or needs to talk.

Not him.

The pathetic crying turns to sobs of despair. He has no right to feel like this. No right to be falling apart like this.

He flinches as two strong arms wrap around him from behind, but relaxes when he sees the familiar Celtic knots tattooed on the back of each hand.

Dillon isn't usually one for hugs or showing emotional weakness, but when Tate holds him, he can't stop the tears. Can't hold back the emotion that breaks out.

When Gregg joins Tate on the stones, and holds him too, Dillon could never be more relieved to have friends like Tate and Gregg in his life.

He never would have asked for help. Wouldn't have admitted he didn't want to be alone. Wouldn't have ruined what was happening with Luke, by telling them he was selfishly devastated Luke had found someone else. Wouldn't have picked up the phone and asked them to just hold him like this, while he falls apart.

But he didn't need to. They knew.

He buries his face against Gregg's chest, sobbing like a pathetic fool, his tears soaking into his friend's t-shirt.

Gregg doesn't care though. He hugs him tighter, Tate supporting the two of them when Dillon collapses back against him.

'It's okay, Dillon,' Tate says, pulling him close.

'We've got you, buddy,' Gregg says. 'We've got you.'

Dillon really hopes so, because right now, he's falling, and he has no idea how to stop.

Thank you for reading **Crushed Rock.**

I hope you enjoyed catching up with the band again. There's plenty more to come!

The next book, **Shattered Rock**, is coming soon.

Do you fancy staying updated with news about my books?

• Join my mailing list at: **www.kafinn.com**

• Like me on Facebook: **www.facebook.com/kafinnauthor**

• Follow me on Instagram:
**www.instagram.com/kafinnauthor**

• Keep up to date with new releases:
**https://books2read.com/ap/nE2Kdj/KA-Finn**

Also, if you have a moment, I'd appreciate if you could review **Crushed Rock** at the store where you purchased it. The band and I would love to know what you thought of the book.

Thanks for your support!


K.A. Finn

Coming soon...

*Broken Chords #5*

# K.A. FINN

www.ingramcontent.com/pod-product-compliance
Lightning Source LLC
Chambersburg PA
CBHW020257030726
47499CB00001B/234